CONTENTS

Adrian Howell's
PSIONIC

Book Four
The Quest

Cover Design: Pintado (rogerdespi.8229@gmail.com)

ISBN: **1482521180**
ISBN-13: 978-1482521184

INTRODUCTION

When you are young, the world looks young. There's right and there's wrong just as clearly as the sun and the moon. There're good guys and bad guys, and the good guys always win in the end. Sooner or later, though, you have to grow up. You have to learn which battles to fight, and which ones to walk away from. Because you can't win them all.

In my experience, you often can't win any of them. At least, not the ones that really matter.

My name is Adrian Howell, but through the years following my sudden leap into the unknown, I've answered to several other names, including but not limited to Adrian Gifford, Addy, P-47, Hansel and Half-head. Sometimes I wonder which one would mark my grave after I die, but then again, people like me often don't get graves. They just disappear. And perhaps that's for the best.

I probably shouldn't have even bothered writing an introduction for this book. It is my fourth, after all. If you have followed my story this far, then I see little point in dissuading you from reading further. Besides, the more you know about us, the better prepared you will be if someday you were to become one of us. It's rare, but it happens.

I have just one warning, however, that I can neither stress nor repeat enough: We are neither heroes nor villains, but we take our secrecy very seriously. So as long as you are still human, don't ever go looking for us. Because you just might find us, and I already have too much blood on my hands, thank you very much.

1. THE MAN AT THE WINDOW

The high-pitched siren went off just as Alia and I had finished eating dinner.

"Oh, not again!" I said irritably as the deafening noise filled every corner of our fortieth-floor penthouse at the top of the New Haven One building.

This made the sixteenth time our panic alarm had been set off in the last two and a half weeks. The first time was the day after Terry's birthday, the next, three days later. From then, they became more and more frequent. Half of them in the middle of the night, the rest invariably at mealtimes and bath times. Sometimes twice or even three times a day. And now this. Another damn false alarm.

Alia was helping me clear the dishes off the table, and I shouted to her over the din, "Could you go get that turned off? I'll take care of the plates."

"Sure, Addy," Alia replied into my head.

My sister always used her telepathy when she was alone with me, speaking with her mouth only when there were multiple people in the room. This time, however, she probably would have used her telepathy regardless, since she would have to shout to be heard over the ear-splitting noise. Shouting wasn't one of Alia's strong points.

Alia scampered off to the game room where Terry and I often played pool. With a solid steel door and shielded walls, the game room doubled as our safe room. It contained an intercom that linked to New Haven One Security, where jumpy Guardian Knights remote-activated our panic alarm every time they heard a mouse fart.

I took the dirty dishes in my hands and levitated the unused clean ones in front of me, carrying them back to the kitchen. I always had to be careful with my telekinetic power when I was distracted or irritated, as was the case now. Losing my focus would mean shattered dishes all over the floor.

I wasn't just upset by the alarm, though.

Alia and I had spent much of the afternoon cooking up a welcome-home meal for Terry, who had returned from a Raven Knight mission today—her first since her return to active duty. But Terry had called in the evening to tell us that she was still in debriefing with her unit leader, Jack Pearson, and that they would be eating out. Cindy was late too. She had been delayed at another Council meeting, and that was after explicitly asking me to prepare a fancy turkey dinner for everyone to eat together.

I huffed as I loaded the dishwasher. Since when had I turned into an angry homemaker?

It had been two months now since the Guardians had returned victorious from their assassination of the Angel queen, Larissa Divine, during the gathering of lesser gods. The Guardians had returned victorious. I had not.

With Terry and Alia's assistance, I had used the Guardian leader, Mr. Travis Baker, to help me sneak into the Angel camp, where I successfully made contact with my lost sister, Catherine. And there I learned that Cat no longer shared my last name. Returning empty-handed, I narrowly escaped execution at the hands of the man Cat now called Father: the Angel queen's nephew, Randal Divine.

Then, before I managed to return to the Guardians, I condemned my former Raven commander, Mr. Jason Simms, to what I hoped would be a slow and painful death. Instead of helping him escape with a broken leg, I had blasted a hole through his elbow. Either he died in the tunnel where I left him, or the Angels found him and put him through weeks of torture. A fitting end to the man who used to brutally murder the children of our enemies. Though I realized that what I had done to Mr. Simms made me not all that different in the ethics department, my only true regret was that Mr. Simms had carried many of the Guardians' secrets, and if he had been found, those secrets might be in Angel hands now.

And then there was Laila Brown... The first girl I ever kissed. The upstanding girl who insisted that good guys should never hide. When the

4

Guardian Knights killed the Angel queen and began their retreat, Laila refused to leave without me. She died with her mother in an explosion that killed both instantly. I wasn't there when it happened.

It had only been eight weeks, and I still frequently had my moments of pain and frustration. The news that Randal Divine had succeeded Larissa Divine as the Angels' new leader, Terry returning to active mission status, and all these recent false alarms weren't helping me in the least.

The panic alarm still refused to stop. What was taking Alia so long?!

I was about to go to the safe room myself to see what the problem was when the alarm finally went silent.

Sighing, I walked back to the dining room to finish carving up the turkey so that it would fit in the refrigerator. Cindy and Terry would be fed on leftovers for the rest of the week.

Alia came back to help me, and I asked, "What took you so long?"

"They didn't answer," replied Alia's voice in my mind. *"I mean, it took more than a minute before anyone said anything to me."*

"That's weird," I remarked.

The security people were usually immediate in their response, and with good reason. Cynthia Gifford, our surrogate mother, was the only psionic hider who could create a hiding bubble large enough to cover the entirety of the Guardians' psionic city, New Haven. Within her invisible bubble, psionics couldn't sense one another's powers, making it nearly impossible for Angel spies to gather information on our settlement. Known among the Guardians as the Heart of New Haven, Cindy was second only to Mr. Baker himself on the priority list of New Haven's security forces.

And yet Alia had to call on the safe-room intercom for a full minute before they even responded?

I put the knife down. "Alia, come with me."

My sister followed on my heels as I jogged to the safe room and hit the intercom button.

"Gifford residence safe room to NH-1 Security," I said into the microphone.

There was no answer, so I repeated myself.

Still no reply.

"What's going on, Addy?" Alia asked in a worried tone.

"I'm not exactly sure," I said quietly. "This one just might be for real."

The last and only time a real alert was issued so far was when a pair of Angel puppeteers (mind controllers who could control people's bodies) hijacked two innocent civilians and used them to attack our building. That was back on New Year's Eve, and it was hardly a real threat to us. Though the puppeteers were never caught, their puppets didn't make it past the lobby.

I called the security team through the intercom again, and finally a voice answered, "NH-1 Security to Gifford residence. Identify please." I didn't recognize the voice, but that wasn't uncommon.

"Adrian Howell," I said.

"Roger that," said the voice. "Is that Hansel?"

"Adrian Howell," I repeated stubbornly.

Ever since my argument with Mr. Baker over his demand that I remain an Honorary Guardian Knight in order to protect his reputation, I adamantly refused to answer to my old call sign. After what I had seen of the conflict between the Guardians and the Angels, I had concluded that while I was probably still better off with the Guardians, I no longer wanted to be a part of their 700-year-old war.

"Hansel?" the voice asked again.

"Adrian!" I shouted. But then I wondered why this security officer would ask to confirm my call sign after hearing my real name.

"What's going on?" I asked into the microphone. "Is this one for real?"

Chances were, it was. Probably another suicide attack. Alia and I were safe up here.

"Negative," said the voice. "False alarm. Knights will be up shortly to double-check."

Alia looked at me anxiously. *"Addy?"*

I heard the front door open and Terry's voice called out, "Cindy! Adrian! Alia! Where are you?"

I rushed back to the living room where I found Terry standing by the front door, panting heavily. Terry was a born and bred warrior who, despite having lost her left arm a bit below her elbow, was one of the toughest Knights in all of New Haven. Rarely did I see her out of breath. Had she decided not to wait for an elevator car and instead sprinted up the forty floors to our penthouse?

"Terry, something's wrong," I said. "I was just talking to the building security and—"

Terry cut me off, shaking her head and saying, "That's not possible, Adrian, because there's no building security left."

"What?"

"They're *in* the building, Half-head! The Angels are in the goddamn building!"

I stared at Terry for a moment. I only had one ear, my right one having been shot off a little over a year ago, but I had heard Terry right.

Angels in New Haven One.

Terry locked the front door as I turned to Alia and said, "Stay close."

Alia nodded silently, giving me her bravest look. I wasn't too worried. Alia knew the drill. We had been through some tough times together and somehow survived them all. At ten years old, my sister was an Honorary Guardian Knight herself, and she often acted the part better than I did.

"Where's Cindy?" asked Terry.

"At a meeting," I replied. "Probably down in the subbasement."

Under the basement parking lot of our building was hidden a secret network of rooms. There was the dojo where Terry taught me to fight, a shooting range, a jail, and meeting rooms of various sizes. Cindy could be in one of those meeting rooms with Mr. Baker and the Guardians' ruling Council, or possibly in another New Haven building altogether. I wasn't exactly sure where she was right now, and it worried me a lot.

"Hope she's okay," said Terry.

"The security guys, or whoever they were, said there are Knights coming up here," I told her.

"Well somebody's coming up," agreed Terry, "but probably not Knights."

The Angels' fighters, known as Seraphim, were on their way up here to either kill or take Cindy prisoner. The fact that Cindy wasn't home wouldn't stop them from attacking anyone else they found.

"Safe room?" I asked hesitantly. I wasn't sure I wanted to barricade myself in a dead end.

Terry shared my concern. "Not yet," she replied, picking up the phone. Then she hung up. "It's dead."

The panic alarm turned on again.

"I'll go check," I said, running back to the safe room, and Terry and Alia followed.

As soon as I pushed the intercom button, the siren went silent again. The intercom crackled to life and a male voice said, "Spider to Gifford safe room."

It was the voice of Mr. Ted Williams, who was a member of Mr. Baker's personal security.

Terry wasn't taking any chances, though. She quickly pushed me aside and said, "Rabbit here. Confirm security code, Spider. This is Rabbit 22-R-31-G."

"Spider confirms Rabbit. This is Spider 13-A-99-L."

"Rabbit confirms," replied Terry.

Security ID codes were a new protocol for the Knights, added but a month ago as Angel-Guardian tensions reached an all-time high. My acquired distrust of psionic powers in general made me wonder if the voice of Mr. Ted "Spider" Williams might still be suspect, but his code was good enough for Terry.

"What's going on down there, Spider?" asked Terry.

"We have retaken NH-1," said Mr. Williams, "but other buildings are reporting disturbances as well. We are not yet sure of the size of the Angel forces. You are under no immediate threat but we strongly advise that you remain in the safe room for now. Are your charges secure?"

In addition to being my personal combat trainer, Terry was our official live-in bodyguard, and her "charges" were Cindy, Alia and me.

"Hansel and Gretel are with me," replied Terry. "Is Silver alright?"

"Roger that, Rabbit. Silver is safe. We have evacuated the Council to a secure location. Please remain locked in the safe room with your charges until further notice. Spider out."

The line went dead, and I could almost touch the frustration radiating from Terry's body. Staying locked in a safe room while Guardian Knights fought Angels inside the borders of New Haven would be a serious test of Terry's self-control. Ever since the Angels had tortured her brother to death, Terry had been itching for revenge.

I couldn't be certain because she refused to give me details, but Terry probably spilled some Angel blood early this year when, in order to cure my blindness, she kidnapped a reconstructive healer from an Angel fort. But aside from that, as a member of the Raven Knights, Terry had so far only fought God-slayers, the non-psionic religious fanatics who were trying to exterminate us. It was the only work Terry could get because she was still too young to learn how to block psionic controllers from her mind. She already planned to transfer to the Lancer Knights to fight psionic Angels as soon as she learned blocking, but in the meantime, she was stuck with us.

Terry looked ruefully at Alia and me before closing the safe-room door, locking us in. I didn't particularly pity her.

"Hansel and Gretel are with me," I mimicked dryly. "Thanks a lot, Terry!"

Terry laughed, and suddenly Alia and I laughed too, letting out our little sighs of relief. It seemed that my sister and I had been holding our breaths ever since Terry burst into the penthouse with her news. It felt good to break the tension.

New Haven was under siege by an as-of-yet-unknown number of Angel Seraphim, but we were safe here and it appeared that the battle had already turned in the Guardians' favor. New Haven One was secured, the Council was safe, and most importantly, so was Cindy, wherever she was.

I sat cross-legged on the floor, meditation style, picturing Cindy's face in my mind. Our adoptive mother took her Guardian call sign, Silver, from the color of her long, straight hair, and I still remembered how it seemed to shine in the moonlight when I first met her one cold night, years ago. I remembered how her calm manner and comforting voice had drawn the fear out of a near-feral child who had been on the run for weeks and might otherwise have kept running until he was caught by the Angels or worse.

Before Terry started living with us, I was Cindy's designated live-in bodyguard, and as an inactive Guardian Knight, Cindy was still officially my charge too. If the Knights expected Terry and me to stay here in this stuffy vault, they had better do a damn good job of protecting Cindy!

Alia had sat down behind me and was just getting comfortable resting her back against mine when Terry asked, "You want to play a game of nine-ball, Adrian?"

"Sure," I said, jumping to my feet.

My sister let out a little shriek as her support vanished and she tumbled backwards. "Addy!" she cried aloud, but she was smiling.

I pulled Alia to her feet. Levitating two cue sticks off the rack, I dropped one into my sister's hands. Alia was horrible at pool, but I couldn't exactly leave her out of the game. Terry grabbed another stick for herself as I set up the table.

Terry made the break shot by threading her cue stick through the metal hook attached to her left stump. Terry had four attachments for her amputated arm: a lifelike prosthetic hand, a heavy metal bar for pounding, a double-edged knife for stabbing, and the pirate captain's hook. The hook seemed to suit her best on most missions and at the pool table.

We played three games. Terry, as was often the case, won them all.

Suddenly Terry asked me, "Don't you miss being a Knight, Adrian?"

Technically, I still was a Knight. I trained regularly with Terry in the subbasement dojo and practiced my pistol work in the shooting range. But I knew what Terry meant.

"No," I replied flatly, "I don't."

"Not even a little?" she asked.

"No."

Terry threw me an exasperated look. "We're in here playing games and people are dying out there."

I shrugged. "It's not my war."

"You don't care in the least?"

I sighed. "Of course I care, Terry," I said patiently. "People are dying. But I only joined the Guardians because I once thought they would lead me to Cat. I'm only here now because Cindy is here, and she only came to New Haven because her idiot son needed rescuing from an underground research facility and the Guardians were the only ones who could help."

Terry frowned. "And you don't think you owe the Guardians anything?"

I shook my head. "We used each other. We're even."

"You are so damn stubborn, Half-head!" Terry spat irately. "Sometimes I feel like I'm talking to my grandfather."

Ralph P. Henderson, Terry's late grandfather, was not the kind of man I enjoyed being compared to.

I grinned at Terry. "I didn't know you ever talked to Ralph."

Terry let out a loud humph.

Then she narrowed her eyes, asking, "When you say you're even, does that include us?"

"What are you talking about?"

"Us, Half-head! You and me!" Terry said emphatically. "You save me on that boat, I cure your eyes…"

"Hey! You're my friend!" I snapped, genuinely insulted. "I never thought of our relationship as a trade!"

"I'm sorry, Adrian," Terry mumbled embarrassedly. "I'm cranky today, I guess."

I smiled. "We're just different people, Terry."

"Addy," Alia said in a small voice, "I have to go."

I was about to ask where but then I saw her shuffling her feet uncomfortably.

"Oh, right," I said, chuckling at the memory of the last time we had been locked in here. "Let's see if the coast is clear."

I pushed the intercom call button and got in touch with NH-1 Security. The voice wasn't Spider's, so Terry went through the security code routine again. We were told that NH-1 was still locked down, meaning no entry or exit until the Knights canceled the alert, but we were probably safe on the upper floors.

We were forty floors off the ground, more than four hundred feet in the air, but I remembered a time when an Angel puppeteer had taken control of my body from miles away, forcing me to telekinetically blast Alia so hard that she had nearly died. The puppeteer had also been a finder and he had latched onto me by sensing my psionic power from afar. Fortunately, that couldn't happen here because we were protected by Cindy's massive hiding bubble.

We let Alia out to run to the bathroom, and while waiting for her to return, I asked the Knight on the intercom for more details.

It had been nearly an hour since the Seraphim first started attacking Guardians inside the New Haven high-rise condominiums. Currently, the fighting was sparse and mostly limited to the NH-2 and NH-4 buildings. In each high-rise, a team of Seraphim had barricaded themselves into a few of the upper floors, and the situation seemed to be turning into a long-term standoff. Local non-Guardian residents had called the police to report hearing gunshots, but Guardian Command had enough connections with the city government to keep police and nosy reporters clear of the New Haven area.

Terry asked into the intercom, "How long is this alert going to last?"

"We're not sure yet," answered the Knight. "Hang in there."

That was when we heard Alia scream.

Terry and I sprinted out of the safe room and toward Alia's high-pitched cries. I heard my sister's telepathic voice desperately calling out my name. We found her lying on the living-room floor, her hands on her forehead, writhing about in agony. She couldn't stop screaming.

Out of the corner of my left eye, I sensed something move.

The sun had set and the overcast sky was dark now, but the light from our living room illuminated a gangly figure levitating just outside, peering in through the window.

Watching us.

Terry shoved me hard from behind. "Damn it, Adrian, no eye contact!"

I had almost felt the controller's power enter my mind, but Terry's quick thinking broke the connection. I telekinetically pulled the curtains over the window.

My sister was no longer screaming, but her whole body was convulsing violently. I grabbed the sides of her head and looked into her dilated eyes.

"Look at me, Alia!" I said frantically. "Look at me! Look at me! Look at me!"

She was completely gone.

"What the hell was that, Terry?!" I shouted, but even before Terry answered, I knew.

It was a berserker. A flight-capable telekinetic berserker.

Alia stopped shaking, but she was still panting like a dog. I knew from direct experience what was about to happen next.

I telekinetically lifted Alia up into the air as she glared at me and let out a low growl. Under the influence of a psionic berserker, even an undersized ten-year-old girl was a frightening sight. Alia's growl turned into hissing and spitting, screaming and snarling as her arms and legs thrashed violently about in midair, looking for something, anything, to hurt. Finding nothing, she then turned on herself, pulling at her own hair and beating her head with her fists. I pumped more of my telekinetic power into her, restraining her arms, and Alia roared even louder.

As soon as Terry saw that I had my sister under control, she dashed back to the safe room to report what had just happened.

Watching Alia, I shuddered as I remembered how a berserker had made my father kill my mother. I remembered my father clawing at my bedroom door like a wild animal.

Keeping Alia safely above the furniture, I glanced at the closed curtain.

Ever since the renovations to the penthouse last year, all the windows were reinforced bulletproof glass. There was no way through, but was the Angel still hovering just behind the curtain?

No. If he was, he could have opened the curtain to look at us again. No doubt his flight up to the fortieth floor and his psionic attack on Alia had used up all his energy, forcing him to make an emergency landing somewhere.

But he could come back.

Alia finally stopped kicking and her whole body went limp. I gently set her down on a sofa as Terry came back into the room.

Terry said angrily, "That curtain was closed when I last saw it."

"He must have opened it from outside," I muttered, looking down at Alia's pale face.

I checked her pulse. It was a little faint, but okay. She was breathing. I pulled open her eyelids and Terry found me a flashlight to check the pupils. Normal responses there.

But I knew from Cindy that many types of psionic mind control carried a high risk of permanent brain damage when used on children, and berserking was particularly dangerous. I had survived two long-range berserker attacks when I was twelve years old, but I sometimes wondered if those attacks might be the reason I often felt so unbalanced and irritable.

Alia was still ten, and the berserker had been right there.

Please let her be okay.

Terry whispered, "I hope her brain isn't fried."

"I should have drained her," I said numbly.

Terry shook her head. "It wouldn't have helped, Adrian. Her balance is too good."

A psionic with "bad balance" was someone who, like me, couldn't stop his psionic power from supporting his physical strength. Metal touching a psionic's body drained all powers, and consequently for someone who couldn't balance his power, it drained physical strength and even emotions. When I had been attacked, I had managed to break the berserker's influence on my mind by touching metal and draining myself. Terry was probably right, though: It wouldn't have worked for Alia. There were disadvantages to being good at some things.

Alia stirred a bit. I thought I heard a whisper in my mind.

"Alia," I called, gently shaking her shoulders. "Ali?"

My sister slowly opened her eyes. *"Addy?"*

"Hey," I said, smiling as she looked up at us. "Welcome back."

Alia threw her arms around my neck, her whole body trembling.

"Addy... oh Addy," she sobbed. *"I—I saw everything but I couldn't stop! I was coming back from the bathroom and something was tapping the window and then the curtain opened and—and he looked at me and..."*

"It's okay, Alia," I breathed, holding her. "It's okay now. It's over."

Terry brought a glass of red wine to calm Alia's nerves. My sister shook her head but Terry forced her to take two sips, and I gratefully downed the rest in one gulp. Then I carried Alia back to the safe room as Terry grabbed the blankets from all of our beds and brought them in.

"I closed the curtains in your bedroom, but stay out just in case, okay?" said Terry as she dumped the blankets on the floor.

Terry had also brought Alia's nightclothes. Alia was totally spent, so Terry and I helped her change into her bright yellow pajamas. As Terry pulled off Alia's shirt, I caught a glimpse of my sister's heavily scarred back: the many crisscrossing lines that told of years of ritualistic torture before Alia was abandoned deep in a forest to die. For Alia, that had only been the beginning. Then there was our capture and interrogation by the Wolves, our time at the Psionic Research Center, near-abductions and dreadful battles after coming to New Haven. Alia had been through so much already that it was a wonder she was sane at all.

We folded two blankets to make a mat for Alia to lie down on. My sister was still shivering a bit. I pulled another blanket over her, up around her shoulders.

"You're going to be okay, Ali," I said quietly, not quite sure who I was trying to comfort. "Just get some rest. You'll be okay."

Alia nodded weakly and closed her eyes.

I kept my hand resting gently on her stomach until she fell asleep.

Terry was sitting with her back against the opposite wall. I noticed her eyes were slightly red as she looked at me and said hoarsely, "Still neutral, Adrian?"

I had no reply to that.

The intercom crackled to life. "NH-1 Security to Gifford residence," called a Knight's voice.

Terry stood and pushed the intercom button. "Rabbit here."

"We haven't been able to locate your berserker anywhere around NH-1," said the Knight. "It's possible that he moved away. We'll stay on the lookout."

"Thanks for nothing," Terry said sourly, and sat down again.

Carefully so as not to wake Alia, I whispered, "He's still here."

"Where?" asked Terry.

"Above us. On the roof. He's resting."

"How do you know that? You can't sense him."

I shrugged. "That's where I'd be."

Terry nodded. "You want to kill him?"

I stared back at her for a moment, and then I looked at Alia's peaceful, sleeping face.

I slowly got to my feet. This wasn't for the Guardians.

The door to the safe room couldn't be locked from the outside, but we closed it and Terry quickly returned from her room with a semi-automatic pistol in her right hand.

We exited the penthouse and locked the front door behind us. All of the elevator lights were off, the whole system having been shut down by NH-1 Security, but that didn't matter. I pulled opened the door to the staircase, and we climbed the last flight of stairs up to the exit that opened onto the roof of New Haven One.

Terry had the key to the roof door in her pocket, but with only one hand, she couldn't use it and hold her gun at the same time. Terry wasn't wearing her pistol holster either, so she slid the barrel under her belt and then silently unlocked the door.

If the telekinetic berserker was on the roof, he'd probably be watching this door in case it was opened by a pack of Guardian Knights. There was little chance of surprising him unless he was already hovering at one of our windows, waiting.

Alia was sleeping off her ordeal, and I didn't want to wake her to heal us if we got injured. It was possible that the Angel was armed, but I doubted it. Flying this high up into the air was no small task even for a powerful telekinetic, and to do that whilst carrying a solid metal gun was really not feasible. No, this man was relying solely on his psionic powers. He had probably been hoping to find either Terry or me behind the living-room curtain, but when he saw Alia, he attacked, knowing that if Alia got away, we'd be warned of his presence anyway.

So he berserked my little sister.

Well, whoever you are, you sick psycho freak, get ready for Terry Henderson and Adrian Howell!

Standing one step behind Terry, I prepared a telekinetic blast in my right hand. In a few seconds, I was ready to fire a single focused shot through my right index finger. I couldn't fire focused blasts very rapidly, and my range wasn't all that great either, but my telekinetic accuracy was always spot on. If I could get within twenty yards, all I'd need was one shot.

"He can't sense you," whispered Terry. "Remember, no eye contact. Ready?"

I nodded.

Terry pushed open the door. A powerful gust of cool night air hit our faces and I involuntarily squinted as I followed Terry out.

Six rapid gunshots.

I didn't even see what happened.

"He jumped the moment he saw us," Terry shouted over the howling wind. Pistol in hand, she was standing at the edge of the roof, leaning over the railing and looking down. "But he's not going to fly very well with blood pouring out of him."

I looked over the railing too. "You hit him?"

"At least twice," confirmed Terry.

The ground was too dark to see where the man had fallen, but I trusted Terry, who was as fast and efficient as ever. The iron in the Angel's blood would have drained his powers the moment it left his body and touched his skin. Even if the Angel could somehow survive two gunshot wounds, he wouldn't have survived his high-speed reunion with the ground.

Terry looked at me apologetically. "I would have let you kill him yourself, Adrian, but he was getting away."

"I don't care," I replied, feeling my telekinetic energy slowly reabsorb into my arm. "Just as long as he's dead."

Terry grinned. "We're not all *that* different."

2. THE SECOND WAVE

The security alert continued into the night. Back in the safe room, I silently watched Alia sleep as Terry sat by the intercom, occasionally getting updates from the Knights.

Alia woke at around 11pm.

Yawning loudly, her first telepathic words in my head were, *"I'm really thirsty, Addy."*

Once Alia was rehydrated, Terry retrieved one of Alia's board games from our bedroom. Terry usually didn't play with us, but this time she joined in. As we sat together on the folded blankets, Alia was soon talking and laughing as if nothing had happened.

It was impossible to tell what long-term damage her run-in with the berserker might have caused, but my sister appeared to be in good spirits, for which I was extremely grateful. Terry and I didn't tell her what we had done while she slept. Alia was a healer, and she never seemed to understand the concept of revenge anyway. I wished more people were like that.

Midnight.

"NH-1 Security to Gifford residence," called the intercom.

Terry stood and touched the intercom button. "Rabbit here, go ahead."

"Rabbit, security code, please."

Terry glanced at me. NH-1 Security hadn't asked for Terry's ID code in a while. Terry read off her code, and the Knight replied with his.

"What's going on down there?" asked Terry.

"Are your charges locked in the safe room?"

"Yes. What's going on?"

"We're not exactly sure yet, but advise you stay there and sleep in shifts tonight."

I wondered if we would sleep at all. Terry tried to get more information, but the Knight refused.

Twenty minutes later, the intercom came on again.

A panicked voice said, "Gifford safe room, respond! Respond, damn it!"

Terry replied briskly, "Rabbit here. Identify, please."

"We're being overrun—they're coming up!" the voice said frantically. "Too damn many! Evacuate now! Get to NH-6!"

"Identify!" Terry said again.

What we heard this time, though, were screams and shouts, and gunfire in the background. Then Mr. Williams's voice came on. "Get out, Rabbit!" he shouted. "They're swarming us! Get out now!"

Terry asked, "Is Silver safe?"

The intercom went dead. Terry, Alia and I stared at each other.

In the weeks following the Guardians' assassination of Queen Larissa Divine, as the tensions between the Guardians and the Angels flared up, we had often discussed the possibility of a major Angel invasion. But the Guardians had prepared for this. Hours ago, after retaking NH-1, the Knights had assured us that they had everything under control.

"Second wave," breathed Terry. "It's happening."

"The Seraphim are in the building, Terry," I said, "so how are we getting out?"

Terry glanced at Alia for a brief instant and then said, "Over the side." Terry unlocked the safe-room door. "Parachutes are on the roof."

I knew that. When the Guardians fitted our windows with bulletproof glass, they had also left a set of emergency parachutes on the roof for just this kind of occasion.

I grabbed Alia's hand and pulled her with us as we sprinted through the living room and out the front door. As soon as we opened the door to the staircase across from the elevators, I heard echoing shouts from below. How close were they?

Her pistol tucked under her belt, Terry led us up to the roof door and opened it.

"Alia's too small for the harness so I'll take her down myself," said Terry as we stepped out of the door and ran across the roof to where our parachutes were stowed. "Help me put on my harness, Adrian. Then you can fly."

Ever since losing her left arm, Terry loathed being taken care of, refusing to be treated like a cripple. It was a testament to how desperate our time constraints were that Terry would ask for my help in something as trivial as strapping on a parachute harness.

Coming to a sudden stop, Terry cursed furiously, and I immediately saw why. The large nylon bag containing all of our parachutes was missing.

"That bastard!" screamed Terry. Score one for the dead berserker.

Terry turned to me and asked, "Can you get Alia down?"

I nodded slowly. "Probably."

Human levitation was one of the toughest things a telekinetic could do, not only because of blood iron, but because of the sheer complexity of the human body. A powerful telekinetic could fly for several minutes or hover quietly for longer, but to lift himself and another person simultaneously was often beyond the capabilities of even the most powerful. When the Angels had abducted Cindy out of our penthouse last year, it took two flight-capable telekinetics carrying Cindy between them to make a controlled descent away from the building.

Soon after the gathering of lesser gods, I discovered that my telekinetic power had grown once again. I could now, for very brief periods of time, levitate both myself and Alia together. Not long enough to carry her up forty floors, but a controlled fall would be easier. All I had to do was keep us from hitting the ground too fast.

"Alright, you jump with Alia," said Terry, looking back at the door to the stairs. "I'll find another way down."

"No!" I said. "We're all staying together."

Alia nodded in agreement, but Terry argued, "I can't protect you two if I'm going to get through the Seraphim!"

Terry wasn't an easy person to kill, but she had limits too. I shook my head. "You'll never get through them, Terry. You're coming with us!"

Even as I said that, I questioned the wisdom of it. Terry was taller than me. How was I going to carry her weight?

"Take Alia down and come back for me, then," said Terry.

I shook my head again. I doubted I would have enough energy to fly straight back up here after escorting Alia down. The Seraphim could be here any moment. "We're going together, Terry," I said firmly. "Together or not at all!"

"You can't carry both of us!"

"Yeah? Watch me!" I shouted back, trying to sound much more confident than I felt. "No metal, Terry. Lose it now!"

After a moment's hesitation, Terry tossed her pistol over the side, followed by her hook attachment. Then, looking down at herself, she quickly pulled off her shoes, belt and jeans. Terry's shoes and belt had metal buckles, and her jeans had a metal button and zipper. Terry wasn't modest at the best of times, and this was an emergency. Wrapping her jeans around her shoes, she threw the bundle over the edge.

Psionics like Alia and myself never wore metal if we could help it. I looked down at the Braille watch on my right wrist. It had been a present from Mark Parnell. I tore it off and threw it over the side of the building.

Then I lightly climbed over the side railing, carefully standing on the few inches of space between the railing and the ledge. Terry lifted Alia over, passing her to me.

Having accidentally peeked over the ledge, Alia cried into my head, *"Addy, I'm scared!"*

She wasn't the only one. "Arms around my neck, Alia," I said as calmly as I could. "Don't look down."

Once my sister was semi-comfortably latched onto me, I said to Terry, "Come on, hurry up!"

But Terry was having second thoughts. "No, Adrian! We'll never make it!"

"Come on, soldier!" I barked.

Terry reluctantly climbed over the railing and put her arms around Alia and me.

I looked down at the distant darkness below and thought that Terry was probably right. We weren't going to make it.

Terry shouted, "So what happens if you can't carry us both? Who gets to die?!"

The roof door burst open.

"I'll decide on the way down!"

I leaned back over the ledge, and felt my stomach jump into my throat as we fell as one. I saw the windows rushing past, and heard Alia screaming over the howling wind. I felt her arms tighten around me. Terry was still with us too. It felt like I was watching a slow-motion replay from far away. I could almost count the floors.

I knew from the start that carrying both Terry and Alia, there was no way to make even a semi-controlled descent. My telekinetic power would never last long enough for that. Instead, I would have to kick-stop in midair just before we hit the ground. I waited until we were less than one hundred feet from oblivion.

Then I roared. Every ounce of power I ever possessed had to come out now. I felt my telekinesis tear through my body. I felt it slice into Alia and Terry. For a micro-second eternity, inside the deepest part of my consciousness, I could feel every hair on Alia's head, every scar on her skin. I felt the awkward stump at the end of Terry's left arm, and the fierce beating of her heart. Here and now, there was nothing else. No wind. No sound. No color. Not even the force of gravity. Just Alia, Terry and myself in motion.

Motion that had to stop. Now!

We smashed into the ground. It was soft, wet earth. I couldn't feel my own body, my senses completely numbed except for a loud, constant ringing in my ears.

Then I heard Alia crying, and Terry said weakly, "Up, Alia."

They were alive, but I didn't even have the strength left to feel relieved. I could hear distant shouts and calls, but couldn't make them out. Where were we? I was lying on my back, unable to even move my head, but I guessed that we had landed behind NH-1. We were safe for the moment, I hoped.

I saw Terry lean over me and peer into my face.

"Alive?" she asked.

I just managed to say, "Uh," and Terry disappeared from view.

Terry's voice from somewhere to my left said, "What is it, Alia? Oh!"

Then, probably replying to something Alia said telepathically, Terry said, "You're right, it's definitely broken. Just don't heal it yet, okay? I've got to straighten your bone first. Here."

I heard Alia yelp in pain as Terry did whatever she did next.

"Okay, do it now," said Terry. "At least you're not bleeding."

Alia didn't respond aloud, but continued whimpering in pain. Whatever she had broken, this clearly wasn't her day either.

Terry came back over to me. "Can you move yet? Come on, Adrian. I need you to get up."

With Terry's help, I managed to pull myself into a sitting position. I tried moving my feet a bit.

"Oh, good," said Terry, "you didn't break your neck. Knowing your luck, I thought you might be paralyzed or something."

"I'm okay," I breathed.

"Can you stand?" she asked impatiently.

"Not sure."

"Rest a minute, then. But only a minute."

Terry went to look for the stuff she had tossed from the roof.

I touched Cat's amethyst pendant around my neck to check that it was still there. The small violet stone was all I had when I first left home after turning psionic. I realized that once again, I had left everything behind. Then I glanced at my sister, who was similarly touching her chest to see if the bloodstone that Cindy had given her was still there. Well, perhaps not quite everything.

"What happened to you, Ali?" I asked. "Are you alright?"

My sister lifted her left arm a bit and said bravely, *"It's a little stiff, but I'm okay."*

"Sorry about the rough landing."

"It's okay."

If it had occurred to me, I might have tried searching for my Braille watch, but it didn't. Terry was gone less than a minute. When she returned, I noticed that she had recovered her hook attachment, belt, jeans and shoes. No pistol, though.

"Time to go, Adrian. Come on, you can stand," she said, roughly pulling me to my feet, which still felt quite rubbery.

"Wait," said Alia, coming up to us. "Don't pretend like you're okay, Terry. Addy, you too."

In addition to healing her broken arm, Alia had already taken care of whatever bruises she had sustained from our crash-landing, and she now spent a few minutes tending to Terry's and mine.

As Alia worked her healing on us, Terry smirked at me, saying, "Nice landing, Half-head."

"We're still alive, aren't we?" I replied gruffly.

My sister finished running her hands over our bruises. My physical pain was gone, but I was still feeling very lightheaded.

Terry didn't care. "Come on," she said, "we need to get going."

Terry grabbed my left hand and Alia took hold of my right. I somehow managed to stagger along with them as we cut across the block, heading away from NH-1.

"I can walk," I said, pulling my hands free, and I found that I could, albeit clumsily. "Where are we going? NH-6?"

"NH-4," replied Terry. "It's closer, and there's a Knight command post there, so if the building is still ours, we might find out where they took Cindy."

"Sounds good."

Alia stumbled, and Terry stopped to pull her up.

"It's alright, Alia," said Terry, crouching down. "Hop on."

It was only then that I noticed that my sister, still in her nightclothes, wasn't even wearing shoes or socks.

Alia climbed onto Terry's back. As we started walking again, I saw that there were many more cars and people on the road than usual for this time of night. How many were Guardians? How many were Knights? How many were Angel Seraphim?

Picking up her pace, Terry looked back at me and said, "Probably no one will attack us in the open, but there's no way to be sure. This may be much bigger than we thought. Stay sharp, okay?"

We entered the large park that ran between the NH-1 and NH-4 buildings. I followed Terry through a clump of trees and across a grassy field. Looking up, I saw the forty-story New Haven Four towering over us. Most of the lights were off in the windows, but a few near the top were still on.

Suddenly I heard a voice cry out, "Terry! Terry Henderson!"

We stopped and turned toward the frantic figure rushing up to us. It was a teenage boy with short blond hair. He was about as tall as Terry, and I had a feeling I had seen him before somewhere.

"Terry!" the boy cried. "Oh God, you gotta help us!"

Terry asked sharply, "What's going on?!"

"We're over there," said the boy, pointing to a line of trees in the distance. "Come on! Hurry!"

We followed him toward the trees, but Terry stopped before we came too close. She put Alia down on the grass and said to me, "Stay here. It could be a trap."

Without waiting for a reply, Terry ran into the trees. A moment later, she called out, "It's okay, Hansel, come on!"

If the boy was being manipulated by an Angel controller, it was equally possible that Terry was also under psionic control now. I didn't remember Terry's security code so I couldn't ask her to recite it. But I had noticed that she called me Hansel.

I looked at Alia and shrugged. We ran through the line of trees, coming into a small clearing.

Alia was hopping up and down, probably having stepped on some sharp twigs or something, but I ignored her, my attention instead on the many pairs of eyes looking at us.

They were all children.

About fifteen or so in number, some looked old enough to be in high school, but most were younger, some even smaller than Alia. The youngest ones looked terrified, and a few were sobbing quietly. I noticed a boy, a little taller than Alia, holding a bundle of cloth in his arms. It was a baby.

The boy who had led us here was saying rapidly to Terry, "They left us in the basement parking lot. The Knights. They gathered us there. They said they'd come back, but they didn't. I don't know where they are."

"You're all from NH-4?" asked Terry.

"Yeah," he replied. "The Angels were coming in from the lobby. We couldn't stay. There were a lot more of us, but the Angels were waiting outside. They started rounding us up. They were putting everyone onto a bus."

A few of the younger ones started crying louder. One of the older girls tried to hush them, and some others helped, but even the baby woke and started screaming.

"We can't leave them here, Terry," I said. "NH-4 is probably lost."

"I agree," said Terry, and then added warningly, "But you better start calling me Rabbit, Hansel. This is no different from being on a mission."

I rolled my eyes. I had always considered Guardian call signs a stupid and unnecessary protocol. It wasn't like the Angels didn't know who we were.

Terry looked around at the crowd and said, "If any of you have psionic combat powers, step forward. Destroyers or controllers, I don't care."

One of the older boys slowly raised his hand, saying, "I'm a pyroid."

"Good," Terry said crisply. "I'm Terry Henderson. Call me Rabbit."

"Yeah," said the boy, "I know who you are. I'm Peter."

"Okay, Peter the Pyroid, you're with me," said Terry. "Gretel, you too. We're going to go get some help. Hansel, you stay."

My strength was gradually returning, but I still felt a bit faint so I didn't argue.

Alia said something telepathically to Terry.

"Oh, right," said Terry, looking at Alia's bare feet. "On my back, then. I'll carry you till we're back on the street. I'm going to need you with us just in case."

As Alia climbed onto Terry's back, Terry turned to me and said, "Stay put, stay hidden. And see if you can get those damn kids to quiet down. If we're not back in ten minutes, Hansel, you get them out of New Haven."

Peter walked up to Terry and extended his hand, but Terry didn't shake it.

"You better be for real, fire boy," said Terry, poking him in the chest. "Let's go."

The three disappeared beyond the trees. The little kids were still crying, but the older ones were doing the best they could to comfort them, so I left them to it and flopped down on the damp grass.

I heard two of the older teen girls whispering loudly.

"Did you see her?"

"Yeah! She had a hook on her arm!"

"That was really Terry Henderson! Oh my God! So *that's* Adrian Gifford!"

The two girls approached me, and one asked timidly, "Are you really Adrian?"

I nodded numbly.

The girl looked at me in awe. "Wow… It's really you!"

Wonderful, I thought savagely. *We're famous.*

In our two years living in New Haven, Alia and I had made no friends except for Terry and Laila. We couldn't even go to a normal school. Because we lived with Cindy, Guardian parents forbade their children from associating with us for fear of being targeted by Angels. I was still bitter about that, and I didn't appreciate our semi-celebrity status at all. It wasn't right that we could be famous and friendless at the same time.

"Was that little girl Alia?" the teen girl asked.

I didn't respond, but her friend said, "Yeah, it must have been. I heard she's a Knight too."

"No way! That cutie?"

I glared up at them both, saying irately, "Would you two please go take care of the little ones?"

Looking wounded, they quickly backed off.

The blond-haired boy who had led us here came up to me and said nervously, "Hi, Adrian. Maybe you don't remember me, but we met once."

"I remember you," I said, finally remembering where I had seen him before. "You're James, the boy who can't catch Frisbees."

James gave me a sheepish smile. "I'm sorry about that time. I really am."

"It's okay," I said quietly. "But leave me alone and let me rest a bit, okay? I just fell off a very tall building and I'm dead tired. Go help that boy over there quiet his baby."

Terry was gone a long time. I had lost my watch, so I couldn't count off ten minutes, but nor did I care. Now that I was feeling stronger, I regretted letting Alia and Terry go off without me. I wasn't going to lead these kids out of New Haven without making sure that my sister was alright.

"*Addy!*" called Alia's voice in my head. "*Terry says get them ready to move. We're at the north exit.*"

I stood up and, trying my best to assume a commanding voice, said to the crowd, "Alright, we're moving out! Everyone get ready to run."

"No way!" said one of the tallest boys. "We're staying right here till the Knights come get us."

He was considerably bigger than me, but I had learned not to worry too much about size.

"I *am* a Knight!" I shouted furiously. "If you want to live, come with me!"

The crowd looked at me hesitantly for a moment, but then James stepped forward, and the two annoying girls followed. Soon everyone was running with me as I led them toward the park's north exit.

Terry met us halfway. She didn't have any Guardian Knights with her, but I noticed that she had acquired another pistol.

"I left Gretel with Peter," said Terry. "You got everyone here?"

"I think so," I said, not breaking pace. "How bad is it?"

"Very, Hansel," said Terry, jogging beside me. "NH-6 was nearly lost when I got there. I tried to get some Lancers to help, but they were too busy. New Haven is overrun. The Knights ordered a full evacuation."

"And Cindy?" I asked worriedly.

"Silver," corrected Terry. "She's safe, I think. She was with the Council when all this happened. They made it to the airport well before the Seraphim cut off that road."

"What about us?" I asked. We were already at the exit. Stopped on the curb with its engine running noisily was an old vomit-green minibus.

"We might just be the last civilian transport out," Terry said grimly as the kids filed onto the bus. "New Haven is falling."

Terry drove, and I sat with Alia in the seat behind her.

"They're not going to just let us drive out of here, are they?" I asked.

"You better believe they won't," said Terry, and then called loudly, "Everybody buckle up. Now!"

The Seraphim were taking New Haven from inside our buildings. There was no visible fighting on the open streets.

"Where are we going, Terry?" I asked, refusing to use her Guardian call sign.

Terry decided to let it slide, replying calmly, "There's an airfield past the river, in the forest just outside the city limits. It's a flight school. The Guardians never go there, so the Seraphim might not have blocked it off."

A few minutes later, Terry said, "We're being followed. There's a blue SUV on our tail."

Our minibus was still in the city, and the Angels weren't going to attack us until we were out of public sight.

"Think you can handle one car, Hansel?" asked Terry.

"Think you can stop calling me that, Terry?" I said evenly.

"Fine, Adrian!" snapped Terry. "The car?!"

"Sure," I replied. "No problem."

"Okay. Let's see if they stay with us."

Terry quietly drove the minibus over a bridge that spanned the wide river at the edge of the city, and soon we were driving along a winding forest road that weaved through some low hills. The road was almost pitch-black and our headlights illuminated very little of it.

Sitting behind the driver's seat, I couldn't see the rearview mirror, but according to Terry, the SUV was still following us at a distance.

"You want me to take care of them?" I asked, unbuckling my seatbelt.

"Not yet," said Terry. "They haven't attacked. Maybe they're not even Seraphim. They could be Guar—"

The rear windshield shattered as automatic gunfire tore into the back of the minibus.

"Heads down!" shouted Terry.

The old minibus's engine roared loudly as Terry floored the pedal, but in terms of acceleration, not much happened. I got out of my seat and, crouching as low as I could, made my way down the aisle between the screaming, terrified children, toward the rear of the vehicle.

It was good that I was crouching, because a moment later, a giant fireball flew in through the shattered windshield and impacted on the ceiling, sending sparks and little dancing flames everywhere. The ceiling was on fire and everything was a bit smoky, but no one had been cooked.

I reached the back and peered over the edge of the broken window. Another burst of gunfire forced me to duck, but I saw what I was dealing with: a dark blue SUV about twenty yards behind us. Its headlights were on high beam, making it difficult to see inside.

"Terry, slow down!" I shouted. "Bring them in closer!"

Terry didn't exactly slam on the brakes, but the minibus shook violently as Terry cut our speed in half.

I lifted my head up again and looked down at the driver and his partner, who were now right up behind us. Then I telekinetically grabbed the SUV's steering wheel and yanked it hard to the left.

The SUV flipped over on its side, turning over twice before disappearing behind another curve in the road. I turned around and happily called up to Terry, "We're clear!"

With the deafening sound of twisting metal and shattering glass, our minibus came to a full and very abrupt stop. I was literally launched off my feet, and only by using my telekinesis to steady myself did I manage to keep from flying through the broken front windshield.

Landing clumsily at the front of the aisle, I looked at the driver's seat to check if Terry was alright, but she wasn't there.

Gunshots outside. I jumped out of the open door and saw Terry as she was finishing off the last Seraph that had been part of a two-car roadblock we had smashed into. There were three other bodies on the road, and both of the Angels' cars had been totaled.

Terry threw down her pistol, which was probably empty.

I said wryly, "Looks like they knew about the airfield."

"Looks like they were sleeping on the job," said Terry, picking up a heavy automatic rifle and resting its barrel on her hook. "They could have pumped us full of lead when we hit their cars. We were really lucky they didn't."

"Lucky," I agreed. "But we're on foot from here."

"It's only another mile," said Terry. "We can leg it."

Terry stepped back into the minibus and called, "Is everyone okay?"

Following Terry back inside, I saw that the baby in the young boy's arms was miraculously alive and unharmed. I wondered how that was possible, but now wasn't the time to ask.

Though quite shaken, everyone was unhurt.

Except one.

Perhaps the pyroid hadn't been wearing his seatbelt from the start, or maybe he unbuckled it intending to help me deal with the SUV. Either way, when the minibus crashed, Peter broke his neck. He was dead by the time Alia got to him.

"Leave him," said Terry, and we did.

The oldest kids carried the littlest ones, and Terry and I took turns carrying Alia as we half-walked, half-jogged down the remainder of the road to the flight school's airfield.

Set in a large forest clearing, there was one runway, two buildings, and two airplane hangars with several small and medium-size propeller planes lined up in front of them. There was a tall iron fence running all the way around the compound, and a locked gate blocked the road, but I quickly levitated everyone over it one by one.

Inside was dark and silent, but we soon put an end to that.

"Stay here," Terry said to the crowd. "We'll be right back."

I started to follow Terry toward a medium-size building next to the hangar, but then we heard the sound of a car engine in the distance.

Terry swore loudly. "These guys never quit!"

Terry called back to our group, "Everyone, get behind that hangar. Stay there!"

Alia led our newly acquired charges to the hangar as I followed Terry to the shadow side of the building nearest the gate.

"They could be Guardians," I said.

"I know," said Terry, checking her assault rifle. I noticed that it had an extra-large scope mounted on it. Terry pressed a button on the side of the scope, and then another.

"Night vision," she explained, aiming the rifle at the gate and peering through the scope. "Now get away from me, Adrian. If they're destroyers or finders, they'll sense where you are. Get up on the roof and stay out of sight. We'll see how they react."

I did as I was told, levitating myself up onto the roof of the three-story building. But Terry didn't wait for a reaction from the incoming vehicle. She started firing the moment the car, which was another SUV, busted through the iron gate. I couldn't see it clearly, but I guessed that Terry killed the driver because the SUV quickly went out of control and smashed into a van parked nearby.

Dropping back down from the roof, I asked, "How'd you know they were Angels?"

"I recognized one of them," Terry said grimly as she jogged toward the wrecked SUV.

I followed two steps behind.

The driver was riddled with bullets from Terry's automatic, but the man beside him was merely knocked out.

This time, I was the one who swore.

It was Mr. Simms.

His clothes were spattered with blood from the driver, but his only injury was a bruise on his forehead. After checking that there was no one else on board, Terry dropped her rifle and opened Mr. Simms's door.

Terry yanked the unconscious Mr. Simms out of his seat and onto the ground as she yelled furiously, "Wake up, you stinking bastard! Turned Angel, didn't you?! Sold us to them! And they don't even have a master controller anymore to make you do it!"

I pointed my right index finger at Mr. Simms's limp body, but Terry grabbed my arm, saying, "No, Adrian! Not yet! We need to find out what he knows, what he told them."

Alia had returned, followed hesitantly by about half of the kids. My sister was staring at me, aghast. I yanked my arm free of Terry's grasp and looked away.

One of the older kids recognized my former unit commander. "Jesus, this guy's a Guardian," he said quietly. "He's a Knight."

"Not anymore," said Terry. "He turned Angel on us."

"Stay with him," Terry said to me. "If he wakes and tries something, then kill him. I'll be right back."

Terry jogged off toward the main building alone. Alia knelt down to heal the bruise on Mr. Simms's forehead.

"Leave it, Alia," I said, looking down at Mr. Simms disgustedly.

My sister shook her head. *"He's hurt, Addy."*

I shrugged. There was no arguing with a healer's logic.

Terry returned a few minutes later with the rest of the kids, a toolbox and a length of rope.

Terry tossed the rope to the two tallest boys. "Tie this man up tightly. Arms behind his back, wrists and ankles together."

Terry opened the toolbox and pulled out a large chisel.

"Keep him drained too," said Terry, tossing the chisel to the boys.

Then she turned to the crowd and commanded, "Everyone stay put. I'll go get us our ride."

Alia stayed behind, but I followed Terry as she jogged, toolbox in hand, toward the row of propeller airplanes parked in front of the hangars. Most were small single-engine planes, only seating four, but a few had an engine on each wing and looked just large enough to carry all of us. But I realized that Terry was forgetting one very important detail.

Walking past the smaller planes, Terry said to me, "I was expecting at least one or two people to be sleeping here, but I think we might actually be alone. We'll have to hurry, though. That Angel car breaking down the gate might have triggered an automatic call to the police."

Terry still didn't seem to realize the flaw in her plan, so I asked, "You're going to steal a plane?"

"No, Adrian, we're all going to sprout wings and fly."

I ignored her sarcasm. "Where's our pilot?"

"You're looking at her," said Terry. "Didn't I tell you I used to fly planes?"

Upon reflection, I remembered Terry mentioning it in passing back when we first met, but I hadn't really believed her.

"Only I haven't flown in five years, and even then, I mostly flew single-engine props," said Terry as we approached the largest twin-engine plane, which looked about the size of our minibus. "But don't worry. I've had some time in twins like this too."

I did some quick math in my head. "You were twelve years old when you learned to fly?"

"No, I was nine. I said the *last* time I flew was five years ago, Half-head."

Terry placed her toolbox on the ground next to the side door at the rear of the airplane.

Gently running her fingers along the edge of the door, Terry mused, "I could pry this open with a crowbar or break a window, but..."

Terry reached up and gently pulled the handle. The door quietly swung down to the ground, revealing steps on the other side of it that led up into the cabin.

Terry grinned at me. "Fortunately, most pilots are complete idiots who don't expect people to steal their planes. Doors are almost never locked."

I couldn't help chuckling.

I grabbed the toolbox and followed Terry inside. The cabin was much smaller than I had imagined from the outside.

"We're going to be terribly overloaded," said Terry, making her way to the cockpit. "I hope the runway's long enough."

That didn't sound at all comforting, especially since I still had a very vivid memory of our last overloaded flight. Terry's next words did nothing to alleviate my anxiety. "Where's the damn ignition?" she muttered to herself.

"Can you hotwire a plane?" I asked, setting the toolbox down on the cockpit floor and opening it for her.

"Sure I can," replied Terry. "It's easier than a car, since planes are built light."

She sat down in the pilot's seat and looked over the cockpit controls. Then she turned her head to me and smiled. "Lucky again. This model doesn't even use a key ignition."

Terry flipped some switches. "There's fuel too. Not full, but I think it'll be enough. Go get the kids. And dump that toolbox. I want to be as light as possible."

"Here we go again," I muttered as I climbed out of the plane.

Jogging back to the crowd of kids, I found them standing in a circle around Mr. Simms. The former Raven commander was still unconscious, his arms and legs bound together behind his back.

I heard the engines sputter to life and said to the crowd, "Come on, let's go. I'll bring the Angel."

I levitated Mr. Simms in front of me as I followed the children back to the airplane. Mr. Simms was extra heavy because he was built like a grizzly bear, not to mention the fact that he had a large metal chisel tied to his arm. Did we really need to take along all this extra weight? Back in the plane, I asked Terry, but she said simply, "We need him. He can tell us a lot. Don't worry. I'll get us up somehow."

I shrugged. The weight issue was Terry's problem this time. I knew nothing about flying airplanes.

There weren't enough seats for everybody, so we got the smallest ones to sit in the laps of the older, and somehow managed to pull everyone's seatbelt on. We left Mr. Simms in the aisle. After checking that the door was properly sealed, I joined Terry in the cockpit, sliding into the copilot's seat and placing Alia in my lap.

"Don't touch anything, okay?" said Terry, and Alia and I nodded.

Throttling up the engines, Terry quickly taxied the airplane over to the very end of the runway before turning us around. She wanted as much distance as possible to the fence at the other end of the strip.

Terry took two deep breaths, and then said, "Okay, here goes nothing. Hang on."

Terry used her hook to push both throttles to maximum. The engines roared in fury. The plane inched forward, and then very slowly gathered speed.

"Come on! Come on!" Terry shouted at the plane, much as she might to me in the dojo.

I looked at her anxiously. The airplane, though moving pretty fast, was still on the ground, and we were rapidly running out of runway. I knew we should never have brought Mr. Simms.

Even in the darkness, I could clearly see the end of the runway now, and the fence and trees beyond. In but a few seconds, we would crash through the fence and die in a massive explosion.

"Addy!" Alia cried in my head as I called out at the same time, "Terry!"

At the last moment, Terry pulled back on the flight controls, and I felt Alia suddenly get much heavier in my lap. We were airborne! Through the cockpit window, I saw the tops of the trees actually brush up against the underside of our airplane as we flew over them.

Within a minute, we had cleared the forest and were flying over farmland. Terry had left the landing lights on, illuminating the fields as we passed over them at dangerously low altitude.

I asked nervously, "Um, Terry, why aren't we climbing?"

"Ground clutter," said Terry.

"Excuse me?"

"Avoiding radar, Half-head. I don't want the Wolves on us. Be on the lookout for high-voltage wires."

I looked around the cockpit at the many gauges until I found the altimeter. The needle was at fifty feet.

Skimming the ground, our plane continued on into the night. Though we lost one brave boy on the road, we had managed to escape the fall of New Haven.

3. A CHANGED MAN

Once we got used to the idea of Terry flying our stolen airplane at just above ground level, Alia and I got out of our seat and faced the passengers. Terry had insisted that I find out who they were and who we could rely on.

It made psychological sense too. Most of the kids were obviously quite traumatized by what they had just lived through, and keeping them busy would help keep their minds off of New Haven, as well as how frighteningly close the ground looked from the windows. It was time to get acquainted with our charges. Including the baby, there were sixteen total.

"I'm Adrian Howell," I said uncomfortably as fifteen pairs of eyes focused on me. "I guess most of you know that already. We're, uh, safe for now."

Some of the younger kids still looked dazed, but most seemed to hear what I was saying.

"This is my sister Alia," I said.

Alia gave a little wave, saying nervously, "Hi."

The annoying teen girls smiled at us.

"I want to know who you all are," I said. "If you could tell me your names and ages, and uh, talents, if any."

A few started to talk at once, so I stopped them and pointed to each of them in turn, going around the cabin like a schoolteacher.

"I'm Daniel Livingston," said a dark-haired boy about my height. "I'm thirteen. No powers of course."

"James Turner," said James. "Sixteen last week. No powers yet."

"I'm Heather," said the girl who had called Alia a cutie. "I'm eighteen. Nothing ever. My parents aren't psionics."

"I'm Candace," said her friend, and I guessed that she was the same age. "I can speak some French."

"That's nice," I said dryly.

The next kid, sitting in Candace's lap, was a little smaller than Alia, and it took some coaxing before he said quietly, "I'm Teddy. I'm seven. I think they took my big sister and my parents."

"You'll find them," I said in a confident voice, lying through my teeth, and Teddy gave me a weak smile.

"I'm Max," said the next boy. "I'm eleven, and I'm a spark!"

"You're already psionic?" I asked in surprise.

Max grinned. "Yeah, I can shoot lightning and everything. I can even—"

"Shut up," I said frostily, and he did, instantly shrinking into his chair. Now that we were well out of New Haven's hiding bubble and I was calmer, I could sense psionic destroyer powers around me. The only one I felt now was a pyroid's.

"Addy, be nice," Alia said into my head, giving Max a reassuring smile. *"He's just scared."*

The next boy was the one with the baby.

"I'm Patrick," he said, holding the infant gently in his arms. "I'm ten, sir."

"Please don't call me 'sir,' Patrick," I said with a wry smile. "Is that baby your brother or your sister?"

"Neither, sir," said Patrick. "I just picked it up. I think it's a girl but I'm not sure."

"Well, you'll find out when you change its diaper," I said briskly. "You picked it up, it's your responsibility. Get some help from the others if you need it."

"Yes, sir."

"And please don't call me 'sir.' It makes me feel even more uncomfortable than flying at this altitude."

Patrick bit his tongue before he repeated himself, and a few of the kids laughed lightly.

Alia went up to Patrick and gently touched the baby's arm. The baby

37

woke and carefully wrapped its fingers around Alia's thumb, smiling up at her and cooing softly.

"It's so little," whispered Alia, gazing down into the baby's eyes.

I asked Patrick, "How did you manage to keep it alive when we crashed back there?"

Patrick looked down at the baby. "Well, when the window broke, I was afraid we might hit something or turn over. I didn't know what else to do, so I put the baby behind me and used my body as a seatbelt."

"That was good thinking," I said, impressed. "You saved its life."

"Thank you, sir."

Alia was beaming at Patrick, and he looked away embarrassedly. As my sister continued to play with the infant, I pointed to the next person, who in appearance reminded me a little of Laila Brown.

"I'm Rachael Adams," she said. "I'm seventeen, and I'm a hider."

"We could use a good hider," I said.

"I'm not very good yet," she said apologetically. "I just came into my power last month. I can only hide myself and anyone within a yard or so."

"Better than nothing."

And so it continued. After the baby, the youngest was only five years old, the oldest, nineteen. I learned that most of them were children of Knights and other important Guardians who had been called out to meet the Angel threat, while a few were from common Guardian families where both parents were simply out of the house when the invasion began. The Knights had been rounding up these strays in the basement of NH-4 and preparing for their evacuation when the Seraphim swarmed the building. In the confusion that followed, more than half of the children gathered there had been taken by the Angels, including the siblings of several members of our group.

This group kidnapping of Guardian children didn't make a lot of sense to me since, without a master controller, the Angels couldn't convert their captives. I wondered if the Angels were hoping to use them as leverage on their parents.

Only two of our escapees had psionic powers. Aside from Rachael, there was the tall boy who had challenged me in the park.

"I'm Steven," he said gruffly. "I'm eighteen, and I'm a pyroid."

I already knew that there was a pyroid aboard, but with everyone packed so closely together, I hadn't known it was him.

I looked at Steven crossly. "Why didn't you say anything back in the park when Terry asked for people with combat powers?"

He shrugged and looked away. "I didn't feel like it."

"I see," I said evenly. "Well, next time your life is in danger, we'll discuss how we feel about it before deciding whether or not to save you."

Steven snorted loudly and refused to look me in the eye. It didn't bother me. I knew a coward when I saw one.

Once I had everyone's name, I returned to the copilot's seat and resumed looking out for power lines. Alia stayed in the cabin for a while longer before coming back and sitting in my lap again.

Terry occasionally brought the airplane up to two hundred feet or more, but for most of the flight, I could see the ground passing swiftly beneath us. The kids in the back were still visibly unsettled by what they saw through their windows, but we had to trust Terry. There was no one else to do this. Time passed slowly.

"The sun will be up soon," said Terry, raising the plane higher off the ground. "Here, hold the yoke for me."

The first time she said that, a little after takeoff, I had thought she said "yolk" and wondered aloud what egg she was referring to. After much laughter at my expense, Terry taught me that the "yoke" was the steering-wheel-like flight control she was gripping in her right hand. There was one in front of me too, for the copilot, and I held it steady for Terry whenever she needed to do something with her hand that she couldn't do with her hook. Terry didn't want to risk using the autopilot at this altitude.

I gently pulled back on the yoke, keeping the nose of our overloaded plane slightly up, and watched the altimeter needle climb to the 150-foot mark. Terry opened the map we had found in the cockpit and flipped back to a page she had been studying earlier.

"We're almost there," said Terry, putting down her map. "Give me back the controls. I need to make a course adjustment."

Terry was aiming for a low mountain range not far from the God-slayers' training camp she had helped destroy with the Raven Knights last year. According to the map, just inside the mountains was a little lake surrounded by forest. Terry planned to ditch the plane there, sinking it to hide our tracks.

Then we could hike back to civilization and make for a small Guardian settlement Terry knew of that wasn't far from there.

It sounded like a good plan until you looked at the fine print.

First off, I wasn't sure how the younger kids were going to swim to shore if Terry sunk the plane too far from it. And what of the baby?

Second, I had looked at the map too. It was a solid forty-mile hike back to civilization, and we had no gear, food or drinking water. Half of the kids were in their nightclothes, and it wasn't just Alia who was lacking proper footwear. Though no one else was barefoot, some of the kids were in light sandals while two had made their escape wearing indoor slippers. We weren't in any way fit for long-distance trekking.

When I pointed that out to Terry, she merely said, "We'll manage."

I shook my head in resignation. Terry had flat-out refused to land on a proper runway, arguing that the police or worse would swarm our plane the moment we did.

Another hour hugging the ground and we were now flying dangerously close to woodland mountainsides as Terry weaved our small airplane between the peaks.

"There," said Terry as the quiet lake, sparkling in the early-morning sunlight, came into view. "It's perfect."

"Are you sure about this?" I asked one last time. "How about a backcountry road or something? Anything closer to civilization."

"If you *must* know, Adrian," Terry said uncomfortably, "I never really soloed until today. And I never landed either. I helped my uncle fly a few times, but I just kept the plane in the air. Charles did all the hard stuff. I'm sorry. I don't want to risk crashing us on a hard surface."

Under less petrifying circumstances, I might have laughed.

Terry dumped our remaining fuel as we approached the water. She tried to ease the plane down slowly, but panicked as she realized that we were coming in too fast and had already overshot half of the lake.

"Hang on, everyone!" shouted Terry as she pushed the yoke forward, tilting us down. "Brace for impact!"

The belly of the airplane smacked the surface of the water once and then the plane glanced off, bouncing back into the air. I could hear our terrified crowd screaming as we began to fall again. The second impact was rattling, but nevertheless smoother, and our plane stayed on the surface of the lake this time, gliding forward like a powerboat. Terry cut the engines, but we were still moving at a fair speed toward the trees that came right up to the water's edge.

Staring out through the cockpit window, Terry said quietly in a panicked voice, "Uh oh, this is bad! Bad-bad-bad!"

"Addy, are we going to hit that?!" Alia cried into my head.

I looked at Terry. "Terry, are we going to hit that?!"

We did. Our airplane ran aground and the nose plowed into the nearest tree, bringing us to another abrupt stop. Our seatbelts kept it from being nearly as painful as our plunge from the fortieth floor, though, and I breathed my sigh of relief with everyone else when I realized that it was finally over.

Unbuckling our seatbelt, I said to Alia, "Go check if anyone is hurt. Check on the baby."

Terry and I got up too and followed Alia.

"Is everyone alive?" called Terry, and most replied that they were okay.

The baby was crying up a storm, but once again was miraculously unharmed. Patrick grinned.

The only one bleeding was Mr. Simms, who had sustained several injuries being knocked around during our semi-crash-landing. He was still unconscious, and Alia healed him again as Terry and I got the kids out of their seats.

The rear of the airplane was still in the lake, and the door splashed down into the water. It was only knee-deep, and soon we were sloshing our way up to the trees. While Alia stayed inside with Mr. Simms, Terry and I gathered everyone at the edge of the water and told them to stretch their legs.

I patted the crumpled nose of our airplane and gave Terry a wicked grin. "Nice landing, Five-fingers."

Terry shrugged. "At least no one broke any bones."

I yawned. "These kids haven't slept, and neither have we. How long would it take for anyone to find this plane? Maybe we could let everyone rest inside for a few hours."

"No, we need to get going. But first I want to talk to Mr. Simms."

I nodded. "Let's go wake him up."

Mr. Simms was already awake when we got back inside. He was glaring up at Alia with bloodshot eyes, but he wasn't struggling. He was drained and he knew he couldn't move.

I asked Alia, "How long has he been awake?"

"I think he was awake when we landed," she replied.

"Go on outside," I said to her.

My sister sensed what was about to happen. *"But Addy..."*

"Just go, please," I said sternly. "Go talk to the other kids."

Alia looked uncomfortably at Terry and me once before quietly exiting the cabin.

Terry and I dragged Mr. Simms farther up the aisle toward the cockpit.

"Talk," commanded Terry.

Mr. Simms stared silently up at us.

"Talk, damn you!" shouted Terry, kicking him in the stomach. "What did you tell them?! What was the price you put on our future?! You're one of the best blockers in the world! You're a Knight! You were our leader! You should have died before giving them anything!"

Mr. Simms slowly replied in a low, growling voice, "I serve the Angels."

Terry froze. Then, staring at Mr. Simms in a daze, she muttered, "No. You can't... It's not possible..."

Suddenly Mr. Simms laughed manically and roared out, "I serve the Angels!"

"What's going on, Terry?" I asked. "What's the matter with him?"

Terry shook her head. "It's not possible. It's just not possible!"

Mr. Simms was drooling a little as he looked at us with eyes that told of nothing but complete and utter victory, and suddenly I knew what it was that Terry couldn't accept.

Mr. Simms had been *converted.*

I whispered, "Who did this to you, Mr. Simms?"

Mr. Simms looked at me and smiled. "I must thank you, Adrian Howell, for leading me to the light. It was a mistake to think that the Guardians could ever—"

"Who did this to you?!" I shouted. "Who changed you?"

"The king," said Mr. Simms, looking up at the ceiling.

"King?" I repeated. "What king?"

"The light of our world. The lord of all peoples. My king..." Mr. Simms's voice trailed off for a moment. Then, taking a deep breath, the newly converted Angel said, "King Divine... King Randal Divine."

Terry stared down at Mr. Simms. "An Angel king?" she asked quietly.

Mr. Simms nodded. "My king."

"No," I said to Terry. "That can't be. Master controllers are always women. Cindy told me."

Terry shook her head. "Cindy told you wrong, Adrian. She was simplifying things for you because you're a wild-born. There was a psionic king once, a long, long time ago. A man who was a master controller. It's said that there's only one every thousand years, but they do exist. The last king lived back when the Guardian Angels were united, and he had complete power. A king's power is much stronger than a queen's. The conversions always last forever."

"King Divine," Mr. Simms whispered emptily, "oh, how I have failed you. But you are greater than us all, and you will be victorious. You will hold the entire world in your hands, and yours will be the greatest kingdom ever. My only regret is that I can help you no further, but I promise you that these self-righteous vermin will get nothing from me."

King Randal Divine... How could we all have been so blind? When Randal took control of the Angels following the death of their queen, everyone wondered how he had done it. Though he was the queen's nephew, he was neither the highest ranking Seraph nor a senior member of the Divine family.

Back at the gathering of lesser gods, when Cat begged Randal to let me return to the Guardians, he agreed. Then, once he was alone with me, he tried to kill me. Randal Divine claimed that he couldn't allow the Guardians to use me as leverage against Cat, who he had taken in as his daughter. He knew he would rise to power one day. When I faced him in the tunnel below the factory, I sensed no psionic powers, so I knew he wasn't a destroyer like me.

But a *master controller?*

Fate had given me the one perfect chance to kill him, but I had spared his life for Cat. How was I to know? But then, had I any sense, I would have killed him even if I hadn't known what he was. He was an Angel. He had tried to execute me. That should have been enough.

"New Haven belongs to us now, young Knights," said Mr. Simms. "The Guardians will never recover. Your pathetic alliances are nothing compared to the love of a true master, to the love of our king, our one true light in the darkness. Soon you will learn this for yourselves, firsthand if you are fortunate."

I looked at Terry, who gave me a slight nod.

Placing my right index finger on the center of the converted Angel's forehead, I said quietly, "Goodbye, Mr. Simms."

Mr. Simms showed no fear. He didn't even lose his sick little smile as he looked up at me and said calmly, "Goodbye, Adrian."

As I released my focused telekinetic blast, punching a hole through the man's skull, I heard a shocked squeal and looked up sharply.

My sister was standing there, mouth open, staring at us with horrified eyes.

"I told you to wait outside, Alia," I said, getting up.

Alia looked down at Mr. Simms's lifeless form, and at the blood oozing from the hole in his forehead. She glanced at Terry, who stood also. Then Alia looked at me again, asking in a quiet telepathic voice, *"Addy, why?"*

"He was an Angel," I said simply, "just like the others who tried to kill us today."

I had once told Alia about the Slayer Charles, who kept me alive, and his sister Grace, who was killed by psionics. But I never told her that Mr. Simms was the man who led the team that routinely killed children in horrible ways. I could understand Alia's confusion, but I wasn't about to make excuses.

Terry said uncomfortably, "Alia, we couldn't leave him here and we couldn't take him with us. He was a dangerous man."

Ignoring Terry, my sister shouted furiously into my head, *"He was tied up, Addy! He was tied up and you killed him!"*

"I did what I had to," I said evenly.

"You didn't have to kill him!"

I shrugged. "That's your opinion."

I looked down at Mr. Simms again. The only thing that bothered me about his corpse was that his shoes were too big to give to any of the kids who needed them.

Alia stared at me for a moment, and then came up to me and quietly put her arms around my waist, her body trembling slightly. *"I don't like it when we hurt people,"* she whispered in a shaky voice.

"I don't like it either, Alia," I said, and it was true. But sometimes it was unavoidable. Alia would just have to learn to accept that.

I picked her up in my arms and carried her off the airplane. Terry followed.

As we rejoined the kids waiting outside, Alia asked quietly, "What's going to happen to us, Addy? Where will we go?"

"We're going to find Cindy," I told her. "Everything will be okay as soon as we get back to her."

But we weren't quite ready to begin our hike back to civilization yet. Patrick was removing the baby's diaper, assisted by Heather and Candace. Apparently the baby's crying wasn't only because of the crash. Patrick had been right: It was a girl, probably not more than six months old. Of course we had no spare diapers, but everyone was doing without basic necessities today, and the baby was no worse off. At least she was clean now.

Heather offered to carry the infant, but Patrick insisted on doing it himself. He removed his shirt and Heather helped him fashion a simple baby harness out of it to put around his neck.

I suggested to Patrick, "You might want to give her a temporary name, just until we find her parents."

Patrick nodded. "I'll think of something, sir."

"And please stop..." I started, but then shrugged. "Oh, never mind."

Gathering everyone together, Terry assigned the younger children to the older ones to make sure that no one got left behind.

"Stay together," commanded Terry. "You get lost in here, you'll die slow, hungry and alone."

Terry led the crowd into the trees. Hoisting Alia onto my back, I followed at the end of the line. As soon as we entered the forest, I felt my sister's arms tighten around my neck, but I had too much else on my mind to make anything of it. Less than twenty paces farther, though, Alia started whimpering and telepathically begged in a frantic voice, *"Addy! Addy! Stop!"*

I stopped walking and asked, "What's the matter, Alia?"

"I can't do this! Please go back! I can't be here!"

Terry called from the front of the line, "Hey, what's the holdup?"

Alia was speaking telepathically despite the crowd, which she wouldn't do unless she was seriously upset. "Just wait a minute!" I called back, and quickly carried her back to the edge of the lake.

I set my sister down onto the ground but she refused to let go of me, her shoulders quivering as she desperately tried to regain control of her breathing.

"Alia?" I said gently. "What's the matter?"

"*I'm sorry, Addy,*" she said miserably. "*I thought I could do it, but I can't.*"

I finally understood her fear. I said as soothingly as I could, "It's just trees and bushes, Ali. Just like a big park."

"*It's not!*"

"Didn't you once come running after me through a forest back when we were living with Mark?"

"*There was a road! Please, please don't make me do this.*"

I would have thought that with everything else we had survived over the years and all that we had just come through, a hike through a forest would have been a cakewalk for Alia, but then again, I wasn't her.

I heard Terry call, "Come on, Adrian! Let's go!"

"I can't fly you over this, Alia," I said. "There're no two ways about it. We have to go through."

Alia shook her head. "*I can't, Addy. I just can't.*"

Gripping her shoulders tightly, I looked into her damp eyes. "Steady, Alia. You're not alone this time. Just hang on to me. Close your eyes if you want."

Patrick came back to us and gave my sister a concerned look. "Are you okay, Alia?"

Alia took a few breaths before answering aloud, "I'm okay. I have to be. Just walk with me."

My sister looked like she was on the verge of another panic attack, but Terry was still calling to us impatiently. I telekinetically lifted Alia onto my back and Patrick walked beside me, holding Alia's free hand as I carried her into the forest once again. I was grateful for Patrick's support. It was difficult walking together, especially since Patrick was carrying the baby and I had Alia, but at least my sister wasn't hyperventilating anymore. Alia knew more than most about facing fear, and to her credit, she made no more complaints.

It was slow going, finding our way through the thick trees. Though it wasn't exactly jungle, nevertheless we could have made good use of a machete to cut through the undergrowth. Terry used the sharp edge of her hook as best she could.

A little past noon, Terry gave us a two-hour break, and almost everyone slept or dozed a little. There was nothing to eat. Alia stayed close to Patrick and the baby girl, caressing the infant's short blond hair.

"We're still not far enough away from the plane," Terry said anxiously. "But then again, the way we're walking, it'll be easy to track us no matter how far we get."

We occasionally followed what appeared to be animal trails, but for the most part we made our own, noisily crumpling leaves and snapping branches as we pushed through the foliage. Alia was kept busy with everyone's cuts and scrapes.

Once, little Teddy fell behind, and we only noticed when we heard his distant cries. Fortunately, it wasn't difficult to retrace our steps, and I wasn't too surprised to discover that the boy who had been put in charge of looking after Teddy was my obtuse pyroid pal, Steven. Terry was equally unimpressed with Steven's attitude, and reassigned Teddy to me.

"Good," said Steven. "I was getting tired of dragging that brat along anyway."

Terry said icily to him, "Keep it up and we'll leave you here."

Steven snapped back, "Don't you talk to me like that, girl! My father's on the Council. You're supposed to be a Knight! If he hears that you treated me like—"

Terry grabbed Steven by the front of his shirt, brandished her hook at his nose and shouted furiously, "Daddy's not here, you arrogant punk! Honorary Knights are just volunteers! Nobody owes you anything here, and if you disobey me again, I swear I'll kill you myself!"

Alia and I exchanged smiles. We were used to Terry and knew quite well that far from killing the boy, she wouldn't even hurt him because that would only slow us down. The others were visibly unsettled, however, and a few began to cry.

Releasing Steven, Terry said to me, "Adrian, bring up the rear and make sure no one falls behind. And that includes the spoiled Council boy."

Then, ignoring Steven's scowls, she walked back up to the front of the line and faced the crowd. "Now, listen up!" she barked. "We're all in this together and we're going to get out of it together. Keep your spirits up and your damn egos to yourselves. Let's go!"

Near dusk, Terry informed us that we had come more than halfway. How she knew this was beyond me. All of the forest looked the same.

Our crew was a ragged bunch. Everyone was sweaty and muddy. Even the kids who hadn't come in their nightclothes were wearing only thin summer clothing, and a full day's march through the forest had reduced them to tatters.

The baby had soiled Patrick's harness, so we took James's shirt next. I asked nicely and James didn't complain. With nothing for the baby to eat, I doubted she would need another change on this trip.

I asked Patrick, "Did you think of a name for the baby yet?"

"Yes, sir," he replied earnestly. "We named her Laila, sir."

"We?"

"It was Alia's idea, sir."

I glanced at my sister, who gave me an apologetic smile. I just nodded and smiled back. Alia had liked Laila Brown a lot. If I was Alia's brother, and Terry very much family as well, Laila had been Alia's first real friend. I looked at baby Laila sleeping peacefully in Patrick's new harness, and realized that I was quite happy with her temporary name.

As we settled down for the night, Terry said to me in an overly casual tone, "So I guess Mr. Simms wasn't all that dead when you passed him in the factory tunnel."

"I guess not," I replied stiffly.

Terry frowned. "So what happened down there, Half-head?"

"That's my business."

Terry looked like she was about to snap at me, but then shrugged. "Fair enough."

I asked her, "Do you believe what he said about New Haven? Did the Angels really take the city?"

"From what I saw at NH-6, it's very possible," replied Terry.

I picked up a dry twig and twirled it around in my fingers. "So much for Mr. Baker's great experiment. New Haven was probably doomed from the start. It attracted too much attention, especially from the Angels."

48

"Well, there's still a chance that the Knights took our buildings back or that they're in the process of doing so now," said Terry. "We won't know until we regroup. Besides, even if the Angels did take the city, there are still plenty of Guardians and Guardian breakaways in other places. We've been divided and scattered before. We'll survive." Terry smiled, adding, "Maybe we'll make a new city somewhere else. A *New* New Haven."

"What would be the point?" I scoffed. "New Haven was hardly a safe haven for psionics. We were always in some kind of danger there."

Once, a pair of Angels had tried to kidnap Alia and me a mere two blocks from NH-1 in broad daylight.

Terry shook her head. "It was only dangerous for us because of who we are and what we did. For ordinary Guardians, that town was a paradise compared to where we're going now. I grew up in the splinter cells, Adrian, so believe me, I know."

I shrugged. Wherever Terry was taking us, I sincerely doubted it would be the worst conditions I had lived in. We would survive.

Terry gazed up at the dark tree branches above us and said quietly, "New Haven isn't my biggest concern right now."

I asked apprehensively, "Then you're sure that Randal is a master controller, the Angels' new, uh… king?" I was still clinging to the hope that it was all some kind of mistake. "I mean, you didn't believe in regenerative healers back when I lost my eyes."

Terry gave me a wry smile. "I never said regenerative healers don't exist. They're just exceptionally rare, and kings are even rarer. But yes, I do believe Mr. Simms. How else could someone like Randal Divine take control of the Angels?"

"Yeah…" I sighed, snapping the twig in my hands. "King Divine… But how could something like that be kept a secret? He was at the gathering of lesser gods, Terry! Why couldn't a finder sense him?"

"He was probably given individual hiding protection, or maybe he's a hider himself."

"But even if your power is hidden, someone who gets really close can sense you," I pointed out. "And yet it's like even the Angels didn't know he was a master until after Larissa died."

"I'm sure the top Angels knew," said Terry. "Guardian finders never got close enough, of course. But as for the common Angels, some of their finders might have sensed his power in passing. The only problem is that masters themselves are so rare that many finders have trouble identifying their signature, or so I'm told. And who's to say exactly when Randal Divine came into his power? It could be fairly recently. Besides, no one would be on the lookout for a male master controller anyway."

Fingering my pendant, I wondered if my first sister had known what her new father was. Cat had insisted that Larissa Divine never converted her, and that she was with the Angels by choice. But what if she had been lying? Perhaps not lying about Larissa, but about conversion? What if Randal had converted her himself? When Randal told me that he had somehow "convinced" Cat to become an Angel, had Cat simply supported his lie? If she had been psionically converted, what would Cat *not* have done for her master?

I asked Terry, "Is what you said earlier about kings also true, then? They're really more powerful than queens?"

Terry nodded grimly. "This is the first time a king has appeared since the schism more than seven hundred years ago. Make no mistake, Adrian, once Randal takes control of the outer factions, he'll come after the rest of the Guardians, and then the whole planet next, just like Simms said. It's too bad you couldn't kill Randal back at the blood trial."

I bit my lip. Terry still believed my story about Randal Divine escaping me. She didn't know that I had spared the Angel king.

Terry looked me in the eye. "Somehow, we're just going to have to stop him."

"We?" I repeated, shaking my head. "What's this 'we' stuff, Terry? My only mission is to find Cindy and get Alia back to her."

"And what then?" Terry asked seriously. "The Angels are more powerful than ever now. It'll only be a matter of time before they absorb anyone who doesn't fight back." Terry glanced over at Alia once and then continued gently, "Listen, I'm with you on finding Cindy, but once we do, I really think you should start rethinking your priorities. Honor? Duty? Loyalty? Any of that ring a bell?"

I narrowed my eyes. "Don't try to prey on my better nature, Terry. I killed a man in cold blood today, remember?"

Terry grinned. "My grandfather would have been proud."

I scowled at her. "Oh, shut up."

4. FAR FROM PARADISE

I looked up at the dim, early-morning light filtering through the tree branches as I slowly stretched my aching muscles. It was hard to locate a single part of my body that wasn't sore. Hiking through a forest might have seemed like a vacation after the nightmare we had gone through to escape New Haven, but now that the former was behind us, I fully appreciated how entirely unaccommodating Mother Nature could be.

It had been a long and restless night. Once the sun had set behind the mountain, it became nearly pitch-black under the trees. Steven had wanted to make a fire, but Terry forbade him, saying that the last thing we needed was a beacon for airborne search teams to see. Steven had seemed like he was about to argue, but then thought better of it when he saw the look in Terry's eyes.

Before we slept, Terry had divided the older kids into shifts to watch out for wild animals and possible pursuit by two-legged predators. Neither came, but in the meantime we were eaten alive by the insects. It had rained a little past midnight, and we managed to catch a sip of water in our hands, but that was our only relief. The little ones took turns waking up and crying all night. Lying between me and Patrick, my sister huddled with baby Laila. I slept very little, and Terry woke everyone at first light.

Once we were all as alert and alive as we could be under the circumstances, Terry called us to attention and we continued our trek through the forest. Again Terry led, and I brought up the rear with Alia on my shoulders.

Patrick had been walking beside me and chatting with Alia for much of the morning, but now he was up near the front of the procession with Heather and Candace. He had finally reached the limits of his endurance and had accepted Heather's offer to carry Laila for a while.

"Looks like you finally made a friend your own age, Alia," I said. "That Patrick is a pretty good boy."

"He's really nice, Addy," Alia said into my head. *"He even tried to give me his shoes yesterday, but they're way too big for me."*

"You two make a cute couple. When this is over, why don't you ask him out on a date?"

Horrified at the notion, Alia grabbed my hair. *"Addy!"*

"Why not?" I chuckled. "You and Patrick can play house together. You even have a real live baby."

Alia pulled my hair until I stopped teasing her.

Well before the sun had reached its zenith for the day, even the oldest kids were showing signs of exhaustion, often stumbling on the uneven path Terry was slowly carving out for us. Terry herself was as steady as ever. Despite carrying Alia, I wasn't too bad off either, since I could fall back on my telekinetic power when my physical strength started to give way. But our group wouldn't manage the pace we had kept yesterday.

Terry had chosen not to take a direct line over the mountaintop, but to weave between two peaks in order to avoid the treacherous climb and descent. She occasionally had me levitate above the treetops to make sure our heading was correct, and I could tell that we were still far from relief.

"The sooner we clear this forest, the sooner we can eat and rest," said Terry, refusing to give more than the absolute minimum in rest stops. "We just have to keep moving."

It made sense too, since without provisions, the longer we stayed out here, the weaker we would become. However, I suspected that Terry's impatience was caused by more than a pragmatic outlook on calorific consumption. She wanted to get these kids off of our hands as quickly as possible so that we could regroup with the Knights and, in the improbable chance that the Guardians didn't yet know the truth about Randal Divine, report it to the Council. I didn't share her loyalty to the faction, but I too was eager to get this leg of the journey over with and find Cindy.

"Laila needs milk," Patrick said worriedly during our afternoon stop. "I think she's getting weak."

Baby Laila hadn't cried in a while now. She seemed to be in a daze, her eyes unfocused. Terry suggested that in the absence of milk, which the teen girls couldn't provide, we at least had to somehow keep Laila hydrated. But even Terry, who could fly a plane and straighten broken bones, knew next to nothing about surviving in a forest, and I didn't have the heart to ask Alia for advice. In the end, at Heather's suggestion, Patrick dampened a piece of cloth with dew drops from the tree leaves and let Laila suckle on it. It worked, and soon everyone was pulling water from their dampened shirts.

At sunset, Terry said, "Maybe another half-day."

My stomach, well past the growling point, was whimpering feebly, so I knew how the others felt about Terry's news.

Steven said angrily, "You said last night that we had come halfway."

"I was exaggerating," said Terry. "But we'll be out tomorrow."

"We damned well better!"

I rolled my eyes. I had survived much worse for much longer, and I knew that this would soon be behind us. While it pained me to see the younger children hungry and tired, I had little pity for the older ones, especially Steven. The Council member's son was by far the loudest complainer, even worse than the littlest kids.

I braced myself for another long night.

It rained off and on all night. The trees gave some shelter, but not enough to keep us dry. Though it was warm rain, I still worried about Laila becoming sick. But I had to trust Patrick to take good care of her. This was his battle, not mine. My primary concern was for Alia. Though my sister did her best to keep her fears to herself, I could tell that she was still terrified of the forest, especially after dark. I could hardly blame her. Alia slept with both hands tightly gripping my right arm, and I didn't complain.

Again, we started walking as soon as it was light enough to see. By now, even Terry was visibly worn down, and the rest of us had been reduced to a procession of zombies, clumsily moving forward at a snail's pace. Still at the end of the line, I kept little Teddy right in front of me where I could see him.

Partly to take my mind off of my aching legs, I thought a lot about what

Terry had said to me two nights ago, about loyalty. No, I didn't owe the Guardians anything. But I owed Cindy. Knowing nothing about me except that I was a lost psionic child, Cindy Gifford found me, took me in and gave me a home. After all the trouble I had caused her, after all the terrible things I had said and done, she still treated me as her son. It would never be even between us. Alia was the same, and I couldn't turn my back on either of them now. My one true mission was finding Cindy and reuniting Alia with her. But as Terry had asked, what then? Would I sit back and watch King Randal Divine slowly take over the world we lived in? Would I really let Terry stand alone?

I almost crashed into Teddy as he suddenly stopped walking and looked up at the sky.

I was about to nudge him on when Alia said worriedly into my head, *"Something's coming."*

At the front of the line, Terry stopped and turned. "Everyone freeze!"

It took a few more seconds, but then I heard it too. A low thump-thump-thump of rotor blades in the distance.

"Hide!" commanded Terry. "Quickly! Adrian, Alia and Steven with Rachael. Get your powers hidden now!"

As everyone pressed their backs up against the tree trunks, I joined Steven at Rachael's side.

"Stay close," said Rachael, closing her eyes in concentration.

The rotor sound was closer now and getting louder by the second.

Everyone remained silent except for Steven, who said, "You know, that could be one of ours."

"It could," agreed Terry. "Now shut up."

Steven snapped back at her, "What's the big deal?! It can't land here anyway."

Terry raised her hook menacingly. "Don't make me tell you twice, boy."

Steven muttered into my ear, "Your friend's a real bitch, you know that? Don't you have a muzzle or something for her?"

I shrugged and whispered back, "She's not my problem, she's yours."

I held my breath as the helicopter passed overhead. It circled around once and then we heard the rotor sound gradually fade away.

"Alright, let's go," Terry said wearily. "We should be out in an hour or so."

It took two hours, but we finally cleared the forest, stumbling out onto a lonely asphalt road that ran along the edge of the trees. Beyond the road was farmland as far as the eye could see.

"Hey," I said cheerfully to Alia as I set her down, "we made it."

"Never again, Addy," said Alia, taking several deep breaths. "No more forests for me."

I asked Terry, "How far to the settlement?"

"A few hours' drive," she replied. "We'll catch our rides here."

It wasn't difficult. After all, who wasn't going to stop for a pair of ragged-looking children alone on the road? Hiding everyone else just inside the trees, Terry picked the two smallest and used them as bait to take the first three cars that came our way. Within half an hour, we owned a shiny silver sports sedan and two rugged SUVs. Their former drivers and passengers were quickly relieved of their money and portable communication devices and were left on the road to hitchhike home. No doubt they'd soon report their cars stolen, but we only needed to get to the nearest town.

Terry drove the sedan, followed by Candace in one SUV and Steven at the wheel of the other. Terry had ordered me to drive the second SUV with Rachael inside to hide Alia, Steven and myself, but when Steven haughtily insisted on driving, I obliged him in order to avoid another argument.

Rachel sat in the front with Steven, while Alia, Patrick, Laila and two others joined me in the back.

"*I really don't like that boy,*" Alia complained into my head.

I chuckled. "What's to like?"

The trip was short. Terry found us a mall just inside a largish town.

Not wanting to attract attention, Terry sent only Heather and Candace inside to do our shopping because they were the least filthy and weren't wearing pajamas. Even so, any casual observer could see that they had been through hell. I feared they would be stopped by the mall's security on suspicion of something or other, but our luck held. We had taken a decent amount of cash from the cars' passengers, and the girls soon returned with clean clothes and shoes as well as desperately needed food, water, milk and diapers.

We ate ravenously in the cars. Then, using wet towels, we wiped ourselves as clean as possible and changed into less conspicuous attire.

"You're on foot from here," I informed my sister.

Abandoning the vehicles in the parking lot, we walked half a mile to a bus station where, using the remainder of our cash, Terry just managed to get everyone onto a cross-town public bus.

Terry was probably the worst off in the low-profile department. With the exception of her pirate hook, Terry had lost all of her left-arm attachments including her decorative prosthetic hand. For the present, she had removed her hook and settled for being a conspicuous amputee, drawing an occasional sidelong glance from other passengers as we rode the public bus to the other side of the town.

"Just another few miles," said Terry once we got off the bus near the end of its line. "We'll walk from here."

That drew quite a few groans from our party. At this point, there was nothing "just" about another few miles.

"Rabbit?" said a man's voice that would have made us jump if we had the energy. "Well, I'll be darned!"

We turned to the voice, which belonged to a blond middle-aged man wearing a dark pinstripe suit.

"Merlin!" cried Terry, and I hoped that was his call sign and not his real name. "It's so good to see you!"

Terry jogged over to the man, and Alia and I followed.

"Welcome back, Rabbit," Merlin said pleasantly, shaking Terry's hand. "I see you brought friends this time. We sensed some psionics heading our way and got worried. It's dangerous to walk about with open powers these days, you know."

"I'm sorry, Merlin," said Terry. "It was unavoidable."

"I can imagine," said Merlin, glancing at our crowd. "New Haven?"

"Yeah."

"How many are you?"

"Nineteen, including one infant," replied Terry. "We really need your help."

"Under the circumstances, I can hardly refuse," said Merlin. "But our finder and I came in a single van and it won't hold everyone. How about I take the psionics in now and then come back for the others?"

"Sounds great," said Terry, and then gestured toward me and Alia. "This is Hansel and Gretel."

"I'm Adrian," I said, shaking his hand.

"Yes, I've heard of you," replied Merlin. "I'll tell you my name once we're in the van."

In addition to Alia, Steven and me, Merlin took Patrick and baby Laila to a black van driven by the psionic finder who had located our party. Rachael could hide her own power, of course, so she stayed behind with Terry and the others.

In a few minutes, we arrived in a quiet residential neighborhood where Merlin, a puppeteer and hider whose real name was Arthur, led us into a large, unoccupied house near the end of the block.

Inside, Merlin spent a few minutes setting a hiding bubble over the house.

"We own all the houses on this block and the block across the street," said Merlin, "but stay here till I get everyone. We'll talk then."

Too exhausted to even bother exploring the house, we flopped down on the dusty carpet and sheet-covered sofas in the spacious living room.

It took two more trips for Merlin to bring everyone to the house, and by then quite a few other residents of the Guardian settlement had come to greet us as well.

"My name is Marjorie Harding," said their leader. She was an aged gray-haired woman who I sensed to be a fairly powerful telekinetic. "Welcome to Walnut Lane, children. Rest easy now. You are safe here."

"Walnut Lane?" I repeated in surprise. The name of the settlement seemed oddly familiar.

"Yes, dear," replied Mrs. Harding. "Have you heard of us?"

"I think so," I said uncertainly. "I'm not sure."

Terry started to ask what happened to New Haven, but Mrs. Harding stopped her, saying, "Rest first, Teresa dear. You will have your answers soon."

Terry looked like she was about to argue, but then nodded compliantly. It was our first break since leaving New Haven, and she wasn't going to cause trouble. I had cringed when the leader called my combat instructor "Teresa." If I had dared to call Terry by her real name, she would have knocked me off my feet.

It was only a little past 3pm, but most of us slept on the living-room carpet as the residents of Walnut Lane kindly cleaned our new house and prepared it for nineteen refugees. Already having rested a bit while waiting for the others to arrive, Alia and I helped out a little, which allowed us to explore the various rooms. This house was owned and maintained by the Walnut Lane Guardians as a guest house, and it was used for hosting occasional psionic gatherings in which representatives of other factions came to discuss everything from the war to the weather. It was a wide, three-story semi-mansion with six bedrooms and two bathrooms, but it would be a tight fit for us. The Guardians brought in extra blankets, mats and folding camp cots from their homes. There was already talk of some of the Guardian families taking in the littlest kids to give them better care, but nothing had been decided on yet.

We ate dinner at a little before sundown. The dining-room table wasn't large enough to seat us all, so two more tables were brought in, leaving hardly any room to move about. Alia and I sat with Terry at Marjorie Harding's table, and we finally learned what had happened to New Haven.

The Angels had come in two waves.

The first was merely a diversion. They attacked several buildings and then retreated into NH-2 and NH-4, barricading themselves into the upper floors. The Guardian Knights had converged on those two locations, leaving the rest of New Haven relatively unguarded.

The Angels' second wave hit the Knights from behind. The invading Seraphim didn't outnumber the Guardian population, but they certainly outnumbered the Knights. With the Knights pinned down in the two buildings, other Seraph units were free to take the rest of New Haven with minimal resistance.

The Guardian Knights had been unprepared for the sheer size and ferocity of the Angel attack. Everyone knew that the Angels were riled up over the death of Larissa Divine, but believing that their head had been destroyed, the Knights hadn't counted on them being very organized. And nobody had expected the Seraphim to attack us with the suicidal determination of newly converted psionics.

"I'm truly sorry, Teresa," said Mrs. Harding. "We believe that less than a quarter of New Haven's residents made it out. The Angels knew that the loss of our greatest city would break our spirit. Of the Guardian survivors, many have already re-separated from the main faction and will probably create their own independent settlements."

"Why aren't we regrouping?" demanded Terry. "What of the Council?!"

Mrs. Harding shook her head sadly. "I'm afraid the Council's airplane never arrived at its destination. We're not yet sure if it crashed or was taken by force."

Steven, who was also sitting with us, swore loudly enough to draw stares from around the room.

Mrs. Harding pretended not to care and continued quietly, "There were a few Council members who escaped by other routes, but we haven't heard from Mr. Baker or—"

"Cindy!" I cried. "Cynthia Gifford! She was on that plane too?"

Mrs. Harding nodded. "I'm afraid so."

Alia gasped and turned to me. I looked down at her face and saw tears welling in her wide, frightened eyes. My sister quickly buried her face in her hands and started sobbing loudly.

Mrs. Harding looked quite uncomfortable. She hadn't known who Cindy really was for us.

Putting my hands on my sister's quivering shoulders, I said as confidently as I could, "She's alive, Alia. I'm sure she's alright. We'll just have to find her."

Alia shook her head and continued crying. I felt pretty horrible myself, but I wasn't going to let myself break down at the table. Besides, I might even be right. No one had found Cindy's dead body, so until we knew for certain, I'd keep my tears to myself.

As for the Angels' new leader, the Guardians of course already knew all about King Randal Divine. Randal had openly declared himself on the night of the attack on New Haven. That was probably one of the reasons why the once-reunited Guardians so easily broke apart again. It was easier to run and hide than to fight a force led by a male master controller.

Terry asked Mrs. Harding, "Do you have a list of known survivors?"

"A very incomplete list," she replied. "I'll have it for you first thing tomorrow. We'll do our best to locate the parents of these children and reunite them as quickly as possible. In the meantime, you may stay as long as you like, provided you obey our rules."

The rules were primarily "don't rock the boat." Three hiders, including Merlin, who was also an official Guardian Knight, made regular rounds to keep all the houses hidden from psionic finders. The street and spaces between each house, however, were not hidden. That meant Steven, Alia and I were not to leave our house without first getting individual hiding protection.

"In addition," said Mrs. Harding, "we would prefer that everyone remain as inconspicuous as possible, since there's always the occasional nosy neighbor that might inadvertently lead Slayers or Wolves our way. We do have a number of Knights here for our security, but it's best to avoid confrontation whenever possible."

I learned from Mrs. Harding that there were twelve other houses on our block, and all of them housed psionic families. The block across the street from which this settlement took its name was also about the same size. All together, there were about twenty-five families in Walnut Lane. According to Terry, this was a pretty typical Guardian community in terms of population. Terry knew Mrs. Harding fairly well, having spent several weeks here last fall after leaving New Haven on account of my blindness.

And I finally remembered where I had heard the name Walnut Lane before: Laila (my late girlfriend, not the baby) had visited this settlement with her mother back in January. Had Laila stayed in this very house? It might sound ridiculous, but I felt as if I had followed her here... that we had been guided to this place by her spirit. But then again, I didn't really believe in stuff like that. I guess I just missed her.

As for baby Laila, one of the Guardian families offered to take her in that very night, and after bidding Alia goodbye, Patrick left with them too. Everyone else was officially put in Terry's temporary guardianship until their parents could be located.

Before bidding us goodnight, Mrs. Harding and Merlin delivered several boxes of clothes to our house. Most of the outdoor clothes were secondhand, donated to us by the families of Walnut Lane, but they had also purchased clean underwear, socks, towels, toothbrushes and other essentials. We were each given a duffle bag to keep our things in, and we thanked Mrs. Harding many times over.

Three of our six bedrooms were on the second floor and the rest were on the third, and the Walnut Lane Guardians had prepared all of them with plenty of extra mats and cots. We originally planned to simply divide the second-floor rooms among the boys and give the third floor to the girls, but there were two strong voices of opposition to that plan.

The first, not surprisingly, came from Steven.

"I get my own room," he said brusquely.

"There are seventeen people here and only six rooms," I said in as reasonable a tone as I could.

"Your problem, not mine," said Steven, raising himself up to his full height and staring menacingly down at me. I wondered if he might actually try using his pyroid powers on me.

I stood my ground and said sternly, "Nobody gets his own room in this house."

Steven grabbed my shirt. "I do. And don't you start playing Knight with me, you little—"

Terry overheard our mounting argument and said, "Steven, relax! You can have your own room. You're more than welcome to it."

Steven released my shirt and looked at Terry in surprise.

Terry strode up to us and smiled at Steven. "We've all had a rough time and I can't bring myself to punish anyone by making them share a room with a brat like you anyway. You'll take the smallest room."

"I'll take what I want!" shouted Steven. "You don't call the shots here! Mrs. Harding will back me no matter what you say!"

Terry bloodied Steven's nose, knocking him down. I smiled to myself. We were no longer in the forest.

"You'll take what I give you," Terry said icily as Steven howled in pain. "Until we can find a place to dump your worthless hide, I'm your legal guardian. You better get used to that quickly, Steven."

Alia tried to heal Steven's nose but he roughly pushed her aside and scampered down the corridor, out of sight. After allowing Steven enough time to recover some of his dignity, I found him and gave him free pick of the rooms. Showing some basic intelligence, he chose the smallest one on the second floor, which wasn't all that tiny anyway, and we dragged the extra bedding to the other two rooms.

The only other person severely dissatisfied with the sleeping arrangements was, also predictably, Alia.

"You can sleep in Terry's room upstairs, Ali," I said when she begged me to let her stay with me. "You like Terry."

"But we've always shared a room, Addy," moaned Alia, giving me her most injured look.

"But my room here is going to have four other boys in it," I pointed out. Alia stamped her feet. *"I don't care!"*

I shook my head and said firmly, "You're ten years old, Alia. You can't be afraid of the dark forever."

"Not forever, Addy," insisted Alia. *"Just until I'm not. Please?"*

I looked at her wearily. "I take it you don't just want to sleep in the same *room* as me, yes?"

I hadn't meant it as an invitation but my sister jumped at the idea. *"Is it okay?"* she asked, her pleading eyes becoming even wider. *"Can I really sleep in your bed again?"*

We stared at each other for nearly a minute. Then I gave Alia a resigned smile. Throwing her arms around my waist, Alia gave me a spine-bending hug.

I remembered how Cat had wanted her own room by the time she was seven years old, and I was only too happy to see her go. I guess most normal kids are like that. Cindy had once told me that Alia would eventually want her own space, but that didn't seem to be in danger of happening anytime soon. I honestly couldn't understand how a ten-year-old girl would want to share a room, let alone a *mattress,* with her brother, but that's just how Alia was. She had her own pace. I suspected that this was simply how she dealt with her past and present, by taking her life slowly whenever she needed to. I had known Alia since she was seven and a half, and I had long since learned not to argue too much with her stubbornness. After all, she was never really selfish. She just had some special needs. Besides, in many ways, I knew that I was much more fortunate than her, so I had less right to complain. I hadn't turned psionic or lost my family until I was twelve. At least I had my memories to fall back on. Alia had been in the fight of her life since she was an infant.

Sharing a bed with Alia again wasn't all that bad for me either. In addition to the cots and mats that the Guardian families had provided us with, our bedroom had a comfortable-looking queen-size bed set against the far wall. Theoretically, I could have simply pulled rank and taken that bed for myself, but with Alia there, I had the perfect excuse. The thin mats on the floor wouldn't be nearly as nice.

The other boys I shared the bedroom with, particularly James, looked surprised as Alia snuggled up against my shoulder, but nobody laughed. I seriously doubted that this was in respect for our status as Guardian Knights, considering how little we must have looked the part. We were all just too tired.

Once everyone was settled, I telekinetically flipped off the light switch. Just enough starlight streamed in from the window for me to see my sister's cheerless eyes staring back into mine.

Gently patting Alia's side, I asked her, "So how are you holding up?"

"I'm okay," Alia said bravely. *"But I don't like this house, Addy. I miss our old room."*

That made two of us. You might think that after days of sleeping outside in a dark and scary forest, just being in a proper bedroom would be enough. And it was, in a way, but that didn't change the fact that this room was nothing like the one we had left behind. The air was different. The blanket felt unfamiliar. It wasn't the first time we had been torn from everything we knew, but that didn't make it any easier.

"We'll just have to make the best of it," I said to her. "I'm sure we won't be here for more than a couple of days, anyway. A week or two at the longest."

"I miss my unicorns."

I gave her arm a squeeze. "I'm sorry you lost your unicorns, Alia."

Alia's side of our NH-1 penthouse bedroom was overflowing with unicorn-themed toys, storybooks, and trinkets of all sizes, including an extra-large stuffed unicorn doll that Alia used to sleep with whenever she was feeling insecure. My sister had recently started to outgrow her unicorn obsession, but I still wished that we could have at least brought along one of her smaller dolls. It would have added a little familiarity to this place.

Alia drew herself even closer and asked quietly in my head, *"Addy, do you really think we'll ever see Cindy again?"*

"Don't talk like that," I whispered back. "I'm sure of it. It's not the first time we've been separated. I promise it'll be okay."

Another promise I had no confidence I could keep. I turned away so my sister couldn't see my face. Staring at the shadows on the walls of this unfamiliar room, I wondered what would happen to Alia if Cindy really was dead.

Or what if we found Cindy alive... *and converted?*

Would Alia join the Angels to be with her? Would I?

No, I couldn't let myself start thinking like that. We were only three days out of New Haven. There was still hope and I had to keep it.

While Cindy weighed most heavily on my mind, she wasn't the only person I was afraid for.

Father Mark Parnell would probably have been at his church or about to head home when the attack started. Mr. Malcolm Koontz, my nocturnal dreamweaver friend from the Psionic Research Center, might have just been getting up from bed. What about Terry's Uncle Charles, or the new leader of the Raven Knights, Jack Pearson? Had they died fighting? Mark, Mr. Koontz, Uncle Charles and Jack P. That made four people. If what Mrs. Harding had said about the number of survivors was true, then statistically speaking, only one of them would have made it out alive.

In a way, I was glad that I hadn't made more friends in New Haven.

5. ONE BIG AWKWARD FAMILY

Alia and I had to endure a fair amount of teasing from the older girls the next morning, but at least my sister was in better spirits and smiled toothily when I reassured her again that we would find Cindy alive and safe.

"And you can still sleep in my bed as long as you stay on your own side and stop trying to strangle me in your sleep," I said, massaging the back of my neck. I would have preferred just to move Alia to one of the cots, but then I would lose my justification to keep the only real bed in the room.

Three Guardian volunteers came to help cook breakfast for the "Refugee House," as we had been dubbed, and Alia and I assisted them in the kitchen along with Heather and Candace. We didn't really need so many people to make breakfast, but the two girls had insisted.

"What are you looking at?" I asked when I caught Candace peering at my face from across the counter where we were cutting vegetables.

"The color of your eyes," Candace replied matter-of-factly. "Or *colors* to be exact."

"Well, stop it, please," I said, trying not to sound too offensive. "I'm losing my concentration here and I might slice off a finger."

Candace smiled. "They're really pretty, Adrian... in a weird sort of way."

"Let me see!" cried Heather, and I sighed as Alia laughed.

After the God-slayers destroyed my eyes by sticking a sharp object into them, Terry had journeyed far to find a psionic who could fix them. (Alia couldn't help me because her power merely accelerated natural healing, and

66

my eyes were too damaged.) Terry eventually managed to return with a "reconstructive healer" who could bring my eyes back to almost their original shape, but after the operation, I discovered that my restored irises no longer matched in color. My right eye was part brown, part reddish purple, and my left eye was a light shade of yellow-green. It didn't matter to me so long as I could see through them, but with two giggling girls staring at my face, it was impossible to focus on the task at hand.

"Come on, girls," said one of the volunteer cooks. "This isn't a playroom. If you're going to help, then help. Otherwise, go set the table or something."

"Sorry," Heather and Candace said in unison, and went back to their tasks.

Mrs. Harding arrived just in time for breakfast, and she had brought Patrick with her as well. Baby Laila was left with Patrick's host family.

"Here's our current list of known survivors," said Mrs. Harding, passing a packet of papers to Terry.

Terry studied the list for a few minutes and then looked at me, shaking her head sadly. I had to see for myself, though. I went over every name twice, but I knew no one there.

"Given a few more days for the reports to come in, I'm sure there will be many more people on that list," Mrs. Harding said encouragingly.

"Yeah," I said, forcing a smile in front of Alia. "No doubt."

Mrs. Harding had also brought another round of donations: an old television set, two radios, several boxes of books and magazines, toys and games. It reminded me of my first few days at Cindy's old house when I was trapped indoors with Alia. We were much more numerous here, but the essence of our lives was the same: stay indoors and out of sight.

Mrs. Harding and the volunteer helpers left right after breakfast, but Patrick stayed behind. Alia played with him and a few others in the living room while the older kids joined Terry and me in the dining room to discuss our future here.

Terry began on a hopeful note, saying, "Probably in a couple more days, the Walnut Lane Guardians will find some of your parents and you can get back to them. In the meantime, we'll just have to get along."

I knew that Terry was itching to dump these kids and return to the main Guardian group, but the fact of the matter was that there wasn't a main

Guardian group to return to anymore. The two largest Guardian factions remaining were led by some unknown Lancer Knights and numbered fewer than a thousand members each. Both groups claimed to be the "true Guardians," as if we didn't have enough enemies without fighting amongst ourselves. Terry had decided that we would stay in Walnut Lane at least until we learned the fate of the Council's plane.

"We're not going to fall apart and I'll tolerate no fighting in this house," continued Terry. "No matter how you're feeling, you will maintain a bare minimum amount of civility here. We'll do the household chores in shifts, and if we end up staying here long term, the older ones should start thinking of getting some part-time work to help pay our way. The little ones can keep house. We're going to be just like one big family, okay?"

Most of the kids nodded, and Terry assigned us our household duties based on age and capabilities as if she was commanding a unit of Guardian Knights.

Steven hadn't joined our family meeting, retreating to his room immediately after breakfast. When seven-year-old Teddy admitted that he was terrified of the big angry boy, Terry smiled reassuringly, saying, "Don't you be afraid of him, Teddy. Inside, Steven is just as scared as anyone. Just ignore him, and if he causes you any trouble, you come straight to me."

Teddy needn't have worried. He was taken into another home before noon that very day, along with two of the other youngest.

"Oh, wonderful!" Alia said loudly in a sarcastic tone that she had picked up from me over the years. "Now I'm the littlest in the house again."

We laughed, and Rachael kindly offered to be Alia's personal hider so that she could leave the house and visit Patrick whenever she wanted.

After Alia, the next youngest left was eleven-year-old Max, the kid who I had snapped at on the airplane. His perkiness had slowly dissipated during our forest hike, and it didn't look like it was about to return anytime soon. Max had slept in my room, and we had been woken twice during the night by his cries.

There were now only fourteen left in the house so our sleeping arrangements changed a bit, but I kept Max with us and asked James to keep an extra-close eye on him. Scott, a good natured nineteen-year-old, agreed to look after Daniel Livingston and the last boy, another thirteen-year-old named

Walter. The three girls' rooms weren't as crowded. Terry shared a room with Rachael while Heather and Candace bunked together in another, and two sisters named Felicity and Susan took the third.

With James, Max, Alia and myself, my bedroom was the most crowded. Heather and Candace offered to take Alia into their room, but Alia refused, much to the amusement of the two girls.

"Is she your sister or your *girlfriend,* Adrian?" Candace asked teasingly while helping me with dinner preparations later that afternoon. With some concentrated effort, I ignored her.

Not to brag too much, but over the years, Cindy had made me into an above-average cook, so Terry had assigned me to the position of head chef. During our morning meeting, we originally considered putting everyone on kitchen duty in turns, but I figured that it would be easier to work with the same people, provided they were willing to help on a regular basis in return for being let off from other household chores such as cleaning and laundry. Heather and Candace volunteered, and so did Scott, who also knew his way around a kitchen pretty well.

This was our first meal to prepare without assistance from the Walnut Lane volunteers, and we had in turn invited them to dine with us tonight as our guests. The good people of Walnut Lane had even stocked our pantry for us, so it was the least we could do to repay their hospitality. I was going for a sure win with something as simple as spaghetti and fried chicken, but even so, I had never been in charge of preparing such a large and important meal. When Candace refused to stop teasing me about Alia, I snapped at her pretty harshly. She recovered quickly, though, and dinner was a success.

Over the meal, we learned from Mrs. Harding that New Haven was now officially under Angel occupation and that the Angels were planning to establish their own capital city there.

"They're calling it Lumina," Mrs. Harding said with a wry smile. "Rumor has it the Angels have already made arrangements with the city government to seize all Guardian assets in former New Haven."

So much for the Guardian Knight money in my bank account.

"Is King Divine going to be living there?" I asked, wondering if Randal and Cat might soon be sharing our old penthouse at the top of NH-1.

Mrs. Harding shook her head. "I'm afraid King Divine probably won't live there permanently, if at all. It's too obvious a target. The Angels will keep their king carefully hidden somewhere else."

"A capital without a king, huh?"

Terry said to me, "If and when the Angels declare themselves the rulers of the world, if any remaining world powers knew where Randal was, they'd lob an atomic bomb or two just to make sure he died. He won't be somewhere as obvious as a giant psionic city."

Mrs. Harding nodded in agreement, saying, "Unfortunately, the chances of finding King Divine anywhere are pretty slim."

That gloomy news, combined with the comfort of a full stomach and the relief of having spent an entire day in semi-normal conditions, compelled me to pull Terry aside after dinner for a quick but important chat.

"I've been thinking of what you said to me on the first night in the forest," I began.

"You mean about priorities?" asked Terry.

"Yeah."

Terry raised her eyebrows. "And?"

"And I still don't care about the Guardians," I informed her. "But I don't plan to live the rest of my life in hiding, and I won't live in a world ruled by a psionic king. Being converted can't be any better than being locked up, and I'd rather die than accept either."

Terry smiled. "Does this mean I can count on you to help me hunt down Randal Divine and save the world from Angel rule?"

"Yeah," I breathed. "I'm in."

I had only spared Randal Divine for Cat's sake, and then only because I didn't know at the time what Randal's true power was. I wasn't going to make the same mistake again. Cat had already lost one father. She'd just have to get over this one too.

"But Cindy comes first," I insisted. "Once we get Alia back to her, I'll help you all you want, but until then, my only mission is finding Cindy and taking care of Alia. The rest of the damn world can wait."

"I knew you'd come around," said Terry. Then she nudged me on the arm with her left stump and asked in mock-surprise, "But could this possibly be Adrian Howell believing in *choices?*"

"Call it what you will," I replied, unamused. "Personally, I don't see it as a choice. There's not much point in trying to be neutral if no one else is."

"That's why it's called a war, Adrian."

Laila Brown had died in that war. So had Ralph Henderson, and Terry's brother, Gabriel. Maybe Terry and I would too. But the Angels' monopoly on master controllers couldn't be allowed to continue. There would be no peace as long as Randal Divine lived.

"So what's the plan?" I asked.

Terry shook her head and smiled wryly. "For now, we do what we're both worst at. We wait."

Over the next few days, most of us found our place in what we hoped would only be a temporary home. But not everyone.

Steven refused to help with any of the chores, so the laundry crew refused to wash his clothes. Terry didn't force Steven to help around the house, knowing that none of the others wanted to share his disagreeable company anyway. We all liked the councilman's son best when he was sulking in his room. Scott even suggested that we deliver Steven's meals there so he wouldn't have to eat with us, but I drew the line there. "Steven shouldn't feel like we're pushing him away," I argued. I agreed with Terry in that Steven was not evil at heart. We all just dealt with our pain in different ways.

Max was as hollow as ever, but James took good care of him, staying close by his side and making sure he ate enough at mealtimes. The sisters, Felicity and Susan, who were sixteen and twelve respectively, often sat with James and Max at the dining table, and I could believe that, given enough time, they were all going to be alright.

I didn't know much of how things were in Scott's room with Daniel and Walter, but the three seemed to get along. Unlike Terry, Scott was almost always calm and relaxed, but nevertheless a natural leader. I was glad that our eldest son was so dependable.

Terry's roommate, Rachael Adams, was a little on the quiet side compared to the other teenage girls, but she was kind to everyone and helped around the house a lot. She also kept her promise to be Alia's outdoor escort. Rachael's power as a psionic hider wasn't strong enough yet for her to give individual hiding protection, so she always walked with Alia to and from Patrick's house, keeping Alia right beside her. Alia liked it better that way too since she hated going outside by herself.

My sister spent much of her waking hours sticking close to me in the house, but nevertheless made friends with the older girls, and also frequently visited Patrick down the street. Whenever she returned from her visits, in addition to updates on baby Laila (who was in perfect health), Alia gave me snippets of information about the Guardians living in Walnut Lane. About half were psionic, and most had pretty normal lives. Patrick's temporary guardians, neither of whom were psionic, worked as doctors at a large hospital.

Several days into our stay, Merlin announced that Walnut Lane had made contact with Teddy's aunt, who had escaped New Haven unharmed, and the following day, we bid Teddy goodbye. It was a brief, happy occasion that brought some hope to the rest of us, but after he left, I'm sure everyone wondered if any more would follow. Teddy hadn't been told yet, but his parents and sister were presumed dead or converted.

Still, Teddy had been the lucky one. July dragged on, and no one else got a ticket home. It looked like we really were going to be here for the long haul.

Despite Mrs. Harding's demand not to draw attention to ourselves, we weren't actually restricted to the house. As long as we were careful not to move about in large packs, the non-psionics among us could come and go during the daytime. The only problem was that no one had any spending money, so movies and recreational pools were out of the question. There was a public park with a sports field that could be used freely, and other Walnut Lane families occasionally invited a few of the kids over for meals and entertainment, but with the summer heating up and few places to go, many of our kids spent the majority of their time at home.

Even so, very few in our house spent their days moping around. Despite (or perhaps because of) the trauma they had suffered, nearly everyone did their best to keep their spirits high. We were all in this together, after all. Either our families and friends would be alive or they wouldn't. Until we knew for certain, it was pointless to grieve. In the meantime, there was entertainment in the form of television, music, secondhand toys, games and books to keep everyone's mind off of their worries. Especially the older girls made extra efforts to keep our home a happy place, and thanks to the cheerful mood they often set in the house, even Max slowly started coming out of his shell. I was grateful for everyone's resilience, which gave me strength in turn. An uninformed visitor probably wouldn't have thought that these were kids who had recently been torn from everything they knew.

As the new "baby" of the house, Alia often got preferential treatment, especially from Heather and Candace who absolutely adored the littlest Guardian Knight. My sister seemed to enjoy the extra attention she was getting—up to a point. At least it kept her from her darker thoughts during the daylight hours. But Alia was used to a much quieter life, and I could tell that she sometimes tired of the girls' lively company. Alia's main problem wasn't so much the fact that she was only ten years old but that she looked even younger, and her honorary title didn't command the same respect that Terry and I enjoyed. No one in our house was ever mindful of Alia's need for peace and quiet, so I could hardly blame her for wanting to spend a little more time over at Patrick's. Terry's idea of law and order was basically the absence of blood on the carpet, so between the boys' roughhousing and the girls' constant chatter, our oversized family often turned the place into a semi-madhouse.

But our fun and games were only during the daytimes. Nights were a very different matter. There was something about the darkening of the sky that unlocked the gates of even the strongest hearts to doubt, fear and pain. Just about everyone had periodic nightmares, and Max was by no means the only one who cried in bed.

I could usually tell when someone had a particularly bad night by how much breakfast they ate the next morning. Most of these kids were lifelong Guardians, and before they moved to New Haven, they had been part of smaller psionic communities just like Walnut Lane. Without their families, however, they were fish out of water, and their strength waxed and waned with the sun and the moon.

As much as I worried about them all, my primary concern was, as always, with Alia.

Candace and Heather often teased my sister about her nighttime attachment to me, but even though Alia was now old enough to be properly embarrassed by it, she still refused their offer to take her into their room. And despite promising to keep to her own side of our queen-size bed, Alia still regularly clung to me at night, which sort of negated the advantage of having a comfortable mattress. Unlike back in New Haven, we didn't have a dreamweaver here that could help pacify her nightmares, so even when I could get Alia to go to sleep on her own side, if she woke in the middle of the night (which she frequently did), I would invariably wake up the next morning with her arms wrapped around me in a way that guaranteed me a stiff neck and shoulders. My sister, knowing full well that she wasn't fooling me in the least, would insist that she had simply rolled over in her sleep.

"If you don't stop being such a bedbug, Alia," I said to her warningly, "I'm going to take a leaf out of Terry's book and tickle you so much you won't have the energy left to roll over in your sleep."

"That's mean, Addy!" said Alia, looking at me in a hurt way.

Of course I was only kidding. I understood Alia's insecurity perfectly well because I felt it myself every night. Once, waking from a nightmare in which I found myself confronted with Cindy turned Angel, I had gone to the bathroom to splash some cold water onto my face and found Scott there doing the same. He actually admitted to me that he had been crying, and we talked for a while about what our futures might be like. We had nothing positive to say.

Once the daylight returned, things were always better.

Midway through July, Mrs. Harding informed us that when the next school year began, all the children would be sent to a nearby school where she knew the principal and could get kids in without proper paperwork. Max didn't look like he was up to returning to a classroom yet, and Alia, who had never been to school, looked pretty apprehensive too. But that was still more than a month away.

Meanwhile, Scott, Heather and Candace had found part-time day jobs at restaurants and cafes, promising enough income between them to keep everyone fed and probably even pay the utility bills. Fortunately, we weren't being asked to pay rent on the house, and the Walnut Lane Guardians would still help us if we couldn't make ends meet. My kitchen crew could no longer assist me for lunch preparations, so when I couldn't get enough help from the others, I often settled for sandwiches which were both nutritious and easy to make.

Steven was as sour and surly as ever, refusing to come out of his room except at mealtimes. Terry finally confronted him, telling Steven to start pulling his own weight or not get fed. After that, he occasionally helped me in the kitchen, silently working in his own corner on whatever task I (very politely) assigned. In all honesty, I would have preferred that he stayed in his room, but I was happy to see Steven making at least a small effort to fit in.

I often felt that Felicity and Susan were comparatively fortunate in that they still had each other, much like Alia, Terry and I did. But Terry had been right when she described us as "one big family." Daniel and Walter regarded Scott as a big brother, and James and I got along pretty well too. Gradually, almost everyone found at least one or two people they could lean on for support when they needed it. There were plenty of loud quarrels over trivial matters, but that was to be expected of even a perfectly normal family, which we most definitely were not. For my part, I found it a refreshing change to be living in a house where I wasn't the only male.

Merlin was our designated house-hider, stopping by every day to repower his hiding bubble around our house. I eventually worked up the courage to ask him to check whether Lumina was hidden under a single giant hiding bubble. Merlin informed me the next day that, according to the Guardian spy network monitoring the Angel city, it wasn't.

"I'll keep you posted, though," promised Merlin. "If Cindy Gifford has been caught and converted, chances are, Lumina will be her station."

"Just don't say anything in front of my sister," I begged. "If Cindy really has turned Angel, I don't want Alia finding out like that." I had no idea how I would break it to Alia if Lumina did someday turn out to be under Cindy's hiding bubble, but I would cross that bridge when I came to it.

At the end of the first week of August, Terry asked Merlin to set up a meeting for us with Mrs. Harding, who hadn't visited our house for several days now.

Terry and I had been restlessly awaiting further news about the missing Council airplane, but now that it had been a full month since New Haven fell to the Angels, Terry was utterly done sitting around. Following their capture of New Haven, the Angels were gaining momentum, threatening to swallow up every last pocket of resistance that the Guardians and every other psionic faction had to offer. If things continued the way they were, in less than ten years, every psionic on the planet might be in the service of Randal Divine. For Terry, the best defense was always a fast and furious offense. Ever since learning the truth from Mr. Simms, there had been no question in Terry's mind that we would somehow have to kill Randal Divine. His death alone might not end this war, but it would certainly bring it down a couple of notches.

Killing the Angel king, however, was like trying to hunt a lion using only a slingshot while wearing a blindfold. The Guardians had spent many long years working toward assassinating the Angels' master controllers, and it had only been through a series of lucky breaks that the Knights succeeded not only in killing Larissa Divine, but her heir apparent as well. But as the last remaining master controller on the planet today, King Divine would be far better protected than any world leader.

Terry and I had discussed this problem at length several times that week.

"You want to find Cindy, and I want to kill Randal," Terry had said to me. "To get help with something like this, there's really only one sure place we can go."

"The cute guy?" I asked innocently. That was how my late girlfriend had once described the never-aging 3000-year-old psionic recluse who lived in the mountains and traded information for favors.

Terry nodded. "This war is history in the making, so the Historian is really our only bet. Even the Angels wouldn't stand a chance if we could get the Historian to fight on our side."

Though technically still flesh and blood, the Historian had been alive so long and had consequently acquired so much psionic power that he was practically immortal. When Terry met the Historian last year, she had been seeking an answer to my lost eyesight. This time, however, our request wouldn't be quite as innocuous.

I looked at Terry uneasily. "But I thought the Historian had vowed never to alter the course of history with his powers. Maybe he'll give us information, but he isn't going to directly help us fight the Angels, is he?"

"That remains to be seen," said Terry. "I told you before that he has a soft spot for underdogs, and even the mighty Historian probably fears what could happen if the Angels really do end up taking over the planet. I'm guessing his neutrality is about to be tested."

I gave a non-committal nod, and Terry continued, "Besides, information alone would be a very good start. With the right information, we might even be able to kill Randal Divine without any direct help from the Historian."

Perhaps, but to get the Historian on our side would require an audience with him and plenty of gifts. The Seraphim would be closely watching every possible route to the Historian's mountain home, and the notoriously fickle and eccentric Historian was unlikely to assist us in breaking through the Angels' embargo on his vast knowledge and powers.

"It won't be easy getting to him," I said warningly.

"I know it won't be easy, Half-head!" snapped Terry. "Since when was anything we did easy? Come on, trust me on this. You remember that I made a second trip to the Historian alone, don't you?"

"Yes," I replied cautiously. "But things are different now."

The Angels would have tripled their guard on the Historian's mountain since Terry had been there last. The balance of power had tilted too far.

Terry said accusingly, "You promised you'd help me find and kill Randal Divine."

"I also said Cindy first," I reminded her.

"I'm going even without your help," Terry said stubbornly, and then grinned as she added, "But if you come with me, who knows? The Historian might be able to tell you what happened to the Council's plane."

I narrowed my eyes. "You're just trying to use me."

Terry laughed. "Well, sure I am, but so what? You don't plan on spending the rest of your life in Walnut Lane, do you?"

It was useless to argue with Terry once she had an idea in her head. Terry wanted Mrs. Harding to lend us the Walnut Lane Guardian Knights, without which our hope of reaching the Historian alive was virtually nonexistent. Merlin strongly doubted that Mrs. Harding would ever grant Terry's request, but he agreed to arrange a meeting nevertheless.

The following day, having received personal hiding protection from Merlin so that I could leave the house, I accompanied Terry to the home of the woman who led Walnut Lane. Old Mrs. Harding lived half a block down from us in a richly furnished two-story house with her daughter, son-in-law and three grandchildren.

We arrived just in time for afternoon tea and cake.

Terry patiently explained her idea and request to Mrs. Harding, who listened with a sympathetic smile as she sipped her tea.

"Oh, Teresa dear," Mrs. Harding said affectionately when Terry finished, "you have grown so much since you stayed with us last winter. But your recklessness has no limit, does it?"

I could never get over how Mrs. Harding called my combat instructor "Teresa dear," and I bit my lip to keep from laughing.

"We have to try, Mrs. Harding," argued Terry, whose facial muscles were hard at work concealing her annoyance. "It is our only hope."

"But we *have* tried, Teresa," said Mrs. Harding. "Do you honestly believe that you are the first to seek an audience with the Historian since the fall of your city? There have been at least six attempts by the Guardians to reach the Historian already, and not one of them has returned. Most of them never even made it to the mountain."

"But we can't just sit around and do nothing," insisted Terry. "That's not how you win a war."

"A war..." mused Mrs. Harding. "Yes, it is a war, alright. Especially these last few weeks, things have been quite crazy right here."

"What do you mean?" asked Terry.

Mrs. Harding sighed. "Teresa dear, you are not even the first to ask me to give away my Knights. We have been contacted by the two so-called 'true Guardians' last month. Both have demanded that I give half of my Knights to them. If I obliged them both, we would have none left at all to protect Walnut Lane."

"Are you going to send any Knights?" I asked.

Mrs. Harding chuckled. "Heavens no, dear. This isn't the New Haven Council we're talking about."

Mrs. Harding took an excruciatingly slow sip of tea, and then said, "The truth is that I have been speaking with the families here and the general consensus is that we should strike our colors."

Horrified, I asked, "You mean *join* the Angels?"

"Oh, no, nothing as dire as that," said Mrs. Harding, smiling comfortingly. "Secession, dear Adrian. The Guardians are on the verge of collapse, and we feel that they may drag us down when they do."

Now I understood why Mrs. Harding had called New Haven "your city" earlier.

Mrs. Harding continued, "Soon after Queen Granados was assassinated, this small community became independent and remained neutral for many years. It was only last year that we decided to rejoin the Guardians and established contact with the New Haven Council. Now, it appears that our trust may have been misplaced."

My first impression of Mrs. Harding had been that of a cookie-baking flower-arranging grandmother, but now I could see the destroyer in her blood. The telekinetic leader of Walnut Lane was actually a tough pragmatist that reminded me a little of Mr. Baker.

Terry's frustration was beginning to show more clearly on her face. "Mrs. Harding, we may be in a state of turmoil, but the Guardians are all that stand between the Angels and a world ruled by psionics. You can't turn your back now. You just can't!"

Mrs. Harding shook her head. "A Guardian councilwoman visited us at the start of this year, shortly after you left us. This Mrs. Brown had come to assure us of the impregnability of your experimental Guardian city. She even suggested that we join her there. And yet New Haven fell to the Angels in just one night." Mrs. Harding took another long sip of her tea before continuing gravely, "The hard truth we must all face now is that our fight with the Angels is a lost cause. The Angels have already won, and we must each do what we can to protect ourselves. I'm sorry, Teresa, but the war is over."

"It's not over!" Terry said furiously. "I'll start my own war if I have to!"

Mrs. Harding gently patted Terry's right arm and asked in an overly understanding, grandmotherly tone, "You and what army, Teresa dear?"

"I'll find help elsewhere!" said Terry, her voice shaking as she stood up. "I'll go to the other Guardian factions if I have to, but I'm going to get to the Historian somehow!"

Mrs. Harding remained calmly seated. "I know you well enough not to try stopping you, but I'm afraid that you may not have much luck anywhere you go. We are all on the defensive now. No faction leader will risk their limited resources for a suicide mission."

Terry bit her lip so hard I thought she might draw blood.

Taking Terry's hand, Mrs. Harding gently forced her back into her chair.

"Besides, Teresa," she said, pouring us more tea, "I have met the Historian four times in my life, and I believe that you are seriously overestimating the potential return on a meeting with him. Even if, by some miracle, you did get to his mountain, the Historian would never actually fight for us. His bending of his vow of neutrality has its limits too. And while there is definitely potential gain from whatever information he might provide on

Randal Divine, even the Historian's lore is not absolute."

I remembered how the Historian hadn't been able to provide the Guardians with the secret identity of the Angels' second master controller, Angelina Harrow. The Historian wasn't omniscient. As for the possibility of him actually breaking his vow and fighting for us, I found Mrs. Harding's levelheaded assessment far more believable than Terry's passionate hopes. Perhaps Terry just believed what she wanted to believe.

Terry was positively fuming when we left Mrs. Harding's home. Merlin had given me strong enough hiding protection to last three solid days, so it was only Terry and me walking back to the Refugee House together.

"Me and what army?!" Terry muttered savagely. "I'll give her what army!"

"Are we leaving, then?" I asked hesitantly.

"No," replied Terry, her eyes suddenly filled with grim determination. "The Historian is still our best bet, but Harding is right too. The Guardians won't keep sending Knights to the mountain if they've already lost six teams."

"Then what are you planning to do?"

"What I should have done the day we arrived here," replied Terry "We've been sitting around playing house far too long."

6. TERRY'S TROOPERS

The living room was in its usual state of chaos when we returned. In one corner were Daniel and Walter throwing paper airplanes at each other. In another were Felicity and Susan in the midst of a heated argument over something or other. Heather, Candace and Alia were sitting together on the sofas, and Heather was teaching Alia how to put on lipstick as the girls talked and laughed noisily over the sisters' shouts and the blaring sound of action-movie gunfire from the TV.

"Attention please," Terry said quietly.

I telekinetically hit the power switch on the TV and then locked onto an in-flight paper airplane, guiding it into my right hand. All eyes turned toward us.

"Is everyone here?" asked Terry.

Heather replied, "Scott just got back from work and said he was going to take a shower. I think everybody is in the house somewhere, though."

"Gather them please," said Terry. "I have an announcement to make. Scott can shower later."

"You want Steven here too?" asked Heather.

"Everyone. This is important."

In less than two minutes, Terry had everybody's undivided attention as they sat on the sofas and on the floor, gazing at us expectantly. I already regretted not confronting Terry before we entered the house.

"You all know it's been more than a month now since we left New

Haven together," began Terry, looking around at everyone in turn. "I heard from Mrs. Harding today that Teddy is doing well with his aunt. I still hope that some of you will find your families. But in the meantime, we are all members of the Walnut Lane community, and it's time we started contributing to it for real."

I looked at Terry uneasily. But as Terry's second-in-command, I knew better than to argue with her in front of the others.

Terry continued, "Scott, Heather and Candace are helping us make enough money now not to be a drain on the other Guardian families living here, and I know that everyone else is helping out in the house one way or another. But we have to do more than that. The Angels are all but unstoppable now, and every small community like ours is at risk. You all know what Adrian and I have been doing downstairs, right?"

By "downstairs," Terry meant the large storage basement under our house. Weeks ago, I had helped Terry clear away the clutter and set up a makeshift training room. Alia had managed to use her connections over at Patrick's to get Terry a set of rusty weights that had been gathering dust in someone else's basement. Though we didn't have proper gym mats to cover the concrete floor, our training room resembled a miniaturized version of the dojo in the subbasement of NH-1. Terry and I had been using the place to keep our skills up, and most of the kids had come down a few times to watch us practice. Seeing Terry's moves, however, nobody ever tried to join in.

Felicity asked hesitantly, "Are you suggesting that we should all become Guardian Knights?"

"No," said Terry. "You don't have to become a Knight if you don't want to. But I'm saying you should at least learn how to defend yourself. Knights or not, we're Guardians, all of us. If you're untrained and get into a fight, you might win, you might die. Two on one, you die. The more you train, the better your odds get. It's really that simple."

Most of the kids nodded. Not every Guardian Knight was proficient in hand-to-hand combat. Many simply fought using their own psionic powers or relied on modern weapons. But these kids didn't have either.

Terry smiled grimly at the crowd, saying, "I'm sure you've all had plenty of time to think about what might happen if you don't find your families again. Most of you will probably gain some kind of psionic power in a few more years.

It might not be a combat power, but that doesn't mean you have to be helpless. If you have time to waste in this house, you have time to train. You might even get one back for what happened to your homes."

Steven snorted loudly. "So who's going to teach us? You?"

"I'll teach anyone willing," Terry replied evenly.

Steven stood up, silently glared at Terry for a few seconds, and left the room.

"Anyone else?" Terry asked challengingly, her eyes darting around the room.

Sitting next to Felicity, Susan seemed to tremble under Terry's fierce gaze. Max just stared emptily back.

Terry said in a softer tone, "I'm not going to force anyone, especially the youngest. It has to be your own decision."

A full minute passed in silence. Then we heard a whisper.

"I'll fight."

The kids looked around trying to find the source of the voice, but Terry and I knew who it was because we were facing the crowd.

"I'll fight," Max whispered again, getting up from the floor and looking at us determinedly.

Scott stood up too. "I'm with you, Terry," he said forcefully. "I'm done running."

James was next, followed by Rachael and then Alia. Slowly, everyone got to their feet.

Susan was last, looking anxiously at her older sister and then at Alia and Max before carefully standing up and saying in a shaky voice, "Me too."

"You're sure, Susan?" asked Terry.

Susan nodded.

"Good girl," Terry said quietly.

Terry faced the crowd again and explained, "What I'm planning to teach you all here is close quarters combat, or CQC for short. It's essentially military-style hand-to-hand and basic weapons training. But you're going to have to build some muscle too, which means a fair amount of all-round exercise and weight training. And if we're all doing this together, we're going to need a much larger room than the basement."

"How about right here?" suggested Scott.

Terry surveyed the spacious living room for a moment, and then nodded. "This will do fine. Move the sofas against the wall and take the TV somewhere where it won't get smashed. Adrian and I will do a quick inventory check downstairs and see what we need to get."

As Scott started to get things organized in the living room, I followed Terry down into our musty makeshift dojo.

Alia came too, and as soon as she shut the door behind her, Terry turned to me and said, "Speak your piece, Adrian."

I shook my head. "You don't want to hear what I've got to say about this."

Terry smiled grimly. "I'll survive it."

"Alright, if you insist," I said icily. "I think that was a pretty impressive pep talk, Terry. I never knew you could be such a *politician.* I suppose it didn't occur to you to tell them the real reason you wanted everyone to learn combat."

"That comes later," said Terry. "Besides, I really did mean what I said back there too. Even if we weren't going to the Historian, it makes perfect sense for them to learn how to fight. Once they're ready, we'll let them decide for themselves whether or not they want to come with us."

"You're just using them!" I said, my temper rising. "Sugarcoat it all you want, Terry, but a lie is a lie!"

Terry gave me an exasperated look. "You want this war to be so damn easy, don't you? First you didn't want to get your own hands dirty, now you don't want to be responsible for anyone else's!"

"They're just kids!"

"Half of those *kids* are older than us," countered Terry. "Some of them are over eighteen, so they're not kids at all. As for the younger ones..." Terry threw a quick nod in Alia's direction and grinned slyly at me. "I think you're forgetting what children are capable of... when they're put to it."

"Damn you, Terry!" I snapped, waggling my index finger at her nose. "Alia never asked for any of this, and neither did I!"

Terry poked me in the chest with her left stump. "Well neither did I, and neither did they. But they're here, they're willing and they trust us."

"Of course they trust us!" I said savagely. "You're the great Terry Henderson, famous hero of New Haven! They'd do anything for you!"

"And you're the famous Adrian Howell now!" said Terry, jabbing me again with her stump. "We lead this rabble whether we like it or not. Get used to it! And get that finger out of my face. I'm afraid it might go off."

I lowered my finger but continued glaring at Terry.

Terry said patiently, "Listen, Adrian, we can either train these kids to defend themselves, or leave them unprepared for the Angels when they come. And the Angels *will* come, make no mistake about that."

"I'm not against them learning to fight," I said, meaning it. "But that's not why you're doing this. What if we're the ones who end up getting them hurt or killed? What then, Terry? Do you really want that kind of blood on your hands?"

Terry gave me a pained look. "Please don't think I ever stopped regretting what I put you through last year. It was my pride that robbed you of your sight. But this isn't about adventure or even revenge anymore. It's about our collective survival. I admit that Peter probably died because I put the fight into him. But this could be our very last stand, and I'm prepared to do anything it takes to give our future a fighting chance. You're the one who doesn't believe in choices, Adrian! We all do what we have to. Not what we want. What we have to!"

Huffing loudly, I turned away from Terry and looked at Alia. My sister steadily gazed back at me with Cindy's quiet eyes. She seemed as if she was about to say something, but then just nodded and smiled sadly.

Terry touched my shoulder from behind. "Please, Adrian. I know I have no right to ask this of you, but I really need you in my corner right now."

I didn't turn around, but replied quietly, "I'm always in your corner, Terry. I never once blamed you for the Slayers. But promise me that when the time comes, you won't pressure these kids to join our quest. They can't feel like they owe us something."

I felt Terry give my shoulder a squeeze as she said, "I promise."

I turned around and gave her a weak smile. "Alright. Let's do it, then."

I didn't want to be the one to mention the brave pyroid we lost on the minibus, so I was glad that Terry did. We would never know for certain whether Peter's death was an accident or if he had removed his seatbelt because he felt duty-bound to help us. And I couldn't help wondering where this unfamiliar road was about to take us. The children of lost Guardian families turned soldier for Terry's secret mission... I wondered how many of them would end up following Peter to their deaths, and how soon.

Terry hadn't really come down here for an inventory check. We already knew what we had, and more importantly, what we didn't have.

"We'll need proper mats in the living room, or maybe several stacked layers of carpet," said Terry.

I asked, "Do you want to leave the dumbbells down here and keep this as a weight room?"

"No. We'll have to move them out. And the shelves too. We're going to use this room as our shooting range. It's way too small, but we can put some targets on the far wall and just use it for short-range pistol work."

The rectangular basement room was only about ten yards long. Hardly ideal for target practice, it was nevertheless the only place you could fire a gun without anyone calling the police.

"Where are you going to get the cash for guns and ammunition?" I asked. If Terry was planning to take away any of my grocery money, she was in for stone soup three meals a day.

"I'll think of something," said Terry. "One thing at a time."

We returned to the living room where Scott and the others had already cleared away the furniture and were waiting for us. I wondered if at least a few of them had been secretly hoping that Terry would offer to train them in combat. For the most part, they were an eager-looking bunch.

"First I want to get a feel for what you can do," said Terry. "Does anyone here have any background in martial arts?"

James raised his hand. "I took karate back in elementary school. I made green belt before I quit, but I haven't done much since then."

"It'll come back," said Terry. "Anyone else?"

It turned out that several did have a basic background in some martial art or another. Scott had been captain of his high-school wrestling team. Rachael had done some aikido. Heather, Felicity and Daniel had attended several classes in basic self-defense that had been organized by the Raven Knights shortly after the gathering of lesser gods. Walter had been commuting to a judo dojo ever since arriving in New Haven two years ago.

"Not a bad start," said Terry. "But I want to see it. When I call your name, please step forward and try to kill me."

After a few seconds of awkward silence, Terry smiled and said, "That was a joke. But of course you're quite welcome to take it seriously."

Candace asked nervously, "Are we going to get seriously hurt?"

"Not today," promised Terry. "Not *seriously,* anyway. And this isn't the army. You're all volunteers, and you're free to quit if you feel this isn't for you. Fighting isn't for everyone. No one will hold it against you if you quit."

Terry gave me a sidelong glance. I smiled back at her.

"If there are no other questions," said Terry, "Scott, you first."

The captain of the wrestling team lasted a grand total of ten seconds against Terry, who easily pinned him using her particular blend of every martial art known to man. Still, I was quite impressed with Scott. The first time I faced Terry, I couldn't remain standing for longer than the blink of an eye.

"That was very good, Scott," said Terry. "With a little work, you might even be a match for Adrian here. I think I'm going to train you myself, but let's see what everyone else can do first."

Terry turned once more to the crowd. "Let's just go down from the oldest. Candace, you're next."

Terry tested each one in turn, squaring off with them and telling them to attack in any way they saw fit. Our students met Terry with a mixture of awe and terror, but even with the older kids, Terry was much gentler than she had been with me on my first day. Terry had learned a thing or two about teaching and motivation. Besides, the living-room carpet wasn't nearly as yielding as a proper gym mat, and Terry had, after all, promised no serious injuries.

In the end, Terry assigned about half of them to me and half to herself. Naturally, she took the stronger ones and left me with the others, promising to train them in person once they learned what they could from me. In addition to Scott, Terry took Rachael, James, Heather, Felicity and Max.

Max looked quite surprised when Terry called his name, but Terry merely smiled at him and said, "I like a strong spirit."

I was left with Alia, Candace, Daniel, Walter and Susan. I couldn't be sure, but it was probably deliberate on Terry's part to separate the sisters and friends as much as possible. Alia was an exception, but I guessed that this was also deliberate. Terry understood about Alia.

Just like Terry, I squared off with each in turn, asking them to kill me.

With his background in judo, Walter was by far the best in my group—if you didn't count my sister. Alia had been down in the NH-1 subbasement dojo with me and Terry ever since we moved to New Haven, and what she didn't have in muscle she made up for in technique. I suspected that if only their sizes weren't so far apart, Alia could beat Scott four out of five rounds any day.

"Enough for one day," said Terry once we had a feel for everyone's drive, nerve and abilities. "We'll start for real from tomorrow. I have to talk with Mrs. Harding first."

There was, of course, no keeping this from the leader of Walnut Lane. We visited Mrs. Harding first thing after breakfast the next morning to ask for official permission to open a combat school.

Mrs. Harding was old but not senile. It certainly hadn't been lost on her that we had begun this on the day she refused Terry's request for Knights. No doubt Mrs. Harding easily saw through Terry's cover story, but she nevertheless agreed.

"You are a trusted and honored Guardian Knight, Teresa," she said gently. "Do what makes you happy."

Mrs. Harding probably doubted, as I certainly did, that Terry could get our students ready for a trip to the Historian for at least several years, and in the meantime, we were doing something that added a little to the desperately needed security of Walnut Lane.

But it seemed that Terry was hoping to set off in a few months, not years. She quickly set up a rigorous training schedule, breaking everyone's free time into CQC sessions, exercise and weight training. The older ones still had their jobs, and everyone else had chores, but even so, most were assigned five hours or more of combat and physical training every day. It would be an adequate test of our students' resolve just to keep up with our pace. Nobody voiced any complaints over the schedule, and I felt a little better about what we had started.

Our training program took into account everyone's personal life, so in practice, Terry and I usually had no more than three students at a time in the living room, and often it was one-on-one, which would be better for the students, but not for the teachers. Whenever I wasn't cooking, I'd have a combat lesson to teach.

"Like this," I said, showing each move as slowly and clearly as I could.

"Focus on your balance and step forward."

Candace, who I was teaching at the time, tripped over herself. I stifled a sigh. Candace seemed serious enough about learning to fight. She just wasn't very coordinated.

"It's alright," I said patiently. "Again."

Though Terry's style of teaching still started with using a move before explaining it, I didn't want my students to think of me as an opponent so much as a guide. I knew from experience that learning combat moves was no different from learning anything else. It required repetition upon repetition upon thorough, painstaking repetition, and then more repetition. It was easier when your instructor wasn't knocking you down every two minutes.

Candace lost her balance again, landing painfully on her hands and knees. All we had for floor padding were a few layers of blankets.

"I'm sorry I'm such a klutz," Candace said unhappily.

I gave her an encouraging smile. "You're a lot better at this than I was when I started learning, Candace. Don't waste your time being sorry. Just get up and go again."

By the end of the third day of training, all our students were noticeably spent, but still no one complained. In fact, Scott and a few others even did extra weight training when they could find the time. The living room constantly stank of sweat but soon nobody noticed or cared. We were definitely off to a good start.

But that wasn't to say that everything was smooth sailing. In addition to her daily chores, Alia was kept busy with everyone's bumps and bruises, occasional bloodied noses and even broken bones. There were so many accidents in those first few weeks that sometimes my sister really was too tired to roll over in her sleep, and we eventually took mercy on her and let her off her other household duties.

Having heard from Alia what we were doing, Patrick asked to join the training program too. Terry had mixed feelings about this. On the one hand, she didn't want to deny any willing hearts, but Patrick would no doubt talk with his foster parents and then Mrs. Harding would get a closer look at what we had started. Besides, Patrick now had a semi-legal home so he didn't qualify for inclusion in Terry's secret plan. In the end, Terry accepted Patrick into our school, but assigned him to me.

With our bare living room so frequently being used for training, our dining room became the new semi-official lounge, though many of us simply retired to our bedrooms when we had time off. Ever since walking out on Terry's offer, Steven was seen even less around the house, and for a while he didn't even help with the cooking.

It was therefore a bit of a shock to find him casually leaning against the living-room wall when I arrived to start my lesson with Daniel and Walter one day. Steven looked down at me, his mouth wired into a tight frown, and said quietly, "Teach me."

I nodded. I neither expected nor particularly wanted a civil tone from Steven. That was just his way.

I squared off with him and showed him what he had been missing out on. It must have been a painful blow to his ego to be knocked down in straight matches by someone three years younger and almost a head shorter, but Steven refused to let it show.

"You're good, Adrian," he said quietly. "I can learn from you."

I smiled and, though I couldn't be certain, Steven seemed to smile a little too.

Steven agreed to join my classes during the times that Terry wasn't sharing the room with us. He was a pretty fast learner and caught up quickly. I knew Terry was doing well with her group, but I wasn't shy about pointing out to her that between the two of us, I was clearly the more skilled instructor. Terry replied tartly, "Popularity and skill are not the same, Half-head."

As word of our training school spread through the Guardian settlement, several families approached us hoping to enroll their children here. They even offered to pay us, but Terry turned them down, citing overcrowding. Terry had six students and I now had seven including Alia, and besides, ours wasn't a weekly or even biweekly course. Outsiders wouldn't be able to keep up. We had only accepted Patrick because his foster parents agreed to let him come for a minimum of two hours every day even after school restarted, which was now only two weeks away.

Now that training had become routine, and no one had quit yet, Terry decided that it was time we got the shooting range set up. Leaving me in charge of the house, she disappeared from Walnut Lane for a week. When she finally returned, she had brought a sizeable collection of handguns as well as a fair amount of money which she decreed was for gym mats and bullets. Terry never told me where or how she got her hands on the money and weapons, and I didn't press her. I trusted Terry enough to know that she hadn't killed anyone innocent for them.

I begged Terry to spare some of the money for the pantry. With everyone training for hours every day, there was a proportional increase in their daily calorific requirements. Or to put it bluntly, everyone ate like horses. I had to find ways to get the most out of our very tight budget. In order to save money on water, we had limited everyone to five-minute showers, much to the dismay of Alia, who was notorious even among the girls for her terribly long baths. We were saving in other areas too, such as turning off nonessential electronics like the TV and air conditioner, but it still wasn't enough.

At my suggestion, we finally accepted six young students from the Walnut Lane families. There were four boys and two girls, seven to nine years old, and we put Alia in charge of teaching them.

"Do I have to?" my sister asked uneasily.

"We've got to eat somehow," I said. "It's only twice a week, and if you make enough money, you can even start taking baths again."

"But most of those kids are bigger than me."

"Don't be ridiculous, Alia!" I laughed. "They're not that much bigger, and you're older anyway. You're a Guardian Knight. I'm sure you can survive a pack of children."

"I don't know how I'm ever going to get them to listen to me, Addy."

I ruffled her hair a bit, saying lightly, "Then you'll learn something too, my brave little bedbug."

Alia scowled.

Admittedly, my sister probably had the toughest crowd. Unlike the kids Terry and I were training, Alia's students were sent here by their parents and consequently weren't as dedicated to learning, especially from a skinny little healer girl. Alia never looked the hero on a normal sunny day, but I knew that my sister was not only capable of fighting but entirely fearless whenever the occasion called for it. Alia's young students would learn respect soon enough, once they looked up at her from the flat of their backs.

Terry soon had a proper shooting range up and running in the basement.

She also managed to find enough secondhand gym mats to cover the living-room floor, turning it into a proper CQC dojo. As I continued to teach my students the basics of hand-to-hand combat, muffled popping noises could be heard from downstairs. In the last month, we had transformed our house into a semi-military camp, and it worried me that everyone seemed to be accepting this as normal. I wondered once again if we were doing the right thing.

"Is something bothering you?" James asked me one evening when he noticed that I was quieter than usual.

I shrugged. "I guess I'm just a bit tired. Tired and scared."

"Scared?" repeated James. "Scared of what?"

"This," I replied, gesturing around the converted living room. "All this insanity. Terry's idea to make you into Guardian Knights. Now you're all shooting guns downstairs as well. I just feel like every day we're digging ourselves deeper into a world of trouble."

James looked surprised. "But you're Adrian Howell," he said with a chuckle. "If even half of what I've heard about you is true, you should be used to getting into trouble by now."

"That doesn't mean I enjoy it," I replied frostily.

"I'm sorry," said James, taken aback. "I just figured that you were use to all this... this 'insanity' as you call it."

I doubted I would ever get used to it. "It's not just me or Alia or Terry this time," I said, shaking my head. "It's everyone. I wish I could believe that you all really know what you're getting yourselves into, but you probably have no idea."

There was something about killing a person, even in self-defense, that took a small part of your own soul with it. It wasn't something you could ever prepare for in the dojo. James would have to learn that the hard way, just like everyone else.

James asked hesitantly, "Do you regret it?"

"Regret what?"

"Becoming a warrior."

"What's to regret?" I scoffed. "It was never my choice. I'm a destroyer. Destroyers fight."

James nodded. "My father said the same thing to me once. My parents were both Lancer Knights. I hope I'll see them again, but that's just hope. They're probably dead."

"You don't know that," I insisted.

"No, I don't," said James, fixing me with a determined look. "But until I find out for sure, I'm going to fight. Maybe you're right, Adrian. Maybe we don't know what we're getting into. But who the hell ever knows that? I'm glad we're doing this. After New Haven, I couldn't just sit around and wait."

I smiled sadly. "You'll make a great Knight someday."

"Terry's an amazing teacher."

"Yeah," I agreed quietly, "she is."

Terry had argued that what we were doing now was an absolute necessity for our very survival, and she was probably right. Times had changed. But I often lay awake at night remembering how suddenly and how easily people can be torn from this world. I lay awake wondering how many more would follow, and how soon.

7. THE CRACKS IN THE SONG

Mrs. Harding stopped by at the end of August to check up on us and make sure that the house was still standing. She pretended not to care about the sweat-stained gym mats covering the living-room floor. At least the walls were undamaged, and we didn't show her the modifications we had made to the basement.

The real reason for Mrs. Harding's visit was to make sure that we continued our schooling. The new school year would start in a couple of days.

Scott, Heather, Candace and Steven were done with high school and weren't about to head off to college just yet. Rachael had one more year of high school left and James and Felicity had two, but where James and Felicity grudgingly agreed to finish their education, Rachael flat-out refused.

"I'll take a high-school equivalency exam and be done with it," she said, and Mrs. Harding agreed to set Rachael up with one as soon as she was ready.

Daniel, Walter and Susan had plenty of classroom years left, and Mrs. Harding accepted no excuses from them.

Max still hadn't recovered enough to return to school. Combat training with Terry had brought the boy significantly out of his shell, but only while he was training. On the mat, Max was ferocious, and Terry, who rarely praised anyone, insisted that Max was a born soldier. However, when resting or at night, Max quickly deflated, and was often emotionally unstable. I knew because I still shared a room with him, and he regularly cried in his sleep. Mrs. Harding, who used to be a math teacher in addition to a Guardian Knight, agreed to take Max as a private student in her home.

Alia also refused to enter school. I had hoped that living here would have made my sister more used to being around people, and it had, up to a point. But Alia was never one to willingly step into a crowded room, and she felt little need to make new friends or seek a normal existence. I explained to Mrs. Harding how Alia had been home-schooled all her life.

Mrs. Harding asked her in a concerned tone, "Are you absolutely certain you don't want to go, dear? You might have a lot of fun, you know."

Alia shook her head, saying, "I don't like noisy or crowded places."

"Well, this house seems quite noisy and crowded," Mrs. Harding logically pointed out. "How can it be so different from a classroom?"

"It's different because I *have* to be here," replied Alia. "Besides, once everyone goes to school, it'll be quieter in the house."

"But you have never even been to a school, child. How do you know it will be all that bad?"

Alia shrugged. "I've seen pictures."

Mrs. Harding laughed. "Well, I suppose Max could use a classmate. I will teach you at my place."

"Okay."

That left just Terry and me.

Terry had dropped out of high school the previous year when Guardian families voiced opposition to her attending school with their children. Like Alia and me, Terry was a prime target for the Angels, and just being near other Guardian kids presented a risk to their safety. That was all before New Haven fell, and I wondered how those parents would feel about where their kids were now. In any case, Mrs. Harding had no chance of convincing Terry to return to school.

"I guess I'm done with it too," I said, referring to both regular school and Mrs. Harding's offer of home-schooling. "With the housekeeping and training, there's just too much to do here."

"Well, I suppose I can't exactly order you," said Mrs. Harding, "but I hope you know what you're giving up, young man."

I knew what I was giving up. In a way, I had given it up years ago. Cindy had tutored me ever since I met her, and I was very grateful for that. But I was a psionic destroyer, and while I still hoped that someday I could settle down and live a quieter life, for the time being, peace would just have to wait.

Once the new school year started, the house did get noticeably quieter. Most of the older kids had day jobs, and the younger ones wouldn't return until the afternoon. Rachael and Steven still hung around, and Terry and I gave them extra training when we could spare the time.

In order to give our students enough training time after school hours, I took on most of the housekeeping during the daytime. Rachael helped out a lot, and Steven occasionally did too. For the most part, Terry left me to play househusband and spent her free time training. Cooking and cleaning for fourteen was no picnic, but that was exactly what I had dropped out of school for, so I kept my complaints to myself.

October was upon us in a blink, but this year, distracted by my many chores and worries, I had completely forgotten that the 12th was my own sixteenth birthday. Alia had to remind me.

Being on a very limited income for so many hungry mouths to feed, we weren't about to celebrate anyone's birthday in this house. Every meal was a bit of a party, anyway. But my sister had taken the time to telepathically tell everyone in the house to wish me a happy birthday, which embarrassed me to no end. The girls, especially Candace, thought it was hilarious.

There were no presents, of course, but Alia had fashioned a colorful card on which she simply wrote "Happy 16th, Addy." Or so it seemed until I noticed that a dotted pattern around the edge of the card were actually Braille letters which read, "From your littlest bedbug, Alia. You are my best-ever unicorn. Thanks for always being there." I stopped insisting that Alia sleep on her own side of the bed. Cindy was right: when my sister wanted her own space, she'd ask for it.

Between housekeeping, hand-to-hand combat training, and pistol practice in the basement shooting range, I felt that we had more than enough going on in this house, so I was decidedly unenthusiastic when, a week after my birthday, Terry suggested that we add yet another item to the program.

"Mind blocking?" I asked incredulously. "Who's going to teach us?"

"Merlin already agreed," said Terry. "Puppeteers are comparatively safe and would be a good start for those old enough."

That would be Scott, Steven, Heather and Candace, who were all over eighteen years old. But Terry announced that she was going to join in too.

"I'm not much more than half a year to eighteen," said Terry. "The age limit is arbitrary anyway. There's always a risk to the mind when someone jacks it, but the only way to learn blocking is by doing."

"Then count me in too," I said.

Terry shook her head. "You're not old enough."

"You just said that's arbitrary," I argued. "Besides, I've already had controllers in my head quite a few times. I'm still sane."

"That's debatable," Terry said with an evil grin. "But I won't stop you. If Merlin agrees, you can join us."

Aside from the added workload, I couldn't deny having some reservations about throwing myself into mental blocking practice. I had repeatedly heard warnings about the possible long-term effects of psionic mind control on people who weren't old enough to take it. But if we were really going to break through an Angel blockade around the Historian's mountain, I couldn't go in wondering when my body would be hijacked by another puppeteer or worse.

And it wasn't just our long-term plans. There were local concerns as well.

While Walnut Lane hadn't yet been the target of any direct attacks, we were hearing of plenty of action elsewhere. We got most of our news through Merlin and Patrick, and it seemed that almost every week the Angels had taken yet another settlement belonging to breakaway Guardians, the Meridian or other independent psionics. We heard how they destroyed God-slayer houses as well as, surprisingly, an occasional Wolf unit. Even the paramilitary group that specialized in hunting psionics seemed to be fighting a losing battle now. In order to keep the existence of psionics concealed from the public, the Wolves had to keep a low profile too.

With a king at their helm, the Angels seemed more bent on capturing their enemies alive than ever before, but that was their one and only disadvantage in combat. Even with their opposition shooting to kill, the Angels were still gaining ground at an alarming pace. The bleakest estimates now put their complete victory at less than three short years away. We even heard one story of how a small breakaway Guardian group willingly surrendered to the Angels and simply walked into their conversion to avoid the bloody inevitable. I had a feeling that others would follow.

One of the few issues Mrs. Harding and Terry were in complete agreement with was that we weren't going down without a fight. A psionic destroyer's greatest weakness was the controller who could turn him against his team. After what I had once done to Alia, I was never going to let that happen again.

But when she learned what I was planning to do, my sister was far more vocally opposed than Terry.

"You know what Cindy said, Addy!" cried Alia when I told her. *"You're still too young. You could really get hurt."*

"I'm sixteen now, Alia," I reminded her. "I know that's not quite old enough, but you were never old enough to do all the things you did either. We all do what we have to, when we have to. I'll be careful, okay?"

Alia gave me a sullen look. *"You're never careful."*

I had no reply to that.

"If it starts to hurt you, please give it up, okay?"

"I promise," I said. "I know this is dangerous. I won't try to hide it if it's hurting me."

"Okay," Alia said resignedly.

My sister clearly hadn't forgotten her experience with the flying berserker.

What with our escape from New Haven, moving to Walnut Lane and opening a combat training school, I honestly hadn't had much time to dwell on what possible damage the berserker might have done to Alia's mind. Outwardly, my sister seemed unchanged, and I knew her to be an exceptionally resilient child so I was hopeful that there was no permanent damage.

As far as the age restriction I was breaking, I hoped that everyone was just playing it safe. After much begging, Merlin grudgingly agreed to allow me to begin blocking training with the other five. Rachael and James both asked to join our sessions too, but Merlin refused. "Terry and Adrian are a special case," he declared. "The rest of you will wait until you're older."

Our first lesson was conducted the next evening when Merlin came by to repower the hiding bubble around our house. We gathered on the gym mats in the living-room dojo, and most of the younger kids had come to observe. Alia was there too, watching me with a worried frown on her face. I tried to give her a reassuring look, but I just ended up making her more anxious.

"It's basically like this," began Merlin, facing his six students on the mat. "All types of mind control are unique, and for the most part, they can all be resisted to a certain degree simply by supplying a conflicting emotion or mental focus. Peacemaking can be resisted through controlled anger. The effects of berserking can be lessened by heavy laughter. Memory alteration can be prevented as long as you are consciously aware of the memories that are being affected. That's why mind-writers prefer to work with people who are asleep. They put up less of a fight."

A few of the young onlookers chuckled at that, but I didn't find it funny. I also seriously doubted that anyone could really force themselves to laugh during a berserker attack. Merlin hadn't mentioned psionic draining as a means for breaking free of berserking and peacemaking, but I guessed that having abysmally poor power balance wasn't considered a viable technique in his book.

Merlin continued, "Dreamweaves can be broken by self-doubt, among other emotions. Puppeteers like me find it hard to control someone who focuses all of his consciousness on reclaiming one body part at a time. But these are all just tricks that reduce the effect of the control, and experienced controllers can usually overcome your resistance. What you all have to learn is that blocking psionic control for real isn't so much a battle of willpower as a cat-and-mouse game of finding the cracks in the controller's song and exploiting them."

By their expressions, I could tell that Terry and the others already knew this. Merlin was speaking for the benefit of the only wild-born of the group, but I was already having trouble keeping up. What the heck was a crack in a song?

"Imagine that you live in a very quiet house," said Merlin, noticing the lost expression on my face. "But then someone in your family, a pesky little brother for example, decides to learn how to play the tuba, and practices twenty-four hours a day non-stop in your living room. You'll at first be very bothered by the noise. It'll make you cranky and keep you awake at night. You may be inclined to take the tuba away and hide it, or better yet, hide your little brother somewhere where he won't easily be found. But sooner or later, you'll get used to the noise and learn to accept your new environment. The annoying tuba will no longer bother you."

Thinking I understood what Merlin was driving at, I asked eagerly, "You mean in order to resist psionic control, we have to get used to it?"

"Quite the opposite," replied Merlin. "You must never allow yourself to get used to it. That's what the controller wants. You must instead constantly be aware and be bothered by the sound of this tuba."

I caught a smirk on Terry's face, and decided to keep my mouth shut so as not to risk making a fool of myself again.

Merlin touched his right temple as he said, "A psionic's control comes from thoughts, and like thoughts themselves, the control consists of waves and rhythm. Much like the budding tuba player, a weak controller's power lacks rhythm, so it is easier to find the bits of quiet in the sounds. Those are the cracks."

Merlin paused once to make sure we didn't have any questions yet, and then continued his metaphorical explanation. "As the tuba player improves, there is more rhythm to his song, so there are fewer silences. But then what if he joins a band and brings them to rehearse in your house? A quartet of beginners is definitely louder, but there are still plenty of cracks if you know where to look."

Merlin paused again, looking around at each of us before continuing in a graver tone, "The strongest of controllers are like one-man orchestras. Their control is refined and multilayered. But even music from a full orchestra has brief moments of silence. With enough practice, you may someday learn to recognize them, though I'll admit that I have never gotten that far myself."

Nobody spoke, but I could tell that they all felt as uncomfortable with this as I.

Merlin smiled reassuringly. "Today, we will start with the tuba."

Being the eldest, Scott was chosen to try first.

With but a quick nod in his direction, Merlin took complete control of Scott's body.

"Shall I make him jump around like a monkey?" Merlin asked playfully.

Before we could answer, Scott was jumping up and down, furiously scratching his head and back. He let out a growl and beat his chest like a gorilla. The younger observers laughed and cheered.

I heard Candace whisper worriedly to Heather, "I don't know about this..."

As Scott screeched and slapped his palms on the gym mats, Merlin calmly explained, "When a controller has your body, it is only natural to feel anger or panic. But strong emotions are not conducive to finding the bits of silence that you are looking for."

Merlin released Scott from his control. Unsteadily getting to his feet, Scott grinned and said, "That was truly amazing. I couldn't find any cracks or even a song anywhere."

"That's because you don't yet know what to listen for," said Merlin.

Then he turned to Candace and asked in a diabolical tone, "And what animal would you like to be, dear?"

Candace took two steps back. "Um..."

"How about a mouse?" suggested Merlin.

Candace dropped onto all fours and spent the next five minutes scurrying around the dojo.

"If a puppeteer is not very powerful, he'll want to keep you moving," explained Merlin as Candace sniffed Heather's feet and lightly nibbled on Alia's legs. "This is to distract you and make it harder for you to focus on the song. As you can easily tell, I am not giving Candace my full attention, but even so, as long as she's squeaking and running about, I doubt she will locate my control anytime soon."

So it continued. Heather was made to do cartwheels and then marched three times around the room, swinging her arms widely while singing campfire songs at the top of her lungs. Steven was fuming after Merlin had him dance ballet, and we all kept our laughter to a minimum. Terry fared no better on her first attempt at blocking: Merlin made her kneel and propose marriage one at a time to James, Daniel and Walter.

Then Merlin turned to me and said, "Adrian, there will be no embarrassing performances from you today, though I guarantee you'll get your fair share soon enough. You are my last contestant, so I'm going to give you a small chance to show the others how this is done."

With that, Merlin took possession of my arms. I quickly discovered that the rest of my body was still my own, and as Merlin made me raise my hands over my head as if in surrender, I asked him, "What am I supposed to do?"

"Lower your arms, of course," said Merlin. "That's all you have to do."

I looked up at my hands and tried to force my arms back down. I wasn't particularly surprised when I found that I couldn't. It wasn't the first time.

Merlin chuckled, saying, "Perhaps it might help if we tickled his armpits."

The crowd laughed loudly. Fortunately, Merlin was only kidding.

I tried focusing on just my right arm, and then just on my left, but still nothing happened.

"Forget your body, Adrian," said Merlin. "Your arms aren't important. Focus your consciousness on the control itself. Listen to its rhythm. Find the cracks."

But Scott was right: There was no song, let alone cracks to find. I looked up at my hands again in frustration. If I could just move one finger…

"Stop worrying about your arms," Merlin said again. "Calm your mind."

Since I wasn't being tickled or jumping around like a monkey, calming my mind wasn't such a hard task even with a crowd of spectators. I had, after all, spent a large part of my life meditating with Cindy and sitting silently with Alia. Calm came naturally to me.

I closed my eyes, and the crowd politely gave me some quiet.

Years ago, when I first learned to sense the powers of other psionic destroyers, I associated them with instruments hidden in an orchestra. A psionic's power flowed a little like music. I wondered if that was what Merlin meant when he talked about the "controller's song."

I thought back to how, when an Angel puppeteer first took control of my body, I had felt his presence at the back of my mind as he looked through my eyes, spoke through my mouth, and forced me to blast Alia so hard that she had almost died. When the puppeteer forced me to speak, my voice had been strangely deep and raspy. That man had been controlling me from a considerable distance, and perhaps that was why his control hadn't been perfect. It was certainly strong enough to keep me from breaking free, but I had sensed his power.

Just as I sensed it now.

With my eyes closed and the room nearly silent, I could feel Merlin's consciousness inside my head, telling my body to keep my arms raised up high. It was like a quiet heartbeat, its pulse slightly irregular but nevertheless constantly pumping something into me. Something that was at the same time both thinner than air and heavier than stone. It was a desire. A pulsing desire to keep my hands held high.

Aiming for the split second between the pulses, I pulled hard on my arms.

My arms stayed up, but worse, I suddenly felt horribly nauseous and fell to my knees.

I heard someone clapping and opened my eyes.

"Very well done," Merlin said happily. "You see? It is possible to find a crack in a tuba song."

Breathing heavily, I looked up at my arms. They were still raised above my head, but not as high as before, and my right hand was clenched into a tight fist.

Merlin released my arms and smiled at the class. "If a sixteen-year-old wild-born can do that on his first attempt, then you know that anyone can learn to block control with enough practice."

Considering what Merlin had done to the others, I was the only one to get a fighting chance, but nevertheless quite a few of the observers applauded as I got back to my feet.

"How are you feeling, Adrian?" asked Merlin.

"Dizzy," I replied honestly. "For a moment there, I thought I might throw up."

I was afraid Merlin might tell me that I was still too young to continue this training, but I had promised Alia that I wouldn't lie about my condition.

Merlin merely nodded. "Disorientation is very normal when you are just starting. You'll get used to it."

We had class twice a week from then on. Everyone got their first breakthrough soon enough, but progress was slow from there. While nobody actually vomited, everyone admitted to feeling on the verge from time to time.

"Every controller's rhythm is slightly different," explained Merlin. "Once a controller knows you're onto his game, he can alter the rhythm, strengthen it, or even deliberately release your mind in a feint and then violently re-establish contact. You have to constantly find your own rhythm of defense to counter the controller's power. Against a professional berserker, that is the deadliest mind game you will ever play."

"Are there any berserkers in Walnut Lane?" asked Terry.

"No," replied Merlin. "And you're not ready to practice with one anyway."

I whispered to Terry, "You're actually disappointed, aren't you?"

Terry shrugged. "We'll need to learn someday."

To our surprise, Scott and I were better than the others at finding the elusive cracks in Merlin's song as he slowly strengthened his psionic control on us each week. Candace was pretty good too, while the worst two were clearly Steven and Terry. I suspected that Steven who was often angry and Terry who was feeling increasingly impatient these days both lacked the calm that was needed to sense the subtle waves and rhythm of Merlin's control. I couldn't help feeling pleased that there was finally something combat-related that I was actually better at than Terry.

"Patience, Teresa dear," I said teasingly.

"I'll give you patience!" barked Terry, chasing me around the dojo and giving me something purplish for Alia to heal.

As the lessons progressed, we discovered that even within the cracks in psionic control, there were paths of greater and lesser resistance. Finding the path of least resistance could mean the difference between breaking free of the control and just feeling horribly queasy.

Furthermore, the lessons were a lot more physically taxing than I had expected. Merlin usually required us to find his cracks "amidst distraction," as he put it, meaning that his students were a regular zoo, circus and freak show combined. The lessons always drew a large number of spectators, often including children from other Walnut Lane families who came here just for entertainment.

"We should be charging admission fees," Scott joked wryly after his failed attempt to break free of a forced duck waddle left visitors breathless with laughter.

It wasn't at all funny for the performers, though. The conscious effort it took to seek out the cracks in Merlin's control often left us very emotionally spent. On days following our evening blocking lessons, I often had trouble focusing on my cooking and other responsibilities. Alia once caught me accidentally refilling the sugar bowl with salt.

"Are you sure you're alright, Addy?" Alia asked anxiously.

"I'm no worse than anyone else," I said, and it was true, though I shuddered to think what might have happened over dinner had Alia not caught my mistake.

Near the end of November, probably due to exhaustion, Heather became sick and had to stay in bed for three days straight. Since her job paid by the working hour, Rachael agreed to fill in until Heather got over her illness. Alia's healing power was useless for things like this.

It was also around this time that Walnut Lane struck its colors. Tiring of the two Guardian factions' repeated demands for Knights, Mrs. Harding officially declared Walnut Lane an independent Guardian breakaway settlement. We were now the Walnut Guardians, or as some of the younger ones joked, the Nutters.

"There's a danger to this kind of move," admitted Mrs. Harding when she invited herself over for dinner to check up on us in early December. "Not only do we pit ourselves against the larger Guardian factions, but if we are attacked by Angels, there's little chance we can ask for reinforcements."

"You can get reinforcements from me," Terry said confidently.

"How are your trainees doing, then, Teresa?"

"Quite well," replied Terry. "The older ones anyway. If the Angels ever do find us, then between your Knights and mine, Walnut will be ready for them."

"I'm happy to hear that, dear," Mrs. Harding said in a slightly strained voice. "But please make sure they do nothing rash. We must keep the peace for as long as we can."

"Yes, Mrs. Harding," Terry said wearily. "We know better than to throw stones at a hornet's nest."

Lately, we sometimes heard rumors about Angel groups passing near or even through our town. I knew Terry was itching to take a few of her Knight trainees out on a patrol and see if they could take one back for New Haven, but Mrs. Harding had repeatedly warned everyone not to do anything that could jeopardize the secrecy of our settlement.

Ignoring Terry's frown, Mrs. Harding turned to Rachael, who was also sitting at our table, and said kindly, "I hear that you have become quite a hider, Ms. Adams."

Rachael smiled back, saying, "Don't worry, Mrs. Harding. The house will stay properly hidden."

"Arthur has every confidence in you," said Mrs. Harding. "But please don't hesitate to ask if you need any help, darling."

"Of course."

Rachael's power as a psionic hider had grown fairly steadily over the last few months, and recently Merlin had stopped coming over except to teach us blocking. It was a big house, and Rachael still had to create her hiding bubble in parts, spending a few minutes on each floor repowering her protection twice a day. Technically, all the detectable psionics here lived on the second floor and below, but Alia sometimes visited Candace and Heather in their room up on the third floor, so Rachael was careful to keep the whole house hidden at all times. Rachael's power was even strong enough now for her to create movable hiding fields around other people. However, not only did this require a lot more effort, but Rachael's individual hiding protection wouldn't last more than a few minutes at a time—a far cry from the two-weeks' worth that Cindy could give. Thus Rachael continued to escort Alia in person to and from Patrick's.

The dinner conversation moved on to our daily lives. I assured Mrs. Harding that everyone was getting healthy, well-balanced meals. Before going home, Mrs. Harding strongly suggested that our younger kids be given a little more time to study academics.

Terry shook her head. "I know you're concerned about their school grades, but in this day and age, we do have to find a healthy balance."

Terry's idea of a healthy balance was that the kids go to school but not waste any time doing homework when they could be training to fight. This was the majority opinion in our house, and Mrs. Harding had no choice but to accept it.

With most of our Knight trainees either working day jobs or going to school, there wasn't enough time to teach them everything they needed to know about surviving a heavy-duty firefight. We were instead giving them a crash course in CQC, teaching the most basic and essential moves such as how to roll and how to wrestle pistols out of people's hands.

Down in the basement, Terry and I taught everyone how to shoot moderately straight and rapidly reload. "Everyone" not only included Susan, Max and Patrick, but also my very reluctant sister, who hated the noise of gunfire even more than I did. Terry had found a tiny pistol for Alia that, when fired, sounded more like a party popper than a gun. But Terry had left me the task of coaxing Alia into using it. Taking Alia down into the basement reminded me a little of the time back when I was desperately trying to teach her how to speak with her mouth, but Alia was older now, and I got her to shoot without making her cry.

But when we started running low on bullets and Terry tried to dip into the money that Alia made teaching kiddie combat, my sister decided that things had gone too far.

"I will not let you do it!" she shouted furiously at Terry over dinner, drawing stares from the other kids who probably never thought she was capable of anger until now. "The money I make here is for food and water and medicine! Not for stupid bullets!"

"Those stupid bullets are going to keep us alive, Alia," Terry countered sternly.

"I'm the one teaching those kids. I'll decide how we use that money!"

Terry stood and glared menacingly at Alia. "Don't you dare forget who taught you those skills in the first place!"

But Alia refused to back down. "I don't care, Teresa! If you want my money, you'll have to fight me for it!"

Terry stared openmouthed at Alia for a brief moment, and then sat down, saying resignedly, "Alia, you are the one and only person on this planet that I'm afraid to fight. I'll get our bullets somewhere else."

The dinner crowd erupted into laughter and cheers for Alia.

Giving my sister a slap on her back, I called out to Terry, "I guess we finally know who the real boss around here is!"

Terry negotiated funding from Mrs. Harding the next day.

Mid-December. Merlin told us to prepare the house for possible visitors. The story was that a family of psionics belonging to the Meridian faction had escaped an Angel takeover of their settlement and was wandering this way. If they came close enough to Walnut Lane, Mrs. Harding might give the word to bring them in.

"We'll have to give them Steven's room," Terry said to me in private. "If you have a problem with that, I'll do it myself."

"Let's at least wait till the visitors arrive before bloodying Steven's face again," I replied. "There's no guarantee that these drifters will ever make it this far anyway."

Steven still refused to acknowledge Terry's presence even during our blocking sessions. I couldn't claim that Steven and I got along even moderately well, but at least he talked to me. If at all possible, I wanted to keep the peace.

A few days later, though it gave me no pleasure at all, I turned out to be right. If Merlin's report was to be believed, the psionic family was simultaneously waylaid by a pack of Wolves planning to take them in for scientific experimentation and by a team of Angels intending to convert them. What happened to the family was unknown, but between the Angels and the Wolves, while there were casualties on both sides, the Wolves came off much worse in the engagement.

Terry said darkly, "If there are any Wolf survivors, they're probably all locked up in some Angel stronghold by now."

I shrugged. "Good riddance."

I felt sorry for the poor Meridian family caught in between, but it gave me some grim satisfaction to know that our two enemy factions were doing each other in.

"You don't get it, Adrian," said Terry. "If the Wolves won, that would have been a good thing. Or at least acceptable to us. Sure, the Angels will torture their captives for information, but they won't kill them. They'll all eventually be converted by Randal Divine. Professional soldiers are a very valuable resource, you know."

"Maybe we should hire us some Wolves," I said dryly.

"Don't be stupid!" snapped Terry, and then mused, "Actually, a team of decent mercenaries wouldn't be such a bad idea, if we only had the money."

"I doubt Alia is about to help you in the finance department."

"Maybe I'll go rob another bank."

I stared at her. "*Another* bank?!"

"I'm kidding, Half-head!" Terry laughed loudly. "I've done some pretty horrible things, but I promise I've never robbed a bank. Not yet anyway."

I laughed with her, shaking my head. "The things we do!"

Then Terry said seriously, "Honestly, I'd prefer a couple of decently trained and dedicated Knights over hired help. Money is a poor substitute for true loyalty."

"Good Knights seem hard to come by these days."

"How are your trainees doing?" asked Terry.

"They're coming along," I said. "Slowly, but they are. Still, they're not as good as yours, I'm sure. You didn't exactly give me the pick of the crop."

"Who's your best? Not counting Alia, of course."

I thought about that for a moment. "Steven is probably my best," I said slowly, "and not just because he's the biggest. He's got some solid moves, and his pistol aim is almost as good as his fire-throwing."

Terry snorted. "He should be good by now, considering he doesn't work and hardly helps with the chores. Maybe he's not a total loss after all."

"Maybe," I agreed quietly. "He's good in training, but I don't know if he has the stomach for a real fight."

Terry shrugged. "No one knows that until they've been put there."

That was for certain.

8. THE BETRAYAL

There was little to party about, but I directed a multi-course dinner for New Year's Eve. Terry handled the midnight toast, saying, "To our great and loyal family. To the hope of better times ahead. And also to peace, may the Angels soon rest in it."

But peace was in short supply everywhere. Terry used everyone's winter vacation time to greatly intensify the training program. We had back-to-back combat training, exercise, weight training and pistol practice. It got so busy, in fact, that almost everyone was looking forward to the end of the holidays and returning to school.

Nobody was counting the days like Alia, though.

"*I hate vacations!*" was my sister's verdict. She had gotten used to the peace and quiet she had during school hours, and winter vacation meant that the chaos of our poorly disciplined family lasted from dawn to dusk every single day. As our dedicated live-in healer, Alia couldn't often seek refuge at Patrick's, so she took to hiding in our bedroom whenever she wasn't absolutely needed.

Terry once said to her, "It really wouldn't kill you to at least try to be a little more normal, you know."

"Nothing in this house is normal," countered Alia. "Why should I be any different?"

As much as I agreed with Terry, my sister had the right of it on that count.

Aside from the daily roughhousing and petty arguments, there were certain other inevitabilities to having so many teenagers under one roof. A week or so into January, we discovered that Scott and Rachael were dating. I have no idea when or how it started, but considering how difficult it was to get any privacy in our house, they probably hadn't been a couple for very long.

"As long as it doesn't distract them from their training, I don't mind it in the least," commented Terry. "And if they fight, that'll be fun too."

Scott's only real crime was that he was keeping a portion of his salary—money that was supposed to be brought home for everyone's needs—as spending cash for his outings with Rachael. It was no great amount, though, so Terry decided to give him a pass. Scott was still our top earner, after all.

Meanwhile, Susan seemed to be getting a little too popular with Daniel and Walter, but big-sister Felicity made sure nothing serious happened.

I agreed with Terry that this kind of thing was none of our business. As long as we were all getting along, or at least getting by, I'd cook and clean and teach CQC and learn blocking, and I wouldn't stick my nose into anything that didn't directly concern me.

"I'm so glad for Rachael and Scott," said Candace one evening as she helped me prepare dinner. "Those two are the perfect couple."

I shrugged. "I suppose it's a good thing."

Candace was my only assistant in the kitchen that day because Scott and Heather were training with Terry. Fortunately, we had all gotten used to the cooking routine and I no longer needed everyone in the kitchen for every meal.

"They look so happy together, don't you think?" insisted Candace.

I gave a non-committal nod, my focus more on the carrots I was rapidly slicing.

"Adrian?" Candace asked hesitantly at my side. "How would you like to go out with me sometime? You know, just the two of us?"

I nearly sliced off my hand.

"Excuse me?" I said, hastily putting the knife down and turning to her. "You—you mean like, going out?" I stammered. "Like a—a couple?"

Candace giggled embarrassedly. "Well, maybe not a serious couple, but yeah. I thought we could just go out and have a coffee or something. I'm sorry. I didn't know exactly how to say it. I've been meaning to ask for a while, actually, but…"

I shook my head and smiled, saying, "I'm deeply flattered, Candace. But I don't think it's such a good idea."

"You don't like me?" asked Candace, visibly deflating.

"It's not like that," I insisted. "I think you're really nice."

Candace blushed. "Then what's the matter?"

"Well, for starters, I'm already psionic, so I'd need hiding protection just to leave the house."

Candace wasn't buying that in the least. "What kind of excuse is that?"

Thinking of another excuse as quickly as I could, I suggested meekly, "I don't date students?"

"Adrian!"

I sighed. "Look, it's just not a good idea, okay?"

"Why not?" pressed Candace, gently fingering my hair. "Is it because I'm older? I heard from your sister that you used to date someone older than you."

I pulled away and snapped angrily at her, "Well, maybe you didn't hear that she was killed at the blood trial last year!"

Candace flinched. As often was the case when I lost my calm, my words had come out in a much harsher tone than I had intended. I stared down at the floor, feeling ashamed and embarrassed.

"I'm sorry," Candace said in a subdued tone. "I didn't know. Alia wouldn't give me any details. I just thought you had broken up or something."

"I'm sorry I shouted, Candace," I said quietly. "I really do like you. It's just that I promised myself that I would never… you know… It hurts too much."

"It's just coffee, Adrian," Candace said soothingly. "It'd be my treat, and we can just be friends if you like."

I picked up the knife and went back to slicing up the carrots, refusing to meet Candace's eyes.

It's not that I didn't see Candace's point of view. There was no telling when Walnut Lane might be attacked, or who might be dead or converted a week from now. Might as well have all the fun we could while we were free and breathing.

And I had meant what I said to Candace. I did like her. I liked her cheerful voice and I liked her gentle, dark blue eyes. Candace had the most angelic smile which she dispensed at every opportunity. She always seemed to find the lighter side of things. While I couldn't deny that something about her personality reminded me just a little of Laila Brown, Candace was more relaxed, more carefree, more the way I wished I was sometimes. In a better world, I would have been the one asking her out, months ago. But in this world, it really scared me. I wasn't sure if I could survive another loss like Laila.

"What was her name?" Candace asked softly. I didn't reply, but she figured it out. "Your sister named the baby after her, didn't she?"

I closed my eyes and nodded.

"Alia says you sometimes cry yourself to sleep," whispered Candace. "Is it for her?"

I wasn't about to answer that for anybody, but I put my knife down and faced her again. "I'm sorry, Candace. I really am. At least I want to wait until this awful war is over."

"I understand," Candace said sadly. Then, before I could react, she leaned forward and lightly kissed my forehead. "But I think you're in for a very long wait."

February.

Merlin praised our progress in mental blocking. Terry and Steven were still lagging behind the class, but even they could break free of Merlin's control given enough time. Of course, there was no way to accurately gauge how much psionic focus Merlin was giving us when he took control of our bodies, so I suspected that our instructor was adjusting the intensity of his control to our individual levels. Merlin talked more freely when he was controlling Terry and Steven.

Terry had to reprimand Scott and Rachael twice for breaking curfew and once for staying out all night. Meanwhile, Felicity's overprotective attitude regarding Susan's relationship with the two boys frequently led to shouting arguments between the sisters. Personally, I agreed with Felicity's view that Susan was being a bit of a flirt, but I kept my mouth shut.

On Valentine's Day, Candace gave me a large heart-shaped card in front of everyone at the dinner table, drawing cheers and catcalls from the crowd. Despite how embarrassing that was, I felt guilty about not giving Candace anything in return. Still, I had to keep this nipped in the bud, and it was better to seem uncaring than to risk Candace thinking that she had a chance with me. It would have been a lot easier if she wasn't so sweet and pretty and… Oh, never mind.

The very next day was Cat's birthday, but this year I forgot it as easily as I had forgotten my own.

I only remembered three days later when Terry asked in passing over breakfast, "Isn't your sister's birthday sometime this month?"

"No, it's next month," I replied, thinking of Alia.

Then it hit me.

"Oh, right," I said awkwardly. "Cat's fourteenth. I forgot."

Terry laughed, but I shrugged it off, saying, "What do I care, anyway? She's Catherine *Divine* now."

"Then why do you still wear that stone around your neck?" asked Terry.

Touching my amethyst pendant, I replied simply, "Force of habit."

That wasn't entirely true, but I didn't want to continue this discussion. Right now, I was much more concerned about Alia than Cat.

My second sister had returned ashen-faced from Patrick's house yesterday evening. She had overheard Patrick's foster parents talking about an airplane that had been hijacked by the Angels last year as it tried to escape New Haven. It was believed that all aboard had been taken captive, and that they were already converted.

I had checked and double-checked the story with Alia, and also with Patrick's parents over the phone. There was no hard evidence that the plane in question had actually carried the New Haven Council. There had been quite a few Guardian planes leaving New Haven that night, and even now, many of them were unaccounted for. Of course, they hadn't all crashed or been hijacked. Most of the Guardians fleeing New Haven by air had probably hidden their tracks just as Terry had done with our plane, and then simply disappeared so as to avoid pursuit by the Angels.

However, "disappearing" wasn't the course of action anyone would have expected of the New Haven Council, which still remained missing in its entirety. I secretly agreed with Alia's opinion that the hijacked plane probably was the Council's. It took hours last night to halfway convince a teary-eyed Alia that there was still hope. I wasn't even sure why I was trying to keep our spirits up anymore. It had been more than half a year. Though Merlin still maintained that Lumina wasn't under a single hiding bubble, that in itself was no guarantee that Cindy hadn't been converted. Cindy had once been the personal hider of the last Guardian queen, Diana Granados. Who was to say she wasn't traveling with King Randal Divine now? If we really wanted to find Cindy, our best bet was to simply turn ourselves in and accept Angel conversion.

"How's Alia doing?" Candace asked me as she helped me wash the dishes later that morning. My sister hadn't been at the breakfast table.

"She's still in bed," I replied. "She said she wasn't hungry, but I'll take something up for her later. Max can go to Harding's by himself today, and if Alia's not up by noon, I'll call up her kids and cancel their lesson."

"I wish there was something I could do," Candace said sadly.

"She'll be okay," I said. "Alia's pretty tough. We'll just give her some time."

My sister did get up for lunch, but she ate very little. I moved her kiddie-combat lesson to the next day so that she wouldn't have to face her students in a weakened condition.

But it was the next day that everything once again fell into chaos.

Steven hadn't come down for breakfast, and I had sent Walter up to fetch him. But Walter returned alone, saying that there was no answer when he knocked on Steven's bedroom door.

"He's not there?" I asked.

"I don't know," said Walter. "I knocked a lot. You didn't expect me to actually open the door, did you?"

Steven was snappish and rude with everyone including me, but particularly with everyone excluding me. Still, that was no excuse. We had lived with Steven for a long time and Walter should have been used to that by now.

I looked at Walter irritably. "He could be sick, you know."

Overhearing us, Rachael said, "Steven is eating at Mrs. Harding's today. He asked me to give him hiding protection so he could go over first thing."

"Really?" I said, surprised.

"Well, he didn't exactly ask," said Rachael. "More like ordered."

That wasn't what had surprised me. "What did Mrs. Harding want with Steven?"

"I don't know," said Rachael, shrugging. "Steven just said that Mrs. Harding had called and asked him to come over."

Terry asked sharply, "Well, who picked up the phone?!"

Rachael shrugged again. "I don't know. Probably Steven."

There was only one phone in a house shared by fourteen, and Steven rarely left his room except at mealtimes and for training. Terry and I stared at each other, no doubt thinking the exact same thing.

Terry grabbed the phone and dialed Mrs. Harding's number, but I already knew what she was about to hear.

Steven was gone.

We didn't expect to find a goodbye note, but we checked his room anyway. There was no note, but further investigation revealed that our jar of petty cash in the kitchen had been removed.

"He's gone home," I said simply. "Back to Lumina."

Steven's father was on the Council. If the hijacked plane really had been the Council's, Steven might soon be reunited with his family.

"That bastard!" Terry shouted in fury, kicking over a chair.

We wouldn't particularly miss Steven, but the real problem was that once the Angels picked him up, he would be made to give away the exact location of Walnut Lane.

Mrs. Harding called an emergency meeting for the Walnut Guardian families that very afternoon. Representing the Refugee House, Terry and I attended the meeting together, leaving the rest at home. I had a feeling that we weren't going to be very popular today.

"We tried to locate Steven before he was out of range of our finders," Mrs. Harding told the visibly disturbed crowd that had gathered in her living room. "The hiding protection he received would have worn off within less than an hour, but unfortunately no one could sense him even after that time."

Mrs. Harding looked quite upset, and paused for a moment before saying slowly, "We believe that Steven never made it out of our town. Most likely he was picked up and taken in by our neighbors."

A few people in the crowd exchanged knowing glances. I didn't know what Mrs. Harding was referring to so I looked at Terry for help, but Terry seemed just as clueless.

"At this time, I would like everyone to remain calm," continued Mrs.

Harding. "All of the information we have suggests that even if the Angels do plan to attack us, they will not be able to gather their forces for at least two or three weeks. We will relocate well before they get to us."

There were murmurs of displeasure and worry from the crowd, and we received more than a few dirty looks. I felt the full weight of what we had done here. Because of us, the entire settlement would have to be moved.

Mrs. Harding talked over the noise, saying, "We all knew that this day would come. It was only a matter of time, and it is fortunate that we were not caught unawares. Now, I have already chartered a bus to move the children to our mountain camp. Everyone under eighteen years old will be evacuated first thing tomorrow morning. I will be asking for a number of adult chaperons to accompany them. The rest of us can take a few more days to wrap up our affairs in this town. With any luck, we will be able to leave Walnut Lane without incident."

"What about them?!" called a furious voice from across the room. The owner of the voice was a middle-aged man pointing at Terry and me. A few others were nodding and staring at us angrily.

Mrs. Harding replied in a no-nonsense tone that quickly subdued the muttering crowd, "If I am not entirely mistaken, these two young Knights will be assisting our evacuation. We all voted for taking Teresa's lost children into our community, so I see no excuse for your tone." Mrs. Harding stared coldly back at the man who had shouted, and when he didn't speak, she continued, "Now, I'm sure that those of you with children will want to get going and prepare for tomorrow. I will be making calls later to your houses to give you details and ask for volunteer escorts."

The crowd dispersed, but Mrs. Harding asked Terry and me to remain.

"We're really sorry," I said once the three of us were the only ones left in Mrs. Harding's living room.

Mrs. Harding smiled. "Nonsense, dear. As I just told the angry mob, it was only a matter of time before we were discovered. There are so many Guardians being converted these days, who is to even say the Angels don't already know exactly where we are? At least this way, I have a good excuse to move the settlement before anything terrible happens."

Terry asked, "What did you mean by Steven being taken by our neighbors?"

"There is a very small Angel outpost on the other side of our town," explained Mrs. Harding. "Just a handful of Seraphim living in one house. It occasionally serves as a staging point for Angel operations in this region."

"You're kidding!" exclaimed Terry. "How long have they been there?"

"Oh, I'm not quite sure, dear. We've known about them for seven years or so. The Angels have long used that house to jail those they capture in their raids until they are moved to their queen—or king now—for conversion." Mrs. Harding chuckled and added, "They never once guessed that they were sharing this town with a Guardian settlement."

Terry stared at her. "And it never occurred to you to shut them down?"

"Certainly, it has," replied Mrs. Harding. "But we've always had to consider that a failed attempt could jeopardize our secrecy. And after all, none of our members have ever been attacked by them."

Terry shook her head in frustration. "So Steven never even made it out of town. He left us with the purpose of joining the Angels, so he'll waste no time telling them everything he knows. Maybe we should—"

"No, Teresa," Mrs. Harding cut across her gently. "I know what you want to say, but we will not attack them. Chances are they have already contacted other Angel units, so destroying their outpost will not blind the Angels to our location. And besides, if Steven wanted to return to his family so much that he would willingly join the Angels, there is little point in trying to rescue him."

As Terry and I walked back to our house, Terry muttered savagely, "I wasn't planning on *rescuing* Steven."

Despite the direness of our situation, I couldn't help but laugh.

Everyone had gathered in the living-room dojo awaiting our return, and Terry quickly explained what was happening. Many used the opportunity to vent some anger over Steven's betrayal, and I suspected that it was probably a good thing we weren't about to get him back.

"We're not exactly a popular bunch right now, so stay indoors," said Terry. "Walnut Lane will be closing permanently as soon as the Guardian families tie up their loose ends. Meanwhile, Mrs. Harding is evacuating everyone under eighteen years old tomorrow morning. The adults will follow at a later date."

"Evacuate?" asked James.

Terry explained about the bus that would take the kids up to the secret mountain camp, adding, "It's just a precaution. We're pretty sure we can all get out before the Angels gather on this location, but just in case they do, we don't want any children in the settlement."

James looked aghast. "You're not going to make us leave with the little kids, are you?! This is exactly the kind of thing we've been training for."

There were nods and murmurs of agreement from our crowd, and even Susan and Max looked determined to stay and help guard Walnut Lane.

Terry smiled. "Anyone who wants to go will have a seat on the bus tomorrow, but as far as making you leave, you won't hear it from me."

Felicity turned to her younger sister and said, "You'll hear it from me, though."

Susan scowled at her.

I pulled Terry aside after the meeting. "We have to get the youngest ones on the bus, Terry," I insisted. "If not James, at least Max and Susan, and maybe Daniel and Walter too."

"They all want to stay," said Terry.

"Of course they want to stay! It's an *adventure* for them. But we can't risk their lives for nothing."

"First off," said Terry, poking me in the chest, "their lives aren't at any real risk. We're sure to get out without incident. Second, James is right in that everyone here has trained for exactly this sort of thing. It's the perfect opportunity for us to test out their nerves in an almost risk-free crisis. Just think of it as a training mission."

"Oh, like mine at the Holy Land?"

Terry winced, and I instantly regretted hitting such a tender nerve. Terry had tried to keep me from harm that night.

"I'm sorry," I said. "It just popped out, and I didn't mean it that way. But do we really have to make these kids do this?"

"We're not *making* them do anything, Adrian," Terry said patiently. "This is what they *want*. Even Max wants to stay here and defend Walnut Lane."

"And what if the Angels really do come?"

"Let them come!" Terry replied fiercely. "We've been training these kids to be soldiers. That just doesn't come without risk."

I shook my head in resignation. I wasn't going to defy Terry and order anyone onto tomorrow's bus. Terry was probably right about the risk assessment, anyway. I couldn't ask for a safer mission for our trainees to get their feet wet in.

Patrick joined us for dinner. He also brought along baby Laila, who had learned to walk just last month. Patrick's foster parents were attending an evening meeting with Mrs. Harding and her Knights.

When he heard that every one of us was planning to stay behind, Patrick announced that he was going to stay as well, adding, "My mom is going to be on the bus tomorrow. She can take Laila."

Alia said something telepathically to him, and he looked like he was about to reply, but just then, Susan and Felicity's so-far quiet argument turned noisy.

"You're not my mother!" Susan shouted angrily at her sister. "You can't tell me what to do! Even Terry said I could stay!"

I had pretty much finished eating, so I quickly retreated to the kitchen to start cleaning up. I had a feeling that the sisters would be at it for a while, and I knew better than to get between them. Susan had made a good deal of progress in her CQC training with me, and I was afraid she might try to get me to vouch for her.

As I scrubbed the plates, pots and pans, I could still hear the two arguing in the dining room, and sure enough, Susan burst into the kitchen a moment later, followed by Felicity.

Susan said in a shaky voice, "Adrian, please tell my sister to stop treating me like a little kid!"

I sighed. "Susan, for what it's worth, I think you're as combat-ready as anyone else in this house. But if it were entirely up to me, I'd have every one of us on that bus tomorrow, including myself."

Susan let out a frustrated moan and stomped out of the kitchen.

Felicity whispered to me, "Thanks."

I grinned. "You're welcome and good luck."

As Felicity started chasing after Susan again, I turned back to my dirty dishes.

Alia came in to help me with the cleaning up, and I was pleasantly surprised to see that she was all smiles.

"What's the good news?" I asked as she joined me at the sink and started drying the dishes.

"*Patrick agreed to take tomorrow's bus,*" replied Alia.

"Really?" I said in wonder. "How'd you manage that?"

"*I told him his mother is going to be too busy to look after Laila by herself, and that the children could use an extra Knight to make sure they're safe at the camp.*"

"Security for the kids, huh? That'd be a good argument for Felicity to use with Susan."

Alia laughed. "*I'll tell her.*"

Alia closed her eyes for a moment, concentrating on sending her telepathy through the walls.

Despite the angry looks Terry and I had to endure at the meeting today, as well as the inescapable guilt of having contributed to the uprooting of an entire psionic settlement, I couldn't help feeling happy seeing my sister in such good spirits. Alia's fears about Cindy's fate were not forgotten, but they were temporarily put on hold to deal with the crisis at hand.

"*There,*" said Alia, opening her eyes. "*But I don't think Susan is going to agree as easily as Patrick did.*"

"Yeah, well, Susan has a hot head," I said.

"*Like you, Addy.*"

"Thanks a lot!" I laughed. Then I said hesitantly, "Would it be pointless to ask you to get on that bus too?"

Alia threw me an exasperated look.

"Okay, okay!" I said, hastily backing down. "You know I had to try."

My sister gave me a quick hug and whispered, "*Everything's going to be okay.*"

How I wished I could believe that.

Early the next morning, Patrick stopped in to say goodbye to Alia, who couldn't see the bus off because her power wasn't hidden. Alia spoke telepathically; Patrick, in whispers. They hugged for a full five minutes. It was hard to believe that they were only going to be apart for two weeks or so.

Susan's departure wasn't as quiet. Felicity, taking Alia's advice last night, had managed to get Susan's grudging consent to evacuate with the rest of the Walnut Lane children, but still Susan protested all morning.

After one last push near departure time, Susan finally gave in, saying crossly to her sister, "Okay, fine! I'll go! But don't bother seeing me off. I'll go with Patrick."

"Oh, no you don't," said Felicity. "I'm going to make sure you really get on that bus."

As Patrick and Susan left with Felicity and a few others who were going to see the bus off, I turned to Max and said, "Last chance, Max. Sure you want to stay here?"

Max nodded quietly.

"Alright," I said. "I guess that's everyone, then."

Mrs. Harding had strongly suggested that Max evacuate today, but Terry had countered that Max was most emotionally stable when he was with us, particularly James, who he was closest to.

Alia looked up at me and said sadly, *"I wish I could've said goodbye to Laila."*

"You'll see her soon," I assured her. "We're only here until the families finish packing up their lives."

After the bus left, Terry had Scott, Heather and Candace quit their jobs, and the younger ones quit school.

"If there's an attack, we want to be here and ready for it," said Terry.

Terry put everyone back on a full-day training schedule, occasionally sending out pairs of trainees to assist the real Walnut Lane Knights in patrolling the settlement. Terry saw this as not only a chance to redeem us a little in the eyes of the angry families, but as an opportunity to give our students some hands-on training. Admittedly, Walnut Lane was just two blocks in size and the kids didn't even know what they were supposed to be on the lookout for, but at least it kept everyone busy.

The days passed uncomfortably. The Walnut Lane families were quitting their jobs, saying goodbye to friends, and selling their material possessions or moving them to temporary storage. To avoid attracting unwanted attention, this all had to be done slowly and carefully. The Wolves especially would be on the lookout for this kind of sudden mass departure, which was a possible sign of psionics on the move.

"It's freezing out there," said Scott, returning to the house with Rachael from an evening patrol.

A week had passed since Steven's disappearance. The winter snows had already melted, but the late-February wind could still bite pretty harshly. I was glad that my psionic power gave me an excuse to stay indoors.

"How is everything outside?" I asked conversationally as Alia passed Scott and Rachael mugs of hot coffee.

"Same as usual," replied Rachael, taking a sip. "More moving trucks. And I think the family across from Harding's sold their house."

"Lucky them," I said.

Actually, it wasn't so lucky. Selling a house this quickly guaranteed that the owners wouldn't get nearly what it was worth. Still, most of the houses were going to be abandoned, so getting any money at all was better than nothing.

"I could use some help with dinner today," I said. "Heather and Candace are still out."

"Late or missing?" Scott asked seriously.

"Nothing dire," I replied reassuringly. "Heather called and said they both were invited to tea at Harding's."

Rachael had her scheduled CQC training with Terry next, but Scott joined Alia and me in the kitchen.

As Scott helped us prepare a large pot of beef stew, he said in a slightly deflated tone, "You know, Adrian, I never thought that being on a Guardian mission could be this mundane."

"What are you complaining about?" I asked with a grin. "I thought you were out there with Rachael today."

Alia giggled, and Scott laughed too as he said, "Well, that part's fun. But you know what I mean. It's not like we're actually helping to defend the people here. It's more like public relations."

"That's important too, Scott," I said mildly. "Besides, I'd take boredom over a battle any day."

Alia nodded vigorously and said, "Only fight when you need to."

Scott smiled at Alia. "I suppose you're right. It's not like I really want to be in a battle."

"That's good to hear," I said. "How are the Walnut residents treating you?"

"They're still not talking to us. At least, not in a civil tone."

I chuckled. "Sounds like a battle to me."

Given enough time, I hoped that the people of Walnut Lane would see us in a better light. After all, we hadn't deliberately treated Steven in a way to make him do what he did. But I could hardly blame the residents for disliking us at a time when their lives had been upturned. Unlike many breakaway Guardian settlements which changed location every few years, Walnut Lane had been around for more than fifteen years.

As we continued adding ingredients to the stew, I said, "Thanks for helping us out today, Scott. It was really Heather's turn."

Despite everyone in our house being out of work and out of school, between extra combat training and pretending to be security guards, hardly anyone aside from Alia helped me with the housekeeping.

Scott shrugged. "It's okay. I had nothing better to do anyway."

"Sure you did!" laughed Alia. "You'd rather be in the dojo with Rachael."

"True," admitted Scott. Then he added happily, "But I got first watch with her tonight."

Terry had set up a night watch, having almost everyone stay up in shifts to guard our house. Though night-watch duty was not something anyone usually looked forward to, Scott had good reason to be happy. Privacy was hard to come by in such a crowded house. Night duty would allow Scott and Rachael to be alone together and out of the biting cold, and theirs was the first shift, which meant that they wouldn't even have to wake up in the middle of the night.

"So you'll be kissing for three hours straight, then?" Alia asked teasingly.

Scott just laughed, saying, "We'll breathe through our noses."

Alia laughed too. "Addy used to be just like that!"

"Really?!" said Scott.

I gave my sister a warning look. "Alia..."

But Alia's next words to Scott were telepathic, and whatever it was that she said, Scott laughed loudly at it.

Just then, Heather and Candace barged in, saying in unison, "Sorry we're late!"

"It's alright," I said, "we're almost done here. But could you girls kindly take my annoying little sister out of this kitchen and tickle her until serving time or until she passes out, whichever comes first?"

"Always happy to oblige," Candace said with an evil grin.

Alia tried to make a run for it but I telekinetically lifted her off of the floor and dropped her into Heather's arms.

"Don't worry, Alia," said Heather. "I promise we won't kill you as long as you tell us what you did to annoy your brother so much."

Once Scott and I were the only ones left in the kitchen, Scott chuckled and said, "You know, even living in the same house for all this time, I can never quite place your sister."

"How so?" I asked.

"Well, she's got guts enough to be named Honorary Guardian Knight, the youngest ever, right? She teaches her own combat classes. But then she hates guns and can't even go to school..."

I raised my eyebrows. "And she still sleeps in my bed?"

"That too," said Scott. "And the fact that she's often silent for hours on end, and then suddenly acts like a regular kid sometimes, like just now."

I shrugged. "Alia's just weird. You get used to it after a while."

After dinner and cleanup, Terry and I taught one last joint CQC class before lights-out.

Before we broke up for the night, Terry reminded the crowd of who was on duty after Scott and Rachael. Second shift was Walter and Daniel, followed by Felicity alone. Scott would wake the boys in his room at around 1am, and they would knock on Felicity's door at four o'clock.

Alia, Max and I were the only ones regularly exempt from night-watch duty, Alia and Max due to their ages, and I because I had pulled rank and refused. Terry probably felt that I should be setting a better example, but she couldn't order me because her original argument for keeping us in Walnut Lane was based on how risk-free it was.

Though I refused to admit it to Terry, over the last few days, I had come to think that I had overreacted on the early-evacuation issue. The Angels at the outpost across town wouldn't dare attack our settlement without reinforcements, and reinforcements wouldn't arrive anytime soon.

The two largest Guardian factions had settled their differences several weeks ago. Though they were still no match for the Angels, the reunited Guardians were nevertheless putting up a very good resistance employing guerrilla-warfare tactics, and the Angel forces were mostly focused on them. If the Angels were planning to strike Walnut at all, it wouldn't happen for a while.

In fact, I now suspected that the only reason Mrs. Harding had even chartered the early bus was so that the adults could concentrate on the task of moving out without having to bother with their kids. At the pace the Walnut Guardians were handling their affairs, it looked like we would be here for another two weeks, maybe more. But I had to agree with Terry that there was no better mission for our trainees than one in which we were pretty much guaranteed our safety.

"Addy! Addy, wake up! Addy!"

Groaning, I opened my eyes halfway in the darkened bedroom and looked up at my sister, who was leaning over me on our bed and shaking my shoulders.

"What's the matter, Alia?" I asked quietly. "Did you have another bad dream?"

I could hear Max and James's quiet breathing, and I didn't want to wake them. Dawn was still at least an hour away, but there was just enough light to see Alia's anxious face.

"Something's wrong," she whispered into my head.

I was about to ask what she meant, but then there was a high-pitched scream from downstairs. Felicity!

"James, wake up!" I shouted.

James sprang up into a sitting position, and Max opened his eyes too.

"What is it?" asked James, instantly on high alert.

"Trouble," I replied. I telekinetically flipped the light switch. Nothing happened. "Big trouble."

I had left my pistol in the basement shooting range, but James had better sense and quickly grabbed his off the top of his dresser.

"Give it to me," I shouted, telekinetically snatching the pistol out of his hands.

Flipping off the safety, I fired two loud rounds into the wall to make sure everyone was awake. I had heard no gunfire from downstairs, and suspected that our attackers were relying solely on psionic powers and silent weapons.

"Let's go!" I said to James, turning to the door. Alia and Max tried to follow, but I stopped them. "Stay here, both of you."

"I'm coming too!" said Alia, and Max looked at me defiantly.

"No you're not!"

"We can fight!" insisted Max. "We've trained for this!"

I heard the sound of footsteps rushing past our door. The rest of our trainees were already on the move.

"You're not ready, Max!" I said, and then turned to my sister. "And you're a healer for crying out loud! Stay here!"

Alia glared at me. "I'm a Knight too, Addy! Stop treating me like a little baby!"

That was rich coming from a kid who was still afraid to sleep by herself, but there was no time to argue the point. I shoved Alia down onto the floor, saying, "You stay here or I'll shoot you myself!"

Then I quickly turned to Max and said, "That goes double for you. Lock the door behind us."

I tossed the pistol back to James. "James, with me!"

As soon as we were out of the room, I caught a whiff of the unmistakable stench of tear gas in the air.

"What is that smell?" asked James, visibly nauseous.

"You'll find out," I replied. "Follow me."

Without lights, the hallway was even darker than our bedroom, but I could see that Scott's room door was wide open. The three boys in that room had already gone down. I could hear panicked footsteps above us, and guessed that some of the girls might still be on the third floor, though Terry would no doubt already be in the fray. I was furious at Alia and Max for slowing us down.

The gas got thicker as we approached the stairs, forcing us to squint and cough as tears welled in our eyes.

"Damn it, Adrian!" James cried in a panicked voice. "I can't see!"

"Neither can I!" I replied, coughing uncontrollably. "Come on!"

There was nothing for it. We had to get down there and find out what was going on. Tugging on James's hand, I pulled him down the stairs with me. The smell of the gas was unbearable here, and I kept my eyes closed tightly, groping along the stairs with my free hand.

I didn't know if James could help me at all in his condition, or even if I would be able to do much. But I had to get down there, and it was easier to do this with James than alone.

Having spent eight months blind, finding my way in the dark was second nature to me, and I had little trouble leading James down to the dojo with my eyes shut. Once we were there, however, I had no choice but to ignore the stinging pain and force my eyes open. The nearly pitch-black room was filled with thick smoke, and I couldn't see more than a yard or two around me. I heard gunshots and shouts, and then a fireball flew past my head.

Suddenly James screamed. I turned but couldn't see him.

In the dark, in the smoke and tear gas, everything had turned to chaos. Even in my panic, I noticed two psionic destroyer powers, one of them a pyroid, the other a frighteningly powerful telekinetic. They were close enough to sense inside Rachael's hiding bubble, and I suspected that both were in this room. And there could be others.

There was another shout, and then, a few seconds later, the sound of a car engine, followed by silence.

I found my way to a window and telekinetically blasted it out. Sticking my head through, I couldn't see any cars on the street, but I noticed that the other houses of Walnut Lane were all quiet. Lights were coming on in the nearest ones, their occupants probably having heard the commotion. They all still had electricity, which meant that our house was the only one under attack. What was going on?

"Adrian!" a girl's voice shouted.

Pulling my head back through the window, I turned to the voice. "Candace!"

"They took her!" Candace screamed through violent coughs, her eyes and nose running horribly. "They took her! They took her!"

"What are you talking about?!"

"Terry! Terry!" Candace cried hysterically. "Oh, God, they took her!"

They took Terry?!

Candace grabbed my shoulders. "Terry! She tried to stop them! I—I think she's dead!"

"Where's Terry?"

"Outside!"

Pushing Candace aside, I sprinted through the smoke to the front door, which was open. Stepping out onto the porch, I saw Terry's body lying facedown on the driveway, unmoving. I wiped my eyes as I rushed to her side.

I carefully turned Terry over onto her back, and she opened her eyes a little. She tried to say something, but then suddenly coughed up a lot of blood. There was a hole in her lower gut, and her shirt was drenched in blood. I pressed my palm against the wound to stop the bleeding. Terry's body went limp, her eyes closed, and I couldn't even tell if she was still breathing.

"Somebody help!" I called out. "Alia! Get down here!"

I heard Scott shout out my name from behind.

"Get over here!" I hollered. "Terry's hurt!"

Terry's blood on my hands was draining not only my psionic power but some of my physical strength too. Scott sprinted up to us, and I said to him, "Scott, put your hands here. Keep pressure on the wound. Press down hard!"

Scott took over for me. Candace had followed Scott out, and I turned to her, saying frantically, "Go get Alia, Candace. I left her in my room."

Candace didn't move.

"Candace!" I shouted. "Go get Alia! Go now!"

Her voice shaking, Candace said hoarsely, "They took her, Adrian."

I looked back at our house, my eyes slowly moving up to my bedroom window on the second floor.

Bits of shattered glass were still stuck to the frame.

9. TEAM LEADER

There were no healers in Walnut Lane, but Candace returned quickly with Patrick's foster father, Dr. Land, who was a surgeon. By now, several Walnut Guardians from other houses had gathered on our lawn, and a few had gone inside to open up the rest of the windows, clear the gas, and help the wounded. Terry was put on a stretcher to be taken to Dr. Land's house where she would be treated.

I was about to follow, but Dr. Land stopped me, saying, "Go see to the rest of your family, Adrian. Make sure they're alright, and bring any others who need help to me."

"But—"

"There's nothing you can do for Terry," Dr. Land said firmly. "Go and see to the rest of them."

"She's going to be okay, isn't she?" I pleaded.

"I can't say," Dr. Land replied grimly. "Now go on."

I watched them carry Terry's stretcher down the sidewalk for a few seconds before turning to Scott and Candace.

"I'm so sorry, Adrian," Candace said between sobs. "I wanted to help Terry but she pushed me back and..."

"It's alright," I said, forcing myself to remain calm. "Terry will be fine, and we'll find Alia too. Come on, back in the house."

If only to subdue my mounting panic, I had to keep myself busy. The dojo still reeked of CS gas, but most of it had cleared.

James had acquired a nasty purple bruise on his forehead, but he was alive and in the process of regaining consciousness. "You were right, Adrian," he groaned, gingerly touching the bruise. "It's not fun getting into trouble."

"It's just a knock on the head," I said reassuringly. "You'll be alright."

But others weren't as lucky.

Having come into close contact with the Angel pyroid, Rachael had suffered second-degree burns on her face and neck, and much of her hair was burned off. Her skin was red and swollen, and I feared she would have permanent scars.

Walter had a broken arm. In the thick smoke, he had crashed into a non-psionic Seraph carrying a heavy hunting crossbow, tussled with him and successfully disarmed him before being thrown to the floor. Fortunately for Walter, the Seraph scampered after he lost his weapon.

Heather had a hole through her right foot: She had accidentally shot herself before she even made it out of her room. That was probably for the better. Much worse might have happened to her had she actually joined the battle.

And two were dead.

The first I learned of was Felicity, who had multiple knife wounds to her stomach and chest, her nightclothes a ghastly, bloody mess. Felicity probably died in seconds.

The other casualty was Max, who we found lying face up on the floor of the bedroom where I had left him. He had a hole through the center of his neck, the result of a focused telekinetic blast. He was killed trying to protect Alia.

Scott and Daniel helped me put both bodies in the basement, where it was coldest.

And slowly, we came to understand what had happened.

There were only four attackers. Three, including the pyroid, had entered through the front door, probably by quietly picking the lock. It had been on Felicity's watch, and when she screamed, one of them had stabbed her to death. As smoke from their grenades filled the first floor and we rushed down to meet the battle, the fourth Angel—the powerful telekinetic that I had sensed—had entered through my bedroom window. Their target had, from the start, been Alia.

Healers were exceptionally rare, and child psionics even rarer. Cindy had told me long ago that because Alia was already a powerful healer at such a young age, chances were she might become the world's greatest someday. Like Cindy herself, Alia had always been a coveted prize for any psionic faction. The Seraphim at the outpost across town knew that the Walnut Guardians would be long gone before the Angels could mount a full-scale attack, so they decided to steal our greatest asset before we could get away.

And who had told the Angels about my sister, what she was and where she was sleeping in our house?

Staring down at Max and Felicity's bodies in the basement, I muttered furiously under my breath, "I'm going to kill that boy myself."

Scott asked, "We're going after the Angels, then?"

"I'm going too," Daniel said quickly.

"No," I replied. "You've both done enough already. Harding is probably organizing her team of Knights right now. I'll join up with them as soon as they're ready to go."

There was never any question in my mind about retrieving Alia. The only question was how and when. It would have to be soon, before the Angels took her to their king for conversion. How quickly could Mrs. Harding prepare her Knights for a counterstrike on the Angel outpost? The Angels didn't know that we knew where they were hiding, so they probably wouldn't be rushed to move their captive. Still, I couldn't take any chances. I wasn't about to lose another sister to the Angels. At least I didn't have to worry too much about how Alia was doing. Her captors weren't going to hurt their prize healer, and Alia knew that I wasn't going to sit by and let her be converted.

At the moment, I was much more worried about Terry. It was intolerable that she was being left at the mercy of human medicine when all she needed was one good healer to keep her from death.

I refused to let any of our injured be taken to Dr. Land's house, wanting the surgeon to focus on the priority case. Fortunately, many of the Walnut Guardians who had come to our assistance knew basic first aid. James settled for an icepack on his head while we made a splint for Walter's broken arm, put cream and bandages on Rachael's burns, and did our best to cleanse and close up the hole in Heather's foot.

We thanked our neighbors many times over. From the way they talked and looked at us, it was clear that most of them still didn't like us very much, but at least they were willing to help. One of them even fixed the severed electrical line to our house, restoring our power.

As daylight crept upon us, Merlin came to our house and told me that Dr. Land wanted to speak with me in person.

Without waiting for Merlin to give me individual hiding protection, I sprinted down the sidewalk to Patrick's house and entered without knocking. The living room was empty, all the furniture already having been removed days prior.

"Adrian!" exclaimed Dr. Land, coming out of another room. "Thank you for coming. I'd ask you to sit, but as you can see—"

"How is she, Doctor?" I asked, dreading the answer. "Tell me she's alright."

"She's alive," Dr. Land replied quietly. "But I'm not yet sure for how long. Terry has taken a very strong telekinetic blast to her chest. Most of her ribs are shattered and the organs beneath them aren't much better. In addition, there's also the focused blast that put the hole in her abdomen. I've closed that up, and I've done everything else I can for now. I'm giving her a blood transfusion, but only time will tell. If she survives today and tonight, I'd say she might have a fighting chance."

"You called me here for a reason."

Dr. Land looked at me uncomfortably. "Terry's awake now. I told her to get some rest, but she refuses. I think she's afraid that she's going to die in her sleep, and under the circumstances, I'm hardly in a position to disagree. She wanted to talk to you, but I want you to keep it as short as possible. Terry really needs to rest now. Otherwise she'll die for certain."

I nodded, and Dr. Land quickly led me into his makeshift operating room at the back of his house.

Terry was lying on a hospital bed, a series of rubber tubes stuck into her. As I entered the room, she weakly turned her head toward me.

"I'm sorry," she breathed. "I'm sorry about Alia."

I shook my head as I stepped up to her bed. "No, Terry. That wasn't your fault. I should've been there."

"How many dead?"

Gazing down at Terry's pale face, I realized that Dr. Land was right:

Terry's life really might end today.

"They're okay," I said softly. "Everyone's alive."

"Liar." Terry grimaced in pain and closed her eyes as she whispered, "I'm so sorry, Adrian. For everything… It was just my damn pride again. I thought they'd be ready. I thought we could teach them."

I watched uncomfortably as a teardrop ran down Terry's cheek. I reached out and gently touched her right hand.

Terry opened her eyes and looked up at me again, saying slowly, "You were right. We should've been on that bus."

I shook my head and gave her hand a little squeeze. "No, Terry. We all do what we have to, remember? Rest now. Everything's going to be alright."

"But Alia—"

"You let me worry about Alia," I said firmly. "I'm going to get her back, she's going to heal you, and you're going to be okay. You've got to hang in there, Terry. You've got to live if we're going to take down Randal Divine together."

Closing her eyes again, Terry mumbled feebly, "Us and what army, right?"

"Terry…" I began, but realized I didn't know what I was going to say. What difference did it make what I said? Max and Felicity were dead. Alia was taken. And Terry… brave Terry who had never lost a fight in her life, had finally met her match. Outnumbered three to one, the Angels had destroyed us in our own house.

I felt Dr. Land touch my arm. "Enough, Adrian," he whispered. "She's asleep now."

Dr. Land escorted me back to his empty living room and asked, "How many others need medical attention?"

I gave him the details.

"I'd go to your house, but I want to keep an eye on Terry too," said Dr. Land. "Why don't you run back and get your wounded over here so I can take care of them."

"Call them on the phone please," I said as I opened the front door to leave. "I'm not going home yet."

Merlin was waiting for me on the porch.

"Is Harding home?" I asked, brushing away his attempt to give me hiding protection.

"I believe so," replied Merlin. "You want something from her?"

Without answering, I jogged over to Mrs. Harding's house, and Merlin followed.

The door was answered by Mrs. Harding herself, and it appeared that she was the only one home. Her three grandchildren were already at the mountain camp, and her daughter and son-in-law were out.

Ushering Merlin and me into her house, Mrs. Harding said to me sadly, "I just got off the phone with Dr. Land, Adrian. I hope Teresa survives. I do love that child dearly."

I decided to cut straight to the chase. "If they haven't left yet, Mrs. Harding, I would like to be on the team."

"Team?" Mrs. Harding asked in surprise. "Oh, you mean the team of Knights that are going to rescue little Alia."

I nodded. "Please, Mrs. Harding. I know I'm not really a Knight, but I want to go with them. When are we leaving?"

Silence. Mrs. Harding looked out the window.

"Mrs. Harding?" I asked uncertainly.

Turning to me again, Mrs. Harding gave me a sympathetic smile. "I'm very sorry, dear, but there is no team."

I was almost certain I had misheard her, but then she added, "We're not going to attack the Angel outpost, Adrian."

"What are you saying?" I asked in shock. "If we don't get Alia back soon, she's going to be converted and Terry is going to die!"

Mrs. Harding's tone remained quiet and miserable. "If it were entirely up to me, I would like to help you, but I can't order my Knights to fight for you when most of my people are still angry over Steven's betrayal."

I had always thought that the whole purpose of Knights was that they could be ordered to fight regardless of their personal issues, but apparently Mrs. Harding's style of leadership was a little different. Once again, I was reminded of the hard pragmatism I had so loathed in Mr. Baker. For all her grandmotherly appearance, Mrs. Harding was a stone-cold politician.

"Then at least tell me where the Angels are," I said. "I'm going with or without your help."

"You are so much like Teresa, my dear," said Mrs. Harding. "But I would never forgive myself if I led you to your death."

"Terry is dying!" I shouted furiously. "Tell me where they are!"

Mrs. Harding remained silent, but Merlin spoke. "I'll tell you, Adrian," he said quietly.

I turned to him, and he added, "I'll join you."

"Arthur—" began Mrs. Harding.

Merlin cut her off, saying, "If you can't order your Knights to fight, you certainly can't order them to stand down. I will help Adrian, and I think I may know one or two more who will join us."

"You're making a mistake," said Mrs. Harding, fixing Merlin with a disapproving look.

"It's my mistake to make," Merlin replied resolutely. "I've worked with Adrian's family now for months. They have trained long and hard so that someday they might be of use to our community. I will not watch Terry die, and I certainly won't suffer Alia being turned into an Angel."

Mrs. Harding nodded slowly, and then smiled. "As our location is no longer a secret, we have nothing to lose but lives, and those belong to the ones willing to risk them. You are welcome to do as you feel fit."

Then Mrs. Harding looked at me with pleading eyes and said, "Do be careful, young Knight."

Merlin and I left her house, and as we walked back to the sidewalk, I muttered savagely to myself, "I'm *always* careful, and despite that, for some damn reason, I'm still alive."

Having overheard me, Merlin laughed lightly. Then he said, "We're going to need more fighters than I can get on my end. I know how you feel about putting your trainees in danger, but—"

"I'll get over it," I promised, and we went our separate ways.

When I got home, James, having already discarded his icepack, was waiting for me in the dojo.

"How's Terry?" he asked anxiously.

"She's dying," I replied. "Gather everyone who isn't injured. Time to get into more trouble."

"Everyone is over at Dr. Land's house," said James.

"Call them back."

James got on the phone, and soon Scott, Daniel and Candace joined us in the dojo.

Scott asked me, "What's the word on the Knights? Has Mrs. Harding prepared a strike team?"

"You're looking at him," I replied grimly. "Harding refused to help."

I gave them a moment to let that sink in.

"She refused?" Candace asked incredulously.

I nodded. "Apparently we're not popular enough for Mrs. Harding to risk her Knights for us."

James let out a soft whistle.

"It's not over," I continued. "Merlin agreed to help us, and he said he might be able to get one or two more."

I stopped there, looking at the faces of the four standing before me. Scott and James were Terry's students. Candace and Daniel were mine. Suddenly I realized that saying what I had to say next would be even harder than I originally thought.

Scott saved me the trouble, looking me in the eyes and saying determinedly, "We're with you, Adrian."

The others nodded.

"I can't ask you to do this," I said, trying hard not to let my voice quaver.

"You don't have to," said Candace. "We're going to help whether you want it or not."

James and Daniel nodded.

"Thank you," I said weakly.

James grinned. "If Terry were here, she would have ordered us."

"She might have," I agreed, "but I won't. Two have already died today because we asked you to be heroes. I don't believe in heroes. I'm grateful for what you're offering, but I want you all to be realistic about this too. These guys are real Seraphim. And that telekinetic..."

I stopped and looked around at them. Terry understood that soldiers' morale sometimes depended upon their ignorance, but I couldn't let these kids risk their lives without knowing what they were up against.

I said to them gravely, "This destroyer is something special. His power is greater than mine, and he knows a lot more about how to use it. He killed Max, who was unarmed, and did more to Terry than anyone has ever managed. Terry might not have been at her best this morning, but I guarantee that this man is going to be very, very hard to kill. I don't know how we're going to do it."

I saw Daniel shuffling his feet uncomfortably. I looked down at the floor for a moment before continuing, "Don't get me wrong. I want every man willing. But if any of you are about to panic or accidentally shoot yourselves in the foot, I want you to be honest with yourself and back out now. No heroes please."

I didn't want to name Candace specifically, but this was aimed mostly at her. Candace had made the least progress among my CQC students, and her shooting wasn't at all reliable either.

I looked around at their faces again, carefully studying their expressions. Nobody spoke, and nobody looked away.

"Alright," I said. "We'll wait for Merlin."

As if perfectly timed, there was a knock on the door, and I telekinetically opened it to Merlin and two others who followed him in: one man, one woman, both in their mid-thirties or so.

"May I introduce Thomas Richardson and his wife, Sally," said Merlin. "They're not Knights, but both are sparks, and they've agreed to join us."

I recognized them both. They were the parents of one of Alia's kiddie-combat students. It was the worst irony possible, but apparently my reclusive sister was the only one who had made any real friends among the residents of Walnut Lane.

After formally introducing my group to the two sparks, I turned to our blocking instructor, saying, "Alright, Merlin, it's your show."

Merlin looked surprised. "Mine?"

"Well, sure," I replied matter-of-factly. "You're the senior Knight here. The *only* Knight, for that matter. You are going to lead us, right?"

"Well, it's your mission, Adrian," said Merlin, scratching his head. "I think it would only be right if you had operational command."

I wondered what insanity had come over him.

"Thanks," I said with a chuckle, "but I think our chances of survival might be greatly improved if we had a real Knight in charge."

After an awkward pause, Merlin said uncomfortably, "Um, might I have a word with you in private?"

"No," I said briskly. "I mean, if this is about our mission, I think everyone should hear it."

Another awkward pause.

Sally Richardson smiled at Merlin and said, "It's okay, Arthur. You can tell them."

"I'm sorry to disappoint you, Adrian," said Merlin, "but you are the only real Knight here, not me. It is true that I am a trained Guardian Knight, but it's also true that I have never been in a real combat situation. Mrs. Harding has done such an excellent job of keeping us hidden that our settlement has never once been attacked, and as you know by now, we don't go around looking for trouble."

I gaped at him.

This was even worse than when Terry had admitted that she didn't know how to land our stolen airplane. Of our entire team, I was the only one who had any experience taking down an enemy stronghold.

We might have stared at each other for a full minute before I finally gulped and said uneasily, "Alright. I'll lead."

I looked around at my team. "Is that okay?"

Everyone nodded or smiled to show that it was.

I took a deep breath and forced a grim smile. "We're going tonight."

It was still late morning. In order to keep this mission from being a complete suicide run, I had to master my desire to rush to Alia's rescue and instead form a passable plan of attack. My greatest fear was that for every hour we waited, my sister might be removed from the outpost or Terry might die of her wounds, but those were chances we would have to take if we were to have the cover of darkness.

Merlin was carrying a large brown envelope from which he pulled what little information the Walnut Guardians had on their Angel neighbors. We gathered in the dining room to look over the documents.

"This is the place," said Merlin, showing us a close-up photo of a square-ish two-story house. The photo looked like it was taken from a speeding car, and was slightly blurry. All of the windows had their curtains drawn, but fortunately the place had no fence around it.

"Here's another," said Merlin, "and this one is an aerial shot."

The second photo was even worse than the first, but the aerial shot confirmed that the outpost wasn't part of a block of houses. It stood alone a short distance from an asphalt road running through a grassy field.

"The next house is more than half a mile away," explained Merlin.

"Gunshots can be heard from farther than that in the open," I said, frowning.

Merlin shook his head. "I don't think we'll need to worry too much about the noise we make. Mrs. Harding pulled some strings this morning with the local police to keep them from coming here when our neighbors reported gunshots fired. I'm sure she'll help us tonight in the same way."

"That may be," said James, butting in from my side, "but even so, we could certainly use the element of surprise."

"That's why we're waiting for night," I reminded him.

"I know that," said James. "But we could do more. What if we all got silencers for our pistols?"

"Silencers?" I repeated. "For our pistols?"

"Yeah," James said enthusiastically. "Keep the guns quiet. That way, if we could somehow sneak into that house, we might even be able to get all the Angels before they wake up."

"You've been watching too many spy movies, James," I informed him.

A sound suppressor, more commonly known as a silencer, was a long cylindrical metal tube that attached to the barrel of a gun to reduce the noise of the rounds. But the important word here was "reduce," and unlike in the movies, real-life silencers didn't bring the noise of a pistol down to those silly little whispering put-put-puts that wouldn't wake a cat in a library. Even with silencers, guns were as loud as jackhammers. That was why the Angels had come at us with only crossbows, knives, tear gas and psionics. They didn't want to wake the neighbors.

James looked quite embarrassed as I explained this to him, but I suspected that most people who had never used sound suppressors before didn't know how ineffective they were. I hadn't known myself until Terry told me during my first year of combat training.

"Unfortunately, silencers are expensive and pretty much useless," I concluded, and then added, "Besides, we already have one silenced weapon."

"What weapon?" asked James.

I raised my right index finger in reply. While my telekinetic blasts did make little whooshing sounds, they were even quieter than the silenced pistols in movies.

"What we really need to get are some quiet radio transceivers," I said.

"I'll handle the shopping," volunteered Mr. Richardson. "How many do you need?"

I wasn't sure yet. "Four, just in case."

"No problem."

"What else you got, Merlin?" I asked, noticing that Merlin still had two papers.

"Map to the location," replied Merlin, "but I have that in my head. And this one here is purely hypothetical." He passed me a set of blueprints mapping out the first and second floors of the Angel outpost. "We've never actually been inside, but this is the design of another house with the exact same size and shape. If the Angels' house follows any logical architectural design, the inside should look something like that."

"This is good," I said, looking over the map. "They'll have made some modifications, though."

"No doubt," agreed Merlin. "Probably a pretty extensive basement, possibly multilevel to hold their captives."

"It's better that way," I said. "Alia will be locked out of the way when the shooting starts."

Looking at the blueprints again, I noticed a back door that led into the kitchen. "Is there a back door on the Angels' house too?"

"Yes," replied Merlin. "We don't have a photo, but our guy who took the aerial shot says there was a door right where it's shown on that paper."

"Two teams, then," I said. "We'll enter from both sides, and try not to shoot each other by accident."

Everyone laughed, but I hadn't meant that as a joke.

"Let me study this map for a while," I said. "In the meantime, you can all rest or go check up on the injured, and Mr. Richardson can go get us our radios."

My team complied without question, and I spent the next hour alone, lying on my bed thinking through various ways in which we might go about taking the Angels' house. I suspected that the Angels would also have a night watch or perhaps an electronic security alarm. Once we were discovered, speed would be everything. I needed to find a sequence of movement that would let us clear the house of threats before the Angels could react.

Staring at the floor plans, I pictured two small teams breaching simultaneously. Team One enters from the front door into the living room, clears the front half of the first floor, and then moves to the stairs leading up into the second floor. Meanwhile, Team Two enters from the rear door into the kitchen, taking the rest of the first floor before heading down into the basement. Team One could follow into the basement after clearing the second floor.

That would keep my teams from bumping into each other, but it was still too slow. The Angels sleeping upstairs could be wide awake before Team One got up to them.

How would Mr. Simms have done this?

When he planned the attack on the Holy Land, Mr. Simms made sure that the first target the Raven Knights hit was the barracks.

Take no prisoners. Kill them in their sleep.

I checked the photo of the front of the house again to confirm what I saw on the blueprints: a second-floor balcony with a glass door that opened into one of the bedrooms. I smiled. This was by far the path of least resistance.

Sally Richardson was putting the final touches on our lunch when I came into the kitchen.

"Chicken soup for the sick," she announced. "Or rather, the injured."

Mrs. Richardson explained to me that Rachael, Heather and Walter had returned from Dr. Land's house and were all resting upstairs in their rooms.

"I'm sorry I didn't help with lunch," I said. "The kitchen is usually my station in this house."

"It's no problem," said Mrs. Richardson. "You obviously have more important things to do today."

I remained silent, and Mrs. Richardson asked, "Are you alright, Adrian?"

"Yeah, I'm fine," I lied.

Mrs. Richardson gave me a sympathetic look. "It's not easy being the leader, is it?"

"How am I doing so far?"

"You look like a natural to me, but I guess you're not exactly feeling it inside."

Time to change the subject. "Can I ask you a personal question?"

"By all means," said Mrs. Richardson.

"Aren't you scared?" I asked. "I mean, you and your husband could both die tonight. Aren't you afraid that you'll never see your son again?"

Mrs. Richardson smiled. "The truth is, Tom and I are more afraid that our son won't see us in the way we want him to see us if we turned our backs now."

I nodded solemnly, but inside, I was sorely disappointed. I didn't appreciate this kind of heroism in the least. People should fight for people, not perception. Still, I wasn't about to tell her that she couldn't come. We didn't have the luxury of being choosy.

I helped Mrs. Richardson deliver her chicken soup to our three injured comrades, and then we set the dining table together. Mr. Richardson had already returned with our radio transceivers, so after a hasty lunch, I announced my revised battle plan.

"Once we're on target, we'll divide into three teams," I began as we sat in a circle around the supposed floor plan of the Angels' house. "We're taking no prisoners, so we're not going to bother with call signs for anyone except Merlin here who we already know as Merlin. Our teams will simply be called Rabbit One, Two and Three."

"Why rabbits?" asked Mrs. Richardson.

I explained to the Richardsons that Rabbit was Terry's Guardian call sign, and then continued, "Each team leader will have one radio. We'll practice using them later. Rabbit One is Merlin and me. We'll levitate onto the second-floor balcony and enter from there. James will lead Rabbit Two, with the Richardsons, and enter from the front. The front door will be locked, but they'll breach from the window to the left of the porch. We don't know what's behind those curtains, so be careful."

I stopped to make sure that James was okay with being a team leader. I had originally considered putting the adults in charge of Rabbit Two, but after what Mrs. Richardson had told me, I decided that James was probably more reliable. He was one of Terry's students, and he knew his CQC stuff as well as could be expected considering the limited time he had spent with us. Besides, I felt a little bad about having publicly humiliated him over the silencer issue earlier.

I continued, "Rabbit Three enters from behind the house. Scott will lead, with Daniel and Candace. There's a back door that opens into the kitchen, but that will be locked too. The door opens inwards, and isn't as heavy-duty as the front, so you'll break it down."

"Kick it?" asked Scott.

"No." I gestured toward two heavy red objects that I had placed by the wall, saying, "Those there are multi-purpose breaching tools."

"They look like fire extinguishers to me," said Daniel.

"And they are," I said, smiling. "Rabbit Two and Three will carry one each. Scott can use his as a battering ram to break down the back door. Once inside, pull the pin, tape down the lever and let it create cover and chaos for you. We don't have gas or smoke bombs, but these will work almost as well. James can turn his on before throwing it through the front window. The smoke will hide you as you enter, but be careful not to breathe in too much of the gas. It's supposed to put out fires, so there isn't much oxygen in it."

"Terry hadn't taught us this one yet," said Scott.

I didn't mention that Terry never expected our students to have fire extinguishers on the Historian's mountain.

I ran my finger along the floor plans as I said, "Once inside, Rabbit One, that's Merlin and me, will start clearing the second floor, where I'm hoping we'll catch most of the Angels in their sleep if we're fast enough. Meanwhile, Rabbit Two clears the living room and adjacent dining room, as well as this room next to it which I don't know what's inside, and then proceeds up the stairs to join us. So far okay?"

James and the Richardsons nodded.

"Rabbit Three clears the kitchen and what I think is some kind of storage room here, and this little hall, and then down to the basement. The basement entrance is here, next to the kitchen." I looked warningly at Scott, adding, "We don't know what's down there. It could be trapped, so take it slow."

I couldn't tell them what kind of traps might be set anywhere in the house. Back when the Guardians had raided the God-slayer house where I had been held captive, one of the Knights had been badly burned by acid.

I said seriously, "Remember that you're looking for my sister and possibly other captives down there, so check your targets carefully."

"We will," said Scott, and Daniel and Candace nodded.

I had some misgivings about putting Daniel and Candace on the basement crew, not only because of the possibility of traps, but because they might accidentally shoot a captive, namely Alia. But as my weakest links, I didn't want them upstairs where I suspected most of the Angels would be. I was counting on Scott to keep his team from causing any real damage.

"Now, most likely there won't be more than four or five Angels," I said in a hopeful tone. "If we're lucky, that'll be one night guard on the first floor and the others asleep on the second, but don't count on it. I suspect that their only combat psionics are the pyroid and the telekinetic that attacked us this morning. If they had a berserker or something, he would have come too. The other Angels would include at least one hider, but the rest might be non-psionic. They'll all be well-trained Seraphim, though, so stay sharp."

"What if we bump into Steven?" asked Scott.

"Use your best judgment," I suggested. "Do what you have to, but stay alive."

"And the monster telekinetic?" Daniel asked worriedly.

"I'm hoping to find him on the second floor," I replied. "But if you do see the telekinetic, stay clear of him if at all possible. Report where he is, and Merlin and I will deal with him."

"What if we get a shot?" asked James.

"You won't," I promised. "If he sees you point a gun at him, he'll take it out of your hands and shoot you with it. At least, that's what I would do."

"Just out of curiosity," said Scott, "what does this man look like?"

"Oh..." I said, suddenly feeling stupid. "Um... Candace? You saw him, right?"

"Actually, I think he was a she," said Candace, "but I can't be sure."

"What do you mean?"

"She didn't look human," Candace replied uncomfortably. "She was really thin and bony, and she looked more like... like a scarecrow, or a witch."

"You mean like someone with bad power balance?" I asked.

"Really bad balance," agreed Candace. "Her hair was all white, and she really looked like a scarecrow."

I had once seen a man at the end stage of bad psionic balance. He had been one of the Angel Seraphim who abducted Cindy from our penthouse two years ago. Despite his formidable telekinetic power, he had been all skin and bones, his physical body entirely reliant on his psionic power for survival. I had only seen him for an instant, but I would never forget his sunken eyes and shriveled, skeletal hands. It was a fate that I myself had narrowly avoided thanks to Terry forcing me to learn power balance.

"A scarecrow," I repeated quietly. "That shouldn't be too hard to find. Again, if at all possible, stay clear and let Merlin and me take care of her."

Merlin said hesitantly, "Adrian, I'm guessing that you want me to take control of the telekinetic's body, but if this Seraph is such a powerful woman, chances are she'll have excellent mental defenses."

"I guessed as much too," I said. "Can you at least buy me a little time?"

"If I can catch her off guard, I might be able to keep her still for three seconds or so, but I can't promise much more."

"That's plenty, Merlin," I said reassuringly.

Merlin stared at me disbelievingly. "Three seconds, Adrian. I mean it."

I grinned. "A lot can happen in three seconds."

Of course, Merlin had promised his three seconds only if he could catch the telekinetic off guard, but I wasn't going to be picky about that. Combat tested or not, Merlin was my only hope in this matter.

I looked around again. "Everyone okay so far?"

Candace asked, "What if they attack us before we even get to the side of the house?"

I shrugged. "Then the plan goes to hell and we storm the place anyway, but nobody shoots till I give the word. Understood?"

Had Mr. Simms been running this show, he would have explained what to do in the event of an abort and retreat. I hadn't forgotten. I had deliberately ignored it. There would be no abort, no retreat.

Once I was convinced that everyone was still with me, I said, "Okay, so once we're in position, I will call the breach. If by some miracle the balcony door is unlocked, Merlin and I will enter silently first. I'll use my telekinetic blasts to quietly clear the second floor and have you all go noisy only after we're discovered. But more likely, you'll hear us breaking the glass door and that will be your signal." I paused, took a deep breath, and finished quietly, "Alright, that's it."

"Sounds like a good enough plan to me," said Merlin.

I stood up. "We're going to practice."

For the rest of the day, we went through every detail over and over.

How to quickly prepare the fire-extinguisher grenades. We decided to keep some tape already on the levers so all James and Scott had to do was pull the pin, press down on the lever and pull the tape around it to keep it in place. That still took nearly five seconds, and I wasn't happy about that in the least.

How to enter through a broken window with drawn curtains. Rabbit Two spent an hour practicing this at the window I had blasted out earlier that morning. To avoid being cut by glass left on the windowsill, Mr. Richardson agreed to carry a thick woolen blanket which he would drape over the bottom of the window frame as soon as James heaved the fire extinguisher through.

How to break open a door with a battering ram. Scott busted the latch on every door in our house with his fire extinguisher, and got better at it each time. Rachael, whose burns were causing her severe discomfort, probably didn't appreciate the noise, but she didn't complain.

How to use the radio transceivers. I knew the protocols, of course, but James and Scott had to use them too. Fortunately, equipped with head-mounted microphones and earpieces, our radios were nearly silent and could be used hands-free.

How to clear a room as quickly as possible without getting killed. Clearing a room wasn't nearly as easy as movie heroes made it look. You couldn't just jump out, pistol drawn, into the middle of an open doorway. Doors were the most obvious of targets, and stepping through one, you could never tell who was hiding behind the wall just inside, ready to empty a scattergun into you. But nor would we have the time to use mirrors to peer into each room before entering. I wanted us to go from breach to clear in thirty seconds or less, which was impossible but nevertheless a nice target to strive for.

We ate another hasty dinner of takeout pizza, and then went back to practicing.

"Everyone study the map carefully," I had said to them over dinner. "Burn it into your minds. Close your eyes and imagine yourself in the house. What is to your left? What is to your right? Where are the doors? Which door do you go to first?"

Though no one complained, I could tell that they were beginning to tire, and I didn't want to burn them out before they got the chance to fight.

"Enough," I said at around 8pm. "Get some rest. Sleep if you can. I'm going to go check on Terry."

I doubted anyone would be able to sleep, but I knew that my team would want to spend some time with their injured friends before we left—especially Scott, who had bravely put his worries about Rachael aside during our hours of practicing.

Heading out to Dr. Land's house alone, I hesitated for a second before knocking on the door. What if Terry was already dead?

The door was opened by Dr. Land, who ushered me in, saying, "I saw you coming from the window."

"How is she?" I asked anxiously.

Dr. Land shook his head. "She hasn't woken. She's been pretty stable, but I'm afraid she might still have some internal bleeding. There's little more I can do in my home office, and considering who she is, I can't take her to the hospital."

"We're ready to go tonight," I informed him. "We'll get Alia."

The doctor remained silent. I wondered if he thought I was crazy, risking my entire team for one life. Maybe I was, but it wasn't just Terry's life that I wanted to save.

I asked, "May I go and sit with Terry for a while?"

Dr. Land smiled. "Certainly. I'll be in my study. Call me if you need anything."

I entered the operating room and, sitting quietly on a chair by the bed, I listened for a while to Terry's shallow breathing. Terry's face was deathly pale, and her every breath sounded like it might be her last.

Was I right in waiting for the night? Would Terry really last another few hours? Would Alia even be there?

Back when I was going over the mission with my inexperienced team, I often wondered where we would all be now had I let Alia and Max accompany James and me downstairs this morning. But I didn't regret what I had done. It had been the right thing to do under the circumstances, just like Terry had done right for me at the Holy Land. Besides, regret wouldn't bring Max back from the dead, keep Alia from being converted, or save Terry's life.

But of what I was planning to do tonight, I had nothing but doubts and fears. Against a team of trained Seraphim, I was going in with only one trained Guardian Knight, two untrained adults and four non-psionic CQC students, and not one of them had ever killed. When Alia had been kidnapped by Dr. Denman at the Psionic Research Center, I had gone after her alone. I knew that I would die, and I had been okay with that. When things got bad, I was usually okay with the possibility of my own death.

But this time, others might die.

Gazing at Terry's almost peaceful expression, I whispered softly, "I've never needed you as badly as I need you now, Terry."

I thought I saw Terry's right hand twitch slightly, but it might have just been a trick of the light. Or maybe I just saw what I wanted to.

Why had I bothered to come here? Terry couldn't even hear me, let alone help me.

I suddenly found my eyes wet with tears. I had promised myself that I wouldn't cry. If I was going to pull this mission off, I would have to be stone hard. But I was never very good at keeping promises, and who would see me here, anyway? I buried my face in my hands to keep myself from crying out loud.

A soft voice called from the doorway, "Adrian?"

I looked up, hastily wiping my eyes and saying weakly, "Hey, Candace."

Candace didn't ask me if I was alright. She just came up to me and gently grasped my hands.

"It's going to be okay," she whispered.

I couldn't let Candace see me break down completely. She had already seen too much. I begged my eyes to dry up, but they gave me only limited control over my tear ducts.

"Everything is going to be okay," Candace said again, crouching down in front of me. "You and Terry are the bravest Guardian Knights I know."

I shook my head and said in a quavering voice, "If I had my own way, I wouldn't even be a Guardian, let alone a Knight." More damn tears! When would they stop?!

Candace nodded sympathetically. "Then you're just as scared as any of us."

"More," I sobbed. "I'm no leader, Candace."

Candace smiled softly. "You had us fooled."

"Mrs. Richardson said the same thing. But I'm just repeating things I heard. And Terry didn't even teach me that fire-extinguisher trick. I just made it up, and I don't know if it's going to work the way I think it will."

"It opened the doors," said Candace. "Just think of Alia. Think of how scared she must be."

I looked up at the ceiling, blinking furiously. "Alia's tough. I'm not worried about her."

"I know she's tough, but she's still just a little girl. And you don't have to be brave all by yourself, you know. We're all in this together."

I stopped fighting. As Candace put her arms around my neck, I let my tears fall freely, soaking Candace's shirt. And with those tears, I slowly felt cleansed inside. The tension I had been feeling all day wasn't lessened, but somehow just a little more bearable.

"Thanks," I mumbled, wiping my eyes.

I felt thoroughly embarrassed by what I had just done, and terrified that no one would follow a coward like me into battle. "Candace, please don't tell the others..."

Candace smiled and gave me a peck on the cheek. "It's okay, Adrian. Your secret's safe with me."

"We should be getting back," I said, hoping I sounded more businesslike and in control. "But give me a moment." I didn't want to return to our house with reddened eyes.

We sat silently together, and I listened again to Terry's shallow breathing, but something was different from a moment ago. I couldn't quite put my finger on what made me so sure, but Dr. Land was either dead wrong or flat-out lying. Terry wasn't stable at all. She was slipping away, and fast.

I stood. "Candace, I think we're going early."

Candace followed me out of the operating room, and I quickly called Dr. Land out from his study.

"Have Terry loaded onto Merlin's van as soon as you can," I said to him crisply. "We're taking her with us."

"That is impossible," said Dr. Land.

I turned my tone to ice. "Kindly do not use the word 'impossible' around me tonight, Doctor."

"If we move her, she could die."

"If we leave her, she'll die anyway. I want her at the target so Alia can get right to her once we're done. You don't have to come with us, but we're taking Terry."

Dr. Land looked like he was about to protest more, so I sternly added, "I don't have time to argue, Doctor. Don't make me force you."

"Alright," he said resignedly. "But don't say I didn't warn you."

As Candace and I hurried back toward our house, Candace said, "Are you sure about this, Adrian? Dr. Land could be right."

"He could, but this is my call," I said firmly. "I'm sorry I lost it back there, Candace. But I'm still the leader of this damn suicide squad, and you're just going to have to trust my judgment."

"Wow," said Candace, looking at me in wonder. "You really change fast."

I was a bit surprised myself, but I shrugged.

We all do what we have to.

10. COUNTERSTRIKE

Things moved quickly once Candace and I returned to the house.

I was elated to discover that two more Walnut Guardians had showed up at the last minute to assist us. Both were fathers of Alia's students and the Richardsons had shamed them into joining us. Neither would actually fight, but one was a peacemaker and the other a mind-writer, and I knew that both would come in handy.

After quickly rechecking our gear, we filed into two vehicles: Merlin's van and the Richardsons' SUV. Placed on a stretcher, Terry was loaded into Merlin's van per my request. Dr. Land insisted on accompanying Terry, for which I was grateful, and he sat in the back of the van with Candace and James while I sat up front next to Merlin. Merlin knew the way to the Angel outpost, and Mr. Richardson followed us in his SUV with his wife and the rest of my team on board.

After an hour's drive, we arrived at the house nearest the Angel outpost, and we quickly subdued the elderly couple living there. Thanks to our last-minute additions, we wouldn't have to leave our vehicles on the side of the road, but could instead use this countryside house as our staging point. It also solved our noise problem, since this was the only house close enough for gunshots to be heard from.

"I'm very sorry for our intrusion," I said to the elderly couple as our peacemaker tied their hands behind their backs with rope. "I promise that you won't be hurt, and you won't remember any of this in the morning."

I knew that altering memory, like other forms of psionic mind control, was as dangerous to the elderly as it was to children, and I had been hoping that the residents would be a bit younger, but it was too late now. Hopefully, our mind-writer wouldn't damage their minds when he erased their memories later.

We wheeled Terry's stretcher into the house, but Dr. Land decided not to try moving Terry to a bed. Terry's breathing was so shallow now that I seriously feared she wouldn't be alive when we returned with Alia.

Looking down the long, straight country road, I could just make out our target house in the distance. Whoever had taken the photos from the passing car had used a telephoto lens, and the aerial shot hadn't shown it either, but the house was on a little rise, almost a hill, about a hundred yards off the edge of the road. There were a few trees here and there, but no real cover to hide our approach. If the Seraphim were looking out through their windows, they would easily spot us in any direction.

"That's not a good thing, is it?" said Scott, standing next to me as I sighed at the distant speck of a house.

"No, it's not," I agreed quietly. "But at least it's dark. That's a good thing."

I wasn't referring to the Angels' house, which fortunately didn't have any light coming from its windows, but rather to the overcast sky. No stars, no moon, and no city lights nearby. As long as we were careful not to trip in the darkness, and if the house wasn't equipped with motion-activated lights or something, we still might get up to it undetected.

"We walk from here," I said, turning to the crowd that had gathered behind me. "Team leaders, get your radios on."

My radio's single earpiece was designed to be clipped onto a right ear, but obviously I couldn't keep it on mine because I didn't have much of a right ear to attach it to. I instead forced it awkwardly onto my left and hoped it wouldn't come off during the raid.

"Radio check," I said into the microphone extending from the earpiece. "Rabbit Two? Three?"

James and Scott nodded.

As we tested our radios, the rest of the team checked their weapons one last time.

The Richardsons weren't carrying guns, preferring to rely on their psionic powers as sparks, which I had discovered earlier that day as being quite impressive. Both could throw little lightning bolts that blackened the paper targets in our basement shooting range. Their electric discharges were by no means exceptionally accurate, but would be plenty effective in close quarters. I was curious whether they ever had a fight between them, but I was too polite to ask.

Everyone else, including Merlin and me, had pistols and spare clips. I preferred my telekinetic blasts to guns, since blasts were always perfectly accurate, but I needed to be able to fire rapidly, and focused telekinetic shots took too long to prepare.

I wore a thin pair of cashmere gloves that not only kept me from being drained by my gun, but gave me a little extra protection from the night chill. I had forbidden my team from wearing heavy jackets that could hamper movement, and I found that I wasn't the only one shivering.

It was now 11:30pm. I had originally planned to get here well past midnight and breach at around 2am, but I wasn't going to wait any longer.

"Last chance to go home," I said quietly, looking around at the grim faces staring back at me.

"Let's do this," said Scott.

Scott and James picked up their fire extinguishers, and Mr. Richardson hoisted his rolled-up blanket onto his shoulder.

We started walking quietly along the side of the road. A minute later, a truck passed us from behind, but didn't slow down. We must have looked pretty weird: eight people on foot on a country road at this time of night. But I doubted anyone would call the cops on us. And if they did, Mrs. Harding had already agreed to keep things under control.

As I led my team through the dark and chilly silence, my mind briefly wandered back to a time when I was younger and naive enough to question the justice of what we were doing.

The people sleeping in that house were responsible for the deaths of two of our children, true enough. But it was equally true that if they were converted Angels, then they had been acting under the influence of psionic control. I knew, of course, that not all Angels were converted, but there was no way to know for certain about the people we were about to attack. If they had been brainwashed by their master to hate us, then that would make them victims of the Angel cause, not much different from ourselves. In the past, that would have bothered me a lot.

But killing Mr. Simms—twice—had taught me what I was capable of. Perhaps the Angels sleeping in that house did deserve our pity, even our mercy. But they wouldn't get it from me. It no longer mattered to me in the least whether our targets were Angels by choice or not. For Terry and for Alia, this had to be done, and so I would do it. It was really that simple.

I couldn't be as certain about the resolve of my teammates, however. No one had spoken openly of it to me, but I suspected that they all felt some hesitation about what we were about to do. They would be less than human not to. As I listened to their soft footsteps following me toward the Angels' house, I sincerely hoped that they were ready to do what was necessary. I hoped that they were ready to kill.

Once we were about halfway to the house, I gestured to Scott, and he led Daniel and Candace off the road and into the grassy field. They were going to walk in a wide arc and approach the house from behind.

A few minutes later, I heard Scott's voice in my earpiece say, "Rabbit Three to Rabbit One, we're at the base of the hill."

"Roger, Three, I hear you loud and clear," I whispered back. "Too loud, actually. Keep your voice down. Start climbing and report when you're in position."

"Roger that, Rabbit One."

Rabbits One and Two were already at the foot of the little hill too. I gestured to start climbing. So far, everything was perfectly quiet except for my thumping heart. I realized that I was no longer feeling at all cold. My adrenaline was kicking in, and I had to wipe the sweat from my brow.

Crouching low, we silently made our way up toward the front of the house. Instead of walking on the asphalt driveway, I kept everyone on the soft ground to reduce the sound of our footsteps, but I felt my whole body hiccup every time someone stepped on a dry twig.

One excruciatingly slow step at a time, we finally made it to the front porch. To the left was the wide rectangular window that James's team would enter from. The curtains were drawn behind the window, and the five of us crept up to it. Right above was the second-floor balcony. The house was completely quiet. Not a single sound or light anywhere.

"This is Rabbit Three," said Scott on the radio. "We're at the rear door."

James replied for me, "Roger that, Rabbit Three. Two is in position. Stand by for One."

I levitated Merlin up onto the balcony, setting him down as gently as I could so as not to make any noise. Then I followed him up.

I whispered into my radio, "This is Rabbit One. We're on the balcony. Stand by for breach."

The curtains were drawn behind the balcony's glass door as well, so I couldn't see inside, but according to the floor plan, this was the master bedroom.

This house obviously had its own hiding bubble, but now that I was standing on the balcony, I could tell that there was a psionic presence close by. It was the pyroid who had burned Rachael, and I was certain that he was just behind the curtain. It occurred to me that I was about to rob Scott of his revenge, but so what? Rachael would be happier if Scott returned alive.

I was about to reach for the glass door to check if it was locked when I heard Scott's voice again. "Rabbit One!" he whispered in a panicked tone. "The kitchen light just came on!"

"Stay calm and silent, Three," I whispered back.

Someone was awake downstairs. Maybe the night watch, or someone grabbing a midnight snack.

I put my hand on the doorknob and slowly tried turning it.

It was unlocked!

I looked at Merlin, who just shrugged.

I steadied my breathing. The cold night air would wake the pyroid sleeping inside the moment I opened the door. This would have to be done in one fluid move. Open the door, step through the curtain, and put a focused blast between the eyes of the pyroid before he could scream or burn me.

I said into my radio, "Rabbit One to Rabbit Two and Three, stand by. Rabbit One is going in quiet. Take your guns off safety, hold position and be prepared to breach on my command."

James's voice answered, "Rabbit Two, roger that. We're ready." He was speaking so quietly that I couldn't hear him except on the radio even though we weren't more than five yards apart.

"The light's still on," Scott whispered frantically. "Rabbit One, the kitchen is still on!"

"Roger that, Rabbit Three," I replied. "I hear you. The kitchen light is on. Stand by."

It didn't matter. If the guy in the kitchen was on night duty, he wasn't going to go to bed anytime soon, and even if he was just getting a midnight snack, I wasn't going to wait for him to fall asleep. Terry was dying. Besides, since I could sense the pyroid, no doubt he could sense me too, even in his sleep, which might wake him at any moment.

I felt my pistol's safety to make sure that it was still on, and then tucked the pistol under my belt. After wiping the sweat from my face again, I gave my pendant a quick tap and then carefully focused a powerful telekinetic blast in my right index finger.

Once my blast was ready, I reached for the doorknob with my left hand, my right hand pointed like a pretend gun in front of me. I looked at Merlin, who had his pistol drawn, ready to back me up if things turned noisy. I had only one silent shot, but I was fairly confident that I could pull this off without waking up the house.

"On three," I mouthed to Merlin. "One..."

Bang! The sudden gunshot made me jump in surprise, and I instantly lost my psionic focus, causing me to release my blast into the air. Where had the sound come from?! Who had fired?!

Drawing my pistol and flipping off the safety, I yanked open the balcony door as I shouted into my microphone, "Damn it! Breach! Breach! Go! Go! Go!"

Sighting down the barrel of my pistol as I pushed through the curtain, I was only dimly aware of Merlin following me in. My attention was fixed on the lone figure that had sprung up into a sitting position on his bed.

"Jesus! No! Please!" shouted the pyroid, and I quickly ended his life with three rounds to his chest.

My peripheral vision caught movement to my right. There was someone else in the room. I spun around on my heel, my pistol held in both hands in front of me so that the moment I faced my target, all I'd have to do was pull the trigger.

I heard a high-pitched squeal. *"Addy, no!"*

I stopped my trigger finger mid-squeeze. Alia was staring down my pistol barrel with wide, frantic eyes.

There was no time to ask her what she was doing in this room.

"How many?!" I shouted.

"Five."

"Stay!" I commanded, shoving her aside and moving toward the door to the hallway.

"Addy, please don't kill them!"

I ignored her. I had heard the sound of breaking glass and now another gunshot from downstairs. Rabbit Two and Three were in the house. Alia was already safe, but I hadn't planned on a retreat, so we were committed to clearing out the house. If we ran now, the Seraphim would hunt us down before we got back to Dr. Land. It would be safer to stick with the plan and shoot everyone. All that mattered now was speed.

"Five in the house! Go! Go!" I shouted.

Pumped on adrenaline, I pulled open the door and, not even bothering to look, jumped into the nearly pitch-black hallway. It was an exceptionally foolish gamble, but it paid off. I was the first one in the hall, followed one step behind by Merlin. A heartbeat later, a dark, shadowy figure appeared from another doorway a little farther down, and Merlin and I rapidly emptied our pistols into it. The man collapsed back into his room, his feet sticking out into the hallway, unmoving.

More gunshots from downstairs.

Letting my empty clip fall to the floor, I telekinetically yanked my spare from my belt and slapped it in as we rushed forward toward the last door at the end of the hall.

Before we reached it, however, the door exploded outwards, the wood splintering into a thousand pieces as if it had been hit from the other side by several shotguns at once.

I felt the telekinetic's full power now, and Merlin didn't need telling.

Skidding to a stop before running into the telekinetic's line of fire, we pressed our backs against the wall next to the doorframe.

Quickly checking my pistol, I was about to peer into the doorframe when suddenly all the sharp little pieces of wood on the floor jumped to life. The telekinetic couldn't see us, but she knew about where we were, and I guessed that Merlin and I had but a moment before we were turned into human pincushions.

"Run!" I shouted, and we scampered back down the hall, stumbling over the corpse as we escaped into his bedroom.

The man's body lying in the doorframe prevented us from closing the door, so Merlin and I both kept our pistols aimed at the hallway as we slowly stepped backwards to the far end of the room.

"You're mine now!" said a harsh female voice in my head.

Hearing the curtain behind me snap open, I spun around, but it was too late.

Through the glass I saw her: a tall, skeletal woman with long white hair whipping about her bony face. Candace was right: It wasn't a person. It was a scarecrow. The poorly balanced telekinetic was only four feet away, levitating just outside the window and pointing her right index finger at the center of my forehead.

I was about to die.

I involuntarily shut my eyes tightly.

"Damn it, Adrian!" shouted Merlin. "Shoot her!"

I fell onto my knees just as the telekinetic's focused blast, which had been temporarily stopped by Merlin, shattered the window and whizzed through my hair. Opening my eyes, I didn't bother aiming as I thrust my pistol upwards and fired rapidly through the broken window. The first two rounds missed, but the third caught the woman's left arm. The impact spun her around, and drained by her own blood, she fell out of sight. There was a soft thud as the woman hit the ground outside.

Getting to my feet, I leaned out of the broken window. The telekinetic was lying facedown on the grass, alive but unable to move. My bullet had only nicked her arm, so if it weren't for her body's total reliance on her psionic power, she might still have been able to escape. Tough luck for her. Taking careful aim, I put a pair of bullets into the back of her head.

Pulling my head back through the window, I saw Merlin on all fours, panting heavily from overexertion.

"Stay here," I said to him, cautiously returning to the open door, my pistol gripped tightly in both hands.

The telekinetic made three. Were the other two downstairs? Had the other Rabbit teams already finished? Rabbit Two was supposed to come up. Where the hell were they?!

Carefully stepping over the dead man's chest, I was about to peek my head through the doorframe when the hallway lights suddenly came on. Squinting, I involuntarily took a step back, almost tripping over the corpse. I held my breath as I heard soft footsteps in the hall. I kept my pistol pointed at the doorway.

Then I heard James say on the radio, "This is Rabbit Two, the first floor is clear. We're upstairs now. We've located Alia. She's alive. Repeat, we've located Alia."

I lowered my pistol as I realized that the footsteps had belonged to Rabbit Two. Properly trained Seraphim wouldn't have turned on the hallway lights.

"Rabbit One, Rabbit One, are you there?" James said again. "We're on the second floor. We've located Alia."

"Rabbit Two, this is One," I said into my microphone. "We're in the room next door. Be advised, there may be more Angels up here."

I quickly returned to the bedroom where we had entered from. James and the Richardsons were there with Alia, who was sitting on a cot that the Angels had prepared for her. Everyone appeared uninjured.

"You okay, Alia?" I asked, clicking my pistol's safety on.

As soon as my sister saw that I wasn't pointing a gun at her face, she pounced on me, wrapping her arms tightly around my waist. This wasn't the time for a teary-eyed reunion, though. The house wasn't officially cleared of threats yet.

Roughly disentangling myself from Alia, I asked James, "How many did your team kill?"

"One downstairs," he replied. "We didn't see the telekinetic, but I think Scott's team got one too."

"That makes five," I said, breathing slightly easier. "We'll need to double-check, though."

"Where's Merlin?" asked James.

"Catching his breath," I said, grinning. "We got the scarecrow."

Then I turned to my sister and said, "Go with James, Alia. He'll take you to Terry."

"Terry's alive?" Alia asked in a surprised telepathic voice. She was still too distressed to speak aloud.

"Not for long if you don't help her. Go now."

"But Addy, there're people downstairs. Under the house. Lazlo showed me. He said he'd put me down there with them if I was noisy. Addy, they're really hurt, and one of them—"

I assumed that Lazlo was the outpost leader currently lying dead on the bed, but I didn't bother asking. Nor was I worried about the other captives in the basement. None of them could be in as dire need of Alia's healing as Terry right now.

"Alia! Listen to me!" I said, crouching down and grabbing her shoulders. "Terry is in a house nearby. She's dying. Go to her now. I'll take care of the people in the basement."

"But Addy, one of the men—"

"Go! James, take her now!"

James grabbed Alia's hand, and Alia didn't struggle too much as she was pulled out of the room. Watching them go, I hoped my Rabbits had done a thorough job of clearing the first floor. I suddenly realized that Scott hadn't called in yet.

"Rabbit One to Rabbit Three, report," I said into my microphone.

There was no immediate reply, and I repeated anxiously, "Rabbit Three, report! Where are you, Rabbit Three?!"

"Rabbit Three here," Scott finally answered. "We're all okay. We've finished checking the basement but we couldn't find Alia."

Apparently Scott hadn't been listening to our radio communications.

"We have Alia," I said. "She's fine. She's heading out to Terry now."

"That's good news, Adrian," said Scott. "We also ran into Steven down here."

"And?"

"He's dead. He tried to burn us, but Candace shot him."

"Roger that," I replied, smiling a bit. "Hold your position. We'll be down after one last check on the second floor."

Merlin joined us in the hall. He, the Richardsons and I went back through each room to make sure no one else was hiding.

It was good that we did, too. We found one more Angel cowering in a closet. (Apparently Alia hadn't included Steven in her count.) This Angel wasn't a member of the Seraphim, but a psionic hider who had been drafted into concealing the outpost, or so he claimed. My first thought was to execute him on the spot, but seeing him looking up at us with terrified eyes, I couldn't bring myself to pull the trigger. My adrenaline had ebbed away, and I remembered my sister's desperate plea not to kill anyone. Alia still believed in sparing our enemies. Though I no longer agreed, I nevertheless found some comfort in letting this man live, especially after killing three people in one night. I didn't want to end up like Mr. Simms.

Leaving the adults to make sure that the Angel was properly tied up, I went downstairs to find Rabbit Three.

Scott was the only one in the living room, and I asked him what had happened on the first floor.

"Rabbit Two killed the sentry," said Scott, nodding toward the charred body of a man lying on the carpet.

The window next to the front door was smashed and Mr. Richardson had used the blanket just like we planned, but I noticed that the fire extinguisher lying on the carpet still had its pin. With the sudden breach, James had probably panicked, but fortunately, so had the sentry. It looked as if James had shot the Seraph at the same time as his two spark teammates released a barrage of lightning. The blackened body was barely recognizable.

Scott continued, "It was Steven in the kitchen. He tried to burn us the moment we made entry. I was still holding my fire extinguisher, and Daniel was a bit panicked, but Candace saved us."

"Where is she?" I asked. "And where is Daniel?"

"Daniel is outside, behind the house. He'll be alright. Candace is with Steven, I think."

In the kitchen, I found Candace staring blankly down at the motionless form of Steven, who was lying in a pool of his own blood on the kitchen floor.

As I stood next to her, Candace whispered dazedly, "I can't believe I killed someone."

"Better him than you," I said, putting a hand on her shoulder.

I looked down at Scott's fire extinguisher lying on the kitchen floor and noticed that it still had its pin inside too. So much for the smoke-screen idea.

Scott had followed me into the kitchen. "I think we were really lucky,

Adrian," he said. "There's some kind of alarm control box on the dining-room wall that looks like it connects to a series of motion sensors around the house. But for some reason, the thing was turned off. I guess the Angels forgot to activate it. I would have thought that after what they did to us this morning, they would've been more careful tonight."

I shrugged. I was still too spent from the battle to find Scott's information particularly interesting, and I didn't share his curiosity about Angel psychology.

Outside, Daniel had been busy donating the contents of his stomach to Mother Nature. Upon returning to the kitchen, he rushed up to me and said frantically, "Adrian, I'm sorry! I'm really, really, *really* sorry!"

"For what?" I asked. Daniel's breath reeked of vomit, but I doubted he was apologizing for that.

It turned out that Daniel was the one responsible for our botched entry. His nervous hands had pulled the trigger that released the gunshot that woke the house.

"It's alright," I said, calming him down. "You didn't shoot yourself or anyone else. We're all still here."

As I said that, it finally hit me that we had pulled off a near-perfect mission.

We hadn't known how many Angels were in the house until after we breached, and though I had deliberately put Merlin and myself at the vanguard of the assault to keep our casualties to a minimum, I had spent much of the day wondering how many of my team would end up dying for Terry and Alia.

Perhaps luck did play a major role, but that didn't change the fact that for a completely inexperienced team, we had done unbelievably well. True, I had almost put a bullet in Alia's head, and the telekinetic had been a microsecond away from blasting a hole through mine, but not only had we avoided losing any of our members, not one of them had even received a scratch. Wait till Terry heard about this!

I wanted to go see how Alia was doing with Terry, but there was other work to be done here. I had promised my sister that I would see to the other captives.

I turned to Scott and said, "Alia said there were injured people in the basement."

"Six men," reported Scott. "Five in one room and one in another. They've all been beaten up, but the solitary one is worst off. I couldn't get them out of their cells because the doors are padlocked."

"If Alia has any strength left after taking care of Terry, she'll be wanting to heal them too," I said, knowing that my sister wouldn't return to Walnut Lane leaving injured people here. "We'll need something to pry the locks off with."

I said to Daniel, "Find us a crowbar or something, please."

Daniel seemed only too happy to be of use, and scampered out of the kitchen. Candace was still in a state of mild shock, so I escorted her to the living room where she could sit semi-comfortably on a couch. I unclipped my earpiece and plopped it onto the couch next to her. Then I asked Scott to show me the basement.

The entrance was by the kitchen door, and a flight of creaky wooden stairs led us down into a narrow, dimly lit concrete corridor.

There were three heavy steel doors, one on each side of the corridor and one at the far end. Each door had a small square window. Through the window of the door on my left, I saw the five men Scott had told me about. They were dressed in tattered shirts and pants, and had long beards and untidy hair. There was no way to tell if they were Guardians or from some lesser faction. I could sense no destroyer powers among them and guessed that this might be the reason they hadn't been express-delivered to King Divine for conversion. I wondered how long they had been trapped down here.

The door was locked with a heavy-duty padlock on the outside, and I wasn't sure a crowbar would be enough to break it off, but we'd try it before looking for something else.

"You guys alright?" I called through the window.

"Yeah," one of them muttered. All of them were looking at me with utter distrust. I could hardly blame them after what they must have gone through down here.

"We're going to get you out in a moment," I told them. "Any of you guys psionic?"

They didn't reply.

"You're safe now," I said reassuringly. "Just give us a moment to get this door open."

The cell across from them was unoccupied, but the one at the end of the corridor contained the sixth man.

He was bound to a wooden straight-back chair by thin ropes, a black cloth tied around his eyes, his head slumped forward as if he was sleeping. His unkempt blond hair and long beard were matted with dried blood. Aside from the blindfold, he was wearing only a dirty pair of shorts, and there were black and purple bruises all over his body. I realized that he had been recently tortured. This was the man who Alia had been trying to tell me about earlier.

"I found a crowbar," said Daniel's voice from behind me. "There was a toolbox hidden in the storeroom."

I didn't reply, my eyes still fixed on the figure sitting in the center of the cell.

"Adrian?" said Scott, touching my shoulder.

I turned to him and said quietly, "I know this man."

I pushed past Scott and Daniel and walked briskly back toward the stairs.

"Wait!" called Scott. "Aren't we going to get them out?"

"No," I said, not breaking step. "They're Wolves."

11. MAJOR EDWARD REGIS

There was no mistaking him, even with the blindfold covering his eyes, even with the longer hair, the beard, the scars and the burns and bruises covering his body. He wasn't just a Wolf. He was *the* Wolf. Alia had recognized him too. That's what she had been trying to warn me about.

I barely made it up to the top of the stairs before I collapsed onto the floor, clutching my chest, hyperventilating and feeling so nauseous I was afraid I might throw up.

I didn't even know his name. But I remembered his boot in my gut. I remembered the tiny metal room, and the excruciating electric shocks running through my body. And I remembered a filthy little girl wearing a tattered hospital gown, dark bruises on her arms and face, so completely lost in her pain and fear that she didn't even recognize me anymore.

I heard Merlin's voice say, "It's alright. Just breathe, Adrian. What's going on here?"

Scott said, "Adrian says the captives downstairs are Wolves. He says he knows one of them."

"I see."

Breathing slowly, I got to my feet and said to Merlin, "Give me your gun."

I had left my pistol somewhere upstairs, and I didn't have the energy left for six focused blasts.

Merlin shook his head. "Adrian, we can't kill them yet. We should find out what they know. That's why the Angels didn't kill them either."

"Give me your gun," I said again, more severely.

"This isn't…" began Merlin, but then we heard the sound of a car engine outside.

I followed Merlin and the others to the living room where, through the broken window, I saw Merlin's van pulling up in front of the house.

The shock of seeing the Wolf who had tortured Alia and me had temporarily driven Terry from my mind, but suddenly I no longer cared about my revenge. That could wait.

We rushed outside where we found James helping Dr. Land get Terry's stretcher out of the back of the van. Alia had come in the van too.

"How is she?" I asked as Alia jumped into my arms.

"She's going to be okay, Addy," said Alia.

Terry was still unconscious, but Dr. Land said, "She's just sleeping. I doubt she'll be walking for a few days yet, but the worst is over."

Candace seemed to have recovered from her shock, and she held the door open for us as we wheeled Terry into the house.

Merlin and the Richardsons had moved Steven and all of the dead Angels to the room with the balcony, where the surviving hider was tied to the furniture. We put Terry in the telekinetic's bedroom at the far end of the second-floor corridor, and I carefully levitated her over to the soft bed. The telekinetic had left the window wide open when she flew out, but at least it wasn't shattered like the door. We closed the window and then nailed a blanket over the doorframe so that Terry's temporary bedroom would remain tolerably warm. Terry stirred a little as we tucked her in, but she didn't wake.

Terry's face was still a little pale, but looked much more alive than it had an hour ago. It was now well past midnight, but I didn't feel at all sleepy. Dr. Land informed me that our peacemaker and mind-writer would join us here once they finished wrapping up our intrusion on the aged couple down the road. But I wasn't worried about them at the moment. My main concern was with the men in the basement.

"Could I have a little time alone here with my sister?" I asked, and everyone complied without question.

Once Alia and I were alone, I asked her hesitantly, "Are you alright?"

"I'm tired, but I'm okay," she replied. *"Did you get the people out of the*

basement?"

"No," I said, and added accusingly, "You could have told me who they were."

"I tried," insisted Alia. Then, letting out a little sigh, she said, *"I should go heal them."*

I looked at her in disbelief. "Alia, they're Wolves. All of them."

"I know that, Addy. I saw them too."

"You saw the man in the end room?"

Alia stared down at her feet. *"Yes."*

"You want to heal him too?"

I realized that I had lost my chance for revenge. At least for now, I couldn't simply go down there and shoot unarmed men in jail cells. But I wasn't about to deliver care packages to them either.

Alia looked up into my eyes, saying quietly, *"He's hurt and alone, Addy."*

I shrugged. "It's no more than he deserves."

"Nobody deserves that."

"Oh, for the—"

Suddenly my sister shouted furiously into my head, *"Adrian Howell, what is the matter with you?!"*

"The matter with—with me?!" I sputtered, "Alia, you—I mean—you honestly—"

"He's hurt, Addy! Don't you get it?!"

"Damn your conscience, Alia!" I spat, throwing my hands up in disgust.

I looked at Terry, still sleeping peacefully. What would she say about this when she woke?

My first thought was that Terry would agree with me. She had lost her brother to the Angels, who had tortured him to death. She knew what it felt like to truly hate. But then again, Terry was a pragmatist. She, like her grandfather, did whatever needed to be done to accomplish the task at hand. And when my thinking was clearest, I was that way too.

I took a deep breath and said slowly, "Alright, you can heal him, but I want to have a chat with this man first. Stay here until I call you."

Alia shook her head. *"Addy, no! Please!"*

"I promise I won't kill him," I said. "Just give me a few minutes. I swear, okay? I won't hurt him."

Alia slowly nodded and hugged me, and I realized once again that there was simply no arguing with a healer. At least not with this one.

It took a few more minutes to convince Merlin and the others of my non-lethal intentions regarding the Wolves, but they reluctantly agreed to let me speak with the solitary one by myself. I wasn't yet certain, but I was pretty sure that this man was the leader. Scott managed to break the padlock on the farthest cell door, and I asked him to leave me and go back upstairs. Scott still seemed to think that I was planning on killing the Wolf, but he obediently left the basement.

The blindfolded Wolf had lifted his head when he heard Scott break the lock, and he seemed to be following the sound of my footsteps as I slowly walked around him once, looking him over.

He wasn't even wearing socks, and I noticed that he was missing two toes on his left foot.

Standing behind his chair, I reached around his head and gently pulled his blindfold off.

The Wolf didn't turn his head. Facing straight ahead, he said in a quiet tone, "You're psionics, aren't you?"

"That's right," I said evenly.

"Meridian?" he asked. "Guardian? Avalon?"

"Guardian," I replied, stepping around to his right side.

The Wolf looked surprised when he saw me, but then said calmly, "I was expecting someone older. Who are you, kid?"

"You don't remember me?" I asked, genuinely disappointed. "I admit I look rather different from the last time we met, but so do you." I lifted my left shirtsleeve up to the shoulder. "Maybe you'll recognize this."

The Wolf looked at my P-47 tattoo for a moment, and then nodded. "Adrian... I heard of your escape."

His composed manner irked me, but I wasn't going to let it show. I kept my tone equally calm as I said, "I never got your name, sir."

"Major Edward Regis," the Wolf replied casually. "You can call me Ed."

I sighed. "And I didn't even have to beat it out of you, Major Edward Regis."

"Names are free, Adrian. Are you going to kill me?"

I slowly shook my head. "I promised Alia that I wouldn't."

"She's here too?"

"Yes. And she also knows that you're here. She wanted to heal you, which is certainly more than I want. I still have nightmares about what you did to us."

"You were a prisoner of war, just as I am here now."

I gave the Wolf a wry smile. "Sometimes I need to be reminded too these days, but there are rules, Major Edward Regis, even in a war."

"Not with psionics," he replied evenly, and then smiled, saying, "Call me Ed."

Despite my hatred, I couldn't help being impressed with this man who so calmly faced me as if speaking to an equal rather than a captor. I certainly wasn't about to call him "Ed" as if he were a friend, but I decided that "Major Edward Regis" was not only too long but far too respectful to continue using on a regular basis.

"You are the leader of your unit, Ed Regis?" I asked.

"That is correct."

"How long have you been locked down here?"

"I'm not sure," he replied, shrugging. "We were caught in December."

"It's almost March now," I informed him. "Why haven't the Angels transported you to Randal Divine yet?"

"King Divine has many duties," said Ed Regis. "We were on a waiting list, but they promised that we'd be sent in a few more weeks."

I raised an eyebrow. "You don't seem very upset by that."

"I wasn't until you showed up."

"What do you mean?"

"We're contaminated," explained Ed Regis. "The Wolves never take a captured soldier back because that soldier could be converted or worse. We would be hunted as if we were psionics ourselves. There was nowhere left for us to go but to join the Angels anyway. But now that you have us, I'm guessing we're all about to be executed after all."

"I already told you that I'm not going to kill you, Ed Regis," I said. "I can't promise anything regarding the other Guardians, but if you're 'contaminated' as you say, well, that makes things much easier for me."

I gazed at the Wolf's face for a moment, wondering if I was really going to say what I had come down here to say. But it had to be said, so I did. "How would you like to join us, Major?"

Ed Regis finally looked surprised. "You're joking, right?"

I wasn't. I had already told Merlin and the others up on the first floor that I was going to ask the Wolves to help us. Without a master controller, we would have to convince them to join us willingly, and for them to do so, they would have to trust us. That's why it had to be me.

"We're putting together a team to get us through the Angel blockade of the Historian's mountain," I explained. "We could use some good soldiers. I assume that you know who the Historian is?"

Ed Regis nodded.

"And you also know that the Guardians are all but destroyed," I said quietly. "We believe that the Historian may be our last hope to find and kill Randal Divine. The truth is, Major, we have common enemies. When the Guardians fall, even the strongest governments of the world won't be able to stop the Angels."

Ed Regis remained silent, but nodded slightly in what I took to be grudging agreement.

Feeling a little more confident, I continued, "Since the Guardians don't even have a master controller anymore, if you join us, you might still make it back to your unit someday if you can convince them that you haven't turned Angel. What better way to do that than by helping us kill Randal Divine?"

Ed Regis still didn't reply. I couldn't be sure if he was thinking it over or simply ignoring me, so I added, "Don't think I like this any more than you. I was a heartbeat away from killing you today. But if Alia can suffer your company, then so can I. This is very simple. You can either join us or you can walk free and go live your life however you want."

Ed Regis gave me a skeptical frown, asking, "You'd let us go?"

I nodded. "If I'm to trust you, then I can't make your freedom conditional on your help. But we could really use your help."

I undid the ropes binding him. Ed Regis remained sitting, but looked at me in astonishment.

"Please," I said, ignoring the horrible pain that word was causing me. "Please will you help us, Major Regis?"

Ed Regis stroked his beard. "If I do this, I will want their master alive."

Not a chance. I wasn't going to let the scientists of any government learn how master controllers tick. But first we had to get to the Historian.

"That's perfectly fine," I lied to his face. "We'll even help you capture him." If Ed Regis was still with us when we moved on the Angel king, I'd personally make sure that the Wolf didn't even walk away with a corpse to dissect. "So will you help us?"

"Yes," Ed Regis replied carefully. "I will need to speak with my team, but I believe they will agree."

"We'll get them out in a minute. Stay here."

As I turned to leave, Ed Regis said, "What I did to you, Adrian... What I did to that girl... It was nothing personal, you know. It was my job to get information."

I rounded on him furiously. "Nothing personal?! You shot me, Ed Regis! You tortured my sister! It doesn't get much more personal than that!"

Ed Regis said quietly, "For what it's worth, I am sorry."

I steadied my breathing. "Alia will be down in a moment to heal your injuries."

"No," said Ed Regis, shakily getting to his feet. "I'm alright. There's no need to put her through that."

"She has survived much worse than you," I told him stiffly. "So have I, for that matter."

"Nevertheless—"

"Alia *insisted*," I said coldly. "My sister is incapable of ignoring any person's suffering, so you will believe me when I tell you, Major, that I'm absolutely sure it's nothing personal. Now sit down!"

Back on the first floor, I found Alia waiting with the others.

"Their leader, Major Edward Regis, has agreed to join us," I announced. "He'll need to talk with his team, so please get them out of their cell now."

Alia looked at me in surprise. She hadn't known what my new plan for the Wolves was.

"Your turn, Alia," I said to her. "I'm going to go check on Terry."

Alia gave me an uncomfortable look. *"Addy..."*

"Hey, don't expect me to watch you do this," I said gruffly. "I'd just as soon shoot them all."

"It's alright," Candace said to Alia. "We'll stay with you."

Scott grabbed the crowbar and headed for the basement, followed by

Alia, Candace and a few others.

Up in Terry's room, I telekinetically pulled an armchair up to the bed. Sitting down heavily, I tried not to think of what my sister was going through as she faced the Wolf again. I knew she was still terrified of him, and I felt guilty about not holding her hand.

But then, what was Ed Regis going through now? The Wolf was a soldier. He might not always follow the warrior's code of honor, but he knew it. I felt that in a strange and sick way, being indebted to Alia was the most fitting punishment possible for a man like him.

I closed my eyes for a moment.

"Addy?"

I first thought that Alia was sending her telepathy from below, but then I felt her hand on my shoulder.

"I'm sorry. I didn't hear you coming," I said, turning my head. "I must have dozed off. So how are they?"

Alia gave me a blank stare. *"They'll be okay."*

"Did you heal them all?" I asked.

Alia nodded. *"And the rest of the team agreed to join us too."*

"Terry will be happy when she wakes."

"I hope so," Alia said sadly.

"What's the matter, Alia?"

"I don't know," said Alia, tears welling in her eyes. *"He said he was sorry for what he did, but I... I..."*

My sister's telepathy hardly ever failed her so I knew how hard this was for her. I asked gently, "But you didn't want to heal him?"

Alia nodded wretchedly as her tears overflowed. *"I'm sorry, Addy. I don't know what's wrong with me. I'm really sorry."*

I held her quivering shoulders and whispered, "Don't ever be sorry for how you feel, Alia."

Alia collapsed onto me, howling at the top of her lungs. I pulled her into my lap and held her tightly. Her loud cries soon brought Candace and a few others to the room, but I told them to leave us alone for a while.

My sister eventually cried herself to sleep in my lap. Not wanting to risk waking her, I decided that my armchair was comfortable enough and closed my eyes too. Somebody thoughtfully brought a warm blanket and wrapped it around us before turning out the light.

Terry was still asleep when the morning light woke me the next day.

Alia woke too, but refused to budge, so I sat silently holding her until Candace came up to announce breakfast.

"The Wolves will be eating with us this morning," said Candace. "If you like, I'll bring something up so you can eat here."

"No," I said. "We'd better get acquainted."

Once Candace had left, I looked down at Alia again, whose eyes were still puffy and a little wet.

I asked uncertainly, "Is this really okay, Alia? Us working with Ed Regis?"

My sister gave me a watery smile. *"It's okay, Addy. I'm sorry about last night. I just felt like crying a bit."*

"It's alright," I said, hugging her. "I kind of felt the same way. You had a long day yesterday. Come on, let's go get some breakfast. We'll probably need to leave this house today. We've got some people back in Walnut Lane for you to take care of, too."

As Alia clambered off of me, I noticed that Terry's eyes were slightly open.

I jumped to my feet and asked excitedly, "Terry? Are you awake?"

Terry's lips barely moved as she croaked, "Where am I? What happened to me?"

"It's a long story," I said, grinning. "Welcome back."

I said to Alia, "Call Dr. Land."

"I already did," Alia replied aloud, and I heard the doctor's footsteps approaching.

After giving Terry a once-over, Dr. Land told me to bring up some breakfast. "Something soft," he said. "And knock when you return."

Alia stayed with Dr. Land as he examined Terry.

Making my way down to the dining room, I was met with the smell of bacon and eggs, and I found the Wolves sharing the table with my team. The dining table was too small for everyone to sit together, so several had taken their plates to the sofas in the living room.

Scott was busy explaining our background to Ed Regis, who nodded curtly to me as I entered the dining room. I saw that Ed Regis had cleaned himself up, shaved, and found some new clothes from the Angels' wardrobes.

His bruises were completely healed too. However reluctantly, Alia had done a thorough job, and I saw that the other Wolves were in equally good condition.

"Terry's awake," I announced, but everyone already knew that from Dr. Land.

Several of my team asked in unison, "How is she?"

I shrugged. "I'm a waiter, not a doctor."

Scott helped me prepare three breakfast trays, and I levitated them with me back to Terry's bedroom. There was nowhere for me to sit at the dining table anyway, so I decided that Alia and I would eat upstairs after all.

Dr. Land was just finishing with Terry when I returned.

"Oh, good," said Terry. "I'm starving."

Terry was not only wide awake, but sitting up on her bed. I suspected that Dr. Land's earlier prognosis that Terry wouldn't be walking for several days was going to be challenged within hours.

I had prepared a bowl of cereal for Terry, but she preferred the bacon and eggs. Taking the tray in her lap, she refused to let Alia hand-feed her.

"I'm okay," insisted Terry. "Dr. Land told me I was out for a day, but he won't tell me where this is or anything else."

Dr. Land smiled, saying to me, "I figured that she should hear it from you. Call if you need anything."

Dr. Land left, and as we ate, I gave Alia and Terry the details starting from the Angels' raid on our house.

Alia had seen Max die, but she hadn't known about Felicity. She shed a few more tears over Susan's sister, but it was Terry that I really felt sorry for.

Terry said dejectedly, "I guess our trainees weren't as ready as I thought. Maybe this whole thing was a bad idea. Maybe they are just kids."

"Oh, they've learned a thing or two from us over the months," I said, and Alia and Terry listened quietly as I told them how our trainees had rallied to save them.

I explained how we spent the day practicing the breach, and how, despite several minor mistakes, we came through unscathed.

"I was expecting to lose at least one or two more," I said honestly, "but everyone made it. Even Candace managed to shoot straight for once."

"You shouldn't have risked them for us," said Terry, and Alia nodded in agreement.

"I didn't," I replied. "They insisted on helping. They're fighters now, Terry. They're not kids anymore. We've trained them well. Give them a little credit."

Terry wasn't convinced. "Well, it's amazing no one died, but I still say you were just lucky."

"You're not giving up on them, are you?" I asked. "After all that they did for us?"

Terry shook her head. "Maybe they'll be ready in a couple more years, but I can't ask them to come to the Historian with us. We need to go soon. It's already been almost a year since we left New Haven."

I smiled. "Well, I don't want to risk them any further either."

Then I turned to Alia and said, "Call the major up."

Terry raised her eyebrows. "Major? What major?"

Ed Regis stepped into the room a few seconds later.

"May I introduce Major Edward Regis of the Wolves," I said to Terry, and laughed as her jaw dropped.

Ed Regis stepped forward and reached out to shake Terry's hand, but Terry was still too shocked to move.

"I found us an army," I said quietly. "Ed Regis here and five more men."

Technically, six Wolves was hardly an army, but it was a good start and I could personally vouch for their skills.

"We're yours to command," said Ed Regis, who already knew from Scott that Terry was our leader.

Terry finally shook Ed Regis's hand, saying, "I don't like Wolves very much, but I suppose beggars can't be choosers."

Ed Regis turned to me. "Well, I guess it's official."

After an uncomfortable few seconds, Ed Regis extended his hand out to me. I glared up at him for a moment, and then nodded and slowly shook his hand.

Alia was next, and she smiled bravely as she shook Ed Regis's hand too.

"Thank you again for healing me and my team, Alia," said Ed Regis.

"I'm a healer, Mr. Regis," Alia said quietly. "It's my job."

"Call me Ed."

Alia shook her head. "I don't think so, Mr. Regis."

I cringed when Alia called the Wolf "Mr. Regis," but I agreed that it was hard to know how to refer to this man. I had settled for "Ed Regis," so my sister was the politer of us.

Before leaving the Angels' house, Terry insisted that we clean the place up so as to leave as little trace of our visit as possible. I was for simply burning the house down, destroying the evidence like the Angels had done with the towboat, but Terry didn't want to cause any more police-related trouble for Mrs. Harding.

We first moved all the corpses from the upstairs bedroom down into the basement. For a variety of reasons that I won't go into here, dead bodies really stink, and I was quite relieved when we got it done. There wasn't much that could be done about the Angels' blood on the carpets, but we vacuumed the floor twice and wiped the house clean of our fingerprints as best as we could.

That left the problem of the single surviving Angel.

Since Walnut Lane was in the middle of an evacuation, we couldn't exactly take the Angel hider with us. Ed Regis offered to take him down to the basement and shoot him, but I stopped the Wolf, saying, "Hey, we spared your worthless hide."

In the end, we decided to let the hider go free. He wasn't even an official member of the Seraphim, and was hardly a danger to us. Besides, this Angel could look after the house and make sure that no one stumbled upon the dead too quickly.

As we exited the house, Terry insisted that she didn't need to be carried on the stretcher, but Alia wasn't having that. Fixing Terry with a stern look, she said, "When people are shooting at us, I listen to you. When you're injured, Teresa Henderson, you listen to me. Understand?"

Terry didn't complain too much. I suspected she probably could walk, but not very well or far just yet.

There were nineteen of us returning to Walnut, and we couldn't all fit in Merlin's van and Dr. Land's SUV, so we took both cars that we had found parked next to the Angels' house.

I sat with Candace and Alia in the back seat of the SUV. It was only when we were halfway back to Walnut Lane that I noticed something missing from my sister.

"Where's your pendant, Alia?" I asked.

Alia occasionally wore her bloodstone under her shirt, and I had assumed that was where it was, but now I saw that there was no leather cord around her neck.

"Oh," Alia said sadly, touching her chest where the pendant usually rested. "Steven took it. He didn't even want it. He just wanted to take it away. And then Lazlo's witch blasted it into a million pieces. She said that's what she'd do to my fingers if I tried to escape."

"I'm sorry," I said. "But better the stone than your fingers."

Alia sighed. "I know."

Like myself, Alia had worn her pendant day and night for years, ever since Cindy had given it to her as a reward for giving up her P-46 tattoo. I knew that she felt it was a part of her body because that was how Cat's amethyst felt to me. Once you get used to something like that, it feels awkward not to have it on you. Maybe not as bad as losing an arm like Terry did, but sort of the same.

"Tell you what," I said brightly, "I'll get you a new one for your birthday, okay?"

"Really?"

I nodded. "And in the meantime," I added, removing my amethyst and putting it around her neck, "you hang on to this one for me again."

Alia fingered the stone and smiled. "Thanks, Addy."

We arrived back in Walnut Lane in the early afternoon.

Her joy in seeing Terry alive notwithstanding, Mrs. Harding blew her top when she discovered who we had brought to town.

"You honestly cannot expect me to allow these men into our ranks, Teresa!" said Mrs. Harding at our doorstep.

The Wolves were already inside the Refugee House, and Mrs. Harding refused to enter.

"Adrian and I will answer for them," said Terry, who was still on her stretcher but sitting up.

Mrs. Harding argued, "We can't take them to the mountain camp. I will not allow it."

"That is no problem," replied Terry. "We're not going to the camp either. We're going to the Historian, and the Wolves will leave with me, Adrian and Alia as soon as we're ready, probably within a few days."

Mrs. Harding gave Terry an incredulous look. "You're taking Wolves to the Historian?"

"That is correct," Terry said evenly.

Merlin said, "I will be going with them too."

Terry and I turned to Merlin, who smiled at us, saying, "You'll need a hider."

"Very well," Mrs. Harding said with a huff. "Make sure your *guests* do not leave the house until they are ready to go."

"Not a problem, Mrs. Harding," said Terry. "I apologize again for all the trouble."

Merlin held the door open for us and I wheeled Terry's stretcher into our house.

Alia was already upstairs tending to Walter, Heather and Rachael, so Terry took this opportunity to try standing on her own legs. She seemed a little off balance at first, but didn't fall over.

The six Wolves were standing in one corner of our dojo, looking uncomfortably unsure where to be.

"You'll all be sharing a single room tonight," Terry informed them, and then turned to me. "Adrian, show them to Steven's old room."

"Why me?" I asked.

"Why not you?!" snapped Terry, which proved she had recovered.

"Alright, come on," I said wearily to the crowd.

The Wolves followed me upstairs to the smallest bedroom. I helped gather the few spare blankets we had left in the house, but informed the men that they were going to be sleeping on the floor without mats.

"That's no problem," said Ed Regis.

Technically, Felicity and Susan's room on the third floor was also open now, but I wasn't feeling generous enough to offer a second room to a bunch of Wolves. Besides, having them stay together would make it easier for us to keep an eye on them.

"What's that in your hand?" I asked. Since returning to Walnut Lane, Ed Regis had been carrying around a small black laptop-like device.

"This?" asked Ed Regis, holding it up. "It's a little toy I reclaimed from Lazlo's house this morning. I thought it might come in handy."

"What is it?"

"It's our portable psionic database," said Ed Regis. "It contains information on known and suspected psionics and faction members. The Angels took it from our APC when they captured us."

I didn't bother asking what an APC was. I was more interested in the database. "Can I see it?" I asked.

"Of course," Ed Regis replied unhesitatingly. "It is password protected, though. One wrong entry and all the data is lost, so you have to type carefully."

Ed Regis opened the laptop and pressed the power button. The nine-inch screen immediately displayed a little window asking for a password.

"Is that what they were torturing you for?" I asked.

"It was one of the things they wanted," said Ed Regis. "They didn't even have a delver, so it took a while before they were convinced that I was telling them the true password."

"You gave them the password?"

Ed Regis shrugged. "I figured I had nothing to lose. In fact, I pretty much answered all of their questions truthfully."

"Then why did they keep hurting you?"

"They were enjoying themselves too much," said Ed Regis, typing in the password.

The screen flashed once and changed to a search interface. There were a number of text boxes for looking people up by name, age, faction, psionic powers, eye color, hair color, facial scars and various other criteria.

"Who are you looking for?" asked Ed Regis.

I shrugged. "I was just curious. Can I try a search?"

"Sure," said Ed Regis, handing the device over to me. "Go nuts."

I knew that Ed Regis had nothing to lose now by giving me his top-secret toy, but I had to (very grudgingly) admit that he was making a first-rate effort to stay on my good side. I found his friendliness thoroughly irritating because I still wanted to hate this man, and he wasn't making it at all easy.

"It's a touch screen," explained Ed Regis. "Just touch the field you want to search in and type in your query."

I tapped my finger on the section for names and typed in "Cindy Gifford." A list of names popped up. There were Cindys and Cynthias of different family names, but no Giffords. I found a Cynthia Anderson, though.

"Anderson?" I asked Ed Regis. "I distinctly remember telling you her real name."

He shrugged. "It hasn't been updated yet."

"In three years?" I said, touching the name on the screen.

Four images of Cindy appeared on the screen, followed by a long section of text. The first of the photos was a mug shot, probably Cindy's old driver's license, and the other three were taken at odd angles through telephoto lenses. None of the photos did any justice to the Cindy I knew. I scrolled down the text and discovered that the Wolves had updated the file in bits and pieces.

FILE ID: *Cynthia Anderson.* ALIASES: *Cynthia or Cindy Gifford; Silver (Guardian call sign).* AFFILIATIONS: *Guardian 1-A, under Baker, Travis.* KNOWN POWERS: *Hider, Finder.* SUSPECTED POWERS: *None.* SUSPECTED EMERGENTS: *None or Unknown.* CURRENT STATUS: *Unknown.*

A detailed physical description followed, including everything from eye color to shoe size, but there was no mention of how comforting her smile was. Then there was a list of relatives, many of whom had either been killed or had mysteriously disappeared. Apparently the families of wild-borns were all alike in that way.

Following the bloodline information were a bunch of addresses and telephone numbers, including Cindy's old home address, Mark Parnell's old house, and Cindy's last known place of residence, the fortieth-floor penthouse of New Haven's NH-1, though of course the database had the actual city name and address. Cindy's file also contained a short history of her time as a Guardian under the last queen, Diana Granados, as well as her disappearance and subsequent reappearance in New Haven. The file noted Cindy's unique position with New Haven's government and touched on her near-abduction by the Angels. At the very end, there was a list of links to closely related people, including Mr. Baker, Mark Parnell, Alia, Terry and myself. But regarding Cindy's current location, the Wolves knew no more than anyone else. There was no information regarding where she might have gone following the fall of New Haven.

Looking down at the list of links to related files, I lightly tapped on my own name, and the screen changed again.

There were two photos attached to my database entry. One was a mug shot, probably from my elementary school file when I was about ten years old. The other was an unflattering photo of me lying half-naked and unconscious on a hospital bed, and I suspected that it had been taken en route to the Psionic Research Center.

FILE ID: *Adrian Howell*. ALIASES: *Adrian Gifford; Addie(?); P-47 (at PRC Site-A)*. AFFILIATIONS: *Guardian 1-A, under Baker, Travis.* KNOWN POWERS: *Telekinetic.* SUSPECTED POWERS: *None.* SUSPECTED EMERGENTS: *None or Unknown.* CURRENT STATUS: *Deceased.*

"Deceased," I read aloud. "You mean I'm dead?"

Ed Regis chuckled. "That entry is probably false. There's been a lot of confusion recently."

I skimmed through the rest of the text, and I was pleased to find that my physical description didn't include my missing right ear or disparately colored eyes. Nor did the Wolves know my call sign, Hansel. In fact, there was no mention at all of me being a Guardian Knight. I was a bit surprised to find "Addie" there, though. How many people knew what Alia called me when she so rarely spoke with her mouth? Dr. Kellogg had known, of course, so perhaps it had been included in his monthly reports to the surface.

"What does 'suspected emergents' mean?" I asked.

Ed Regis explained, "Based on family histories, we tag people who might develop psionic powers in the future."

"I see," I said, nodding. Most psionic powers were hereditary. The children of telekinetics were often telekinetic too.

"And what is 'unknown'?" I asked. Cindy's suspected emergents had included that too.

"That's a common tag for wild-borns. It simply means we can't predict what powers will develop because we can't trace the family history."

My annoyance with Ed Regis's helpfulness was reaching its boiling point.

I decided to test him, asking, "If I was at PRC Site-A, would it stand to reason that there is a Site-B out there somewhere?"

"It would, and there is," said Ed Regis. "But I can't tell you where it's located."

"Why not?" I asked harshly.

"We're just hunters, Adrian. We don't deliver the psionics ourselves."

"Some help you are."

"I am sorry."

I slapped the device closed and thrust it back into Ed Regis's hands. "Write the password onto the back with a marker and leave it where I'll find it later."

"As you wish," he replied calmly, but I was already walking briskly back toward the stairs.

How I wished I had at least punched him once when I could!

12. LEAVING WALNUT LANE

That evening, Scott and Candace helped me cook up an extra-special multi-course feast to celebrate our new alliance with Ed Regis and his Wolf pack. And no, I didn't spit in their soup, though I admit that I was sorely tempted.

It was also a thank-you meal for the parents of Alia's students. Alia was heartbroken to learn that she wouldn't even be able to say goodbye to her kiddie-combat class, but she wrote a long message for the parents to read to them at the mountain camp.

It wasn't easy, but we managed to squeeze everyone into the dining room. Alia had finished healing Walter's broken arm, the hole in Heather's foot, and Rachael's burns. Rachael was left with permanent scars on her neck, but at least her hair would grow back.

We hadn't forgotten our two casualties, for which there would be no proper funeral or burial. Max and Felicity's bodies would eventually be taken to the mountain camp and placed in unmarked graves. For the time being, they were quietly moved to a local morgue to be kept in cold storage.

Terry led the toast, saying, "To absent, brave friends."

Earlier that morning, Merlin had discovered a large stash of cash at the Angel outpost, so in addition to soldiers, we now had more than enough money to make the journey to the Historian's mountain. Terry broke that news over dinner too, and predictably, Scott and the others insisted upon accompanying us on our journey.

"Oh, no you don't," said Terry. "You guys have a more important mission. You're going to help repay our debt to Mrs. Harding and the Walnut Guardians. You're all trained Knights now, and I expect you to act like it. I will, however, choose one of you to join us at your own peril."

"Who gets to go?" asked Scott, who probably thought it was himself.

Terry smiled. "I will speak privately with this person so that there is no pressure to accept. But it's not you, Scott. I need you to lead this rabble, and make sure Susan is okay."

Poor Susan had parted with Felicity in anger. Now she would be reunited in grief. I didn't envy the messenger, and I was almost glad that I wasn't going up to the mountain camp.

After dinner cleanup, I went up to my room where I found Ed Regis's database leaning against the corridor wall next to the door with a little note stuck to it that read, "I disabled the security completely and recharged the battery. Hope you find something useful. —Ed"

Picking up the database and entering the room, I noticed that someone had attached a blue plastic sheet over our broken window. The glass probably wouldn't get replaced since the house was soon going to be abandoned anyway, but at least the plastic sheet would keep the wind and insects out.

It was still not much past 8pm, and the light was on, but Alia was already curled up on her side of our bed, fast asleep. That was hardly surprising considering how she had spent the previous night and this afternoon healing one person after another. Unlike her telepathy, which was second nature to her, healing was always taxing on her physical strength.

I quietly plopped the database onto the bed and turned to James, who had been lying on his cot reading a magazine. "You up for another adventure?" I asked.

James looked stunned. "It's me?"

I nodded. "Terry believes in you. So do I. But it's got to be your own choice. Where we're going next, it's unlikely we'll come through without losing a few."

James slowly gulped once and then nodded. "Count me in."

"Good man," I said.

"Um, I think I'm going to go take a walk outside."

Watching him leave, I called out behind him, "Take your time."

Then I sat down on the bed carefully so as not to wake Alia. Resting my back against the headboard, I opened the database.

Who would I look up this time? I touched the screen to activate the search field for names, and carefully typed in the one that was heaviest on my mind.

FILE ID: *Randal Divine*. ALIASES: *Flash (Angel call sign)*. AFFILIATIONS: *Angel, under Divine, Randal*. KNOWN POWERS: *None*. SUSPECTED POWERS: *Finder, Master Controller*. SUSPECTED EMERGENTS: *Spark, Delver, Mind-writer*. CURRENT STATUS: *Unknown*.

I found it slightly amusing that the Wolves had updated the bit about Randal Divine being the new leader of the Angels but then forgotten to move "master controller" to the "known powers" slot. There were probably thousands of entries in this little device, and I wondered how much outdated information it contained.

Reading Randal's file further, I learned that the former-queen's nephew had been inching his way up the Angels' ranks through a combination of skill and name. He had been bitter enemies with Riley O'Neal, which explained why he thanked me for killing Riles. Randal's file contained a fairly extensive list of previous sightings, but that was back when he led the Seraphim in battle. Ever since declaring himself king, Randal Divine had turned into a ghost.

One of the names on the "related files" list at the bottom caught my eye. I touched it and the screen changed.

FILE ID: *Catherine Howell*. ALIASES: *Cathy Divine*. AFFILIATIONS: *Angel, under Divine, Randal*. KNOWN POWERS: *None*. SUSPECTED POWERS: *None*. SUSPECTED EMERGENTS: *Telekinetic or Unknown*. CURRENT STATUS: *In care of Randal Divine*.

Like mine, Cat's mug shot was probably also taken from her old school file. I noticed that she was wearing the amethyst pendant our uncle had sent her on her eighth birthday. There was nothing in her personal history that I didn't know already, and the Wolves had no information about what happened to her after she was taken by the Angels.

New search.

FILE ID: *Alia Gifford*. ALIASES: *Alia Anderson(?)*; *P-46 (at PRC Site-A)*. AFFILIATIONS: *Guardian 1-A, under Baker, Travis*. KNOWN POWERS: *Healer, Telepath*. SUSPECTED POWERS: *None*. SUSPECTED EMERGENTS: *None or Unknown*. CURRENT STATUS: *Committed to PRC Site-A*.

Here was another file that needed updating. Apparently my sister was in two places at once, and neither of them existed anymore.

The only photo on the file showed a bruised and terrified Alia, her wrists and ankles bound by iron chains. She was sitting inside what appeared to be a cargo plane. Alia had been awake when we were transported to the PRC, and if it hadn't been for her memory of the upper floors, we might not have made it out alive. Seeing the battered Alia in the photo made me shudder, and I quickly returned to the search screen.

I glanced over at the real Alia, who had wrapped her arms around her pillow and was holding it tightly to her chest as she mumbled incoherently into my head.

Using psionic powers during sleep was common to child psionics, and Alia still spoke telepathically almost every night. Back in New Haven, I used to wake up hovering several times a month, usually resulting in painful crash-landings and mild bruises when I woke. I realized that I hadn't sleep-hovered in many months now, and thought happily that perhaps I was finally becoming an adult. It was about time.

I looked at the database again and typed in another search.

FILE ID: *Teresa Henderson.* ALIASES: *Terrie or Terry(?) Holloway; Rabbit (Guardian call sign).* AFFILIATIONS: *Unknown. Previously Guardian 1-A, under Baker, Travis.* KNOWN POWERS: *None.* SUSPECTED POWERS: *Light-foot, Graviton.* SUSPECTED EMERGENTS: *Windmaster, Peacemaker, Finder, Berserker.* CURRENT STATUS: *Unknown.*

This was an interesting one. The Wolves didn't have a photo of Terry after I had hacked off her left arm, but her handicap was noted in her physical description. They had properly updated her file to show that she had escaped New Haven, but they also suspected her of already being a psionic, which was utterly wrong. Perhaps the Wolves simply couldn't believe that a one-armed teenage girl could fight as well as Terry could without having psionic powers.

Her file also claimed that Terry had some berserker in her blood. Had one of her parents been a berserker?

Suddenly I felt horribly ashamed of myself for reading up on Terry like this. It was like I was peeking at her school report card, but worse. Terry probably would have agreed had I asked, but nevertheless I should have obtained her permission before doing this.

I had been toying with the idea of looking up Laila Brown next, hoping I might find a nice photo of her, but decided against it.

I was about to shut the database off when I realized that there was just one more person I had to look up before I put this amazing little toy away: Nightmare, the mystery psionic who had turned the entire Psionic Research Center into a swirling muddy hole in the ground. In a way, he had saved Alia and me from being killed by Dr. Denman, and I wanted to know who he was.

But when I typed "Nightmare" into the names field of the search screen, all I found was a deceased Guardian Knight who had once used Nightmare as a call sign.

I brought up a new search. Looking at each text field, I found one labeled "Groups and Categories" and typed in "PRC Site-A."

What followed was a list of forty-seven names, each marked with a number before it. Scrolling down to the bottom, I quickly spotted Alia and myself at the end.

I scrolled back up through the list and discovered that Nightmare wasn't the only mystery man at the PRC. In fact, there were several entries simply listed as "Unknown Male" and "Unknown Female." What had been Nightmare's psionic ID number? Hadn't Nightmare been brought to the PRC a little after Mr. Koontz? If I could find Mr. Koontz, I might know which of the unknowns was Nightmare.

Before I spotted Mr. Koontz on the list, however, my eyes stopped dead on another name.

P-26: Denman, David Percy

My finger was shaking a little as I touched his name on the screen.

FILE ID: *David Percy Denman, MD.* ALIASES: *P-26 (at PRC Site-A).* AFFILIATIONS: *PRC Site-A, under Otis, Reuben, MD.* KNOWN POWERS: *Graviton, Hider.* SUSPECTED POWERS: *None.* SUSPECTED EMERGENTS: *None or Unknown.* CURRENT STATUS: *Deceased.*

I stared at the old, wrinkled face of Dr. Denman in the photo, at his hawk-like eyes and fierce scowl. They had known what he was from the beginning, and Dr. Denman had been a prisoner there himself.

After my escape from the PRC, I had thought very little about Dr. Denman aside from a few sighs of relief that he was dead and gone. But now I realized that in his last moments, Dr. Denman had said two things which seemed almost self-contradictory. On the one hand, he claimed that he was "trying to find a cure to this insanity." That pretty much summed up Dr. Denman for me. He hated psionics because he himself was one, and the scientist in him was repulsed by it. But then he also claimed that Alia was worth more than the rest of us put together. I wondered if perhaps Dr. Denman, who, after all, had a medical background, was secretly fascinated by Alia's ability to heal. Was Alia the exception to his rule? Could he tolerate psionic powers so long as they were limited to peaceful uses? I didn't like entertaining this thought because it was identical to my own feelings about psionics, and I hated to think that I shared ideals with Dr. Denman. But there was no denying what he said, or that he had risked (and consequently lost) everything to keep my sister from being rescued by the Guardians. Why was Alia so important to him?

I could understand the Angels giving Alia preferential treatment at their house because of who she was, but Dr. Denman?!

"Addy?" said Alia, breaking into my thoughts.

I turned to my sister. She had opened her eyes and was yawning quietly.

"Sorry," I said, "did I wake you?"

Alia sat up on the bed. *"It's okay."*

I closed the database and carefully levitated it over to the desk. Alia watched me silently for a moment and then asked, *"Did you tell James?"* My sister had been there when Terry asked me to invite James on our quest, so she knew of Terry's decision.

"I told him," I replied. "And yes, he's coming."

"That's good," said Alia. *"When are we leaving?"*

"I don't know yet. We'll go as soon as we're ready."

Alia peered carefully into my eyes. *"All of us?"*

I couldn't help smiling a little as I said, "You're thinking that I want you to stay with the rest of the kids up in the mountain camp while Terry and I go to meet the Historian."

Alia stared at me, unblinking.

I raised my eyebrows. "Whatever put that idea into your head?"

Alia scowled. *"Stay here or I'll shoot you myself."*

I ruffled her hair a bit, saying, "You deactivated the security system at the Angels' house, didn't you?"

She nodded. *"And unlocked the balcony door, too."*

"So what makes you think I wouldn't want you on this mission, soldier?"

Alia smiled broadly. *"Thanks, Addy."*

My sister had proven herself time and again to be more than anyone ever expected of her. To Dr. Denman, Alia had been but a prize, perhaps the key to some great mystery. To me, she was family, and that was the key to everything. Even now, as I wondered how insane I was to allow my ten-year-old sister to join a mission that would take us into who-knew-what dangers and quite possibly death, I also knew that there were preciously few people in this crazy world to whom I could unhesitatingly entrust my life, and this unlikely girl was one of them.

Putting my hands on her shoulders, I said seriously, "Alia, I really do want you to come with us. But I also want you to promise me that you'll do as you're told."

"I promise," Alia said lightly.

"I mean it! No arguments in the middle of a battle! Understand?"

"Okay. I promise."

"Alright," I said, shaking my head. "Go on back to sleep if you can. I have a feeling we're going to be pretty busy from tomorrow."

James wasn't back yet, but that was okay. No doubt he had a lot on his mind, too.

Over the following week, we got our joint Wolf-Guardian team ready for the long-anticipated push to the Historian's mountain. Terry, with the assistance of several members of Ed Regis's team, acquired the gifts that we would present to the Historian to beg his assistance. What could a 3000-year-old all-powerful psionic want that he couldn't provide for himself? The answer to that question was surprisingly simple.

"Nothing," Terry had said to me with a confusing smile. "There is nothing the Historian can't get for himself if he really wanted to. But the Historian hates leaving his mountain, and he hates using his psionic power when he could do without. In a way, he's a little like you, Adrian. He finds his own power burdensome. He prefers to deal in information. So people bring him food, money and entertainment."

"Entertainment?" I asked, chuckling at the thought of the great and wise Historian playing computer games in his mountain retreat.

But Terry was serious. "The Historian loves stories. He collects them. And he speaks every language on the planet so there's never a shortage of things we can take to gain his favor."

Even so, we weren't about to carry stacks of books and magazines on a mad rush to the Historian's mountain through hoards of deadly Angel patrols. Heavy boxes of expensive wines were equally out of the question. With the assistance of the Wolves, Terry made contact with some under-the-table gemstone dealers and converted a large portion of our newly acquired funds into rubies and emeralds.

"A symbolic gift," explained Terry, "but it'll be enough."

Meanwhile, Ed Regis was kept busy arranging our covert transportation. Over land and sea, we would have to cross multiple international borders without proper passports or paperwork. "Trust me," he said confidently, and we had little choice but to.

Merlin had an easier but equally important assignment: the acquisition of our mountain trekking gear, including clothing, boots, tents, tools, and consumables such as food, water and medicine. Once on site, the narrow footpath through the mountains—several days' hike—would be as unforgiving as the Angels who guarded it. We had to be ready for setbacks and detours.

While we waited, the rest of us continued to keep house, train, and assist the Walnut Knights in patrolling the neighborhood. James "the Chosen One" acquired a new status in the house, but to his credit, he didn't abuse it. Alia also got much more attention than she probably wanted from Candace and Heather, who both felt that my sister should accompany them to the mountain camp. As for myself, I quickly settled back into the role of designated househusband and Terry's semi-loyal second-in-command.

Ed Regis had originally requested a month to prepare our trip to the Historian's mountain. Terry had given him seven days, and though I have no idea what corners Ed Regis had cut to manage it, it looked like he would actually meet Terry's deadline. This meant we would probably be leaving Walnut Lane in a day or two, so Terry had ordered me to field-strip all of our guns one last time and make sure that they were in top condition.

Terry usually cleaned her own guns, refusing to trust her weaponry in anyone else's hands. Thus I took her command as praise, and despite my continuing dislike of firearms, I accepted the task without argument. I knew how important this was, too. One of the reasons I was alive today was because an Angel's pistol had jammed before it could put a bullet through my head.

Therefore, a little after lunchtime, I went around the house gathering up all the pistols we had, but not the ones that we had supplied to Ed Regis and his men. The Wolves could clean their own damn guns.

Retreating to the kitchen, I draped a white bedspread over the counter so I wouldn't lose sight of any small parts when I started disassembling the pistols. Then, sitting on a stool, I slowly, methodically started working on the first one, which was James's.

I heard the door open and looked up from my work.

"Addy?" said Alia, looking at me from across the room.

"What is it?" I asked.

"Have you seen Terry?"

"I think she's still out. Why?"

"Mr. Regis was looking for her."

"It's not that big a house," I said, annoyed at the mention of Ed Regis. "They'll bump into each other eventually."

Closing the door behind her, Alia came up to the counter and gingerly fingered the bedspread. *"What are you doing?"*

I gave her a nasty smile. "I'm playing golf, Alia. What does it look like I'm doing?!"

Ignoring my sarcasm, Alia hopped up onto a stool and silently watched me work. Though she knew how to handle a pistol if the need arose, my sister still hated guns even more than I, so she didn't offer to help, and I didn't ask her to. Personally, I felt that cleaning a gun was still far preferable to actually killing someone with it.

I was almost through reassembling James's pistol when there was a knock on the door. I telekinetically pulled it open, and Ed Regis stepped into the kitchen.

Alia asked him, "Did you find Terry, Mr. Regis?"

Ed Regis shook his head. "Scott told me that she'll be back in an hour or so." Then he gave me a smile and said, "I have good news, Adrian. We'll be leaving first light the day after tomorrow."

"Terry will be happy," I said indifferently, returning to my work.

"Do you need any help with those?" asked Ed Regis.

"No," I said flatly.

"I've got nothing better to do at the moment."

"Suit yourself."

There were only two stools, occupied by Alia and me, so Ed Regis stood at the counter next to Alia and took Terry's spare pistol, removing the clip and checking the chamber before starting to work on it.

I kept silent and focused on my own work.

Over the last few days, I had forced myself to get to know Ed Regis and his team a little better, but I prudently remained wary of what I said in front of any of them. After all, we all knew that this was a very temporary and shaky alliance. When Terry first learned that it was Ed Regis himself who had tortured Alia and me, she was just as disbelieving of my decision to spare the Wolf as I had been. ("Never knew you could be such a *politician,* Adrian!") Although pragmatism always trumps ideology in times of crisis, that didn't mean any of us were particularly thrilled with the setup. Furthermore, word of who we were harboring in our home had quickly spread through Walnut Lane, and tensions between us and the neighborhood remained uncomfortably high.

Thus I found it annoying that my sister seemed to have forgotten that she was living in the company of people who ordinarily hunted our kind from helicopters. Ed Regis had made a second apology to Alia three days ago, and Alia, unbelievably, seemed to accept it as sincere.

Even now, sitting between Ed Regis and me, my sister looked far more at ease in the presence of the Wolf than I felt.

"Your brother still doesn't like talking to me," Ed Regis stated the obvious.

Out of the corner of my eye, I saw Alia shake her head and smile. "He doesn't like you, Mr. Regis."

"Someday soon, Alia, I hope at least you will call me Ed," replied Ed Regis, his hands busily cleaning Terry's pistol.

Having finished with James's pistol, I next began to work on my own, but I was finding it increasingly difficult to concentrate on the task.

Alia asked the Wolf, "Why do your men call you 'Major'?"

"It's because I'm a major pain in the neck," joked Ed Regis.

Alia giggled. "Addy says that about me sometimes."

"Well, that makes you a major too," said Ed Regis. "Major Gifford. Major

Pain-in-Addy's-Neck."

I rolled my eyes as the two laughed loudly.

Then Ed Regis explained to Alia, "Actually, 'major' is just a rank title. It shows that I'm a soldier, kind of like your Guardian Knights."

Alia smiled, saying, "Addy is a Guardian Knight, but he's not a major."

"I didn't know that your brother was a Knight," said Ed Regis, sounding genuinely impressed.

"I am too, sort of."

"You're a Knight too?"

Alia nodded happily.

"Now that's something!" said Ed Regis. "How did you become a Knight at your age?"

Halting my work, I turned to the two and said dryly, "Low recruiting standards. Alia, would you please go find something better to do?"

Alia jumped down from her stool, stuck her tongue out at me and made for the door. "See you, Ed," she said lightly, and disappeared.

I telekinetically slammed the door behind her and then glared up at Ed Regis. "If I didn't know you better, Major Pain, I'd say you're enjoying your stay here."

"I'm just trying to be nice," said Ed Regis.

"Well, stop it."

"Are you telling me to stay away from your sister?"

"Who Alia giggles with is her business," I replied icily. "But you stay away from my sister. And everybody else, too."

"It would be very hard to make friends if I did that."

I narrowed my eyes. "What the hell do you want to make friends with us for?"

"If we're going to survive a trip to the Historian's mountain, we're going to have to be a team," Ed Regis pointed out logically. "I don't like it either, but it's not a matter of liking. On a mission, you do whatever you have to do to succeed."

"Oh, you're going to fit right in with us," I said with a huff.

Ed Regis sighed. "After what we did to you, Adrian, I would never expect you to like or trust me in the least. But do you regret sparing my life?"

I shook my head. "Alia spared your life, not me. And you're right, Ed

Regis. I neither like nor trust you. Not in the least."

We both worked silently for a while longer, and I eventually asked in a slightly more civil tone, "So how did you become a Wolf, anyway? I mean, you almost seem like a decent person when you're not beating up little girls."

Ed Regis kept his eyes on his work as he explained, "I was in training for Special Ops when I was approached by a bunch of black suits who promised me the opportunity to make 'an important contribution to society' as they put it. They wouldn't give me any details. Hell, they wouldn't even take off their damn sunglasses, and I actually wondered if all the nonsense I had heard about aliens landing on Earth might just be true. Anyway, they said I'd have to become a ghost, but that if I survived my tour, I'd be set up for life."

I gave Ed Regis a wry smile. "And you just jumped right in?"

"I was young and reckless," he replied. "I had no family and very few friends outside the military. It seemed like the right thing to do. When I discovered what my new assignment was, I did have certain reservations, but being a Wolf isn't your average police work. You can't just hand in your resignation, you know."

"I always thought you hated psionics," I said quietly. "You said we weren't even human."

"Just words, Adrian," said Ed Regis, shaking his head. "It was my job to hunt down psionics and to take information from the ones we captured. You were a child and I decided to present myself to you in an animalistic way so that you would be more afraid of me. You've grown since then, and I'm sure a professional soldier like yourself can understand that."

Having finished reassembling my pistol, I slapped the clip back in, saying sourly, "What makes you think I'm a professional, Ed Regis?"

Ed Regis looked thoughtfully at me for a moment. Then he replied, "A true professional puts the mission first. When you met me down in that basement, you didn't even hit me once. I don't know many people who would have had that kind of restraint under the same circumstances. Honestly, I'm not sure even I would have."

I raised my eyebrows. "You expected me to hurt you?"

Ed Regis shrugged. "I would have understood."

"Well, it's not like I didn't consider breaking your nose," I said, "but I guess I've lost my opportunity now."

"If it would make you feel any better, you're still welcome to. I promise I won't resist."

I laughed. "I'll keep that in mind."

It truly irked me that, in a few short days, Ed Regis and his Wolves had become borderline friends with many of my team. This was way beyond unfair. Ed Regis had apologized, making me feel guilty for my refusal to forgive him. I wasn't sure I could ever forgive him for what he had done to my sister, but Alia herself no longer seemed to mind his company in the least, so I had little choice but to stow my mixed up emotions and accept the former Wolf as one of our own. Ed Regis was a Guardian now. A temporary one, but a Guardian nevertheless, brought into our faction by a combination of fortune and misfortune, no different from myself. It was better to think of it that way. As Ed Regis had said, we had a long and dangerous road ahead of us, and it wouldn't do if we couldn't get along. Besides, it had been my bright idea to recruit the man.

Apparently pleased that he finally got me to stop frowning, Ed Regis pressed his advantage, saying, "So you tell me something now, Adrian. What's with the new look?"

"It hides this," I replied, telekinetically lifting my hair to reveal my jagged right ear.

"Ouch," remarked Ed Regis. "Looks like you've been put through the paces."

"The Slayers said that too."

"And what happened to your eyes?"

I was about to tell him, but then I checked myself. I had already been too careless showing him my lopsided head, which hadn't been marked in the Wolves' database yet. I decided that it would be safer not to go into details about my blindness, so I replied simply, "Mistakes have consequences, Ed Regis. I'm sure a man with only eight toes can understand that."

Ed Regis nodded and chuckled. "I've made many mistakes."

I tapped my upper left arm. "So have I."

Ed Regis asked seriously, "Do you think you can find it in you to survive my company, at least for the duration of our joint assignment?"

"I'm not about to forget what you are, Major," I replied. Then I forced a smile and added, "But as I told you when we met, I've survived worse than you."

Ed Regis was faster than me at field-stripping weapons, and we finished the work before Terry returned to the house. Though she refused to show it much, Terry was clearly pleased with Ed Regis's news. So was I, of course. I agreed with Terry: we had waited much too long already.

Later that evening, when I managed to get a moment alone with Alia, I said as casually as I could, "So you call him Ed now, do you?"

Alia just shrugged.

Knowing how hard it was for my sister to trust people, I didn't want to discourage her from making new friends, but I felt that this was going a bit too far.

"Don't play with him, Alia," I said warningly. "You know what he does for a living."

"You brought him here," Alia reminded me.

"That's not the point!" I said. "That man is very dangerous."

My sister shrugged again. *"He's just like you, Addy."*

I glared at her. It was one thing to accept Ed Regis into our ranks, but I wasn't going to be compared to him by anybody. "I am nothing like Ed Regis!" I said through clenched teeth.

Alia didn't reply. She just stared blankly back at me until I got too uncomfortable and turned away.

The next day, our last supper in the Refugee House was a comparatively quiet affair. Merlin joined us, but not Mrs. Harding, who was busy elsewhere. We sat together, Wolves and all, and Scott led the toast, wishing us a safe journey. Considering where we were going and the nature of our company, it would have been unrealistic for him to wish us a pleasant one.

With Scott as unit commander, Rachael, Candace, Heather, Daniel and Walter would stay here a few more days, at which time the last transport out of Walnut Lane would take them to the mountain camp. There they would officially be absorbed into the breakaway faction under Mrs. Harding, who seemed grateful for the reinforcements. I hoped that, in time, the other Walnut Guardians would accept them too.

Alia was late coming down to the dining room because she had been writing two long letters. The first, which she showed to no one, not even me, was addressed to Patrick. Knowing how close they had been, even Candace and Heather kept their teasing to a bare minimum. The second letter was addressed to baby Laila, in care of Patrick until Laila was old enough to read it. Alia knew that the chances of Laila ever being reunited with her parents were next to nil. She asked me to proofread this letter, which I did, correcting a few spelling mistakes but keeping the message unchanged. As for what my sister wanted to say to the baby, that is between her and Laila, and I will not share it here. Alia handed both envelopes to Scott. "I'll make sure Patrick gets them," Scott promised her.

For my part, I had only one painful goodbye to make, which I delayed till the morning of our departure.

"Keep training with Scott," I said to Candace as the first cold rays of sunlight splashed across our front lawn where two dark vans were waiting to take us to an airport. "Remember, like Terry keeps saying, your skills are only as good as you keep them."

Candace smiled. "Don't worry about me, Adrian. I'll be okay. We all will. You just take care of yourself. And take care of your sister, too."

"Always," I replied. Then, stumbling over my words a bit, I said, "I'm really sorry that you had to kill Steven."

"It's okay," said Candace. "I mean, it was horrible, and I'm still getting used to the idea that I killed a person, but this is the kind of thing you were training us for, after all."

I shook my head. "I never did want you to come on that raid, you know."

"I know that," said Candace, laughing embarrassedly. "I knew I wasn't ready to fight. I'm not exactly your star student."

I smiled. "That's true, but that's not why."

Candace looked at me for a moment, and then asked uncertainly, "Are you saying what I think you're saying?"

I was, albeit clumsily. "You once told me that I'd be in for a long wait, Candace. The truth is, waiting was never one of my strong points."

Ignoring the giggles and catcalls from the crowd, we let our lips touch for a moment, and then a few moments more.

Breaking apart from her, I said quickly, "I'll be back."

Candace grinned. "You better!"

And we were off.

Merlin was driving the van carrying all the Guardians, leaving Ed Regis and the other five Wolves in the second van.

As we pulled out of Walnut Lane, Terry nudged my shoulder and asked, "Don't you ever go for someone your own age?" Then she added nastily, "Or height?"

I ignored her, but then she asked more seriously, "Do you really think you're going to see her again?"

I shrugged as I gazed through the windshield at the Wolves' van. "Stranger things have happened."

Terry snickered. "You're still a dreamer."

Terry, James, Merlin, Alia and I, along with Ed Regis and his five Wolves, made us a party of eleven to the Historian's mountain. I sincerely hoped that all of us would make it safely there and back, but that was probably just the dreamer in me.

As our vans left the small town where we had lived and trained for eight months, I couldn't help thinking about the quirks of fate that had finally brought us to our attempt at making contact with the great Historian and asking for his aid in the Guardians' last stand against the Angels.

We had trained the lost children hoping to build us a private army, but things rarely turn out as planned. Two had died defending our home. While several of our trainees had made progress enough to storm a small Angel outpost, Terry and I agreed that only one was potentially up to the task we had been preparing them for. And even James wasn't nearly as ready as we wanted him to be.

But training the refugees had paid off in other ways. Taking down the Angel outpost saved Terry's life and kept Alia from being turned into an Angel. We found the allies we needed for our journey, thus sparing our charges, and even acquired the money that would buy us the Historian's favor. All in all, I had to conclude that training the children had been the right course.

But for Max and Felicity to not have died in vain, we would have to somehow succeed in our mission. And that wasn't just getting to the Historian, but all the way to Randal Divine. All the way to a world without master controllers.

This would be Terry's third trip to the Historian's mountain, but never had the approach been as heavily guarded by the Angels as it was now. I hoped that Terry could still find a safe (or at least non-lethal) path for us. But before she could do any guiding, Ed Regis would have to get us halfway around the world, which would be a difficult and dangerous journey in itself. I had never even crossed a border legally, and we weren't applying for passports for this journey.

What dangers would we face over the next few weeks? Were James and Alia really up to this? Was I? My primary motive behind this journey was still entirely personal, selfish even, but I considered it to be worth whatever risks we encountered. If anybody could help me find Cindy, or at least tell me what happened to her, it was the Historian.

By now, you might be wondering why I haven't mentioned the names of any of Ed Regis's Wolves. I was first introduced to the five soldiers back at the Angel outpost, and I did learn all of their names.

It's just that none of them lived long enough to really matter.

13. THE MOUNTAINS

I peered out of my small oval window on the left side of our dirty little twin-engine passenger plane. The desolate mountains far below had jagged peaks that looked like monstrous claws, and I didn't like how the engine on the right wing kept sputtering loudly as if it was getting ready to give its rusty propeller a permanent holiday.

Sitting in the pilot's seat in front of me, Ed Regis calmly flew our ancient, poorly maintained aircraft, with Terry on his right as copilot. Behind Terry sat Alia, who had been silently gazing out of her window at the sputtering engine for most of the last two hours. James and Merlin, sitting behind us, had been equally quiet, and I suspected we were all feeling the same tension about this flight.

Through Alia's window, I could see the second plane flying in close formation. Piloted by Ed Regis's second-in-command, it was carrying the Wolves and much of our supplies. The Wolves' plane looked just as likely to fall apart as ours did, and the only comfort I had was in the knowledge that if we landed safely, we would finally be on our very last step of this journey, just a few days hike from the Historian's mountain.

We had been traveling for two weeks now without major incident, by road, rail, sea and air. We had crossed seven international borders, but not once at an actual border checkpoint. Ed Regis certainly knew how to unofficially navigate the world.

That isn't to say it had all been easy. We once had to wade through a leech-infested swamp to evade border patrols. On another occasion, Ed Regis bribed a shipping company to slip us through customs, and we were stuffed into coffin-size boxes for nearly thirty hours. Still, as uncomfortable as our journey sometimes was, we were making definite progress.

The only real threat we encountered so far had been six days ago, when a group of Seraphim picked up our trail as we left the cover of human civilization. It was a member of Ed Regis's team that first spotted them coming, and thanks to the Wolves covering our escape, there were zero casualties on our side. Even Terry was vocally impressed with the efficiency of Ed Regis's men. The Wolves were, after all, an elite paramilitary unit specializing in anti-psionic operations, and we had been right to employ their help. Without them, we might never have made it this far.

Yesterday, in a sweltering, smelly trading post where people spoke in multiple languages I couldn't decipher, Ed Regis had rented two eight-seat passenger planes to get us to an unmarked airfield at the edge of the Historian's mountain range. Both planes were so frighteningly old and grimy that even I, who could telekinetically fly if the need arose, felt apprehensive about boarding. Unfortunately, it was either this or weeks on camel-back.

There were only two licensed pilots among us: Ed Regis and his second-in-command. Ed Regis agreed to fly the plane carrying us Guardians while his Wolves followed in the second plane. "I shall be your hostage," he had joked, but considering that he was our pilot, it felt like the other way around.

I had only just started getting comfortable with the sputtering right-wing engine and thinking that perhaps we would make it safely to the airfield after all when suddenly a loud bang jolted the cabin. At first I thought it was from the plane, but then I saw a puff of black smoke through my window.

Ed Regis shouted, "Incoming fire! Everybody hang on!"

We didn't need telling. As more bangs and black smoke filled the sky, I realized that they were exploding rounds of anti-aircraft fire. So far, we hadn't been hit, but each bang rattled the cabin so violently that I thought we might break apart in midair. Across the aisle, Alia looked as terrified as I felt, and I telekinetically yanked her seatbelt tight enough to make her squeal.

Through Alia's side window, I caught a glimpse of our second plane banking hard to the right, its underside exposed to us. But the next moment, the Wolves' plane turned into a giant, bright orange fireball, burning my eyes as the massive explosion rocked our plane.

Ed Regis put our plane into a steep dive twisting to the left. I felt my stomach jump into my throat as I clung on to my seatbelt for dear life.

"Hang on, everyone!" Ed Regis shouted again. "We're going to keep changing our heading and altitude till we're through this." Ed Regis pulled the plane out of its dive and into an equally steep climb. "Who the hell is shooting at us?!"

Who indeed? We couldn't be sure they were Seraphim since we didn't expect the Angels to have access to anti-aircraft guns. But according to the news, there were no human wars going on in this part of the world this month. Besides, we weren't illegally crossing any borders today and most normal people at least radio a warning before shooting down a civilian aircraft. Most likely, our attackers knew who they were trying to kill.

There were more bangs and pops as Ed Regis weaved our plane through the fire, and I expected to blink out of existence at any moment. But a nerve-racking minute later, the exploding rounds were left behind us as we cleared the gun range. Our plane was still banking to the left, though.

"We're in trouble," said Merlin from the seat behind me.

I looked out my window and saw what he was referring to. The left propeller had ground to a halt, the engine billowing black smoke. Worse yet, part of the wing beyond the engine had been torn away, leaving the left wing slightly shorter than the right.

"Losing oil pressure," announced Terry.

"I see it," replied Ed Regis, his voice tense but in control.

I looked diagonally behind me to see how James was doing. He just stared blankly back at me.

"Sorry, guys," said Ed Regis. "We're not going to make it."

"Keep her steady," commanded Terry as she unbuckled her seatbelt and stood from the copilot's seat. "We're going to jump."

Knowing the dangers, Terry and Ed Regis had prepared for this too, but not enough. We had only managed to get our hands on six parachutes at the last outpost, which meant that there were only three on each plane.

Quickly making her way to the rear, Terry announced, "Three chutes, six people. We're going tandem."

She passed one of the packs to Merlin, who said anxiously, "I've never used one of these before."

"I'll explain," said Terry. "Go get your weapons out of your bags now! Leave the rest. We're going as light as possible. Merlin will jump alone. I'll get James down. Major Regis, Alia. None for you, Adrian. Hold the plane for us."

"Typical," I muttered, unbuckling my seatbelt and standing up.

Grabbing my arm, Alia said in a shaky voice, "I'm scared."

"It'll be alright," I said, pulling free of her. "You go with Ed Regis. I'll meet you on the ground."

Terry had chosen the two jump pairs out of a pragmatic weight calculation. Alia, the lightest, with Ed Regis, the heaviest, which would be roughly the same weight as James and Terry combined. On principle, I really didn't like the idea of putting Alia's life in Ed Regis's hands, but I had to admit that the Wolf was the best qualified. Merlin was a first-time jumper, and we were so high up that I didn't trust myself to get Alia down safely.

I took the copilot's seat beside Ed Regis, saying crisply, "Get your chute on, Major. Try not to drop my sister."

"You can count on it," said Ed Regis, standing up. "See you on the ground, Adrian."

My heart was racing as I grabbed the yoke of our crippled plane. Back during our escape from New Haven, I had piloted our stolen airplane for a grand total of less than thirty minutes, and though I had the basics down, flying a broken antique solo wasn't supposed to be in my job description. Without its left-wing engine, the plane felt horribly sluggish and wouldn't fly straight.

I heard Alia cry into my head, *"No, Addy! I want to go with you!"*

"No arguing!" I called back, fighting the controls to keep the plane level. "You promised, Alia! Go with Ed Regis!"

I heard Ed Regis say calmly, "Don't worry, kid. I'll get you down in one piece."

Suddenly there was another loud bang. Turning my head, I watched in horror as the engine on the right wing also sputtered to a halt. Whether it had been damaged by the guns or had simply failed due to stress was anybody's guess, but we were losing airspeed fast.

"Make it quick!" I shouted, feeling the controls becoming increasingly unstable. "I don't know how long we have."

Behind me, Terry was giving Merlin a crash course on how to use his parachute, saying, "Here's your pull string. Yank it hard, but not till you see the rocks rushing up to meet you. If the Angels see you floating down, that's where they'll shoot you."

"Is there a reserve chute?" asked Merlin.

"Yes, but if you do this right, you won't have time to use it. Delay your pull to the last second."

"I don't know if I can do this, Terry," Merlin said worriedly.

"Relax. It's not like you have a choice. Just keep your cool and you'll be okay."

I didn't have time to worry too much over the fact that Merlin was being asked to perform a dangerous low-altitude pull on his very first jump. The whole airplane was beginning to shudder.

Suddenly a high-pitched alarm filled the cockpit, and Terry called to me, "Stall warning, Adrian! Bring the nose down a bit. Watch your airspeed."

I did, and the alarm turned off. But our lopsided plane kept trying to bank to the left, and if I stopped countering it, I feared we would quickly be upside down or worse.

The cabin filled with swirling wind as somebody opened the side door. I could barely hear Terry shout over the noise, "Alright! Merlin first! Go! Go! Now, Merlin! Come on! Jump now! Major Regis, you next!"

Alia was shouting something into my head, but I ignored her, my concentration focused on the yoke and pedals, and Alia's telepathic voice faded away a moment later.

"Terry, tell me when you jump!" I shouted. I didn't want to turn my head.

"Hold on!" said Terry. "A couple of last-minute things."

"We don't have a couple of minutes, Terry!"

Terry ignored me, shouting, "James, throw those bags out. We might find them later."

The plane began to shudder again.

"I think we'd better go too, Terry," said James, his voice understandably panicked.

"Just wait!" said Terry. "I'm looking for something!"

But our airplane wasn't in a waiting mood. The left wing suddenly dipped sharply, and I heard Terry and James lose their balance and tumble onto the floor. I tilted the nose down a bit more and restored some airspeed, but there was no way to level us out anymore. The mountain peaks were looking dangerously close now.

Terry shouted, "Damn it, Adrian! Can't you keep her steady?"

"Do I look like a pilot to you?!" I shot back furiously. "What the hell are you looking for back there, anyway?"

Instead of answering me, Terry cursed loudly and then cried in a panicked voice, "No! No! No! It's not here!"

"Then get out *now!*" I hollered.

"Alright, alright! We're going!" said Terry, and then asked, "But how are you going to get to the door?"

"I'll think of something! Just go, Terry!" I begged. "Go now! I'm losing her!"

"Alright! James, hang on to me!"

I waited another ten rapid heartbeats, which I hoped was enough time for Terry and James to get out. Then I jumped out of the copilot's seat, scrambling madly toward the open cabin door.

But before I took two steps, the whole cabin began to swirl around me. The plane had gone into a spinning nosedive with me still in it! Something mildly soft shoved my left arm, and then I hit my forehead against something much harder. Everything was a blur, and I felt like I was in a washing machine's spin cycle. Where was the exit?!

Almost entirely by chance, my right hand caught the edge of the open door and, with some help from my telekinetic power, I managed to pull myself through. As soon as I cleared the door, I used my telekinesis to kick-stop in midair. A second later, the airplane smacked into the rocky mountainside and exploded. I found myself close enough to the ground to feel the heat of the flames.

Distancing myself from the wreckage and dropping safely to the ground, I looked around at my new surroundings. The mountain slope was moderately gentle here, but there were high peaks in every direction. The terrain reminded me of pictures I had once seen in a science textbook—specifically pictures of the surface of Mars. We had literally fallen into a world of yellowish-brown earth and jagged rocks, with hardly any vegetation and not a single tree in any direction.

I saw only one parachute—Terry's—touch down several hundred yards away. Where were the other two?

Due to Terry's unexpected delay, Merlin, Alia and Ed Regis could be far behind us, either on the other side of this mountain or on another one entirely. I couldn't even be sure which direction we had been flying.

Still moderately high on adrenaline, I used my telekinesis to push off from the ground and fly over to Terry and James, who were busy freeing themselves of their parachute.

"Adrian!" called James. "Are you alright?"

"I'm fine," I replied, landing beside them. "Where are the others?"

Terry took a quick look up at the sun and then pointed to the nearest peak. "Behind that, I think."

"Then let's go find them," James said hurriedly.

"We will, James," said Terry. "Just calm down. We have to sort ourselves out first."

Worried about my sister, I felt just as impatient as James, but I agreed with Terry. Considering what we had just come through, a minute of calm thinking was definitely in order. Though lucky to be alive at all, we had lost all of our supplies, including...

"The stones," said Terry. "We lost the stones."

"What stones?" I asked. There were rocks and stones in every direction.

"The box wasn't on our plane. It was on the Wolf plane."

I stared at her until I understood what she meant. Then I gasped. The bag containing the jewels for the Historian was gone! We had hidden it inside a wooden crate containing our bottled water and hiking food. That was what Terry had been looking for before she jumped, but in order to balance the load between the two airplanes, I had stowed that crate on the second plane myself.

Terry let out a dejected huff. "I can just imagine some goat herder finding the wrecked plane and making off with our fortune."

We had lost more than food, water and gemstones. Ed Regis's entire team had burned up in midair, instantly cutting our numbers nearly in half. But even if I had it in me to mourn the deaths of five Wolves, I certainly had no room for such thoughts now. I was still getting used to the idea of still being alive, and wondering how we were going to stay that way for the foreseeable future.

James asked hesitantly, "So, um, what now?"

"We're going to the Historian," decided Terry. "We've come this far so there's no sense in turning back now. Who knows what he'll say to me when I arrive without gifts for the second time, though."

That was something to worry about later.

Terry turned to me and said, "Get yourself a bird's-eye view and see if you can't find the bags we tossed."

I did, levitating myself up fifty yards or so, but I couldn't spot any lost luggage.

"See anything?" Terry called up to me.

"No," I called back. "But there are a lot of big rocks and our bags might be behind or between them."

"Okay, forget it," said Terry. "Come on down before someone sees you."

As I landed, James asked Terry, "You think there are people living on these mountains?"

"People live just about everywhere," replied Terry, "but I'm more worried about the Angels right now. We'll have to assume that those guns were fired from an Angel-controlled camp, and that they know we're here, and about where our plane crashed."

"That's a lot of assumption," I remarked.

"Better than being caught with our pants down," said Terry. "We're sniper bait here."

I looked nervously around at the surrounding peaks. Were there Angels heading our way even as we spoke? Without Merlin to hide me, my psionic power would be a beacon for the Angels to home in on, whereas any Angel patrol approaching us would be protected by their own hiders. Playing cat and mouse was never fun for the mouse, but especially so when the mouse had to wear a beeper collar and the cat was invisible.

Easily reading my mind, Terry said, "Hopefully we'll find Merlin's group on the other side."

"So what do we have?" I asked.

"Not much," replied Terry, shaking her head. "Food and water were on the other plane, and since you couldn't spot our bags, we lost the tents and stuff too. Still, I got my pistol and two spare clips."

I smiled. "And your hook."

James also had his pistol and spare clips. I was the only one unarmed, having left my pistol in one of the bags. The lack of food, water and shelter was troubling, but that, like the gemstones, was something to worry about later. At least we were already dressed for hiking, boots and all.

"Let's get going," I said. "The sooner we find the others, the sooner you can lead us all to the Historian, and the less time we'll spend being hungry, thirsty and cold."

"Agreed," said Terry. "But what makes you think I know the way to the Historian?"

I froze solid. "Excuse me?"

James looked just as shocked, asking slowly, "Are you saying that you don't know the way from here, Terry?"

Terry shrugged. "The last time I came, I entered these mountains from the other side."

"We're lost?!" I asked, horrified at the thought.

"Not if you can show us the way," answered Terry. "I'm not the guide here, Adrian. You are."

I just stared at her until she asked, "Can't you feel him?"

I slowly turned around on the spot, calming my breathing. Then I pointed to the northeast and said confidently, "That way."

"Good," said Terry, nodding. "Then I was right about the general direction."

Now that I was tuned in, the Historian's multiple and exceptionally potent destroyer powers were easily identifiable. So much so that even I, who usually couldn't tell the actual direction of a psionic power, could point to the Historian as easily as if I had a psionic compass in my head. It was actually harder to accurately gauge the distance this time because the Historian's power was so intense. I suspected that he was at least a hundred miles away, possibly much more.

"Merlin and company first," said Terry. "Let's go find them."

By the position of the sun, I guessed that it was a little past midday. The air was dry and chilly, but refreshingly clear. Breathing deeply, I scanned the mountain range as we climbed, looking out for any signs of movement.

Despite our precarious situation, I couldn't help being inspired by how beautiful and utterly merciless the terrain looked. Only the highest peaks were snowcapped, but the air was somewhat thin, making it hard to walk quickly. Some dry and thorny bushes were growing here and there, but they just added to the desolation. Looking up, I saw a few scattered clouds not far above us, and the sky was a deeper blue than I was used to. This was a truly different world from the one we had left back in Walnut Lane.

We plodded steadily on without talking, making our way westward up to the lowest part of the gap between two peaks. I couldn't be sure about Merlin, but I was confident that Ed Regis would know which direction to lead his group in order to meet up with us. With any luck, we would rendezvous with them at or near the gap. The slope got steeper as we went, and Terry and James had to crawl on their hands and knees to get over some of the rockier parts of the climb. I simply levitated myself over the hard parts.

"Don't tire yourself out doing that," said Terry, clearly annoyed at how easy it was for me. "You never know when you'll need your power for something more important."

"Don't worry," I said, grinning at her. "I'm pacing myself."

It made sense too, since I couldn't risk cutting myself on the rocks for fear of losing my power completely. But even I couldn't simply fly up to the top of the mountain. It was too far up, and though I was worried about Alia, I didn't want to lose sight of Terry and James. Whenever possible, I walked.

As the sun began its slow descent toward the western peaks, the three of us cleared the gap and found what was on the other side, which was...

"Nothing," I breathed, desperately looking around for my sister. Where had Alia and Ed Regis landed? Where was Merlin?

James asked Terry, "Are you sure they landed over here, Terry?"

Terry shook her head. "Pretty sure, but not certain. It kind of depends on how straight the plane was flying when we jumped. Maybe they landed on this slope, but had to move elsewhere to evade capture."

Or maybe they *had* been captured. Shaking my head, I quickly forced the thought out of my mind. There was nothing to be gained by entertaining my fears when we still had no idea what really happened to them.

"Alright, change of plan," announced Terry. "We're going straight toward the Historian. Merlin and Alia can sense him too, so we can all use the Historian as our magnetic north. If we're lucky, we'll meet up with them somewhere on the way."

I wasn't at all happy with this plan, but unable to suggest another, I agreed. Terry suspected that my sister's group was slightly ahead of us rather than behind, but there was no way to be sure.

As we started walking again, James looked at me and said quietly, "I really hope Alia is okay."

"Alia is with Ed Regis," I replied in as confident a tone as I could muster. "I'm sure she's fine."

James chuckled. "I thought you didn't like that man."

I gave James a grim smile. "You don't have to like someone to respect their skills. That Wolf just lost his whole team. He knows better than to lose another."

With Ed Regis and Merlin to take care of her, my sister's chances would be no worse than ours.

Terry said, "At least Merlin can hide Alia's power, so those three won't be as easily hunted as us."

I remembered Ed Regis's words about how professionals always put the mission first. "Maybe you guys will be better off if I'm not here," I suggested. "There's no way to hide my power from the Angels."

"Together or not at all, remember?" said Terry, repeating what I had said to her before we jumped from the roof of NH-1. "Besides, how are we going to find the Historian without you to guide us, dummy? Don't worry. We just need to get to Merlin before the Angels find us."

We turned northeast now, heading in the general direction of the Historian's power, and soon we were carefully making our way down a moderately steep, boulder-infested mountainside. I quickly discovered that descending wasn't any easier than climbing: It used a totally different set of muscles and there was a greater risk of slips and falls. In less than two hours, we had to stop for the night. The night sky was nearly cloudless and the moon was just beginning to wane, which meant that it was bright enough for us to see each other's faces without flashlights, but too dark to walk safely on the rocky slope.

"Break a leg out here and you're dead for sure," warned Terry.

Our trekking clothes were thick and warm, but not enough to keep us from shivering a bit in the cold night air. We took cover behind the largest boulder we could find, but it did little to shield us from the biting wind which began to blow soon after sunset. We huddled as closely as we could, shoulders touching, curled up and hugging our bodies to keep warm.

"It's not so cold that we'd die in our sleep," said Terry, "so we'd better sleep. I'll take first watch. James can have the midnight shift, and then wake up Adrian. Try to sleep as much as you can. It's going to be a long day tomorrow."

"I thought it was a pretty long day today," I said, and then suddenly I couldn't help laughing to myself.

"What is it, Half-head?" asked Terry.

"Nothing," I said, still chuckling. "I was just imagining Alia huddled up somewhere out there with Merlin and—and Ed Regis!"

Terry laughed too. "That kid has no fear."

I stopped laughing and said quietly, "Only in the daytime."

"We'll find her, Adrian. Just get some sleep."

It's hard to stay warm on an empty stomach, and I doubt James and Terry slept any better than I did that night.

The dawn was cold and uninviting, but at least the wind had died down during the night.

"Let's get going," said Terry, and we did.

We plodded steadily along all day, mostly without talking, doing our best to ignore our parched mouths and rumbling stomachs. There was nothing edible to be found on these barren mountains, but early that evening, we were fortunate enough to come across a narrow river running between two slopes. The icy water was clean and refreshing, and I took hope in the knowledge that if Alia's group was heading toward the Historian, they would no doubt have crossed this river too. We didn't have any bottles to carry the water in, but the outer layer of our hiking clothes were nylon raincoats which, once we made some crude adjustments, worked nearly as well.

Water was a poor excuse for sustenance, however, and that night felt even colder than the first.

"I'd like to find Alia before her birthday if at all possible," I said as I stretched out my painfully cramped muscles in the chilly morning sunlight.

Alia's finding day, March 24th, was the day after tomorrow.

"She's going to be eleven, right?" asked James.

"Theoretically," I said, since no one knew exactly how old she was. "And assuming she's still alive."

But we didn't see Alia's group that day or the next. Fortunately, we met no Angels either.

Terry had a theory on the lack of pursuit: "First off, we're still a good long distance from the Historian, and very few people attempt to reach him from this side of the mountains. Most of the Angels are probably guarding the common access route from the east. They know we're here, though, so it's only a matter of time."

"What about the guns that brought down our plane?" asked James.

"I still think they were Angels or hired by Angels," replied Terry. "But they may be non-psionic, in which case they won't be able to sense Adrian's power. Or perhaps they can and they're trailing us at a distance as they wait for reinforcements. Who knows?"

From then on, James kept looking over his shoulder as he walked. I didn't have the energy left to bother. We had been going without meals now for three days, and it was taking its toll. I no longer had the strength to levitate myself over the difficult parts of the journey, and my legs felt as heavy as the boulders we had to navigate. Even Terry was running on vapors, and I feared for my sister's group, which had also jumped without supplies.

We had no maps, and really no idea where we were. All we had was a heading, and there was no straight line to the Historian. Without ropes or any proper mountain climbing equipment, we had to carefully choose our routes, which often took us in wide arcs around the jagged peaks. Sometimes we would get to the top of a relatively mild slope only to discover that the other side was a sheer cliff, and I wasn't about to attempt another controlled descent with Terry and James hanging on to me. The going was slow and we still saw no sign of the rest of our team. We spent another cold night on the rocks.

In the mid-afternoon of Alia's eleventh birthday, as we reached the top of yet another gap between two peaks, Terry asked, "How far do you think the Historian is, Adrian?"

"I can't tell," I replied honestly. "We're getting closer, but I don't think we've even come a quarter of the way."

"We need food," said Terry. "We're not going to make it much farther if we can't find anything to eat."

James, who had so far refused to complain about this basic problem with our forced march, nodded weakly. "I feel like we're walking in circles. These mountains all look alike."

We weren't, but James had a point. And I knew that Terry's real fear wasn't dying of starvation, but how weak we might be when the Angels finally decided to pounce.

"We'll just have to keep going," Terry said resolutely. "We still might find something beyond the next mountain."

That didn't sound very promising, but as I let my eyes wander down the slope, across the miles of desolate yellowish-brown terrain that we would have to cross before we could even begin climbing the next mountain, I saw something that made me do a double take before I believed it.

"Alia has been here," I said quietly.

"How do you know?" asked Terry.

"It's written in the rocks."

Terry stared at me. "Have you lost your mind, Adrian?"

I pointed downward to a collection of seventeen large brown rocks set in a pattern on the ground near the bottom of our slope. Terry couldn't read them but she recognized the writing. "Braille," she said, nodding. "That's her alright. What does it say?"

"Hansel," I read.

"There's probably a message near it," said Terry. "Let's try to get down there before nightfall."

We did, but only just. In the fading light, we discovered hundreds of little holes carefully patterned along the bottom of my Guardian call sign. The Braille dots looked like they had been made by pressing the tip of a bullet into the soft earth. Alia had chosen her words carefully just in case someone aside from me out here could decipher Braille, and I couldn't help smiling as I read her secret message.

"Well, tell us what it says already!" Terry commanded impatiently.

"Happy birthday to me," I read aloud. "Already got two presents yesterday, but I think more are coming. This morning I'm taking my dog to the swimming pool first and then we'll head to the party. Hope to see you there. Gretel."

"What the heck does that mean?" asked James. "Is there a lake around here or something?"

Terry shook her head. "Today's her birthday, so they were here this morning. There was a swimming pool a few blocks east from New Haven One. They're headed east around the mountain before continuing toward the Historian."

I glanced at the eastern slope, which was by far the easier climb compared to the steep north face.

"Clever girl," commented James, shaking his head in wonder.

"Too clever," I said dryly. Alia's "dog" was no doubt the Wolf, while "presents" were probably Angels.

"She didn't mention Merlin," said Terry. "She thinks he's with us."

"Damn," breathed James. "I wonder what happened to him."

"He may still be alive," said Terry, though she didn't sound very convinced herself. "More importantly for us, if Major Regis bagged a pair of Seraphim, they'll probably have food and water."

"We're a day behind," I said. "We'll have to double-time it tomorrow if we're going to catch up."

"Especially if they're moving on full stomachs," agreed Terry, "but that should be incentive enough for us to pick up the pace tomorrow."

Incentive it was, but willpower alone couldn't speed up our legs very much the next day. We were out of water again, and I'm sure that I wasn't the only one feeling dizzy with each step we took. We didn't realize it at the time, but our average elevation was gradually increasing with every mountain we crossed, so the air was getting thinner.

But even altitude sickness, gnawing hunger, thirst, and the pain in our legs were not the worst of our problems on the mountains. To varying degrees, we had all learned to deal pretty well with physical discomfort. The real problem was the sheer monotony of the landscape compounded with the fact that we had to take each step carefully to avoid slips and possibly fatal falls. That, combined with the constant strain of not knowing if and when we might come under fire, stretched our nerves to their limits.

Stumbling, occasionally crawling, we reached the top of the eastern slope in the early afternoon. I wanted to stop and catch my breath, but not until I had a look down the other side of the mountain where I hoped to see the distant shapes of Alia and Ed Regis.

"They're following you," said a rough voice from my left that nearly stopped my heart.

James and I spun toward the source of the voice, James drawing his pistol as I prepared to throw a blast from my right hand.

Ed Regis, sitting calmly on a large boulder, merely smiled.

Terry, equally composed, said, "I know that, Major. They've been following us for the last three days. But I don't think they're actually Seraphim. Just common Angels, or maybe even hired guns. They're waiting for reinforcements."

"Which will come soon, I'm guessing," said Ed Regis. "The two scouts we ran into the day before yesterday were unmistakably Seraphim, and I'm sorry to report that they managed to give our position away before I got them."

I had many questions, but the most pressing one was, "Where's my sister?"

"Taking a nap under the sun," replied Ed Regis, pointing at a large rock formation behind him. "We saw you three coming toward our little message yesterday afternoon and decided to wait for you here."

Wanting to see for myself, I ignored the pain it was causing my weakened body and levitated myself up several yards. Alia was lying curled up on a sleeping bag spread out over a large flat rock. Next to her were two tall, dark gray backpacks.

"I'd let her rest, Adrian," said Ed Regis. "I'm sure she could use it."

I agreed and let myself drop back down. Then I said crossly to Terry, "You should have told us that we were being followed."

James nodded in agreement, but Terry said coolly, "And the two of you should have noticed. They weren't all that hard to spot, you know."

I scowled at her, but James hadn't seen anything either so at least I didn't have to feel like a total idiot.

Terry continued, "Anyway, I didn't want to worry you over a non-threat. They've been keeping their distance, always one mountain behind us. I'm pretty sure there're only three of them."

I asked Ed Regis, "You haven't seen Merlin, have you?" After reading

Alia's Braille message yesterday, I wasn't very hopeful, but I still had to make sure.

"We haven't seen Merlin since our jump," replied Ed Regis. "We had been hoping that he joined up with your group."

"Our jump was delayed," I explained. "Merlin should have landed closer to you."

"He did, but not close enough," said Ed Regis, shaking his head. "I pulled my chute pretty close to the ground, but I think Merlin opened his up the moment he left the plane. I saw his chute in the air. The wind took him over a different peak from where we landed."

I narrowed my eyes. "And you didn't try to find him?"

"The terrain was too rough in that direction to cross without our gear," said Ed Regis, looking at me apologetically. "I had to look after Alia, too. And I figured that since Merlin could home in on the Historian just like you and Alia could, if we all set off in the same direction, we would meet up in a day or two. But the truth is that I'm not even sure if Merlin landed safely."

"I hope he's still alive," said James.

"Me too," said Ed Regis.

There was no reason to doubt the Wolf's sincerity. He had, after all, brought Alia this far. I forced a smile, saying, "Hopefully we'll meet up with Merlin soon."

As worried as I was for Merlin's safety, his continued absence presented a serious problem for us too. How were we ever going to get through these mountains without Merlin's hiding protection? We were already being followed by a team of Angels or mercenaries or whatever, and no doubt more were on the way.

At the moment, however, we had far more pressing physical issues to resolve.

"We haven't eaten in five days, Major," said Terry, and James and I nodded fervently.

Ed Regis grinned. "I have some canned food."

"We'd love some canned food."

Ed Regis quietly retrieved one of the backpacks from Alia's side and produced some processed meat that looked a lot like dog food but tasted divine. Ed Regis didn't join our meal, explaining that he and Alia had already eaten just before Alia lay down for her nap.

As we ate the food Ed Regis had taken from the Angel scouts, I wondered if Alia had tried to stop the Wolf from killing them. What had my sister's journey been like? Without Merlin, Alia's only company in these mountains all this time had been Ed Regis. Though I hated to admit it, I now felt grateful to Ed Regis for having taken extra pains to get to know Alia before leaving Walnut Lane.

"Try to eat slowly," said Ed Regis. "Alia says we're still a good long ways from the Historian. We'll have to ration this carefully."

In addition to the canned meat, Ed Regis had acquired a fair supply of beef jerky, wheat crackers, chocolate bars, dried fruits, nuts and other hiking foods, but it was hard to guess how long the five of us could make it last. Fortunately, my stomach had shrunk so much that it didn't take a lot to fill me up, and though I still felt physically weak after eating, at least my telekinetic power was nicely recharged.

"I suppose we should get going," said Terry, and Ed Regis nodded in agreement.

"I'll go wake her," I said, levitating back up to Alia's rock.

Landing beside my sister, I gently shook her shoulders, saying, "Rise and shine, sleepyhead."

Opening her eyes, Alia instantly threw her arms around my neck, but I had been ready for that, so we didn't go tumbling off the rock.

"You made it, Addy!" Alia cried in my head. *"You're here!"*

"Happy birthday," I said, holding her tightly and rubbing her back. "Sorry we were late."

"I'm so happy you're okay."

Breaking apart from her, I gingerly fingered her horribly dusty hair. "You need a bath, Ali."

Alia touched my chin and laughed. *"You need a shave."*

My sister was equally thrilled to be reunited with Terry, and even gave James a hug.

Once Alia calmed down a bit, she looked around at us hesitantly, and I knew what she wanted to ask. Having seen us from this mountain yesterday, Alia already knew that there were only three of us.

"We haven't seen Merlin either," I told her quietly. "We always thought he was with you and Ed Regis."

Alia nodded dully, and I wondered if she was about to sink into one of her silences.

Grasping her hands, I said firmly, "Don't give up on him yet, Alia. We don't know what happened to him, so there's no use worrying. We still might run into him somewhere in these mountains. Who knows? We might even find him waiting for us at the Historian's house."

Alia slowly nodded, giving me a weak smile as she said, "I hope he's not hurt."

"Me too," I said. "For now, we'll just have to keep hoping for the best, okay?"

Alia nodded again, her smile a little more confident, and I breathed a silent sigh of relief.

Terry nudged me with her hook and said, "Hey, aren't you forgetting something, Adrian? Something small, green and needlessly expensive?"

"Oh, right," I said, grateful for the change of topic. I hastily pulled out a wrinkly paper package that I had kept hidden in my pocket ever since leaving Walnut Lane. It was fortunate that I had it on me when our planes came under fire.

Passing the package to Alia, I said, "Happy eleventh, Alia. You probably think you know what's in this, but you don't."

Carefully opening it, Alia pulled out her new bloodstone pendant. Hanging from a thin leather cord, the dark green stone speckled with red spots had been cut and polished in the shape of...

"A unicorn!" Alia exclaimed in delight. "It's so pretty!"

"Happy birthday," I said again.

"Oh, thank you, Addy!"

This hadn't been an easy present to get, not only because I had to sneak out of the house in the daytime without Merlin's hiding protection, but because unicorn-shaped bloodstones weren't commonly sold at the local rare-stones dealer. I had my sister's new pendant specially designed and made just for her, and the expedited service needed to get it done before our departure came only with Terry's grudging consent to use some of the money that we had taken from the Angels' house.

"Now that's from both me and Terry," I informed her.

"Thank you, Terry!" said Alia, holding the little unicorn up. "I love it!"

Terry laughed embarrassedly, saying, "Well, hurry up and put it on."

"Yeah," I agreed, "and give me back mine already."

Alia returned Cat's amethyst, which felt comfortingly familiar around my neck. Then we resumed our northeasterly march, beginning yet another slow and painful descent.

The two backpacks that Ed Regis had taken from the scouts were heavy even for the Wolf, who had been carrying both by himself for the last two days. James and I agreed to take turns carrying the second pack, but it was James who ended up doing most of the carrying. He was bigger than me, after all.

Our new supplies included one small tent, two thick sleeping bags, hiking food, bottled water, miscellaneous mountain gear, and the warm mountain clothes Ed Regis had stripped from the dead bodies. "We can use them as blankets," said Ed Regis. The clothes had bullet holes and dried blood on them, but that kind of thing wouldn't matter when you were cold at night.

As we carefully walked down the mountainside, my mind briefly wandered back to our last moments in the crippled airplane, to the fear in Merlin's voice as Terry explained to him how to use the parachute. Had Merlin been injured in his landing? Had he fallen from a cliff? Had the Angels caught him and sent him to Randal Divine for conversion? Under the circumstances, it was hard not to imagine the worst.

But as I had just said to my sister, worrying wasn't going to solve anything. Besides, Merlin was a hider and a puppeteer, and a trained Guardian Knight. He had saved my life in the Angels' house. He certainly wasn't helpless, and who was to say we wouldn't run into him tomorrow or the next day? It was even possible that we really would find him waiting for us at the Historian's home.

Always assuming, of course, that we made it that far ourselves...

"I'm almost afraid to ask," I said to Alia, who was walking beside me and occasionally grabbing on to my arm for support as we descended the slope, "but how are you enjoying your adventure so far?"

My sister looked tired and weathered, but nevertheless in pretty decent condition under the circumstances. Perhaps too out of breath to speak aloud, she replied telepathically, *"I don't regret coming, if that's what you're asking. But I'm not enjoying it. I really missed you, Addy. Terry too. And I'm still worried about Merlin, and sad about what happened to Ed's friends."*

I grimaced at Alia's mention of "Ed's friends." More concerned with our immediate survival, I still hadn't given much thought to the five Wolves who had perished with the second airplane. But those men had been an important part of our team too, and unlike Merlin, there was no chance of finding them alive. I did feel bad about that, but at least for now, Alia could keep the damn handkerchief.

"It was pretty scary at night," said Alia. "But Ed always kept me safe."

"He's a soldier," I said brusquely. "That's his job."

Ignoring my tone, Alia continued, *"It wasn't easy getting over some of the really rocky parts of the mountains we climbed. Ed had to carry me a lot. After the Angel scouts, sometimes he had to make two trips, one for the extra backpack and one for me."*

I let out a resigned huff. "You really like him, don't you?"

Alia walked a few steps in silence before answering, *"I know you don't trust him, Addy. It took me a long time too, and I still don't know if we're really friends. It's not like I forgot what he did to us. But I think he's changed."*

I gave a non-committal, "Hmm."

Alia looked away. *"Maybe not a whole lot. I mean, he shot the two Angels, one of them while he was running away. But you and Terry kill people too. And I've helped."*

"You have, and I'm sorry you had to."

"Ed doesn't like hurting people any more than we do."

I stopped walking and looked at her. "You still think he's like me?"

Alia gazed thoughtfully into my eyes for a moment, and then said carefully, *"Maybe you can't believe that, but I think there's just something inside him. Something that hurts him, Addy. Something really sad. That's why I said he was kind of like you."*

I didn't know how to reply to that, so I just smiled and said, "I'm glad he took good care of you."

Alia nodded. *"We're still alive. My feet really hurt, though. Ed isn't the kind of person you ask for a piggyback ride unless you really need it."*

"You can have one now if you like," I offered, noticing that Alia's legs were a bit wobbly. "You're probably lighter than James's backpack."

14. THE HUNT BEGINS

We made fairly decent progress for the rest of that day, completing our descent and getting more than halfway up the next slope before sundown. It wasn't easy finding a flat space big enough for our tent, small as it was, but we did. Designed for two, the tent was just barely large enough to squeeze four of us in, but that was okay since one would always be on watch outside.

We couldn't have made a campfire even if there was wood to burn, but nobody complained about the cold dinner. We did our best to eat slowly.

"If we're careful, we might be able to stretch this for another five or six days," said Ed Regis, "but water is going to be a problem sooner. Hopefully we'll find another river on the way."

"Hopefully we'll get to kill a few more Angels and take their supplies," said Terry.

I couldn't be sure if Terry was being serious, though, because we weren't equipped for a major confrontation.

Like Terry and James, Ed Regis was armed only with a pair of pistols, and Alia and I had nothing. Ed Regis offered me one of his, but I declined. In such a large, open area, the comparatively short range and poor accuracy of a handgun were going to be mortal disadvantages against anyone carrying a proper rifle, so I saw little point in carrying Ed Regis's spare. Terry knew this too, of course, but her assault rifle, along with everyone else's, had been on the second plane with the Wolves. To make matters worse, the two psionic scouts that Ed Regis had killed hadn't been armed with conventional weapons, relying solely on their psionic powers.

"So what were they?" I couldn't help asking over dinner.

Ed Regis replied, "One of them was a telekinetic, fairly strong, but not enough to fly. I can't be sure, but I think he was the finder. The other guy was a puppeteer like Merlin. It was pretty hard blocking him."

I looked at him in surprise. "You can block controllers?"

"Of course. Blocking is a standard part of training for all Wolves."

"So where do they get the training dummies?" I asked accusingly.

But it was Terry who answered, "There are plenty of traitor psionics who help the Wolves in return for money and protection."

Ed Regis shook his head. "We do have some collaborators on our side, but it's also true that not all of our teachers are willing participants in the program."

I wondered if some of those unwilling participants were former inmates of the PRC, but I didn't ask. Nor was there reason to pass too harsh judgment on the Wolves. The Guardians had done plenty of equally deplorable things over the years. Besides, had Ed Regis not known how to block controllers, my second sister might already be en route to Randal Divine to join my first. It was time to change the subject.

I asked, "Do you think those guys following us are ever going to attack?"

Earlier that evening, James and I finally got to see the group that had been trailing us for the last few days. There were three men, mere specks in the distance, one mountain behind us just as Terry said. Ed Regis got a closer look at the trio through a pair of binoculars he had taken from the scouts, and he told us that all three of our pursuers were armed with scoped rifles, not military grade, but probably semi-automatic.

"They'll attack alright, but not until they're good and ready," said Terry. "We really should take them out before they get reinforced."

I knew Terry had been itching to do just that for days now, but it was impossible to get close to them without their seeing us. And they had the range advantage. Even with Terry and Ed Regis's formidable battle skills, we couldn't hope to remove our pesky tail without a fair amount of risk. Besides, killing them wouldn't blind the Angels to our position. Any decent finder could easily locate Alia and me on these mountains.

"I could try taking them from the air during the night," I suggested.

"They probably wouldn't be able to hit me if I was flying."

Terry shook her head. "If those hunting rifles could shoot a bird out of the air, I'm sure they could get you too. Just because you're a runt doesn't mean you're smaller than a bird."

I was used to Terry's cracks about my size so I didn't let it bother me. "A bird doesn't know bullets," I countered in a reasonable tone. "And it'd be dark and they wouldn't be expecting me."

"It could work," said Terry, smirking. "If you're that willing to risk your life, you're welcome to give it a shot. But you might want to ask Alia first. After all, she's the one who's going to have to heal your gunshot wound."

I took one look at the expression on my sister's face and deflated. "Maybe not tonight."

I was still hungry after eating, but I suppose we all were, and not even Alia complained aloud. Terry assigned the night watch. I was to go first, followed by Ed Regis, then James, and Terry last. Alia was given a pass due to her age.

Also by virtue of her age, Alia was automatically given one of the two sleeping bags, which looked far more comfortable than the dead men's clothes. Terry suggested we draw lots for the other bag, and James won.

I said jokingly, "I'm second youngest. Doesn't that count for anything?"

Terry laughed. "No, but you're welcome to snuggle in with Alia like always."

Not that I hadn't considered it, but the sleeping bags weren't all that roomy. There was no telling when we would have to spring into action, and the thought of trying to wiggle out of a bag while being pounded by gunfire wasn't very attractive.

Even so, I guessed that just being inside the tent and shielded from the wind would be a vast improvement in comfort, especially since the body heat of four people in a two-man tent would keep us all plenty warm. As the others sealed themselves in, I bid them goodnight and sat on the uneven ground between two boulders.

I was shivering slightly, but comforted by the notion that, even though we still weren't psionically hidden, we were now five strong, fed and sheltered. In but a moment I heard my sister's familiar telepathic mumbling. It might have been impossible to hear approaching footsteps over the sound of the wind and Alia's voice in my head, but fortunately none came during my watch. At nearly midnight, I unzipped the tent door, reached in and shook Ed Regis's foot until he woke.

Silently crawling out of the tent, Ed Regis stretched and asked, "How has it been?"

"Quiet," I answered.

"Go on inside," said Ed Regis. "I'll take it from here."

When I didn't move, Ed Regis asked, "What is it, Adrian?"

I opened my mouth to speak, but then closed it again. Ed Regis looked at me quizzically.

Gazing up at his weathered face, I remembered how hard it had been for me to beg this man's assistance back in the basement of the Angels' house. But sometimes you just have to stow your pride and say something that needs to be said.

"Thank you, Ed Regis," I said quietly. "Thank you for watching over my sister."

Ed Regis smiled. "You're welcome."

"I'm glad you're with us. And I am sorry about your men."

"They knew the risks," Ed Regis said matter-of-factly. "But thank you. I hope your friend is okay."

I nodded. "I'm sure Merlin knew the risks too."

Ed Regis asked hesitantly, "Are you sure that you're glad I'm here?"

I shrugged. "Mission first, right? Nothing personal?"

"That's right."

"Alia likes you a lot."

"She's a good kid," Ed Regis said softly. "I wouldn't hurt her again."

"Then I'm glad you're here," I assured him.

Ed Regis chuckled. "You want to know something funny? I spent three years learning mental blocking, but for the life of me, I can't keep your sister's telepathy out of my head."

I laughed too. "Join the club."

"The kid never stops talking about you, Adrian. Addy this, Addy that. She even told me how your eyes changed color. She told me what the Slayers did to you."

"Yeah, well, Alia is a big blabbermouth."

"So it's true?" asked Ed Regis. "You were actually blind for several months?"

"I didn't learn Braille for my health, you know," I said wryly.

Ed Regis grinned. "So I'm guessing that's why you consistently run your fingers along every wall you pass."

I stared at him incredulously. "I don't do that! Do I do that?"

Ed Regis nodded. "Part of my job involves spotting people's habits."

I cringed. "I can't believe I still do that."

"Most people don't realize half of the things they do," Ed Regis said casually. "Like you probably don't know what your hand is doing right this instant."

I stopped fingering my amethyst and narrowed my eyes at Ed Regis. "When you get back to your unit, are you going to write all this stuff in my database entry?"

Ed Regis frowned. "Well, technically, everything I learn here should count as being off record. But most likely, yes, I will."

I laughed. "At least you're honest about it."

I really was glad that Ed Regis was with us, but that didn't mean I was about to give him a hug. I valued his expertise as a soldier, but he was a Wolf and that wasn't going to change. At least it kept our relationship simple and straightforward.

We stood silently, side by side, looking out over the dark mountainside for a few more minutes. Catching me stifling a yawn, Ed Regis said, "Why don't you get some sleep now, Adrian."

I had one last question for him. "Do you really think we're going to survive this trip?"

"Our chances do seem pretty slim right now," Ed Regis replied gravely. "But stranger things have happened. Who knows, right?"

I nodded. "Goodnight, Ed Regis."

Slipping into the tent and zipping the door, I carefully crawled over Alia's sleeping bag to Ed Regis's former space between my sister and the wall. Terry was asleep on Alia's other side and James's sleeping bag occupied the sliver of space between Terry and the opposite wall. We really were packed like sardines in here, but at least I was out of the wind.

The night was painfully short.

I felt I had barely closed my eyes before they snapped open again to the sound of a gunshot echoing out across the mountain.

"Wake up!" shouted Terry's voice from just outside.

The dim light filtering in through the fabric told me that it was nearing dawn. On the other side of the tent, Ed Regis was already in a sitting position, awake and alert. He shook James awake as I quickly woke Alia.

Another shot rang out, followed by a third.

"Come on, out of the tent!" Terry shouted again, but her voice sounded calm and in control. I guessed that our attackers were not yet on our doorstep.

Yanking Alia out of her sleeping bag, I followed James and Ed Regis outside.

"What's going on?" asked James.

"Our buddies decided they want to play," replied Terry, leaning her back against the boulder that was shielding our tent from the gunfire. "They're about three hundred yards down."

"Let me see," said Ed Regis, grabbing his binoculars and peering over the boulder. "They're pretty well dug in," he observed. "It won't be easy taking them out. But at least they're still too far away to get a good shot at us."

"Looks like the Angels finally caught up with us," I said.

"Yeah," Terry said grimly.

Terry knew that I wasn't referring to the three riflemen approaching from below, but James didn't. "We can still escape," said James, looking up toward the top of the slope. "They're enough boulders around here that we can use as cover to get up over this mountain and—"

"No!" Terry and Ed Regis said in unison.

"We can't escape that way," I said patiently.

"Why not?" asked James.

We had trained James pretty well in combat, but not at all in battle strategy. I explained to him, "The other side of this mountain is crawling with Angels. Those three down there aren't trying to kill us. They're trying to run us into a trap."

"How the hell do you know that, Adrian?"

"Because that's how you hunt people," I replied matter-of-factly.

"He's right," said Ed Regis. "There's no escape over the mountain."

Terry nodded. "We need to go back down."

James looked horrified. "Into the fire? But they have rifles! With scopes! It's insane!"

I secretly agreed. If we charged down the mountain, chances were we'd all be dead well before we got into pistol range.

"I suppose we could inch our way down using the boulders for cover," Ed Regis said uncertainly, "but it would take a lot of time. As soon as those bastards see that we're not running away from them, they'll probably radio their ambush team. We need to get down quickly if we're going to stay ahead of the pack."

"Everyone just stay put," I said, peeking over the boulder to get a feel for the distance and direction of the riflemen.

"What are you doing, Addy?" asked Alia, though she probably guessed.

"What I should have done last night when it was darker."

"Not smart, Half-head," warned Terry.

Probably true, but I felt that if I delayed this any longer, I might lose my nerve.

"We can argue tactics later if I'm still alive, Terry," I said, and inhaled deeply.

"No!" cried Alia, but I was already airborne, jumping ten yards up above our camp.

Then, swooping down the mountainside, I gathered speed as I made a controlled diagonal descent toward the rocks that the riflemen were using as cover. When I had crossed about half the distance, one of the men appeared from behind his boulder and took careful aim at me. As I saw the puff of smoke from his rifle, I pumped more power into my telekinetic levitation, raising my body a yard higher. Another rifleman took a second shot, and I quickly dropped down low against the slope and shifted my heading to the left for a moment before veering back. This was no different from flying an airplane through anti-aircraft fire. Keep changing trajectory.

I felt a bullet slice across my left shoulder blade, tearing through the back of my jacket. I was yanked a little to the left, but surprisingly uninjured. Had the round cut into my skin at all, my psionic power would have drained and I would probably have broken my neck smashing into the rocks below. I didn't have time to appreciate this semi-miracle, though. With less than fifty yards left to my target, I finally realized my big mistake.

I was unarmed!

Had I taken Ed Regis's pistol, I could have simply put a few bullets into the riflemen from the air. I was even wearing gloves so there was no excuse for my blunder. Nor was there the option of turning back.

I saw two of the three men throw down their hunting rifles and reach for their pistols as I passed overhead and landed a few yards behind them. There was no time for me to prepare focused shots. Thrusting my right hand out, I released two rapid blasts, knocking the pair onto their backs before they could train their pistols on me.

The two men weren't dead, of course, but I had more pressing business to attend to. Through the corner of my eye, I saw the third man about fifteen yards to my left. He had reloaded his rifle and had just finished leveling it on me. I telekinetically snatched the rifle out of his hands, spun it around in midair, and shot him in the face with it.

That was when I felt a bullet enter my right arm, just below the shoulder. The force of the impact made me lose my balance, and I fell onto my back and slid several yards down the rocky slope. But the hot stinging pain in my arm was nothing compared to the fury and fear I felt as my telekinetic power drained away.

Clutching my right arm to stop the bleeding, I half-crawled, half-slid my way farther down the slope and took cover behind a boulder. I heard the remaining two men shouting and cursing as their footsteps approached.

Before I could move again, one of them, a dark-skinned man with a shaggy beard, popped around the left side of the boulder and grinned. "There you are!" he said nastily, bringing his pistol right up to my nose.

A bullet exited his right temple, and he fell forward, unmoving. A few more rounds rang out in rapid succession, and then I heard more footsteps.

"You okay?" asked Ed Regis, looking down at me over the corpse of the man he had just shot from behind.

"There was one more," I said, wincing.

"'Was' is correct," reported Terry, who had come around the other side of my boulder. Then she saw the blood on my arm. "You're hit!"

"Tell me something I don't know!" I said angrily. "Where the hell is Alia?!"

"Running her little legs off trying to catch up," replied Terry. Then she said to Ed Regis, "Go find James and collect whatever supplies you can from these guys. We've got to get moving quickly."

"You got it," said Ed Regis, and disappeared.

Then Terry yelled over the boulder, "Alia! Get your butt down here right now! Adrian's got another gunshot wound for you!"

Terry helped me pull my jacket off and then used her hook to tear away the bloody sleeve of my shirt. My sister arrived a minute later, out of breath and furious.

"I can't believe you, Adrian!" she shouted into my head. It was always a bad sign when she refused to call me Addy. *"What were you thinking?!"*

Terry couldn't hear Alia's telepathy, of course, but she guessed what my sister was saying. "Just close up the wound, Alia," Terry said impatiently. "Once we escape, I'll hold him down and let you kick him as much as you like."

"The bullet's still inside," Alia said aloud. "Can you get it out, Terry?"

"Leave it in," I said. "Just close the hole for me."

"No," said Terry. "Alia is right. We should get it while it's fresh. The less metal in you, the better."

Terry ducked back around the boulder for a moment and returned with a small knife. "Now you get to pay for your stupidity, Adrian."

"Hey, it worked, didn't it?" I said defiantly, and then howled in pain as Terry started digging.

Alia put her hands on her hips in full-blown angry-mother mode. *"You could've died, Addy!"*

"Well, I didn't!" I said through clenched teeth. Terry was holding my arm in place with her hook as she dug deeper into the exposed flesh, and it was all I could do to keep myself from wailing like a baby.

"Actually, it wasn't such a bad move," said Terry, still working her knife on my arm. "Certainly saved us a lot of time, and they may not even have radioed their buddies. But did you really have to go without a gun? What the hell are you trying to prove?"

"It wasn't like that," I insisted, though I wasn't about to admit that I had simply forgotten.

My sister gave me an exasperated look. *"I thought you promised Cindy you'd stop getting shot."*

"When's the last time I kept a promise, Alia?" I said, and then let out another loud yelp as Terry finally located the bullet and pulled it out.

"Be quick," Terry said to Alia. "We need to start running again right now."

Terry disappeared again, presumably to help Ed Regis and James gather supplies.

"I'm sorry, okay?" I said.

Alia silently put her hands up close to my bullet hole. I felt guilty about putting her through the fear she must have felt for me when I charged down the mountain. But Alia was a soldier too now, and she knew that risks were an unavoidable part of getting things done. At least we were all still alive and the Seraphim on the other side of the mountain none the wiser.

"All done, Addy," said Alia, removing her hands. There was an ugly scar left and my right arm was still a bit stiff, but I could move it without any real pain. After quickly wiping the blood off of my body, I put my jacket back on.

Having lost a fair bit of blood, I felt dizzy when I stood.

"Think you can carry this?" Terry asked me, holding out one of the backpacks taken from the riflemen.

I stared at her disbelievingly.

Ed Regis said, "I'll carry it till Adrian has recovered his strength."

As much as I hated being helped by the Wolf, especially just after he saved my life, I didn't argue. Ed Regis wore my backpack on his chest. Combined with the bigger pack on his back, it made the man look like a walking boulder.

It turned out that Terry, before sprinting down the slope to catch up with me, had ordered James to bring down our two backpacks. There hadn't been time for James to take down our tent, but we still had our food and water, and James had even managed to bring one of the sleeping bags. Then, while Terry and Alia were taking care of my arm, Ed Regis and James had combined the riflemen's supplies with ours. We now had five packs, one for each of us, a three-man tent, four sleeping bags, ropes and other mountain gear, as well as additional food and water that might even be enough to last us to the Historian, if we ever made it that far. Our three new rifles went to Terry, James and Ed Regis, and I took two of the riflemen's pistols for myself, including the one that shot me.

"Let's get moving," said Terry. "The Angels haven't seen us yet. They might not even know what's going on."

"Let's keep it that way," said Ed Regis, taking his rifle and firing it once into the air.

Occasionally firing a few rounds behind us to make it appear as if the riflemen were still driving us up the mountain, we double-timed it down the slope, slipping and sliding down the steeper parts. It was a harrowing descent, but we made it back to the bottom by mid-morning, and miraculously without injury.

"Keep going," said Terry, nodding toward the slope rising to the west. "Once we put enough distance between us, we'll work our way around."

"Look!" cried Alia, pointing back up to the top of the northeastern mountain.

My eyes had trouble focusing on the distant peak, but I could just make out the tiny moving shapes, like ants on a hill.

Looking through his binoculars, Ed Regis said, "Twenty. Maybe more."

If they decided to charge down the mountain at the same speed we had done, they could be here before we got sufficiently up the next slope.

"Couldn't expect them to be fooled by the gunshots forever," muttered James. "They can sense us."

"Give me my pack," I said to Ed Regis. "I'll carry it from here."

"First you need to eat, Adrian," said Ed Regis, looking down at my unsteady legs. "I think we all do."

I had forgotten that we had skipped breakfast.

"Alright," conceded Terry. "Ten minute break. Then we go."

We ate hurriedly and nervously, keeping a watchful eye on the Angels gathering on the distant peak. Ed Regis assured us that even a professional sharpshooter wouldn't be able to land a bullet in our midst at this distance, but I was more worried about the possibility of a long-range psionic-based attack. The range of psionic controllers varied considerably: some required eye contact, others didn't. I doubted they had any finder-controllers among them, since if they did, they could have locked onto Alia and me from much farther away, but now that the Seraphim had line of sight on us, there was no telling what might happen. And neither James nor Alia had any mental blocking training. Keeping my consciousness guarded against sudden intrusion,

I watched my team carefully. But no mind attacks came, nor did any flight-capable telekinetics try swooping down the mountainside.

"They're well hidden," I said, popping a handful of mixed nuts into my mouth. "I can't sense any of their powers."

"At least they're not coming down the mountain yet," said James.

It was strange considering how utterly they outnumbered us, but if anything, it looked like the Angels were just observing and debating what to do.

"Whatever they're planning, it wouldn't hurt to put more distance between us," said Terry, standing up.

"Five more minutes, Terry?" pleaded Alia. "My legs really hurt."

That was my sister's first and last complaint of the day, but Terry replied unsympathetically, "Your legs will stop hurting when you're dead, Alia. On your feet. Now!"

I took my new backpack from Ed Regis, who turned around and offered to carry Alia's next.

But after a quick glance in Terry's direction, Alia shook her head, saying resolutely, "It's okay, Ed. I can carry it."

We had given Alia the lightest load possible: Hers was the backpack without the sleeping bag, heavy gear or bottled water. But even so, Alia's backpack, like the others, had been designed for adults, and even with all the straps pulled tight, my sister had a lot of trouble walking with it.

"Once we've eaten through enough of our food, we'll combine everything into four packs," promised Ed Regis.

The western slope, though not as steep as what we had just descended, was a serious challenge for our exhausted crew. The going was not only slow and painful, but nerve-racking with the knowledge that we now had a large audience one peak away. The Angels still hadn't moved from their vantage point, and I constantly felt their eyes on my back as we made our way up the rocky mountainside.

In the early afternoon, we finally managed to leave the Angels behind as we began our descent down the other side of our mountain, turning slightly northward. It should have been a relief, but I soon came to the conclusion that it was even worse on this side since we couldn't see the Angels and thus had no clue what they were doing. Still, we kept to a safe pace this time, and reached the bottom within a few hours.

"We still have some sunlight left," said Terry. "Let's see how far we can get up the next mountain."

My sister kept her mouth shut, so the rest of us did too.

We made our way northwest, climbing steadily until near sundown. That was when Alia pointed behind us again.

The Angels had been following us, carefully keeping their distance just as the riflemen had been doing. They had gathered at the top of the slope that we had descended in the afternoon, and again they refused to come any closer while we were in view. In the rapidly waning light, I watched them uncomfortably, wondering what they had in store for us. Was this the cat playing with the mouse before eating it?

"What the hell are they playing at?" said James.

"I'm not sure," said Terry, "but we're stopping here for the night."

"But we're only another two hundred yards or so from the top," argued James. "Shouldn't we at least get to the other side today?"

Ed Regis shook his head. "Terry is right. These rocks here will give us plenty of cover, and if the Angels decide to attack us during the night, we'll be able to see them coming and have a decent tactical advantage."

"What if there's another team on the other side of this mountain?" asked James. I was wondering the exact same thing.

"Then either way, we're dead," said Terry.

Fair enough.

My sister had been almost entirely silent today, even during our breaks, but I couldn't be sure if she was in one of her moods or if she was simply dead tired like the rest of us. As we settled down for the night, I asked her timidly, "Are you still mad at me, Alia?"

Alia shrugged, replying quietly, "I'm too tired to be mad. But I should be. I just can't figure out what you're thinking sometimes."

"It's not like I enjoy getting shot, you know."

Alia finally smiled. "Four times, Addy."

Ed Regis and James set up our tent in a relatively flat space between several large rocks. Our new tent, though still a tight fit for four, was definitely an improvement on our last one, and this time we even had enough sleeping bags for everyone who wasn't on night watch. Alia fell asleep almost instantly.

I had first watch again, but Ed Regis, who was second, joined me. I suspected that he was afraid I might fall asleep on the job, but it was hard to feel insulted because I wasn't so sure myself.

"So what *were* you thinking, Adrian?" asked Ed Regis, his eyes scanning the dark slope.

"I wasn't," I admitted meekly. "Thanks for saving my life, by the way."

"What goes around comes around."

"I already told you that wasn't me," I said stubbornly. "It was Alia."

In the short silence that followed, I wondered if Terry might have had a point this morning when she accused me of trying to prove something. I hadn't *deliberately* flown down the mountainside without a pistol, but I *had* flown down the mountainside. While even Terry had agreed that, under the circumstances, our lightning attack had been the best possible tactic, that wasn't why I had done it.

Was I competing with Ed Regis?

The Wolves had taken care of us all the way from Walnut Lane to these mountains, and then for five days Ed Regis had taken my place as Alia's protector. I was grateful, of course, but in all honesty, it irked the hell out of me.

Ed Regis said hesitantly, "Adrian, can I ask you a personal question?"

"Is this for your database?" I asked warily.

"No," he said, chuckling. "I promise to keep it off the record."

"Shoot."

"What's your deal with Alia?" he asked.

"What do you mean?"

"Well, you're not really her blood relation, but that's pretty hard to believe considering the way you two get along. What turned you into her brother?"

I shrugged. "I owe her multiple life debts."

Ed Regis wasn't buying that. "Oh, come on."

"What do you care?" I asked gruffly.

"I'm just curious."

That made two of us. After a moment of thought, I said slowly, "The truth is, Ed Regis, I'm not exactly sure myself how it happened. I was just taking care of her because I had to." I threw him an evil grin. "Because some bastard stuffed me in an underground prison with her. But then one day, I realized that we were family. When I think back, it was probably long before the PRC. Maybe even the first day we met. I don't know."

"You'd die for her?"

"Any day," I replied without hesitation. I wasn't being brave or showing off. It was just true.

"I envy you, Adrian," Ed Regis said quietly. "It's good to have someone like that in your life."

"You've never had someone you'd die for?" I asked.

"Yes, I have," said Ed Regis, who seemed to grow a little older in the starlight. "I just never got the chance."

I was debating with myself whether or not I wanted to hear more about this when suddenly we heard a high-pitched scream from behind us. Ed Regis and I ran back to our tent. Telekinetically unzipping the tent flap, I stuck my head inside.

Alia, sandwiched between Terry and James, had pulled herself out of her sleeping bag and was sitting up, wide-eyed and panting heavily. Terry and James had been woken by her scream too.

"What happened?" I asked, crawling into the tent and peering into my sister's terrified face.

"He was here, Addy!" Alia cried into my head, her body trembling all over. *"He was right here!"*

"Who?" I whispered. "Who was here?"

Alia just stared forward, mouth open and eyes unfocused.

"She probably just had a bad dream," James said sleepily.

I shook my head. "What did he tell you, Alia? What did he want?"

"He wanted..." Alia's telepathic voice trailed off. Then she gulped and said aloud in a shaky voice, "He wanted us to give up. He said that if we gave up now, they wouldn't kill us."

15. PREDATOR AND PREY

Over the following days, we gave the Seraphim a wide berth and continued to inch our way northeast toward the Historian's mountain. Though we remained on the lookout for Merlin, we saw no sign of our lost hider anywhere, and before long, we had all stopped wondering aloud whether he was dead or alive. Merlin's fate wasn't our primary concern right now.

Every night, the Angel dreamweaver sent us grisly warnings to surrender or be destroyed. Alia was the only one who couldn't block him at all, so she had it much worse than the rest of us. I could tune down the horror factor of these psionically induced nightmares, even block them entirely in my sleep, but my sister frequently woke screaming in the night.

Why didn't the Angels simply attack and kill us? First, though the Seraphim were certain to win, an all-out battle could mean losses for them as well. Since we were still many days away from the Historian, it made sense for our pursuers to wait, just like in a siege, until all negotiations had failed. But more than that, they wanted us alive. Or rather, they specifically wanted one of us alive.

"I'm putting you all in danger," Alia said miserably. "They wouldn't be doing this if I wasn't here."

"You're as dumb as your brother sometimes, Alia," said Terry. "You're the one keeping this a stalemate. The only reason they haven't wiped us out already is because they're afraid they might accidentally kill you."

The twenty-plus team of Seraphim was still trailing us at a distance of one mountain. They had maintained this distance for more than a week now, but the only real question was how much longer they were willing to wait before they attacked—because there was no way we were about to surrender.

As we trudged forward, ever keeping a watchful eye on our dogged fan club, the dreamweaver's proposals had become increasingly accommodating. He had first merely promised that we wouldn't be killed. Then he said that only the psionics need be converted, while the other three could walk free provided they turned back. Now his dreamweaves told us that the Seraphim would let everyone go as long as we gave up the healer.

"I wish I could answer him," I said savagely after yet another long night of threats and promises. "If only to tell him that I think he's full of—"

"Save your breath," said Terry. "There's nothing to negotiate."

I glanced at Alia, whose eyes were so red and puffy that I wondered if they would ever look normal again. Years ago, dreamweaving had been the answer to her bad nights, but now she was learning firsthand that that door swung both ways. This was particularly hard on my sister not only because the Angel dreamweaver seemed to take special pleasure in tormenting her with nightmares, but because he had repeatedly promised her that if she alone gave herself up, the rest of us would be spared.

"Don't you believe a word of it, Alia," warned Terry. "They're not about to let any of us go."

"I know," said Alia, though without any conviction in her voice.

Terry asked me, "How much farther to the Historian, Adrian?"

I shook my head. "I can't be sure. We're close, though. Alia, what do you think?"

"I don't know either," said Alia. "He's really strong. Maybe another four or five days."

"That feels about right," I agreed, taking a little comfort in the knowledge that my sister still had some of her wits about her.

We had managed to replenish our water at another clear river, but our food supplies were getting dangerously low. It was unlikely that they would last more than another three days, but at least we'd be traveling light when the Angels finally charged us.

"They won't keep their distance much longer," Ed Regis said grimly. "No matter how much they want Alia, if they think we're actually going to reach the Historian, they'll attack."

Terry turned to him. "You do know what we have to do, don't you?"

"I'm well aware of what we must do, Terry. I'm just not sure how we're going to go about doing it."

James gave the Wolf a questioning look. "What are you talking about?"

"There's only one sure way to stop being hunted," Ed Regis said quietly.

"Which is?"

Ed Regis didn't immediately reply, so Terry answered for him, "Become the hunter, James."

"Whoa!" exclaimed James, his expression even more incredulous than when we had told him that we'd have to break through the riflemen. "We're outnumbered what, at least four to one, right? Maybe even five to one."

"Maybe," Terry said evenly. "But if we don't make a stand, they'll run us down on their own terms, and we won't have a chance."

"Adrian?" said James, possibly hoping to get my support against this suicidal tactic.

I shook my head. "Terry and Ed Regis are right. We'll have to fight them."

We didn't fight them that day, though. Despite our new rifles and the formidable combat expertise that our team was blessed with, James had a point too. This just wasn't a fight that we could win.

That evening, we stopped near the top of yet another slope spanning two high peaks. At the lowest point between the peaks, which was where we were headed, it was very rocky but the slope itself relatively gentle. We always tried to end our hikes on a place like this so that we had a good view of the Angels following us.

"Any day now," said Ed Regis, looking out toward the specks of Seraphim on the mountain behind us.

"Hope they got my message," I muttered. Against better judgment, I had left a rude two-word reply in the dirt for the Seraphim to find.

That night, the Angel dreamweaver finally issued us an ultimatum. Each of us dreamt it one after another, and while the form of the nightmares varied, the message was the same: another step toward the Historian and the deal was off.

Comforting a trembling Alia in the dim, early-morning light, I looked around at the other three who were sitting silently, wide awake, all wondering the same thing.

"Is this really a good idea?" whispered James.

"Probably not," replied Ed Regis, "but it'll be better than being shot in the back while trying to escape."

Catching my eye, Ed Regis hastily put his hands up in defense. "I didn't mean it that way, Adrian. It's just true."

I laughed and shook my head. "I wasn't thinking of that, Ed Regis. Actually, I was thinking that maybe there's a way to even the odds just a bit."

"Are you suggesting a plan?" asked Terry. "I hope it's saner than your last one."

"No promises," I said. Chances were that this would be the worst one to date. "They want Alia and me alive, right? Well, maybe Alia more than me, but they want us both alive."

"So?"

"So we give them what they want."

"Don't start talking like Alia," said Terry, rolling her eyes. "They won't let us go just because you sacrifice yourself."

I grinned at her. "Who said anything about sacrifice? I thought it was your job to keep us alive, bodyguard."

A look of understanding slowly spread over Terry's face, and then she smiled slyly. "A calculated risk?"

"A lack of options," I countered dryly.

Terry nodded. "You're right, Adrian. It'll even the odds a bit. Maybe a lot. But are you sure you're up to it?"

I shrugged. "Better than being shot in the back."

By the time the sun had risen high enough to warm our horribly grimy faces, the Seraphim looking out at us through their binoculars saw Alia and me sitting with our backs against a large, semi-comfortable boulder. And attached to the top of the boulder was James's undershirt, which served as our white flag of surrender.

I sat silently with Alia all morning, occasionally nibbling on the last of our beef jerky as we watched the specks approach and finally start climbing our slope. Alia seemed dazed but in decent control of her emotions. She knew the plan and what we were up against. She knew she might die today. I only wished that I could feel as calm about it as she behaved.

About a quarter of a mile down the slope, the Angels, which I counted to be twenty-three in number, stopped once and looked up at us. I raised my right hand and gave them a little wave.

But then something happened that we hadn't planned for: The group split into two. Twelve men started climbing toward us as the rest stayed put, keeping their distance. I wasn't yet sure if this was a blessing or a curse, but there was no turning back now.

As the men slowly approached, I looked over their gear. Three of them were carrying assault rifles while two had regular hunting rifles with scopes. The others weren't armed as far as I could tell. We knew that at least one of them was a hider, another a dreamweaver. They were still too far away for me to sense any of their powers under their hiding protection, but the rest of the Seraphim were no doubt destroyers and non-psionics, with possibly a controller or two mixed in.

I turned to my sister and whispered, "Alia, are you still with me?"

Alia gazed back at me, her eyes finally betraying her show of bravery.

"I'm a little scared too," I said gently.

Putting her arms around my neck, Alia said shakily, *"I don't know about this, Addy."*

I didn't either. I had pretty much conscripted Alia into my insane plan, much like Mr. Baker had once done, forcing her to help us do the one thing she hated most. I had no excuse for my hypocrisy.

Holding her tight, I whispered into her ear, "Whatever happens, stay close to me. Trust in Terry, Alia. And James and Ed Regis. We'll be okay." Releasing her, I gripped her shoulders and looked into her nervous eyes. "Steady now."

Alia swallowed hard, and then nodded. *"I'm right here, Addy. Whatever happens."*

Once the welcoming committee was only about fifty yards away, I slowly stood up and pulled Alia to her feet, standing her in front of me. Then I quickly drew my two pistols from my belt, pressing the one in my left hand up against the bottom of my own chin as I touched the barrel of my right against Alia's head. Alia didn't flinch.

"That's far enough!" I called down to the men. "One false move and I'll kill the healer and myself."

The men stopped and stared up at us. I half-expected them to laugh at me, but they didn't. One of them, who I assumed was their leader, took a slow step forward and asked, "What's your name, kid?"

"Adrian Howell," I replied. "And don't you think for a second that I won't pull these triggers."

"I've heard of you, Adrian Howell," the leader said evenly. "Where are the others?"

"They're on the other side of this mountain," I said, my voice surprisingly steady despite my fear. "Not far, and not going any farther. You honor your promise to let them go free, and they will turn back and you can have this healer and me alive."

"Put down the guns and willingly accept your fate, and I promise that you won't be harmed."

"First promise me the safety of my friends," I demanded.

The leader didn't reply, but instead slowly started walking up toward us, followed by two others behind him. The other eight stood watching.

"Stay back!" I ordered, keeping my pistols firmly on Alia and me. I pulled both hammers back. "I swear to God I'll blow us both away if you come any closer!"

I felt Alia tense up, her breathing fast and uneven. I could hardly blame her. This wasn't entirely an act, after all. The guns were loaded, and I was fully prepared to put a bullet through Alia's head, and my own, if that was what it took to keep us from being taken by the Angels. But not just yet.

The three stopped once, and the leader said calmingly, "Put the guns down, kid. You don't want to die here."

"You still haven't promised me my friends," I said. "You will let them leave these mountains."

"You have my word," replied the leader. "Now give yourself up and we can all go home."

The three started approaching again. Contrary to my threat, this was exactly what I wanted. I wanted them as close to Alia and me as possible, and I knew that as long as my only threat was suicide, the Angels wouldn't be too afraid of me despite the fact that I had two drawn pistols in plain view. In a few seconds, I would spring the trap.

Come closer, I thought to myself. *Just a little closer.* It was fortunate for me that the Seraphim didn't have a delver who could read my mind from this distance.

But something was wrong. Three approaching, eight waiting, eleven far away. Only twenty-two Seraphim.

I sensed motion to my left. Turning my head, I found myself staring into a pair of floating eyeballs not more than three yards away. I almost pulled both triggers in surprise as the phantom turned visible. Then I felt my limbs suddenly become rigid as this phantom, who I realized was also a puppeteer, took control of my body.

I thought the phantom puppeteer would force me to hand over my pistols, but he didn't. Instead, maintaining the distance between us, he just kept my arms locked in place so I couldn't shoot anyone. I quickly discovered why.

Meanwhile, the leader and his two minions quickened their pace, smiling in victory.

"Good work," the leader called up to the phantom puppeteer. Then he turned his head and shouted down to the rest of his team, "Come on, let's go! We still have three more to bag."

As his men started up the slope, I shouted at the leader furiously, "You promised you'd let my friends go!"

The leader, now less than five yards away from me, merely laughed. "Once you're properly converted, you'll want your friends to be with you. On our side."

I turned my head back to the puppeteer. "Let go of me!"

The puppeteer shook his head. "It's for your own safety, kid."

He should have been more worried about his own.

Merlin had taught me well. The phantom puppeteer thought he had my arms and legs good and tight. He thought I was a child who hadn't yet learned how to block a controller's song. But he was the one who was untrained. This amateur puppeteer's song was uneven, cluttered, nothing like Merlin's. The cracks were so obvious I almost felt sorry for him.

Reaching out to take the pistols from my hands, the Seraph leader said pleasantly, "Welcome to the Angels, Adrian Howell."

I put a bullet between his eyes with my right-hand pistol. Then, quickly shifting my aim, I fired two more rounds: one for each of his two pals. The phantom puppeteer was busy turning invisible again, but when a pair of bullets from my left-hand pistol entered his chest, he quickly reappeared on his back, twitching.

From there, it was controlled chaos.

Alia knew to hit the ground when the first shots were fired. I had actually missed my third headshot from my right-hand pistol, failing to kill the leader's second minion, but that was only because the man suddenly staggered sideways, having caught a round from Terry's rifle. As the Seraph fell to his knees, I put a few extra bullets into his upper body, and he collapsed backwards.

Well before the sun had risen, Ed Regis and Terry had carefully crawled just over fifty yards to my left and right, while James had taken position above and behind me. The remaining eight members of the Seraph advance team, now less than thirty yards from Alia and me, opened up with automatic rifles, telekinetic blasts, spark electric charges, and everything else they had. But they hadn't expected to be fired upon from three different directions.

I dropped to the ground beside Alia as a powerful electric surge shot over my head, singeing my hair. I saw the spark preparing another thunderbolt in his left hand, but then the right side of his head blew apart. I guessed that round had come from Ed Regis.

What felt like an unfocused telekinetic blast smacked into my forehead, but I wasn't injured. At this distance, the blast wasn't half as painful as being hit by Terry in the dojo. Stretching my arms forward, I emptied both of my pistols into the group of Angels, but I couldn't tell if I actually hit them. Some of the Seraph leader's blood had spattered onto my face, draining me, but I was too far away to effectively use my telekinetic blasts anyway. Once I was out of bullets, I turned my eyes away from the carnage as Terry, Ed Regis and James used their rifles to quickly dispatch the remaining Seraphim. It was over in seconds.

Using my sleeve to wipe the blood off of my face, I turned to my sister and asked, "Alive?"

Alia's eyes were wide and frantic, but at least she didn't appear to have any holes in her. She tried to stand up but I grabbed her and pulled her back down. There were still eleven Seraphim approaching from below, already within rifle range.

Ed Regis called out, "You kids okay?"

"We're good!" I yelled back. "Run or fight?"

"Run!" shouted Ed Regis. "Up to James! We'll cover you!"

We didn't need telling twice. As our rifle team fired several rounds in the direction of the approaching second wave, Alia and I scrambled up the slope toward James's cover. Ducking behind his boulder, I heard the unmistakable sound of bullets ricocheting off the rocks.

Terry and Ed Regis joined us there.

"What have you got?" Terry asked James.

"I'm empty," said James, breathing heavily.

"Two rounds," reported Ed Regis.

"I have one left," said Terry.

"Nice shooting," I panted. "Good thing they split up."

"Not good," said Terry. "Only three rounds left and they won't fall for that again."

Terry was referring specifically to our rifle ammunition. Our original plan had included Terry, James and Ed Regis charging out with their pistols once their rifles were dry. But without the element of surprise, our pistols would be of little use against the remaining Seraphim, who could pick us off one by one from a safe distance. Nor was there enough cover below us to retrieve the weapons the first-wave Seraphim had dropped when we killed them.

"Light and fast," said Ed Regis. "Dump the rifles and packs."

We did. Ed Regis transferred the remaining food and water into his own backpack, which he kept. The rest of us now had nothing but our tattered clothes and a few pistols between us.

"Three days, right?" Ed Regis said to Alia. "We can still make it."

Up we went, using the terrain for cover, occasionally having to dash or crawl between the rock formations as more bullets greeted us from below. Fortunately, we were already so close to the top of the slope that, within only a few minutes, the Angels no longer had line of sight on us.

I was bringing up the rear with Ed Regis so I didn't immediately see what caused Terry to swear as loudly as she did the next moment. Anxiously making my way around the rock that was blocking my view, I saw the cause of her frustration.

The descending slope was so steep that it could hardly be called a slope at all.

"This is a cliff!" shouted James. "You led us onto a goddamn cliff!"

"Shut up, James!" Terry and I shouted in unison.

James looked like he had been slapped. I felt a bit sorry for him, being thrown into this horrid mess on only his second mission. He was much like I had been: unstable and panicky. But we didn't have the time to nurse him through it.

"There's got to be a way down," I said, looking down over the edge. But there wasn't. Not without the ropes and gear we had just dumped.

"Nothing for it," said Terry. "We'll just have to keep going."

She meant keep going north along the edge of the cliff, which ran all the way to the next mountain peak where the slope was gentle enough to descend without dying. Until we got there, however, we would be easy targets.

It wasn't much more than half a mile, though, and I hoped we might make it before the Seraphim behind us reached the top and re-established line of sight. Our path between the two peaks quickly turned into a knife's edge, with dizzying drop-offs on both sides. We jogged forward as fast as we dared, single file, Terry first, followed by James, Alia, then me, and Ed Regis last. To our rear left, I could see the mountainside where we had ambushed the Seraphim. Fortunately, the curvature of the mountain kept us out of view from the Angels who were no doubt scrambling up the slope, and the jagged mountainsides were so steep here that our pursuit would have no choice but to follow our roundabout route.

A rifle shot rang out behind us. We stopped and turned, wondering how the Angels could have already reached the top of the slope. But there were no Seraphim yet to be seen on the path behind us.

"Look!" shouted James, and he didn't have to point for us to know what he was talking about.

One Seraph, a flight-capable telekinetic, was hovering high up above the spot where I had shot their leader. The telekinetic was holding a bulky scoped rifle in his hands.

"So they did have a flyer," muttered Ed Regis.

The Angel telekinetic was smarter than me so he wasn't about to rush at us without the rest of his team. But there was nothing we could do to keep him from sniping us from the air. Praying not to catch any bullets in our rears, we kept going as fast as we could.

Fortunately, it takes an extraordinary amount of psionic focus to levitate yourself and a big metal rifle at the same time, and the telekinetic wasn't finding it easy. He fired several more rounds, but none of the bullets landed close enough for us to even hear the ricochets.

I was certain that it was only a matter of seconds now before the telekinetic ran out of psionic energy and would have to give up and land, but then Ed Regis suddenly let out a surprised yelp behind me. A lucky bullet had hit Ed Regis's backpack, and in his surprise, Ed Regis had lost his footing. Turning around, I tried to grab him, both with my hands and telekinetically, but it was too sudden. Ed Regis toppled over the edge and slid down the near-cliff more than thirty yards before coming to a stop on a little ledge. If he had fallen over that ledge, it was another one hundred yards or more, but this time really straight down.

"Ed Regis!" I called down.

He didn't reply, but he seemed to be moving a little.

I glanced back up toward the Angel telekinetic, but he had already dropped out of view. Most likely he'd need a good long rest before he flew again.

Terry wasn't taking any chances, though. "Come on!" she shouted, leading us forward several more yards to one of the few rock formations on the narrow edge that we could use for cover.

"Ed Regis!" I shouted again, and Alia joined me, cupping her hands around her mouth and shouting, "Ed! Are you okay?!"

Ed Regis finally turned his head and looked up at us. "I'm alright!" he shouted. "Get moving!"

"He's not alright!" I said angrily. "He's got nowhere to go. The Angels will shoot him as soon as they get up here."

"We can't get down to him," Terry logically pointed out.

"I can," I said through clenched teeth, all the more furious because it was true. If I didn't, it would mean I had deliberately refused to, and that wasn't about to happen.

I turned to my sister and said quickly, "Alia, you're the leader now. You get Terry and James to the Historian for me. If we both survive this, I'll see you there."

Alia shook her head. "No, Addy! You can't go!"

"He saved my life and yours," I said, putting my hands on her shoulders. "I'm not leaving him."

Alia gave me an anguished look. I knew what she was going through because I was going through it myself. "I know you're scared," I said gently, "but you wouldn't leave him to die, either. You know you wouldn't."

Alia grabbed my right arm. She looked like she was about to say something, but then she just nodded acceptingly.

"You're an idiot, Adrian!" spat Terry. "You'd do this for a Wolf? For *that* Wolf?!"

I nodded. "Yes, Terry. For that Wolf. Take care of Alia for me."

Without waiting for a reply, I jumped over the edge, using my telekinesis to slow my descent only when I was almost at the ledge. I had to carefully save my strength for what I was about to do next.

Landing lightly beside Ed Regis, I asked, "Are you injured?"

"No," groaned Ed Regis.

"No broken legs or anything?" I asked. "That was a hell of a fall."

"What are you doing down here, Adrian?"

I scowled at him. "What goes around comes around."

"You can't lift me and yourself back up this slope," said Ed Regis.

"There's no going back up," I agreed. "But there's always down."

Now that I was down here standing on the edge of the cliff, I wasn't at all sure I really could save this man. Despite his months in Angel captivity and all this time rationing our limited food supplies on the mountain, Ed Regis was a big and muscular man, and I suspected that he weighed as much as Terry and Alia combined.

"Just hang on to me," I said. "We'll jump together. I'll get you down safely."

Ed Regis caught the uncertainty in my voice. "Have you ever done this before?"

I looked at him for a moment, wondering if he preferred the truth or a lie, especially considering the good chance that we were both about to break our necks on the rocks below.

"Not successfully," I answered honestly. "Throw your backpack over the side. Your boots, guns, belt and jacket too."

Ed Regis did as I requested, and I also threw everything metal I had on me over the ledge.

Once we were as light as we could be, I took two deep breaths and said to Ed Regis, "Alright, arms around my neck. Time to fly."

Ed Regis looked at me, suddenly afraid. He shook his head and said, "You don't have to do this for me, Adrian. It's okay. Just go."

I punched him in the face. Not a nose-breaking punch, but hard enough to knock him back to his senses. Grabbing the front of his shirt, I hollered, "I am not going to let you die here, soldier! Put that in your goddamn database!"

16. THOSE WITHOUT REASON

Like the last time, it was more a controlled crash than a controlled descent, but when my ears stopped ringing and I staggered to my feet, I discovered that we had both survived the fall. It was hard to feel happy about this. Though I wasn't bleeding, I felt horribly drained and weak, my head spinning, and I could barely limp the few steps I needed to gather my scattered gear. I had hit the ground sideways, and my whole left side felt like it had been pierced by thousands of knives.

Ed Regis wasn't much better off but he helped me put my boots back on and, shouldering his backpack, grinned down at me. "That was one hell of a fall."

"We're alive, aren't we?" I mumbled weakly.

"Let's keep it that way. Come on, up you get, Sir Knight."

"Please don't call me that," I said as Ed Regis helped me to my feet.

The slope that stretched downwards from the bottom of the cliff was still pretty steep, but we didn't have time to be careful. The Angels would soon be able to spot us from above, and I couldn't put it past their flying telekinetic to chase us down if he saw that there were only two of us. Ed Regis was limping slightly too, but he helped me along until I recovered enough strength to keep up on my own. We somehow made it down the slope without falling or hearing any more gunshots from behind.

We knew that Alia's team should have descended somewhere to our north, but the terrain was exceptionally rough in that direction so we decided

250

to continue toward the Historian rather than attempt to regroup with them.

"If we're really lucky, their finder is dead," said Ed Regis.

"What difference does it make?" I said, pulling along my deadened left leg as quickly as I could. "They still have destroyers who can sense me."

"True," said Ed Regis, "but what are the chances of them having a healer who could track your sister?"

The chance was small, but not comfortingly small. The Seraph leader had probably split up his team suspecting an ambush, and, in doing so, he would have left any healer he had behind. Besides, a telepath, if they had one, could track Alia just as easily as any finder or healer. Still, that was Terry's problem now. Mine was getting Ed Regis and myself to the Historian.

Despite having only two uninjured legs between us, we made fairly good time and didn't stop for the night. The moon was the thinnest sliver possible without being gone altogether, but the sky was cloudless and the starlight seemed just a little brighter than usual. We had several dangerous slips and falls in the darkness, but since there was hardly a place on my body that didn't already hurt, a few extra bumps and bruises couldn't make much difference to me anymore.

Whenever I could, I used my telekinetic power to augment the strength in my left leg, which, along with my left arm and side, had turned deep purple and throbbed with every step. Ed Regis had to rely solely on his own tired muscles, but whatever pain he was in, he kept it to himself. As we pushed ourselves forward one mind-numbing step at a time, I felt as if we were daring each other to be the first to give in and ask for a rest. I kept my mouth shut.

It was only well after dawn of the next day that our strength finally gave in and we rested several hours. Ed Regis offered to take the first watch, but when I woke in the early afternoon, he was fast asleep.

We ate one last meal, and then Ed Regis dumped everything but the last of our water, putting the remaining two small bottles into his jacket pockets. It looked like even the mighty Wolf had finally reached the end of his endurance. Even without his backpack, Ed Regis's pace didn't improve much, for which I was grateful since I was still struggling to keep up.

Near nightfall of that day, we stumbled upon a small crack in the mountainside. The cave was only a few yards deep, and Ed Regis and I debated the merits of staying there for the night. If the Angels found us, the narrow opening would nullify their advantage in numbers, giving us a fighting chance. On the other hand, we would be trapped inside and they could just wait us out.

"Being underground would hide my power a little," I suggested. "They'll have more trouble pinpointing us."

We carefully dragged ourselves in through the crack.

It was pitch-black inside until Ed Regis turned on a little flashlight that was designed to be mounted under the barrel of one of his pistols. The white light illuminated the rough walls and low ceiling of this claustrophobically tiny space, which was even smaller than the two-man tent we once used. We couldn't even sit up properly in here, but at least the cave was dry and had a moderately flat floor.

We both groaned in pain as we stretched our stiff bodies on the hard, dusty ground, lying face up, side by side, with our heads toward the cave's entrance. Once we were settled, Ed Regis turned off his light, leaving us in total darkness.

"How much farther is it?" asked Ed Regis.

"We're making good progress," I replied. "Just not in the right direction."

As always, we weren't traveling in a straight line to the Historian's mountain, and today's hike had taken an especially long detour around yet another un-climbable peak.

"How much farther?" pressed Ed Regis.

"Two days," I said. "Two days in a straight line."

"You could have flown there by now."

"I can't fly more than a few minutes at a time."

"You know what I mean, Adrian."

By taking frequent breaks to recharge my strength, alone, I could have easily crossed more difficult terrain. But that wasn't an option in my mind. "We're going together or not at all, Ed Regis."

"You already saved my life on the cliff," said Ed Regis. "You don't owe me."

"I do owe you," I said firmly. "Your life isn't saved till I get you to the Historian."

I didn't want to argue that point any further, and by Ed Regis's silence, I assumed that he understood.

Technically, I could hardly claim to have saved his life (or my own for that matter) simply by getting us to the Historian alive. We had no gifts to trade for information, and even if the Historian did answer our questions, it would be another mad run against the Angels to get back to civilization. Unless we could replenish our supplies and get some proper gear and weapons, our chances of returning alive were next to nil. Right now, however, the mission was simply to get to the Historian. After that, what was unknown couldn't be helped, and I hadn't the strength left to worry about it.

I realized that I was so dead tired, my nerves so stretched, that there was no way I could simply close my eyes and fall asleep.

Ed Regis seemed to be in the same situation. "I'll take first watch," he said.

I asked playfully, "Like you did this morning?"

Ed Regis laughed embarrassedly. "Sorry about that, Adrian. So much for professionalism, huh? I'm okay now."

"Actually, I'm not that sleepy right now either."

"Still, one of us should sleep," said Ed Regis.

"Let me have that light again," I said, pulling myself up slightly and resting on my elbows.

Ed Regis held the light for me as I pulled off my belt and stuffed the buckle under my shirt.

Watching me, Ed Regis asked, "What are you doing?"

"A little trick I learned from the Slayers," I said as I lay back down, feeling extra dizzy from the draining. "This will make it harder for the Angels to find me."

"Doesn't that mean you won't be able to get a good rest?"

I scoffed. "We're hiding under a rock in the middle of nowhere with nothing to eat and hunted by Seraphim who might catch up with us in the middle of the night and throw a grenade in here. What makes you think I'm about to get a good rest either which way?"

"You've got a point there," laughed Ed Regis. "Still, it must be pretty uncomfortable to remain drained for so long. Especially when you're injured."

"Don't worry about me, Ed Regis," I insisted. "I can deal with it."

"I know you can," Ed Regis said quietly. Then he shook his head slowly, looking at me in wonder as he said, "You know, even when we first met, years ago, I really was very impressed with you. It took a while before I realized that I wasn't dealing with some dumb little kid that I could scare into submission."

"Which is why you threatened to kill Alia," I reminded him.

"Yes, but we would never have actually done it."

"I know that," I said with a grimace. "I really kicked myself for believing you." Then I smiled and added, "But you never got Cindy."

Ed Regis smiled too. "No, we didn't."

Ed Regis turned the light off again, and I whispered into the darkness, "It all seems so long ago. If someone had told me when I was twelve years old that soon I'd be flying and getting shot at and killing people and traveling around the world to meet a 3000-year-old man, I would have wondered what drug he was on."

I heard Ed Regis chuckle. "I wouldn't have believed it either if someone had told me last year that I'd be joining a team of Guardians to seek out the greatest psionic in all history."

"What's so great about psionics, anyway?" I muttered.

"You tell me," said Ed Regis. "You're the one who can fly and use your fingers like guns."

"So what?"

"That doesn't register as being special in any way?"

Ed Regis couldn't understand because he wasn't psionic. "Not really," I said. "I mean, what's it all good for, anyway? My power never saved my life or anyone else's. At least, my life would never have needed saving if I weren't psionic. They call me a destroyer, but a bullet from a gun is far better than anything I could shoot from my hands. My powers didn't help us in that ambush. What good is being telekinetic aside from being able to jump out of an airplane without a parachute?"

Ed Regis replied, "The greatest minds in the world want to know how psionic power works. It's got to be worth something."

Dr. Otis had said something similar to me on my first day at the PRC. I frowned, but Ed Regis didn't see it in the darkness.

"Besides," continued Ed Regis, "you're forgetting why we're here. Maybe modern weapons have nullified a psionic destroyer's advantages in combat, but master controllers can rule empires. That's the power everyone is interested in today."

"I'm not interested," I said stubbornly. "Today or any other day."

"Then you're the exception to the rule. After all, what is the one thing all powerful people want?"

"More power?"

"That's right," Ed Regis said matter-of-factly.

"The point is, Major, I never asked for this power, and I don't like being hunted for it. All I wanted was to live in peace. Is that really so much to ask?"

Ed Regis remained silent for a moment, and then said apologetically, "You're right, Adrian. It shouldn't be."

"I wasn't talking about the Wolves, you know," I said.

"I do hope you find your peace."

Cindy had said the same thing to me last year, but I never expected to hear it from a Wolf. "It'll depend on what the Historian tells us," I said wearily. "But most likely she's already dead."

"Who?"

Ed Regis's question threw me for a moment. Then, realizing what I had just said, I let out a frustrated huff. That's what I get for blabbing.

"Why *are* you here?" pressed Ed Regis. "If not to find Randal Divine, then why?"

"Alright, you got me. King Divine was Terry's mission, not mine," I admitted. "I came here looking for Alia's mother. She was with the Guardian Council when our city was taken. We haven't seen her since."

"Cynthia Gifford, was it?"

"That's right."

"You came all the way out here hoping that the Historian might tell you where she is?"

"I know that sounds ridiculous," I said, sighing. "She's probably long dead or converted by now. But Cindy was the only real mother Alia ever had, and mine too after my parents died. I have to know what happened to her."

"This woman must have been something really special for you to risk your life like this," said Ed Regis.

I smiled to myself, remembering the embarrassingly cute clothes Cindy used to buy for me. But I would happily wear those girly outfits for the rest of my life if only I could find her again. "She had her faults, Ed Regis, but yes, she was very special."

Ed Regis asked in an incredulous tone, "You have no interest at all in the Angel king?"

"You sound like Terry," I said, chuckling. "She once accused me of the same indifference. Of course I care about the king. I don't want to live in a world ruled by psionics. Especially by Randal Divine. Getting Alia back to Cindy would be pretty meaningless if we're all going to end up serving the Angels together. I already promised Terry that I'd hunt the Angel master with her as soon as we find out what happened to Cindy. I've broken many promises but this one I plan to keep."

"You sound pretty serious," said Ed Regis.

"I am," I said forcefully. "And it's not just about the Angels or Randal Divine, for that matter. I've seen enough of this war to know that psionics should never rule the world. I will do anything to make sure that doesn't happen. Anything at all."

"You know, Adrian, sometimes I wonder if the Angels might have a point. Maybe if all countries were united under a single psionic king, there would be less conflict. But I wouldn't want to live in that world either. People should always be free to govern themselves without fear of psionic influence. That's what the Wolves are about, more or less."

Now *that* struck a nerve. I replied icily, "Don't kid yourself, Major. The PRC was never just about researching psionics for defense or peaceful uses. They wanted to create soldiers that could fly and shoot lightning and heal themselves in combat. Everything was about power and control and who gets to have it."

Ed Regis mumbled awkwardly, "I wasn't suggesting that it's a perfect world."

I didn't want to get into an argument with this man. Drained and dizzy, I didn't have the energy for it, and there was little point anyway. It was time to change the subject.

Ed Regis seemed to feel the same way, and asked me, "Just out of curiosity, what does the Historian's house look like?"

"You know what? I have no idea," I admitted embarrassedly. "Terry's been there, of course, but I never asked her. I just assumed that we'd know it when we found it. Honestly, I don't even know what the Historian looks like."

"You don't?" Ed Regis sounded surprised.

"Call it a lack of imagination, Ed Regis, but I never really thought about it. Maybe because I was blind when I first heard about him. Why? Do you know what he looks like?"

"We have some, uh... theories, but I guess not," said Ed Regis.

"My old girlfriend once described him as being really cute."

"Ha!"

"It was before we were dating," I said defensively. "Why? Do your theories not ring well with the Historian being cute?"

"The database doesn't classify subjects by cuteness, Adrian."

We both laughed. My body really hurt from it, but laughing eased my nerves a lot. So much, in fact, that a moment later I found myself yawning loudly.

Ed Regis asked, "Are you sure you don't want to sleep first tonight?"

"I don't think we even need a night watch," I said, yawning again. "If they find us, either way they'll kill us."

"You might have a point," said Ed Regis, yawning also. "I don't know if I could really stay up half the night and then get through tomorrow. Do you want to just put your trust in fate?"

"Fine."

"Just promise me you won't die with that belt buckle under your shirt."

"No promises, but I'll probably be okay."

"Goodnight, then. Hope to see you alive in the morning."

I tried to shift my position a little to get more comfortable, but it didn't help. I didn't like sleeping on my back, but it was too painful on my side.

"Ed Regis, you never told me who you would have died for," I said, closing my eyes. "Tell me now."

"No, Adrian," whispered Ed Regis. "That's just for me."

If there was more to that conversation, I didn't remember it in the morning.

When I woke, I discovered that I wasn't being drained. My belt was lying on the ground next to me, and I suspected that I must have pulled it out of my shirt during the night. For a second, I wondered if perhaps Ed Regis had done it, but I doubted that.

The Wolf was still asleep at my side. Turning my head, I looked out the cave entrance and saw that the day was just beginning. The early-dawn light looked cold and uninviting, but I pulled myself out of the hole to stretch my body. Much of the pain had receded, perhaps due to my continued inability to balance my power very well. I felt numb all over, but at least I could walk.

I felt pretty thirsty, and was about to go back into the cave and wake Ed Regis when I heard a whisper from behind me say, "Hey there."

I spun around, but it was too late. It was the Angel telekinetic who had shot Ed Regis off the mountain. He had been hiding his footsteps by levitating a few inches off the ground, and with his left hand he grabbed my neck while pressing the tip of his right index finger painfully against my lower chest. I knew what that meant.

"Where are your friends?" he hissed.

His grip on my neck was so strong that I could hardly have answered him even if I wanted to, but I somehow managed to spit in his face in reply.

The Angel's grip tightened even more. "Where?!"

Two rapid gunshots. The Angel released me, and I fell to my knees.

As I slumped down onto the ground, coughing violently, I dimly saw Ed Regis standing over the fallen Angel, pointing a pistol at his face.

"Where are *your* friends, buddy?" asked Ed Regis. "Tell me now and I swear I'll call out our healer and have her take care of you."

"Don't worry," croaked the Angel. "They'll find you soon enough."

"Have it your way," said Ed Regis, double-tapping him in the head.

Then he turned to me. "Adrian? Are you..." his voice trailed off as he caught sight of the blood trickling out from between the fingers of my right hand pressed hard against my chest.

"Twice in as many days," I mumbled feebly. "Alia is going to kill me."

I coughed up some blood as Ed Regis helped me lie face up on the ground. The Angel's focused blast hadn't gone all the way through me, but it had gone deep enough. He hadn't been a flight-capable telekinetic for nothing.

"Oh God, Adrian, I'm sorry!" said Ed Regis, looking down at me frantically. "I should have known he wouldn't be drained instantly."

I moaned in pain when Ed Regis pulled my hand away from my chest. After using a small knife to quickly cut my shirt off, Ed Regis poured some water over the wound to clean it.

"He was just a scout," I breathed. "Because he could fly. The rest are still far behind. They would have heard your gunshots, though. You have to get going."

"We will," said Ed Regis, "as soon as I plug the hole."

Ed Regis began fashioning my torn shirt into a bandage as he said, "It missed your heart, but it's pretty close. Still, at least it's a straight line. A blast doesn't churn you up inside like a bullet does."

"Doesn't make a difference," I panted. "I'm not going to make it like this."

Even if I wasn't being drained by my blood, I doubted I could even stand up, let alone walk. Alia wouldn't get the chance to scold me for my stupidity this time. Ed Regis needed to get moving before the rest of the Seraphim caught up with us.

Ed Regis pressed the cleanest part of my shirt against the wound and carefully wrapped it around my body. He had to lift my back a little to get the makeshift bandage around me, and I screamed in agony.

"Stop it, Ed Regis!" I pleaded. "Just stop! There's no way. If you want to do me a favor, give me your gun."

"I can't do that, Adrian."

"Then go! Stop wasting your time." I coughed up more blood. "What makes you think I'd want to die in your company?!"

"You don't have a choice. I'm taking you with me." I felt his arms under my back and legs, and then Ed Regis lifted me up as he said, "You're my guide, remember?"

I didn't need this. Not from a Wolf! Not from anybody when it was clear as day that we wouldn't make it over another mountain together. Ed Regis couldn't even carry his own backpack. How could he possibly escape the Angels carrying me?

"You already know the way," I said, groaning as my blood soaked through the bandage. "Don't pretend like you don't. I didn't jump off that cliff with you so you could throw away your life for nothing."

But Ed Regis refused to put me down. "Not for nothing, Adrian. Never for nothing."

"What's your malfunction, soldier?!" I growled through clenched teeth, desperately hoping I wouldn't pass out before I could talk some sense into him. "Mission first, Major Edward Regis! Professionals put the goddamn mission first!"

Ed Regis looked down at me with eyes that, for the briefest of instances, reminded me just a little of Mark Parnell, and of Alia, and of Cindy. As I closed my eyes, I heard him say gruffly, "What the hell makes you think I'm a professional?"

From there, I faded in and out of consciousness. Sometimes I saw the deep blue sky above me as I lay on the ground next to Ed Regis. Sometimes I woke on his back. Once, I heard several gunshots, but I couldn't be sure if they were real or part of a dream or hallucination. I didn't even have the strength left to care. I remember Ed Regis asking me how much farther it was to the Historian. I don't remember answering. I had found myself a private little world beyond pain or thought or emotion, and I tried my best to stay there. My whole life didn't flash before my eyes. That doesn't happen in real life. But I did see bits of it. For the most part, the better bits of it.

My clearest waking memory was at night, after how many hours or days I couldn't tell, but there was Ed Regis crouching behind a boulder. I was on his back, my arms wrapped loosely around his neck. Voice trembling, Ed Regis said, "I don't know if you're still alive, Adrian, but if you can hear me, know that I'm sorry. I really thought we'd make it."

There were more gunshots. I was pretty sure they were real, but I still didn't care. As far as I was concerned, we were already dead, and I had no desire to go back through the pain it had taken to get here.

Ed Regis was carrying me, this time in his arms, running. I saw the star-filled infinity above us. It reminded me of sitting in a car with Cindy, Alia sleeping in the back.

I fell onto the ground. It didn't hurt. Ed Regis was shouting something. There were several other voices too.

But there was only one voice that I could actually hear and understand. It was a clear, calm voice, strong yet gentle. It made me think of autumn leaves. The voice echoed through my head, and as it did, I knew that everyone on the mountain had heard it at the same time. It said simply, *"Some of you are here without reason."*

I felt myself pulled sharply backwards, as if someone had grabbed me around the waist and yanked hard. For an instant, my whole body felt as if it had frozen solid. It was a sharp, stinging pain, and I wondered if this was perhaps a normal part of dying.

17. THE PRICE OF A HISTORY

When I opened my eyes, they snapped into focus so quickly that I wondered if I had been asleep at all. I was lying on a soft mattress, under a comfortably heavy blanket, the back of my head resting on a large, slightly overstuffed pillow. My hazy memory of the last few days felt more like a fading daydream than reality.

I had been cleaned up and dressed in a thin blue robe much like a hospital gown. I carefully felt around for the blast wound on my chest, not entirely sure that I ever even had one. My fingers found some light scarring there. Yes, it had been real.

Alia, wearing a simple light brown shirt and matching cotton pants, was sitting on the far corner of my bed. Noticing me moving, she looked over at me with a slightly dazed expression and said quietly into my mind, *"Hey, Addy. Welcome back."*

"Am I where I think I am?" I asked slowly.

Alia didn't reply.

"Depends on where you think you are," said a voice to my left. It was Terry, also dressed in a plain cloth shirt, and without her left arm attachment. "No, you're not dead."

I let out a quiet sigh. "This is..."

"The Historian's home," confirmed Terry. "Or rather, his guest house."

"Where are..."

"James and Major Regis?" Terry smiled. "They're in the common room, just outside."

I turned my head, slowly taking in the bedroom. It looked like something out of a strange dream. The walls were each a different color: red, yellow, blue and green. The carpet was deep purple with wavy white stripes across it. The furniture was an awkward combination of leather couches, white marble chairs, a folding plastic picnic table, mahogany bookshelves along one wall, and a modern metal office desk in one corner. A large oil painting of a tiger attacking a mammoth hung above the desk, its frame tilting slightly to the left. The room's lighting was provided by a tiny chandelier hanging from the ceiling and several colorful electric lamps mounted on the walls.

"What is this?" I asked, bewildered by the utter lack of congruity.

"It's all like this," said Terry. "I told you the Historian was eccentric."

"How did I get here?"

"Major Regis carried you to the mountain, and the Historian let you in," Terry replied simply. "From what I heard, the Historian didn't take too kindly with your fans, though. He doesn't allow anyone without official business on his doorstep."

"What do you mean?"

"The Seraphim accidentally followed you too far, past the boundary set by the Historian. Tough luck for them."

There was still so much to take in that I didn't particularly care what fate had befallen the Angels. It was enough that they were no longer chasing us, and that we were safe.

Wondering if it was day or night, I looked again around the room, but not only were there no clocks, there weren't any windows to see if the sun was up.

"Is this some kind of basement?" I asked.

"You could say that," replied Terry. "We're *inside* the mountain, Adrian. Pretty deep, too. That's how the Historian keeps unwanted visitors out. He only allows you in if you have official business with him."

"Then how did we..." I began, but then I understood. "He teleported us into the mountain."

"That's right. That's really the only way in or out of this place."

I had heard of psionic teleporters, and it made sense that the Historian would be one, but I had never expected to experience teleportation firsthand. I stared up at the ceiling for a moment, wondering how far it was to the surface.

Looking again at Alia, I realized that she hadn't spoken at all. She was still sitting motionless on the far corner of my bed and staring emptily off into space.

I said to Terry, "Could I have a moment alone with Alia?"

"Sure. I'll be in the common room," said Terry, and quietly let herself out.

My sister looked a little older than I remembered, and she had definitely lost some weight during our journey, making her even skinnier than she usually was. Aside from that, however, she was the same old Alia. Her unicorn pendant, hanging from its leather cord around her neck, rested lightly on her chest.

Using my telekinesis to give her pendant a gentle tug, I said quietly, "I'm sorry I got shot again."

"James got shot too," Alia said in a monotone. *"And Ed, twice."*

"Are they alright?"

"They're both alright now."

"Are you?"

Alia took a minute, silently fingering her pendant, but then she gave me a quiet Cindy-like smile and nodded. *"I'm sorry I was scared, Addy. I didn't want you to leave us, but I'm really glad you saved Ed."*

"We saved each other," I said. "I don't know if we'll ever be friends, but you were right, Alia. Ed Regis is okay."

"Why don't you start calling him Ed like he wants?"

I shook my head. "I'm just used to calling him Ed Regis. I don't mean anything by it." As I said that, I was a little surprised to discover that it was true. "Ed Regis knows that too, I think."

Alia lay down beside me on top of my blanket. *"We almost didn't make it, Addy,"* she said, staring up at the little chandelier. *"I didn't think I'd see you again. But I guess you guys had it pretty rough too."*

"You could say that," I said, putting an arm around her and patting her side. "How long was I sleeping?"

"Only about a day. Terry, James and I got here yesterday evening. You

and Ed were brought in a few hours after us, at night."

"So have you already talked with the Historian?" I asked.

"We didn't bring any gifts, remember? The Historian hasn't decided if he'll actually talk to us yet."

"But didn't you meet him when he pulled you down here?"

"We were teleported straight into this guest house," explained Alia. *"The servants told us that we'd have to wait for the Historian to decide what he's going to do with us."*

"I see."

"But teleporting really hurt. It was like we were frozen all over."

That part I remembered.

"You said James and Ed Regis were shot," I said. "How bad?"

"James got one through his arm, but I took care of it then and there. Ed was shot in his shoulder and leg, but he didn't lose as much blood as you did. He was up from this morning."

"You know, you're really amazing, Alia," I said. "Thanks for bringing me back from the dead again."

"You don't have to thank me for that, Addy," Alia said quietly. *"You're my brother. I'm just happy you're alive."*

"I'm hungry," I said, noticing my empty stomach for the first time.

"I think it's almost dinnertime. The servants will call us when it's ready."

"One more question," I said, gingerly pulling myself out from under the blanket.

"What?"

"Where are my clothes?"

Alia laughed. *"Over there, by the table."*

I discovered that I could stand without feeling too dizzy. I carefully walked over to the plastic picnic table where a neat stack of clothes lay on a marble chair. Resting next to the chair was a rolled-up sleeping bag. I guessed that Alia, not wanting to bother me, had slept on the floor last night.

Alia had gotten up off of my bed too, so I politely shooed her out of the room and changed out of my robe. There was a pair of cotton underpants and trousers and a thin but comfortable long-sleeve shirt. The clothes had no metal buttons or zippers anywhere, nor any tags or markings of any kind. They fit me as if they had been tailored precisely to my measurements.

My bedroom had a second door which led to a toilet, sink and bath, just like in a hotel. Seeing my own weathered face in the mirror above the sink, I almost gasped in surprise. Whoever had cleaned me up had even given me a shave, but it was still the face of a stranger. My long hair covering my ears had become dry and brittle, and I had lost so much weight that my features looked borderline skeletal. I had long since gotten used to my disparately colored eyes, but now they seemed to sit deeper in my eye sockets, more severe and hawk-like, uncomfortably reminding me of Dr. Denman. Alia had apparently healed my sunburns, but the result made my skin pale and lifeless. In short, I looked like a vampire.

Turning the faucet on and filling the sink, I splashed some cold water onto my face. Then I cupped my hands under the stream of water and took a sip. It was wonderfully refreshing. I didn't wonder too much about how there could be electricity and running water down in the center of the middle of nowhere. It was the Historian's home, after all.

As I studied my face in the mirror again, a strange feeling came over me. It was a combination of wonder and relief, with a touch of grim satisfaction mixed in.

I'm here, I thought to myself quietly. *I'm at the Historian's mountain.*

Or rather, *in* the Historian's mountain. But it was the same. My hope of ever getting this far had been steadily eroding away ever since we had jumped from the crippled airplane. When the Angel telekinetic blasted a hole in my chest, I had given myself up for lost. But once again I had survived. Just as I had somehow survived the Psionic Research Center. Just as I had survived the raid on the towboat. And the Slayers' basement. And Randal Divine. I had survived them all, and here I was, still alive. Alive in the Historian's mountain.

I'm here, I thought to myself again. *I'm here and I'm alive.*

What next? The answer was surprisingly simple: my stomach was beginning to growl.

Opening the door to the common room, I was met with cheers and applause from James and Ed Regis, who knew from Alia and Terry that I had regained consciousness.

"Good to see you alive, Adrian," said Ed Regis, standing up to greet me.

"You too, Ed Regis," I said, shaking his hand. "Thanks for carrying me all the way out here. I hope I wasn't too heavy."

Ed Regis shook his head. "You were actually walking for almost half of it, but I guess you don't remember."

That wasn't very easy to believe, but now that he mentioned it, I did remember a few moments of stumbling along on my own feet.

James said, "We didn't expect you up so soon."

Ed Regis nodded. "You were white as a sheet when we arrived. I was almost certain you were dead."

"He still looks pretty dead," commented Terry.

I agreed, but it wasn't just me. Now that I saw James, Ed Regis and Terry together, I realized that they all looked quite thin and weathered. Though noticeably skinnier, Alia was nevertheless the healthiest among us, probably because back when we were rationing our food supplies, she was given equal-sized portions. I supposed that if we could all get a few days of healthy eating and rest, we would soon return to our normal selves. I wondered how long the Historian would let us stay before sending us on our way, though, especially since we had nothing to offer in return for his hospitality.

"Alia mentioned dinner," I said hopefully.

"Probably in a few more minutes," said Ed Regis, and then gestured to one of the sofas set around a low table. "Why don't you sit down?"

We all sat, and I looked around the common room in wonder. The long rectangular room was at least four times the size of our old living-room dojo in Walnut Lane. Along the walls I counted ten doors which probably led to individual bedrooms. Alia's mention of "servants" and this being just a "guest house" made me wonder how big the Historian's underground compound was. Perhaps it was even larger than the PRC.

Terry had warned me, but I was still shocked at the chaotic interior decoration. The common-room walls were, like my bedroom, each painted a different color. There were three large tables surrounded by chairs and couches, and not one of them matched any of the others. The low square coffee table where we were sitting was made of black marble. The next one over was an old oak dining table, while the farthest one belonged in a school cafeteria. The chairs and sofas were all different sizes and colors, some made of wood or stone or plastic, others covered with leather or various types of cloth. At the far end of the room stood three massive grandfather clocks, side by side. The place was a cross between a museum and a showroom. Each of the bedroom doors was of a different style and color. Mine was painted dark blue with a large red circle in the center. On the walls between the doors hung several landscape and portrait paintings, but not only were these paintings each following very different artistic styles, their frames were all slightly crooked, tilting to the left or right. I could only assume that this was deliberate.

"So what do you think?" asked Terry, clearly amused at the look on my face as my eyes wandered around the room, stopping at a bright green grand piano in the far corner.

"I'm trying not to," I said. It wasn't my place to judge the tastes of a 3000-year-old man.

"That's my room," said Terry, pointing to a green door with a vertical yellow stripe down the middle. Then she pointed to two more, explaining, "That's Major Regis's and James's. There are no other guests here at the moment except us."

"So I guess Merlin never made it this far," I said quietly.

Terry silently shook her head.

Ed Regis said, "If Merlin had been traveling alone and undetected, he could have arrived much sooner than us. But without supplies..."

I nodded. I had already assumed that Merlin was either dead or captured, so I hadn't expected to find him here anyway.

But that isn't to say I didn't care. I would never forget the words Merlin had spoken to Mrs. Harding when he chose to side with us. Merlin owed us nothing, and yet he gave us everything. He was a true friend, the truest kind possible. But we never did find out what happened to him.

To keep my mind off of my hunger, I asked James and Ed Regis about their injuries.

Helping Terry hold back the Angels, James had taken a round in his right forearm. The bullet hadn't hit his bone, but from the scarring on his skin, I could tell that a fair chunk of flesh had been torn off.

"Congratulations, James," I said wryly, looking at his scar. "You've survived your very first bullet. Not many people do."

James smiled. "I still have a long way to go before I catch up with you."

"If you have any sense at all, you won't try," I said seriously.

Ed Regis didn't show me his scars, but according to him, two Angels caught up with us within hours of my passing out. Ed Regis had taken a round to his right shoulder fighting them off. I still couldn't remember it, but apparently I had offered to walk as much as possible after that. The Seraphim that had failed to stop Alia's group met us on the Historian's doorstep. Still bent on capturing us alive, they shot Ed Regis in his right leg as he carried me up the slope, causing him to drop me onto the ground, but moments later we were whisked away into the mountain. Ed Regis refused to describe in detail what the Historian had done to the Angels, stating simply that, "They died horribly."

"I still think it was stupid of you to take me with you, Ed Regis," I said.

Ed Regis shrugged. "You would have done the same for me."

"Don't bet on it."

We laughed loudly and without reservation. I was wrong earlier when I said to Alia that Ed Regis and I might never be friends. It might only be until our mission ended and Ed Regis returned to his Wolf unit, but here and now, we were friends. It was impossible to come through what we had and not be.

Though we had all done our parts to get this far, it was mostly thanks to Alia that we actually made it to the Historian's mountain. The Angels had issued their ultimatum with what they believed to be plenty of distance to spare, but if it hadn't been for their desire to take my sister alive, they could have killed us all much earlier.

Sitting next to me on the sofa, Alia was leaning her back against my side and giggling annoyingly every time my stomach moaned. I was contemplating giving her a good whack on the head when the door at the far end of the room opened and an elderly man wearing a dark suit entered.

The man gave a little bow and said, "Master Regis, Master Turner, Master Howell, Mistress Henderson and Mistress Gifford, dinner is served."

As we approached him, the servant bowed to me and said, "Master Howell, it is good to see you back on your feet so quickly. Benjamin Havel, at your service."

Something about his name seemed strangely familiar to me but I couldn't quite put my finger on it.

"It's nice to meet you, Mr. Havel," I said, shaking his hand.

"Just Havel if you please, Master Howell," the servant corrected gently. "If you are ever in need of anything, call my name or think it loudly, and I will come."

It felt odd being called "Master Howell" by this old and dignified man, but I suspected that it was part of his job. I bowed my head and mumbled awkwardly, "Thank you."

The servant gave me a warm smile. "You must be hungry, Master Howell. We have prepared a special meal for you to help you recover your strength. Good masters and mistresses, please come with me."

As we followed the servant down a corridor lined with more crooked paintings, I asked the man, "How did you know to prepare a meal for me, Mr. Havel? I only just woke up."

"It is our honor and pleasure to care for the guests here. I try my best," the servant replied, and then politely reminded me again, "Just call me Havel, Master Howell."

I whispered to Terry through the corner of my mouth, "How *did* he know?"

Terry shrugged. "The servants here usually know everything that's going on, so watch what you say and do."

Terry's warning made me more self-aware, and I suddenly realized that I was running my right hand along the corridor wall. Ed Regis laughed as I shoved my hands into my pockets.

A few twists and turns later, we arrived at a massive dining room with enough tables and chairs to seat fifty people. I was used to the chaotic decor by now, so it didn't bother me that we were seated at a table shaped like a giant guitar.

We had no sooner sat down than a team of servants entered the room carrying large wooden trays of steaming hot dinner. The servants, I observed, were all different ages: one was a girl who looked only a little older than Terry, while the oldest was a man with a wrinkled face and a long gray beard. They looked and spoke like they came from all different parts of the world, but they nevertheless worked quickly and efficiently together. Our guitar-shaped table was soon overflowing with platters of every evening dish known to man.

I stuck to what looked familiar: diced steak, fried chicken, baked potatoes, bread and salad, keeping clear of the mysterious-looking stews, pâtés, and anything I couldn't identify or pronounce the chief ingredients in. As a semi-professional cook, I would, under more normal circumstances, have jumped at the opportunity to try out new and interesting tastes. But at the moment, I wasn't feeling very adventurous and I knew that I wouldn't be able to eat very much on a shrunken stomach anyway, so why take chances? My sister took a bite of just about everything on the table and reported that it was all perfectly delicious.

"I'll take your word for it, Alia," I said, backing away from her recommendation of what appeared to be tiny purplish raw fish eggs. "I really don't want to have an upset stomach when we meet the Historian."

"If we meet him," corrected Alia.

"If," I repeated, smiling. "But he saved our lives. Even if he won't give us information, I'd still want to thank him."

As I expected, it didn't take much to fill me up, but I felt immensely better for it. And with my senses running on a full stomach, I also finally realized something about this whole place that I had been feeling ever since I had woken but couldn't quite identify, being too distracted by all the ridiculous furniture and paintings: there was absolutely nothing underground-ish about the Historian's home.

I had been underground a lot, and in many places. This wasn't like any of them. It wasn't stuffy, claustrophobic or unnaturally wet or dry here. The air was cool and fresh, not the kind you could get from a mechanized ventilation system, and there always seemed to be a gentle spring breeze blowing from somewhere. The lights were a combination of modern electric lights, oil lamps and candles that were neither too bright nor too dark, didn't cast uncomfortable shadows, and reminded me of sitting in the shade of a tree on a lonely hill. It was as if time itself had frozen at that precise afternoon moment when everything about the day is perfect.

And then there was the Historian. Not the man, but his power. I had felt it strongly from miles away, but here it permeated every room and corridor, seeping through our bodies, an almost tangible flow of psionic energy. I could only sense his destroyer powers, of course, but I nevertheless felt the combined effect of his many others. It soothed my mind and body. My own psionic power seemed to be resonating with the Historian's, feeding off of it, and I strongly suspected that this was the reason I had regained consciousness in but a day after being so close to death.

As we continued our meal, I suddenly felt the Historian's energy surge through my body, making me gasp in surprise.

Ed Regis put down his fork and smiled broadly. "Is this the Historian?"

"You feel it too, don't you?" said Terry. "He's happy about something. When you're this close and he's excited, you don't have to be psionic to feel the Historian's powers."

"This is amazing," James whispered in awe.

Alia had her hands pressed to her chest as if she was having some trouble breathing. Catching my concerned look, she said, "I'm okay. It's just a little too much."

In a moment, the Historian's power flow returned to normal, and Alia and I breathed our sighs of relief.

"What happens when he gets angry?" I muttered.

Terry laughed. "You don't want to know."

We had eaten almost to the bursting point when the servants next began bringing in trays of fruit bowls, ice cream, cookies and cake.

One female servant had come without a tray. She looked about thirty years old and spoke in a slight Swedish accent, saying carefully, "Master Howell, Mistress Henderson, if it pleases you, the Historian will meet with you now."

Everyone looked surprised except Terry, who calmly stood up and said, "It would please us greatly."

"This way, please," said the woman.

"What about us?" asked James.

"Eat your dessert," suggested Terry.

Alia looked even more upset than James at not being invited, but Ed Regis kept a politely unconcerned expression as the woman led Terry and me out of the dining room.

"Why only us?" I asked Terry as we followed the servant, weaving our way through a maze of rooms and corridors.

"We're about to find out," said Terry. "Just remember, the Historian is a very fickle person. Try to stay on his good side." Terry's voice seemed to have a touch of—was it fear? No, it was more like apprehension or nervousness, but it still didn't suit Terry at all.

After a few more doors and corridors, Terry informed me that we were already inside the Historian's residence, but I couldn't tell when we had officially left the guest house. The Historian's mansion was no different: a deliberately outlandish combination of colors and styles.

We passed through a room full of shelves and showcases crammed with ancient-looking pots and small stone figurines. The servant's pace was quick so I didn't get a good look, but I guessed that most of the artifacts here were at least a thousand years old.

The woman brought us to a small waiting room. There was a pair of closed double doors on one wall and a few couches along another.

"Please remain here," she said, gesturing to a couch. "The Historian will be with you shortly."

The servant bowed herself out of the waiting room through a small side door. Terry didn't sit down, so neither did I.

Glancing at the double doors, one green, the other blue, I said nervously to Terry, "I feel like I'm about to get a tooth pulled or something."

Terry grinned. "Anything can happen."

The side door opened again. I was expecting the Historian, but instead another servant came in. I nevertheless stared at him in surprise: This servant was a very young blond-haired boy, even smaller than Alia. Wearing a light blue tunic that matched his baby blue eyes, he looked only about six or seven years old. I guessed that he was the son of one of the other servants, perhaps even the child of the woman who had just led us here. Did the Historian's many servants live here all their lives, taking care of this underground mansion one generation after the next?

The servant boy silently opened the double doors for us and stood to the side, motioning us to enter. We did, and the child followed us in, quietly closing the doors behind him.

Aside from the predictably colorful walls and mismatching furniture, the Historian's office looked fairly ordinary, with a large wooden desk at the far end, several exotic-looking potted plants in the corners, and two long sofas and an armchair set around a rectangular coffee table near the entrance. Never mind that the desk was bright orange.

"So where's the damn Historian?" I whispered to Terry.

Terry promptly smacked me over the head.

Then she bowed low to the child and said, "It is an honor to see you again, Mr. Historian."

I finally got the joke.

Like Alia and me, the Historian had gained his first power, complete physical regeneration, at an age much younger than normal for psionics. He then spent the next three thousand years in his little body, not only unable to grow old, but unable to grow at all. And yes, he was very cute.

Terry looked like she was about to formally introduce me, but the Historian spoke first. "Adrian Howell, it is a pleasure to finally meet you in person," he said in clear if somewhat accented English. "I see your vision is fully restored."

"It is an honor, Mr. Historian," I said humbly. "Thank you for helping Terry find a cure for my blindness."

"Thank Terry," said the Historian. "She paid quite dearly for my help that time."

The Historian's accent was impossible to place. I could only guess that he had moved from language to language over the millennia, resulting in a combination of hundreds of styles and dialects.

"Thank you for seeing us, Mr. Historian," I said uncomfortably, "but we lost the gifts we had meant to bring you."

"Yes, I know," said the Historian. Then he turned to Terry and, telekinetically levitating himself up so that he was eye level with her, said with a frown, "Teresa Henderson, you have returned to me through many dangers to learn about the Angels' new master, but I fear your journey may have been in vain. Once again you stand before me bearing nothing to exchange for my services. There will be no deals or promises with you this time."

Terry roughly poked my side with her left stump. "I brought Adrian, didn't I?"

I stared at Terry and silently mouthed, "What?!"

Terry ignored me, saying to the Historian, "I offer one Adrian Howell in exchange for your assistance in destroying King Randal Divine, or at least information leading us to him."

I looked back and forth between Terry and the levitating Historian, feeling confused and embarrassed. What the hell was Terry doing?!

The Historian waggled a finger at Terry. "Now, now, Teresa. You know perfectly well that I will never fight for either side in this pointless conflict. As for your offer, young Adrian here is not really yours to give, now is he?"

Terry countered, "I'm the one that convinced him to come here and meet you, Mr. Historian. My training and my team kept him alive. I think that makes him mine to offer."

"What is going on here?!" I demanded.

"Negotiation," Terry replied playfully. I glared at her.

Gently touching down onto the floor and looking up at me, the Historian explained, "I wanted to meet you, Adrian Howell. I have been following your progress through the mountains, and I was afraid that you would not survive your journey. I had so very much wanted to speak with you, and that would have been impossible had you arrived as a corpse."

"*You* wanted to speak with *me?*" I asked incredulously.

"I did indeed," the Historian replied with a smile. "Your visit just might be the highlight of the year for me."

At the moment, I had no interest in why the Historian wanted to meet me as opposed to the other way around. Suddenly I was too angry to care. "We lost half of our team on the way here, Historian!" I said, my temper and tone rising rapidly. "I almost died too. We all did! You could have helped us! If you really wanted to meet me so much, why didn't you help us?!"

"It was my choice not to," the Historian replied icily. "Just as you are now choosing to bark at me in my own home."

The little Historian's baby blue eyes were suddenly cold and menacing. His power had grown again, but this time the energy flowed erratically, making my head throb.

I quickly checked myself and took a few controlled breaths. Then I said in a subdued tone, "I'm sorry, Mr. Historian. I know you are sworn to neutrality. I am just frustrated after our long journey."

The Historian nodded, and then smiled, his power instantly returning to normal. "No matter, Adrian. I am hopeful that our meeting will be mutually beneficial."

"Thank you for killing the Angels in the end, by the way," I said.

The Historian shook his head. "They were needlessly on my mountain."

Then, after a sidelong glance at Terry, the Historian said lightly, "Still, at least your combat instructor can indeed claim some credit for your presence here today. You, on the other hand, have arrived without any gifts at all."

Except myself, I thought wryly.

"Are you making an offer?" asked the Historian, apparently delving my thoughts.

"I don't know what I'm offering," I answered honestly. "What do you want with me?"

"It is my belief that you may be able to help me fill in a gap in my knowledge that has been troubling me for the last two hundred years."

"I've only been alive for sixteen," I reminded him.

"It matters not," said the Historian. "You have come with questions you wish me to answer, yes?"

"I have come with one."

"Cindy Gifford?" asked the Historian, still delving my consciousness.

"That's right."

"I shall answer your question, Adrian. But only if you allow me to read your history."

"My history?"

"Your memories, your thoughts, your very essence," said the Historian, levitating himself off of the floor again and looking me in the eyes. "Everything about your sixteen short years of life, from the moment of your birth to the moment you stepped into this room and shouted at me."

I frowned. "I'm guessing that if you wanted, you could read these things without my consent."

"Of course," said the Historian, gliding slowly backwards and setting himself down onto the armchair facing the coffee table. "But once again, I choose not to. Allow me to look inside you for the answers to my questions, and you may consider yourself to have paid for my help in full. The Angels have been so generous of late that I am in no real need of material gifts anyway. I am far more interested in what may be locked inside you."

"What about Terry's questions?" I asked. "What about the location of the Angels' master?"

"I don't think so," said the Historian, shaking his head. "Your history for the answer to your question, nothing more."

I bowed my head and said quietly, "Then, Mr. Historian, I must respectfully decline."

Though he remained sitting, I felt the Historian's anger surge up again. "Not very wise, young Adrian," he said in a chilling voice.

"Perhaps not," I said, still looking down at my feet, "but my information has a price too."

I had no doubts about his claim that he could read me without my consent, and perhaps I was a fool to parley with the notoriously fickle Historian. But I wouldn't be here today if it weren't for Terry and Ed Regis, and their questions were just as important as mine. I was still angry at Terry, of course, but not enough to betray her.

"This is your last chance," the Historian said warningly. "Your history for the location of Cindy Gifford."

"I am deeply sorry to have wasted your time," I said, turning to leave.

Suddenly the Historian laughed loudly. "You are quite a negotiator, young Adrian!" he said jovially, lightly hopping down from his armchair. "It is not often that I must submit to someone else's demands, but in this case I shall have to agree to your terms."

"Thank you, Mr. Historian," I said, breathing a deep sigh of relief as I realized that the Historian's power was once again at peace.

Terry nudged me with her stump, saying happily, "You're better than a bag of gemstones, Adrian."

I replied frostily under my breath, "We are going to have words later, Terry."

I still had no clue what the Historian hoped to gain by reading my history, but it sounded harmless enough, and if that was what it took to get the answers to our questions, then I would happily give him everything I had.

Just to be extra sure, I pressed the Historian, asking, "You will answer all of our questions about Cindy and about the Angel king? And you're not going to mess up my mind or anything when you read it?"

"I promise it will be safe and painless," said the Historian.

"What if you don't find what you're looking for?"

"I may appear to be a child, Adrian, but I am mature enough to honor my promises."

I threw one more dirty look at Terry and then nodded to the Historian.

"Good," the Historian said curtly. "We have a deal."

"How are you going to read my history?" I asked.

"I have just finished reading it," the Historian informed me. "And I thank you."

"That was fast," I remarked. No wonder the Historian was regarded by many as a living god.

"I will have to consider this information very carefully," said the Historian. "One of my servants will escort you back to your dining room now. I can sense the child healer fretting over you."

"Alia can wait," I said. "You have my history so now it's our turn."

"All in good time. Go finish your dessert."

"But you promised to answer our questions!"

The Historian's eyes flashed with anger again. "I will answer them, young Adrian. But I never said that I will do so today. Return to the guest house. Rest and recover your strength. We will speak again when I deem you ready."

I was about to protest further, but Terry painfully twisted my arm and, bowing low, said to the Historian in a humble voice, "Thank you, Mr. Historian. We are greatly in your debt."

Terry dragged me out of the Historian's office. The female servant was waiting for us just outside the double doors.

As we followed the woman back through the maze of rooms and corridors, Terry said mildly, "That was some gutsy negotiation, Adrian, but you really do need to be more polite when dealing with a god."

"Don't you lecture me about being polite, Terry!" I spat furiously. "What the hell was that all about, anyway?!"

"I don't know for sure," Terry replied in an irritatingly calm tone. "Back when you were blind, I told the Historian a bit about you. He seemed a little surprised by your name and said that he wanted to meet you someday."

"And you couldn't tell me this earlier?" I asked sourly. "You couldn't have given me one little warning before you offered me to the Historian like a lump of meat?!"

Terry said defensively, "Hey, it's not like I planned it that way. I offered you to him as a joke because we didn't have anything else to give. I didn't think he'd actually go for it."

I let out a resigned huff. "You're unbelievable, Terry."

Terry laughed. "I'm sure he saw right through me. There's no cheating him, you know."

"I wonder what he was looking for in my history," I said.

"Hopefully something about Randal Divine. Maybe something you didn't notice when you met him last year."

I shook my head. "That doesn't make any sense. The Historian said he was looking for something from two hundred years ago. That's before Randal was born."

Terry shrugged. "Well, at least he agreed to answer our questions. That's all that really matters."

"I thought you were going to push him a lot more to fight for us. He could easily kill Randal if he had a mind to, couldn't he?"

Terry replied in an uncomfortable tone, "Under those circumstances, I honestly didn't have the nerve. It was scary enough asking him just once, and unlike you, I really do want to stay on his good side."

I laughed and said teasingly, "Since I'm the one paying for the Historian's help, you had better stay on my good side too, Teresa."

Terry narrowed her eyes, but she didn't hit me or even offer a nasty rejoinder. She knew that I had scored a point on her. That didn't happen often enough.

Ed Regis, James and Alia had finished their desserts and were patiently waiting for us when we returned to the dining room.

"How did it go?" asked Ed Regis.

"The Historian agreed to answer all of our questions," Terry reported happily.

James looked stunned. "How'd you pull that off?"

Terry smirked. "We traded him a one-eared idiot."

We sat down and I let Terry explain in better detail. Alia had saved me some cake, and I found that my stomach had expanded a bit to make room for it. My dessert and Terry's explanation finished at about the same time.

"We would like to be there when the Historian answers your questions regarding the Angel king," said Ed Regis, and James and Alia nodded in agreement.

"That's really for the Historian to decide," said Terry, "but we can ask."

Havel, the elderly servant who had led us to the dining room, came now to lead us back. "Masters and mistresses, I hope you have enjoyed your meal," he said, smiling around at us.

Alia giggled and whispered into my head, *I really love how they call us here, Addy. It's like we're princes and princesses.*

I grinned at her. "Don't get used to it, Mistress Gifford."

Getting up from the guitar-shaped table, the five of us followed Havel back to the common room.

When we arrived, the servant turned to us and bowed, saying, "Your rooms have been better prepared for your stay. You will find clothes and other necessities provided, but if there is anything further that you require, please don't hesitate to ask."

Then he looked down at Alia. "Mistress Gifford, now that Master Howell no longer needs your constant attention, we have prepared a room for you next to Master Turner's." He gestured to a bright yellow door. "I hope young mistress will find it more comfortable than the sleeping bag on Master Howell's floor."

Alia looked like she was about to argue, but then just smiled and said, "Thank you, Havel."

Once the old servant left the common room, curiosity dictated that we have a quick look inside our bedrooms to see what had been added. We found several sets of clothes in the dressers. The bathrooms had been stocked with soap, towels and other amenities. Havel ran the guest house like any decent hotel. It wasn't exactly five-star, but cozier.

I felt tired but not yet sleepy, and as I sat with the others in the common room, I wondered again what the Historian had been looking for when he read my past. Perhaps it did have something to do with Randal Divine, but it was equally possible that the Historian was after something I had seen or heard during my months at the PRC, or in Slayer captivity, or even in my relationship with the one-of-a-kind hider Cindy Gifford. Some little piece of information that would only have significance within the context of the Historian's vast ocean of knowledge.

Maybe something about Nightmare, I suddenly thought to myself.

Back when I was looking through Ed Regis's psionic database, I had been distracted by Dr. Denman and hadn't read the file on the PRC's mystery psionic. I really wanted to now, but unfortunately I had donated the device to the Walnut Guardians, leaving it in Scott's care.

Telepathically breaking into my frustrated thoughts, Alia asked me for more details about the Historian, so I described him to her. Hearing what he looked like, Alia was now dead set on seeing the 3000-year-old child for herself.

My sister found it hilarious that the Historian had accepted "one Adrian Howell" as payment for our information, but she wasn't as curious as I was regarding what the Historian wanted from my history. Alia's main concern was, like mine, much more personal. "Do you really think he can find Cindy for us?" she asked.

"Let's just say that I'm optimistic," I replied cautiously. It wouldn't do to get Alia's hopes up again only to hear from the Historian that Cindy's current location was a cemetery.

Alia gave me a hesitant look. "Addy? Do you think the Historian would know who my parents are?"

Her question threw me for a moment. Then I gasped. "I can't believe I didn't negotiate that into our deal. Oh, Alia, I'm so sorry! I wasn't thinking at all!"

"It's okay, Addy," Alia said lightly, shaking her head. "I was just wondering, that's all. Cindy first, right?"

My sister rarely mentioned her birth parents so I didn't know how she really felt about them. To say that she was indifferent might be going too far, but I guessed that my sister, like me, cared more about the people who were an actual part of our lives. Of course that didn't excuse my oversight, but what was done was done.

"I'm really sorry," I said. "I don't know if the Historian will answer, but you can still try asking when you meet him."

Alia shrugged. "I might. I'm not sure I really want to."

Ed Regis and James eventually retired to their rooms, citing exhaustion. According to the three grandfather clocks, it was only about 9pm, but our bodies hadn't yet readjusted to a normal life.

Catching me yawning, Terry said, "I guess we should turn in, too."

As we stood, I gave my sister a reassuring smile and said, "It's alright, Ali. You can bunk with me if you want. Just go get your pajamas from your room."

To my utter surprise, however, Alia shook her head, saying, "You only have one bed in your room, Addy."

I shrugged. "That's never stopped you before."

Alia smiled up at me. "Thanks, but I think I'll sleep in my own room tonight."

I wondered if I had heard her right. "Are you sure you'll be okay, Alia?"

"I'm eleven years old, Addy," she said, giving me a resolute look. "Like you said, I can't be afraid of the dark forever."

I looked long and hard at her, and then nodded and whispered, "Good girl."

"I want to take a bath before bed," said Alia, and then laughed, adding, "A really, really long one." She gave me a quick hug and then disappeared into her room.

As I watched her go, Terry said teasingly, "You're actually disappointed, aren't you?"

"Of course I'm not!" I replied forcefully, but not entirely truthfully.

On the one hand, I was exceptionally relieved to see my sister finally acting her age. It put to rest some of my fears regarding the psychological trauma she still carried from her past, including the berserker and everything else that had happened since the fall of New Haven. But I couldn't deny that I would miss her stubborn attachment to me.

Noticing my mixed-up expression, Terry giggled and said, "Well, she couldn't be your little girl forever, Addy-daddy."

"Please don't make fun, Terry," I said quietly. "I am happy for her."

Alia's nighttime murmuring would probably still carry through the walls, but someday she would grow out of that too. Terry occasionally joked that I was more Alia's father than her brother, but perhaps she had a point. I wondered if this was how my own parents had felt when they were watching Cat and me grow up.

Terry smirked. "You might want to keep your door unlocked tonight, just in case."

"Goodnight, Terry," I said, retreating into my room.

"Aren't you at least going to tuck her in?"

"No," I said flatly, closing the door in Terry's face.

18. ANSWERS AND STORIES

I woke early the next morning.

Half-expecting Alia to come sneaking into my bed in the middle of the night, I had taken Terry's advice and kept my room unlocked, but she hadn't come. After changing and splashing some water onto my face, I stepped out into the common room where I found my sister sitting alone on a bright green sofa. The grandfather clocks showed a little past 6am.

"Did you have a good night?" I asked hesitantly as I sat next to her on the sofa. Alia was still in her nightclothes, and I wondered how long she had been sitting here. "No bad dreams?"

"Just one," Alia admitted quietly. *"But I'm okay now."*

I gave her shoulders a quick squeeze. "I'm really proud of you, Alia."

"Thanks."

Alia's tone and slightly unfocused eyes told me that she wanted a little silent time, so I obliged her and we sat together listening to the tick-tocks of the three clocks until they all struck seven.

Suddenly returning to normal, Alia smiled and said, *"I haven't slept in a room all by myself for so long. It felt so strange."*

"It's got to be better than the kind of places we've been sleeping for the last few weeks, though," I said. "You'll get used to it soon enough."

Alia nodded. Then she gave me a slightly embarrassed look as she said, *"I'll sleep in that room while we're staying here, Addy, but if we ever get back home, can I please share a room with you again?"*

"*When* we get back home," I corrected. "And yes, as long as you really want to, we can share a room. But you have to sleep in your own bed, okay?"

Alia gave me a toothy smile. *"Deal!"*

"Now go on and get dressed."

Alia skipped into her room and reappeared a moment later wearing a plain, dark green dress. In sharp contrast to our colorful rooms, all our clothes were basic in design and of quiet shades. I was certain now that they had been specifically tailored for us by the servants of the house who didn't share the Historian's eccentric style.

Havel arrived to announce breakfast at precisely 8am, by which time Terry and the others had been up for half an hour. Alia seemed happy that no one made a big fuss over her finally being able to pass the night on her own.

Breakfast wasn't an insane feast like last night, but there was plenty of ham and eggs and surprisingly fresh milk. In addition to my telekinetic power, which had already been fully recharged, I felt my physical strength well on its way to making a full recovery.

The servants seemed hell-bent on seeing to our every need, constantly watching over our table to make sure nothing was lacking. Alia still found it amusing how everyone insisted on calling her "Mistress Gifford." I didn't particularly care for the fancy titles, but after months of playing househusband at Walnut Lane, it felt wonderful to be waited on for a change.

Delivering us back to the common room, Havel announced that the Historian would probably meet with us again in a few days or possibly a few weeks, but in the meantime we were free to go and do as we pleased.

"Weeks, Havel?" I asked in dismay. "How many?"

Havel merely smiled. "The Historian does not mean to be rude, Master Howell. He merely operates in his own time."

Terry had her own theory. "He's punishing you for insulting him, Half-head. I told you to be careful. Now we're stuck here thanks to your bad manners."

"Who's paying the bills, Five-fingers?" I retorted nastily. "So bite me!"

Even so, I did regret not being more polite. Whatever the Historian's real reason for the delay, our days spent waiting for his answers passed painfully slowly for me. We were granted access to an extensive library as well as a small movie theater in the Historian's home, but restless for news about

Cindy, I wasn't in the mood for entertainment.

Our guest house was also equipped with a training room, complete with mats and various exercise machines, and I wondered when Terry would suggest that we resume our combat training. We would need to keep our skills razor-sharp if we hoped to get back through the Angel-infested mountain range alive.

"Rest first," said Terry, uncharacteristically relaxed.

"We've been resting for almost a week," I said grumpily.

"And you seem much more human for it."

Terry had a point there. At least I had lost the vampire look, and the rest of the team looked much healthier too.

I was also relieved to see that my sister wasn't spending too much time in her silent moods since arriving at the Historian's mansion. She still hung around me a lot during the daytime, but she continued to sleep in her own room and looked like she was finally developing some notion of personal space.

"It's about time," remarked Terry, and I agreed wholeheartedly.

I only gave it a fifty-fifty chance that Alia would really want to share a room with me again when we returned to civilization. Cindy's "give her time" tactic had finally paid off. I doubted Alia would ever be completely free of her many scars, but even so, despite the fact that we were living in a demented mansion deep inside a mountain in a lost part of the world, my sister was finally acting like a normal kid.

Now all I had to do was get her safely back to Cindy.

While waiting in the common room to be called to breakfast on our ninth day in the mountain, Terry finally suggested that we resume our training.

"Who knows how much longer we'll be allowed to stay here," she said. "And the Angels won't easily let us leave."

"We have no supplies and no hider," I reminded her. "How are we going to get out of these mountains alive? The Historian isn't about to help us in that department, is he?"

"No, but the servants will if we ask nicely. I'm sure they'll give us some equipment and maybe even some hiding protection too. It'll wear off, but at least we'll have a head start."

James said sarcastically, "I can't wait to get shot at again."

"I can," I said darkly. "But we can't hide here forever."

"Masters and mistresses," called Havel, who had quietly entered the common room. "Breakfast is served."

"Breakfast is fine, Havel," I said grumpily, "but when can we meet the Historian?"

"Master Howell..." Havel began patiently.

I cut him off, saying sharply, "It's been more than a week, Havel! Might I remind you that we have already paid the Historian for his services?"

"And the Historian is grateful, Master Howell," Havel replied with infinite politeness. "I was going to wait until after breakfast, but I see young master will be happier to know now that the Historian wishes to meet with you today. I am to escort you to his office after your meal."

"Oh," I said, taken aback. "I'm sorry."

"Not at all, Master Howell. I do hope you are satisfied with the Historian's information."

"I'm sure I will be," I said. "But is it just me or all of us this time?"

"The Historian did not specify, young master."

"Then we will all go together," I said curtly.

"Very well."

We ate a rather subdued breakfast, each of us lost in our own thoughts.

For Terry, this was probably all pretty straightforward. Find Randal. Kill Randal. Rid the Angels of their king, and their kingdom would fall apart, restoring the balance of power between the Guardians and the Angels. And it wouldn't hurt to kill a few more Angels along the way.

For James, this might have felt more like the eve of a personal victory. Of the Guardian children we had rescued from New Haven, he alone had made it this far. James clearly took after his parents, who were both Guardian Knights. If this led to the destruction of the Angels, James Turner would be honored by Guardians for generations to come.

Ed Regis would be the first Wolf to ever meet the Historian. What he learned today might very well be his ticket back to his former life. He could go back to hunting psionics and pretending that he was making the world a safer place for everyone. After all he had done for us, I couldn't deny him that.

For Alia and me, this was the deep breath before the plunge. Either Cindy was alive or she was dead. If alive, either she was converted or she was free. As with all hard truths, knowing might hurt at first, but it would ultimately be better than living in ignorance. We had been in limbo far too long. One way or another, I wanted to move on with my life. I think Alia felt the same way.

Once it was clear that we weren't about to finish all of our breakfast, Havel quietly led us to the Historian's office. Even from the dining room, the Historian's energy flow had felt strange to me. His power wasn't particularly happy or angry or excited in any way, but nor was it at peace.

"Remember your manners," whispered Terry as we entered the waiting room.

She didn't have to remind me. I was going to be a good boy this time.

Havel opened the double doors and ushered us inside. The Historian was waiting for us, seated on a tall chair at his desk. Silently bowing once to the Historian, Havel left us, closing the doors behind him.

Levitating up from his chair, the Historian glided over to us, smiling broadly. With all that had happened during our first meeting, I hadn't noticed it then, but the great and wise Historian was missing his two upper front teeth.

Still levitating, the Historian shook hands with James, Ed Regis and Alia in turn. "Welcome to my mountain," he said. "I hope your stay here has been a pleasant one so far."

"Thank you for seeing us, Mr. Historian," I said humbly. "I want to apologize again for how I acted before."

The Historian shook his head. "Did you have a good rest?"

"A very good rest. Thank you." I managed to say it without a trace of sarcasm, but of course the Historian could read my thoughts.

"It was not as punishment that I made you wait, young Adrian," he said, touching down onto the floor. "There was certain information I wished to verify, and I wanted you properly rested before I gave you the news that it is my unfortunate duty to share."

"I'm in pretty good shape now," I said evenly.

"That is good. But I feel compelled to suggest that you will not want an audience for what I am about to tell you."

I glanced around at the four standing beside me.

"We can leave," suggested Ed Regis, but Alia shook her head.

"No," I said, turning back to the Historian. "Thank you for your concern,

Mr. Historian, but they all have a right to be here." If Alia was going to hear that Cindy is already dead, she might as well hear it now, directly from the Historian himself.

"As you are the one who paid for this information, that is your decision. I hope you do not regret it." The Historian gestured to the sofas around the rectangular coffee table. "Won't you please be seated?"

"No disrespect, but I prefer to stand," I replied.

"Do sit down anyway," said the Historian, gently puppeteering me down onto a sofa. He gestured to the rest of my team, and soon I found myself sandwiched between Terry on my left and Alia on my right. James and Ed Regis sat on the other sofa across from us, and the Historian hopped up onto the armchair at the end of the table.

Releasing my limbs from his psionic control, the Historian said, "Now that we are comfortable, would you like your answer first, and the story behind it later, or would you prefer the story first, and allow it to lead you to your answer? My personal preference is always to tell the story first, as I am very fond of stories. However, you are the client, so you may decide."

"The answer first please, Mr. Historian," I said. I didn't care about the story. I wanted to know the ending, and we had waited long enough.

"Indeed you have," said the Historian, again reading my thoughts. "But you will not like what I am about to tell you."

Alia was holding my right hand. I gave her a comforting smile and then said to the Historian, "I think we can handle it."

"Very well. Your answer first," said the Historian. "As you have already guessed, your Cynthia Gifford is currently converted and bound to the service of Randal Divine, self-proclaimed king of the Angels."

I felt Alia's grip tighten on my hand. I squeezed back a little.

"Where is she?" I asked.

The Historian replied, "She currently lives in your old penthouse at the top of the building formally known as New Haven One."

"In Lumina..." I breathed. "She hides Lumina?" But that didn't make sense. Merlin had insisted that Lumina wasn't being hidden by a single hiding bubble.

"Merlin's information is a little outdated," explained the Historian. "Cindy moved back into her penthouse three weeks ago. She had traveled with Randal Divine as his personal hider for a few months following her capture, but now she is in charge of the Angel city."

"How did she get captured?"

"The story?" asked the Historian.

I nodded.

"Very well. The Guardian Council's plane, after a botched hijacking attempt by the Angels, crashed into the ocean, killing about half of the passengers. The survivors, including your Cindy Gifford, tried to return to shore on inflatable rafts, but were rounded up by the Seraphim before they could make it."

The Historian paused, allowing us to take this in.

Cindy's capture could hardly count as good news, but it was still better that she was alive and in Angel captivity rather than dead and irretrievable.

Perhaps after reading my consciousness to make sure that I was ready for the rest of the story, the Historian continued, "Even after being converted, Cindy searched for you and Alia. She was hoping to bring you into the Angels with her, but Randal Divine kept her busy with other work. I am not entirely certain, but she may have later been told that you and Alia are dead."

"Cindy would never believe that," I said.

"She may have been psionically forced to," the Historian suggested delicately.

Alia's hand was trembling slightly, but my sister wasn't crying or defocused. We had both known and accepted this as the most probable explanation for Cindy's disappearance. The Historian wasn't telling us much that we hadn't already suspected. Cindy was bound to the Angels. As a male master controller, Randal's conversions would be permanent even on adults, but there was still one way to break the connection.

Destroy the master.

"Looks like this war just got very personal for you, Adrian," Terry said grimly.

"Very," I agreed quietly, turning to her. "I know I said Cindy first, Terry, but I guess there's no way around it. Getting Cindy back will just have to be our reward for saving the world from Randal Divine. Whatever it takes, I'll help you kill him."

"You're sure?" asked Terry.

I nodded. "It's probably better this way. At least now I know what I'm fighting for."

I turned back to the Historian, who was sitting calmly in his armchair, his hands folded neatly in his lap. "Thank you for telling us about Cindy, Mr. Historian," I said. "Now could you please tell us where to find the Angel king?"

The Historian shook his head. "Alas, I cannot."

"You don't know?" I asked, trying not to make it sound like a challenge.

"Answer first or story first?" asked the Historian.

"Answer," I replied without hesitation. I wasn't interested in Randal's story. All I wanted to do was kill him, now more than ever, and if the Historian really didn't know where the Angel king was, then at least he owed us whatever information he did have.

"I really think you should hear the story first this time, Adrian," the Historian said warningly.

"Answer," I insisted, sensing Terry's impatience as strongly as my own. "Please, Mr. Historian. We need to know."

The Historian sighed. "Very well. The answer is simple: There is no such thing as a psionic king, and therefore I cannot tell you where to find one. There is not now, nor ever was, a male master controller. The few cases in our recorded history were actually women posing as men. Reports of their powers surpassing those of other queens are merely decoration added by the men who passed the history on. Men simply wanted to believe that a man's power was greater than any woman's. But it is all just decoration. I was there in person so you will believe me when I tell you that psionic kings are nothing more than a hopeful myth."

I stared at him, gaping. We probably all did.

Terry blurted out, "But Randal—"

"Randal Divine," the Historian cut across her in a slightly annoyed tone, "is a mind-writer, Teresa. A powerful one, no doubt, but merely a mind-writer. While it is true that most of the recently converted Angels are bound to his service, he is not the one doing the converting."

"Then who?!" I asked.

"But you already know who, Adrian," the Historian said matter-of-factly. "You have known all your life."

I blinked back at him, shaking my head.

"Your sister," said the Historian. "Young Catherine Divine is the current queen of the Angels."

For a frozen moment of eternity, I wondered if what the Historian had just said could actually be true. Then I leapt up from the sofa, shouting furiously, "You lie!"

The Historian telekinetically slammed me back into my seat, his voice suddenly deep and menacing as he growled, "Now you wish you heard the story first!"

I struggled against the Historian's telekinetic field pinning me to the sofa. Alia was saying something in my head but I couldn't make it out. My head was spinning so horribly that I felt like throwing up. "You lie!" I shouted again. "It's not possible!"

"Your history was quite an interesting read, young Adrian," said the Historian, his tone calmer but cold and businesslike. "Your power came slowly. Unnaturally slowly for a psionic. Even the doctors who studied you at the research center found it strange, but you never cared to know why. Gradual psionic development is a little-known trait of a very unique power. One that, for better or for worse, we are both incapable of attaining."

I was barely listening to him. I couldn't breathe well and I felt horribly lightheaded as I continued to push vainly against the Historian's telekinetic grasp.

"Stop struggling, Adrian!" commanded the Historian. "I do not wish to hurt you or alter your state of mind. Do not make me force you into submission! You asked for truth. I am but the messenger."

"I'll keep him in his seat, Mr. Historian," said Terry. "Please let him go."

I felt Terry take hold of my left hand while Alia put both of her hands firmly around my right arm. The Historian released my body. I tried to pull my arms free but Terry and Alia refused to let go.

"Addy, please don't!" Alia cried into my head.

I stopped struggling and rested my back against the sofa, trying to regain my breath.

"You have always been a good brother for little Cat, haven't you, Adrian?" said the Historian. "Your father often complimented you for that. Did it never occur to you to question why your sister always seemed to get the better of you when the two of you were growing up together?"

I shook my head, still unable to accept what the Historian was telling me.

The Historian continued mercilessly, "And you never once wondered why, when you were separated from Catherine, you became so attached to young Alia here that you could lay down your life for her without so much as a second of thought? Just as you had grown up accidentally knocking things off of shelves and not knowing why, Catherine had been unknowingly using her power on you. When you lost your master, to preserve your sanity, you turned to Alia in her stead."

"You lie," I whimpered, no longer able to see the Historian through my tears.

"Search your heart, Adrian," the Historian said quietly. "Catherine Howell was your one true master. Not Alia Gifford."

I finally stopped struggling. I let my head fall back onto the cushion as I sobbed, "I tried to save her. I had to save her from the monster. But they took her. They took her away." Terry had let go of my left hand, and I brought it up to my chest, feeling the amethyst under my palm as I thought wretchedly, *I'm so sorry, Cat. I'm so sorry I let you go.*

"It hurts to lose a master," said the Historian. "Just as it hurts to lose family. But you were twelve years old. You need not blame yourself for your failure."

I slowly wiped my eyes with my left palm. I noticed that the sofa where Ed Regis and James had been sitting was now empty. Exactly when I couldn't tell, but they had quietly let themselves out of the office. I felt just a bit grateful, and a little calmer.

"Your conversion was never very deep or complete," explained the Historian. "If it had been stronger, you would have jumped out of the window with your master when your home was attacked. As is usually the case with weak or untrained psionic conversion, your commitment to your master faded in and out. That is why you remained so undecided about searching for her. During your first few months living in Cindy Gifford's house, Alia helped you overcome much of your separation anxiety. You still pined for Catherine over the years, but by the time you met her at the gathering of lesser gods, your conversion had weakened enough for you to walk away. While you may never be completely free of her, I doubt very much that she has any serious hold on you anymore."

My mind flashed back to the moment Cat had pulled a gun on me inside Randal's motorhome. I wondered if she already knew what she was.

The Historian was following my thoughts, and he said, "I do not know exactly when Catherine came into her full power, or if she had been forewarned that she would become a master. Randal Divine has gone to great lengths to shelter her from the outside world."

"Cat called him 'Father,'" I said disgustedly.

"They are quite a team, Adrian. After Larissa Divine was killed, Randal stepped up to the Angel throne, claiming to be a psionic king. In reality, young Catherine is the one doing the converting, binding new arrivals and rebinding those whose conversions have been broken with the death of Larissa Divine. Once Catherine binds her subjects to the Angel faction, Randal alters their memories, making them think that he is the master controller."

Terry asked disbelievingly, "How could something like that be kept a secret?"

"Deep down, many of the converts probably know that Randal isn't their true master, making for some very confused Angels," the Historian said with a chuckle. "It is nevertheless a viable short-term solution. In order to perpetuate the belief that he is a psionic king, Randal Divine employs hiders such as Cindy Gifford to keep his power and Catherine's well hidden. To be extra safe, however, when she isn't converting people, Catherine keeps herself constantly drained by wearing a thin silver chain around her neck."

I touched my amethyst again. This stone had once been on that chain.

The Historian continued, "That, combined with her youth, is why no one has yet felt her power from afar. Catherine is probably much better than you at power balance, Adrian, but it must still take a fair amount of dedication to willingly live in a drained condition."

"Randal is just using her," I said, trying desperately to believe that it was true.

"That is possible," said the Historian. "But it is more likely that Randal does indeed love Catherine as a daughter. He doesn't want people to know what your sister is until she is ready to take on the risks and responsibilities of a psionic queen. And Catherine in turn supports Randal Divine and the Angel cause. Her allegiance to the Angels is not based on psionic control. After all, she could hardly convert herself. Whatever you may think of her, Catherine is doing this of her own free will."

As much as it hurt, I nevertheless knew that the Historian was right. Even after Cat had told me that she had joined the Angels willingly, I often toyed with the idea that either Larissa or Randal must have psionically converted her. But now that excuse no longer worked. Cat was the queen. She was the one behind the Angels' new order. It no longer mattered whether I accepted that or not. It was simply the truth, and now I knew.

"So now you have your answers, Adrian and Teresa," said the Historian. "Everything except the current location of Catherine Divine, which I do not have. But I nevertheless feel compelled to ask you both: if I could tell you where Randal and Catherine are, would you really want to know?"

"I don't know," I replied honestly. It was still too early to know for sure what I wanted. I still couldn't deal with where this discovery was trying to take me. Terry remained silent.

"Then perhaps you will listen to the story now," suggested the Historian. "It may help you to make up your minds."

I nodded dully.

The Historian smiled. "As you well know, I am a collector of histories, of facts and events and stories. But my personal favorite is family histories, and most specifically, psionic family histories. It was for my collection that I asked to read your history, Adrian, and my suspicions turned out to be well founded."

I wasn't sure I cared for a history lesson right now, but at least it allowed my mind to think of something aside from what I had just heard about my first sister.

"In relatively modern history," began the Historian, "that is, these last three hundred years or so, there were only five known bloodlines that could spawn a master controller, including the family of Divine for the Angels and the family of Granados for the Guardians. Master-controller bloodlines are actually much easier to trace than those of other psionics, because while it is true that only females can become master controllers, the potential for this power can only be passed down the male side of the family."

I hadn't known that, but it made sense: that was why certain family names such as Divine, Harrow and Granados were tied to master controllers.

"I had been following all five bloodlines with considerable interest," continued the Historian. "But then, by a combination of chance and foolish error on my part, I lost track of one: the Gelsons." The Historian gave me a curious smile. "I suppose you have never heard of the Gelsons, young Adrian."

I shrugged. The name meant nothing to me.

The Historian slowly leaned forward in his armchair, saying quietly, "Nearly two hundred and fifty years ago, Eldridge Gelson was the last surviving member of his bloodline that had any chance of having children, and he did have many with his wife, Holly. Nineteen children to be exact. But then Eldridge was accused of devil worship, not an uncommon thing for psionics of that time. He was hunted down and killed along with his wife and several of their children. Those that escaped hid their identity by adopting Holly's maiden name, Havel."

Havel? As in the servant Benjamin Havel?

"That is correct, Adrian. But despite changing their names, all but two of the remaining Havel children were eventually found and killed. Of the two, one evaded capture through skill and cunning. Benjamin Havel is the last of his bloodline, and so that one will end when Benjamin dies. The other Gelson child, Kenton Havel, changed his name a second time, and by now you must have guessed what he changed it to."

I gazed back at him for a moment, and then nodded slowly.

The Historian gave me an approving smile and continued, "When you were a baby, your grandfather took it upon himself to compile an extensive history of the Howell family name. At ten months old, you watched through the bars of your crib as your grandfather, your father and your uncle worked on this project. They came across the name Kenton Havel and wondered if he really was the very first Howell, but they were never quite as certain as I was when I saw them through your eyes."

The first memories I could recall for myself were from kindergarten, but I didn't particularly care to know how the Historian managed to read an event that happened when I was crawling around in a crib. In light of what he had told me earlier, all of this information now seemed entirely trivial, and I was never one to care much for history anyway.

But I did have one question. "Why did no one ever find us before?"

The Historian explained, "Eldridge Gelson's psionic blood was already fairly thin due to intermarriage with non-psionics. His marriage to the commoner Holly Havel resulted in only six children with any psionic ability. The Gelson-Havel bloodline soon fell into darkness. Dormant bloodlines are difficult to track. There are many people with the surname Howell in this world, and they are not all descendants of Kenton Howell. Only when your power grew strong enough to be sensed by finders did anyone take any notice of your family name."

I stared at him. "The Angels knew all along exactly what was in my blood, didn't they, Mr. Historian?" I said accusingly. "They knew because you told them!"

I couldn't help the resentment I felt toward the Historian. There was nothing neutral about the Historian's lifestyle. He was undoubtedly the one who had provided the Angels with the information that led their berserker to my home that night.

The Historian's power flow remained at peace as he said calmly, "You are very perceptive, but nevertheless not entirely correct. You see, the Gelsons were not the only family hunted to extinction. By the time Diana Granados was killed, only two families capable of producing master controllers remained: the Divines and the Harrows. And the Harrows now belonged to the Angels too, so the Angels had little need for another master bloodline. Thus it was not an Angel, but rather the second-in-command of the largest remaining Guardian group, none other than Teresa's grandfather, who approached me years ago seeking my knowledge of lost master bloodlines."

"You mean Ralph Henderson was looking for a new master controller to reunite the Guardians?" I asked.

"That is correct. I didn't know where your family was, of course, but I gave Ralph all that I knew at the time, including your surname. When your power grew strong enough to be sensed from afar, it wasn't hard for him to put two and two together. The once-dormant Gelson-Havel bloodline had finally been reactivated by the union of your mother and father, and any female offspring could very well turn out to be a wild-born master controller."

"Adrian Havel," I said, suddenly remembering. "That's what Ralph called me when we first met."

"Your memory serves you well," said the Historian, smiling. "Ralph of course knew your real surname, but it must have slipped his mind in his excitement at finally finding the bloodline that, to his mind, might still save the

Guardian cause."

I asked, "But if you had told this only to Ralph, then how did the Angels find out about us?"

"Due to difficulties on the road, Ralph Henderson arrived here alone with nothing but the clothes on his back, much like yourselves. He had nothing to offer me in exchange for the information he sought, but in the spirit of giving the Guardians a little extra help in their time of need, I made a deal with him. Ralph would get your family name, but in return, he would have to pass it along to the Angel queen. Ralph agreed to my terms, knowing that the Guardians had more to gain than the Angels who already had a master. I gave Ralph your family name and he later mailed it to Larissa Divine. Such was the price he paid for my information. It was the only fair way."

Fair way? What about the price I paid?! My mother, my father, my uncle... how many others had died for the Historian's neutrality? How many lives had been destroyed by this 3000-year-old child's sick little games? I sensed Terry bristling at my side, but she remained silent. With extraordinary effort, I kept my outward calm too, and if the Historian was reading my furious thoughts, he didn't comment.

Instead, the Historian said, "The Angels didn't need another master bloodline, but nor were they about to stand back and allow the Guardians to take it. When your bloodline was rediscovered, in order to keep her monopoly on master controllers, Larissa Divine immediately sent one of her very best Seraphim to bring you and your sister in."

"The berserker..." I breathed.

"This particular Seraph, a highly trusted member of Larissa's personal guard, had a unique combination of long-range finding, telepathy and berserking which allowed him to attack psionic minds from great distances," explained the Historian. "His power wouldn't work on Ralph, however, as Ralph was far too skilled at blocking mind control. Thus the hunt for you and your sister began, and as you remember, it turned into a very close race."

"But that doesn't make sense, Mr. Historian," I said, shaking my head. "If the Angels were trying to get my sister alive, why did their berserker try to force me to kill her?"

The Historian rolled his eyes, saying, "Because, young Adrian, Larissa Divine's primary objective was to stop the Guardians from getting a new master, no matter the cost. When the berserker learned that Ralph Henderson was after him, he decided that it would be better to kill your family from afar than risk letting Ralph take you and Catherine into the Guardians. He first used his long-range berserking on you, hoping you would kill your sister. Later, when he was close enough to use his power on your father, he tried to kill your whole family."

I still vividly remembered how the berserker had grinned at me just before Ralph shot him through the throat with his crossbow. But the race hadn't ended there. Ralph had to get me out of my house quickly. He had known that there were more Seraphim fast approaching.

"Eight Seraphim, to be exact," said the Historian, still reading my mind. "You see, Larissa Divine had originally sent only the one Seraph berserker to intercept your family, wishing to keep your bloodline a secret even from the top members of her own faction. But then, when she learned that Ralph was on her berserker's trail, she reluctantly sent in a whole team. Impossibly outnumbered, Ralph had little choice but to give up your sister and escape with only you."

"Ralph saved me only because he failed to get Cat," I muttered, feeling the full weight of the irony. I had spent years thinking that Cat had just been a sideshow for the Angels. I had thought that they kidnapped her simply because she was the sister of a wild-born telekinetic and that someday she might become telekinetic too. But, in reality, my sister had always been the true target.

The Historian shook his head. "You were both important targets, Adrian. As I told you earlier, the power of master controllers can only be passed from father to child. Your sister's future daughters will never become masters. Only yours can. Thus, in a way, you are far more important."

"But Ralph wanted my sister," I insisted. "He asked about her when he came for me."

The Historian chuckled. "Of course, for Ralph Henderson, Catherine was indeed the greater prize. He wanted a master for the Guardians as soon as possible, after all. But having lost your sister to the Angels, Ralph hoped that one day you might grow up to have a daughter who could become the next Guardian queen. Thus, when you were captured by the Wolves and Cindy asked Mr. Baker for help in retrieving you from that research center, Ralph volunteered to lead the assault because he valued your blood too much to trust to anyone else."

And yet old Ralph didn't force me into the PRC's elevator when he had the chance, allowing me instead to go after Alia. I would never really understand Ralph Henderson.

The Historian said lightly, "Ralph was eccentric, like me."

"How do you know all this?" I asked.

"It is just my business to know."

"Mr. Baker said he never wanted a master controller in the Guardians again," I said. "Did he know what I was?"

The Historian shook his head. "Ralph never told him, fearing that if he did, Mr. Baker might have you killed."

"Would he have?"

"Who is to say?" the Historian said with a shrug. "But had he known, he certainly would never have let you cross into the Angel camp at the gathering of lesser gods last year. Fearing for your safety, Ralph never told anyone your identity, aside from Larissa Divine of course. He never even told you, and now he is dead. Very few people alive today know what is in your blood, Adrian, or what your children might someday become."

"That secret won't last forever," I said darkly.

"It will last awhile yet," replied the Historian. "Perhaps fortunately for you, Larissa Divine also carefully hid your surname from the rest of the Angels. The team of Seraphim that captured your sister mysteriously disappeared shortly thereafter, never to be seen again. Meanwhile, young Catherine was placed in the care of Larissa's trusted nephew, Randal. Now, with Larissa gone, it is very likely that Randal and Catherine Divine are the only Angels who know that the family of Howell has master controller in its blood."

Listening to the Historian's story about Ralph and the berserker, I had actually managed to temporarily subdue my unhinged emotions, but the Historian's mention of Randal and Catherine Divine threw me back into the icy water.

Back at the blood trial, Randal had said that he was going to execute me because he couldn't allow the Guardians to use me against Cat. Now I understood what he had really meant. But that brought me to another unanswered question. "Why didn't Larissa Divine try to catch or kill me when I was living in New Haven?" I asked. "Wasn't she worried that I would provide the Guardians with a new queen?"

The Historian replied, "When Larissa Divine discovered that you were living among the New Haven Guardians, she certainly feared that someday you would give them a new master. But since you were no longer a solitary wild-born, she couldn't directly order a hit on you without the risk of arousing new suspicions about your bloodline. In order to protect your sister's identity, she decided to wait, hopeful that her faction could absorb the Guardians completely, along with you and any daughters you might have, well before they were old enough to come into their powers."

Considering the pace at which the Angels were gaining ground, it was hard to disagree with that line of thought.

The Historian looked into my eyes, saying, "You have another question about Larissa Divine."

I did. "Mr. Baker told me that the only reason Larissa called for a blood trial last year was because she was without a successor after the Guardians killed the Angels' second master, Angelina Harrow. If that's the case…"

The Historian nodded. "I'm only guessing, but Larissa Divine probably didn't think that your sister would become a viable successor for many years to come. And it's quite possible that Catherine only came into her power shortly after the old queen's death."

"Talk about timing…" I muttered.

The Historian leaned back in his chair and said slowly, "Once Catherine is old enough, she will officially take over the faction, and if she continues to believe in her father's cause, the Angels will soon rule the entire world. You are already a very powerful telekinetic, Adrian. It stands to reason that Catherine is an equally talented master."

"Is she really the last of the master bloodlines?" I asked.

"You and she are the last," corrected the Historian. "The two of you are the last living descendants of Kenton Howell, son of Eldridge Gelson and Holly Havel. There still are, of course, Divines and Harrows within the Angels, but none of them carry the potential to spawn master controllers. The Guardians saw to that when they killed Angelina Harrow shortly after your rescue from the God-slayers. During the raid on the second master's settlement, the Guardian Knights, acting under Mr. Baker's orders, made sure to kill every other Harrow that could potentially give rise to a new master."

I had to be absolutely sure, so I pressed the Historian, asking, "So if I die without children, there will be no more master controllers left anywhere? Forever?"

The Historian gave a little shrug. "I cannot guarantee that there isn't another lost, dormant bloodline somewhere, but I have studied these matters extensively and I am fairly confident in my findings."

I nodded and shakily got to my feet, mumbling, "Thank you for your time, Mr. Historian."

"It was my pleasure, Adrian Howell," said the Historian, hopping down from his armchair and gently shaking my hand. "I'm sorry it had to be such difficult news for you. If you don't mind, I may wish to speak with you again before your departure."

"Fine," I said.

Terry and Alia had stood up too.

The Historian shook Terry's hand, saying, "You and your companions are welcome to remain in the guest house for a few more days if you like."

"Thank you," said Terry. "We will."

Then the Historian turned to Alia. He reached out to shake her hand, but Alia refused to take it, staring blankly back at him.

The Historian smiled and nodded understandingly. "Take good care of your brother, young Alia."

19. THE BALANCE OF POWER

Ed Regis and James were not in the waiting room outside the Historian's office. As Terry closed the doors behind us, I looked at her and asked quietly, "So, what now?"

Terry just sighed and shook her head.

"Master Howell," called Havel from the waiting room entrance, "Mistress Henderson and Mistress Gifford, I have already escorted Master Regis and Master Turner back to your common room. Please allow me to take you to them." Catching the look in my eyes, the old servant bowed deeply and said, "My apologies, Master Howell. It was not my place to speak of it."

Now more than ever, I hated how he called me "Master Howell," but that was just how he talked. I wondered how long he had been a servant here.

We knew the way by now, but Havel insisted on guiding us. As we walked, I looked down at Alia. She was loosely holding my hand as she stared off into space. With her free hand, Alia was fingering her unicorn pendant, gently stroking the polished bloodstone.

So overwhelmed by what the Historian had told me, I hadn't given any thought to how Alia had taken the Historian's information. I wondered now how she had felt about the Historian's claim that I had used her as a security blanket when I lost my psionic master. Was that really the only reason I had refused to escape the PRC without her? Was conversion the basis of our so-called family relationship?

"Alia," I whispered, squeezing her hand.

Alia looked up at me, her eyes a little damp as she asked into my head, *"Are you alright?"*

I didn't know how to answer that.

"I'm really sorry, Addy," she said, holding my hand tightly.

"So am I," I said quietly. "Thanks for always being with me."

Alia gave me a watery smile.

I stopped walking and turned to her. "You are my sister, Alia," I said, suddenly entirely sure that it was true. "I don't care how this started or what that boy thinks he knows about us. You are my family. Don't you ever doubt that."

"I don't, Addy. I was just afraid that you did."

I shook my head. I refused to believe that my actions were dictated by the fading remnants of untrained psionic control. Even the Historian had confirmed that I was no longer under the influence of Cat's conversion, and if I was faced today with another situation like the one at the PRC, I knew exactly what I would do.

Ed Regis and James stood up from their chairs as we arrived back in the common room.

"Are you alright, Adrian?" asked Ed Regis. James chimed in with the same question too.

I wished everyone would stop asking me that because I still didn't know. I replied instead, "You two didn't have to leave, you know. But thank you."

Ed Regis nodded. "We heard enough."

After telling us that he would return when lunch was served, Havel bowed himself out of the room, and I said to Terry, "Could I please have a little time alone?"

Terry gave me an uncharacteristically sympathetic look. "As much time as you need, Adrian."

Alia was the only one who understood that I wasn't asking for "time alone" in the physical sense. I was grateful for her presence as she quietly followed me into my bedroom and sat beside me on the edge of my bed.

As we sat there listening to each other's breathing, I don't know what was going through Alia's head, but mine was still struggling to come to grips with the new world that I found myself in. I had already accepted the Historian's information as true. Everything was utterly, painfully clear now.

Catherine was Randal Divine's secret weapon: a young queen who could psionically rule the planet for years to come, consolidating governments and setting up a new world order that would keep the Angels in power forever. That much I understood. The only question that remained was what, if anything, we were going to do about it. That question felt like a jackhammer on my skull.

Staring down at my empty hands, I sat there thinking in circles, trying to grasp a solution that simply didn't exist. But I had known from the moment I learned what Cat had become that there was no way around this. Even Terry couldn't bring herself to say it out loud, but she knew it as well as I did.

Catherine Divine would have to die.

And it wasn't because of who she was. It wasn't because of her choices or her allegiances or even who she called her father, but purely because of *what* she was. It was for the same reason that we had originally wanted to kill Randal Divine. It was the same reason I had been blinded by the Slayers, the same reason Cindy was so valued by the Guardians and the Angels alike. It was the same reason Alia bore the crisscrossing scars on her back. Cat's only true crime was that of being born.

Yet my first sister's very existence was the difference between a world with a master controller and one without.

That was the difference Terry had wanted to make. It was the only Guardian cause I believed in anymore. That the world's last psionic master turned out to be my own flesh and blood made no real difference in what we were fighting for.

Though Cindy and all the other Angels had been tricked into believing that they were bound to the service of Randal Divine, the only way to break their conversions quickly was to kill the true source, which was Catherine. Unlike a mythical king's, Queen Divine's conversions would someday wear off, but not for many years to come. Meanwhile, Alia would either grow up without her mother or she would be turned into an Angel herself when we were finally hunted down.

Ralph Henderson had known that as long as there were multiple masters ruling multiple factions, the balance of power could be maintained. In a world with only one master, that one master would rule everything. I cared no more for the Guardians than I did for the Angels, but this wasn't about which side would win the psionic war. Nor was it a choice between Cindy, Alia and Cat. To restore the balance of power and protect the future of psionics and non-psionics alike, somebody would have to kill my sister.

Would that somebody be me?

Cat… Catherine Howell… Cathy Divine… Queen Divine. It was still difficult to see them all as the same person, but there was no denying what my sister would eventually become, and what she was already in the process of becoming. What had happened between her and Randal that she had come to uphold the Angels' purpose to dominate the world with psionic control? I might ask her when I found her again.

I heard the door open and looked up. Terry quietly let herself in, saying, "Havel just announced lunch. I told him you probably weren't hungry, but he insisted that I check anyway."

I remained silent. Terry closed the door and took a few uncomfortable steps toward my bed. I was glad that she didn't ask me if I was alright.

"I won't do it, Adrian," said Terry, not meeting my eyes. "I swear I didn't know it would be like this."

"I know you didn't," I said softly. "But you will do it. And so will I."

Terry looked at me in surprise. "You can't mean that."

Ralph had once claimed that I was "destined for greatness." What he had meant was that someday I would father the child who would become the next Guardian queen, and in doing so, I would restore the balance of power between the Guardians and the Angels. But it wasn't going to be that way.

I stood up from my bed and looked Terry in the eye. "I am going to kill the Angel queen, Terry, and you are going to help me."

Terry slowly shook her head. "This is crazy, Adrian. This is completely crazy."

I sighed. "That's what I first thought, too. But you know something? If we turn away from this now, then they all died for nothing. Felicity and Max, and Merlin… and your grandfather, and your brother, Gabriel, and Mr. Barnum… and Laila and her mother… they all died for nothing."

"This won't bring them back," said Terry.

"You're right, Terry. It won't. But if I wasn't going to let Randal Divine rule the world, then I won't let Cat…" I gulped hard. "I won't let Catherine Divine have it either."

"You would kill your own sister?"

"No," I said sarcastically, "I'll go hide under a rock and wait for a complete stranger to kill her."

"Maybe that would be better," Terry said uncertainly.

I shook my head. "This started in my family. That's where I'm going to end it."

"Are you sure about this, Adrian?" asked Terry, stepping closer and peering into my face. She slowly placed her right palm onto my chest, pressing my amethyst up against my heart. "Are you absolutely sure?"

This is why I don't believe in choices. Not the ones that really matter, anyway. The horrible irony of it was that if Randal had been the master, it would still have been possible for me to just walk away. But I couldn't do that with Cat. She was my sister, and nothing is more important than family. Whether you love them or hate them, whether you die defending them or murder them in their sleep, family is the single most powerful connection in the world. I had already failed Cat once. I certainly wasn't going to turn my back on her now. If anyone was going to kill Catherine Divine, it was going to be me.

"I'm sure," I said, strangely relieved at my own resolve.

Terry lowered her hand and looked at me sadly. "You've really changed, haven't you? Whatever happened to the boy who didn't want to kill?"

I shrugged. That frightened little child had died so long ago I hardly remembered what he looked like.

"I'm beginning to regret teaching you to fight," said Terry, looking away.

"If it's any consolation, Terry, I'm not all that grateful."

Terry gave a hollow little laugh.

I asked her quietly, "Will you go to war with me, Terry Henderson? Will you help me finish this? Help me rid the world of its last master controller?"

Terry looked back into my eyes and slowly nodded. "I will."

"Thank you," I whispered.

I saw Terry glance past me at Alia, who was still sitting on my bed. Alia must have said something telepathically to her, because Terry suddenly looked at me uncomfortably and said, "I'm going to go get you some fruits or something so you can eat here, Adrian. You'll need your strength."

As Terry hastily let herself out, I turned to my sister. Alia had gotten down from my bed and was staring up at me, her eyes brimming with anger, horror and betrayal. I had expected no less from her, as it would not have been Alia otherwise. After all, this was the girl who was torn to tears over her own reluctance to help a man who had once tortured her.

"Spit it out, Alia," I said, sighing heavily.

Alia looked down at her feet. *"You don't want to hear what I have to say about this, Addy."*

Lightly stroking her hair, I whispered, "Now where have I heard that before?"

"Addy, I know you kill people. I've watched you do it, and I've helped you do it. But this is different. This is your sister."

"That's right," I said evenly. "You heard the Historian. My sister is Queen Divine."

Alia stamped her feet angrily. *"This is wrong, Adrian! You know it's wrong!"*

"What would you have me do, Alia?" I asked, doing my best to maintain my calm. "Catherine is a master controller. I can't rescue her from that."

"If I was a master controller, would you kill me?"

"Ask me when you become one," I said gruffly.

Alia hid her face in her hands, sobbing. *"Terry's right. You really have changed."*

I knelt in front of her and carefully pried her hands away from her tear-stained face. "Look at me, Alia," I said gently. "I know that this is wrong. But do you really want to leave Cindy with the Angels? Do you want to live the rest of your life in hiding, moving from town to town and wondering when you'll be attacked in the middle of the night? Tell me, Alia, what would you have me do?"

Putting her arms around me and pressing her face onto my chest, Alia whispered shakily into my mind, *"I don't want to lose my unicorn, Addy. I love him too much."*

"He loves you too," I whispered back, holding her tightly. I tried hard to blink back my tears, but my voice cracked as I said, "I just don't know what else to do anymore, Alia. Do you?"

Alia shook her head, but said no more.

For a long time, we just held on to each other, the both of us crying like two little children lost in a deep, dark forest. And why not? The Historian had turned my already convoluted world upside down, and now I had to hunt down and kill my own fourteen-year-old sister. Over the years, Alia had watched me slowly turn into a killer, and in a sick way, we had both gotten used to it. But what would it be like to take my own blood? Could I really blast a hole through Cat's head as easily as I had done to Mr. Simms? Alia had it right: This was utterly wrong. It was unfair and unwarranted and unreasonable, and there wasn't a damn thing anyone could do about it. Crying would solve nothing, but Alia knew, as did I, that tears were soap and water for the spirit. We were probably loud enough to be heard in the common room, but I didn't care. There was no shame in being hurt and confused.

Once our tears ran dry, I carefully led Alia back to my bed and sat beside her, hugging her from the side as I said quietly, "I don't like what I do, Alia. I don't like hurting people. I don't expect you to either."

"I'm sorry I was so mean, Addy," Alia mumbled into my mind. *"I know you don't want to kill your sister. But I still think it's wrong."*

I patted her back as I said, "I'm glad that you do. At least one of us is still normal. You don't have to be a part of this if you don't want to."

Alia scoffed. *"Where would I go?"*

"I could deliver you to the mountain camp, or wherever Mrs. Harding is staying now," I suggested. "Candace could take care of you, or you might be able to stay with Patrick's family, with Laila."

"I almost wish I could do that, Addy. But I can't. If you have to go, then I have to go too."

"It doesn't have to be that way. This isn't your fight."

Alia shook her head. *"I want Cindy back. I want to live in a world without nightmares. I'm tired of running away. This is my fight."* She looked up at me and forced a smile. *"Besides, how many times have you been shot?"*

"Four bullets, one blast," I replied automatically.

"You're going to need a healer. Gretel always goes with Hansel."

"I can hardly argue with that," I said with a chuckle. Then I looked into her eyes and said seriously, "There's no happily ever after where we're going, Alia. Chances are we won't survive this."

Alia nodded solemnly. *"I'm okay with that, Addy."*

"Then you're in," I said evenly. "You're a greater Knight than I'll ever be, and you've certainly earned the right many times over. Let's go tell Terry."

Exiting my bedroom, we found the common room empty. A large decorative fruit platter had been left on one of the tables, and though I wasn't feeling particularly hungry, I took a bite out of an apple.

"Master Howell?" Havel called from behind me, making me jump a little in surprise. "Mistress Gifford," he continued, nodding to Alia, "the others are in the dining room. Lunch is almost finished, but if you like, you may join them for dessert."

I glanced at Alia, but she shook her head. "We're fine," I said.

"Very well," said Havel, turning to leave. "Please call if you need anything."

"Actually, Havel, could I ask you something?"

Havel turned back toward me, asking, "You wish to know why I live here?"

I nodded.

"There isn't much to tell," said Havel. "I was in my early thirties when I arrived here seeking asylum. You see, my great-grandmother was a master controller."

"Guardians or Angels?" I asked.

"Neither," replied Havel. "Hers was a small group of psionics and common townsfolk in a farming community in Wales, or so I heard. I never met my great-grandmother, but that didn't stop a number of people from trying to hunt me down for, um… breeding purposes."

"I can imagine," I said. Once more people found out what I was, I would have to be careful too.

Havel continued, "I found my way here, and the Historian graciously allowed me to stay. I have served him ever since. In fact, for one reason or another, all of the servants here are asylum seekers. If you ask it of him, the Historian will most likely allow you to remain here too."

"Live down here for the rest of my life?" I asked, shaking my head. "That might not be so bad under the circumstances, but I have to go do something horrible first. If I'm still alive when it's over, I'll think about it."

Havel nodded, and then asked, "Are you certain you won't join your companions for ice cream and cake?"

I looked at Alia again. Her eyes were still red, as no doubt were mine. I smiled and said, "I think we could both use some ice cream and cake."

The Historian's servants had a knack for timing and, sure enough, when Alia and I arrived in the dining room, the table had just been set with dessert.

"What's the verdict?" asked Terry as Alia and I sat down.

"Against better judgment," I replied, taking a slice of dark chocolate cake, "Alia will be joining us again."

"So will they," said Terry, nodding toward James and Ed Regis.

James I could understand. He was a born and bred Guardian Knight, and after he had taken a bullet to help get Terry and Alia safely to the Historian, I could hardly deny him the right to choose his own doom.

The Wolf was another matter entirely.

"I'm sorry, Ed Regis," I said, "but I lied to you when I said that you could have the Angel master alive. Even if it had been Randal Divine, we would never have let you take him into custody."

Ed Regis merely smiled, saying, "I know that."

"You already have more than enough information to deliver to your Wolf unit to regain their trust," I pointed out. "I can't stop you from telling them about Catherine. Once we get back to civilization, you can use what you learned here to get your life back and go hunt the Angel queen with your own people. You don't have to come with us."

Still smiling, Ed Regis shook his head. "Assuming that we actually get through the Angels and return to civilization alive, I can guarantee that the Wolves will never take me back."

"Why not?" I asked. "All you have to do is prove that you haven't been converted, which should be pretty easy since you'll be spilling the secrets of the only master controller left."

"But I have been converted, Adrian," Ed Regis said seriously. "By you, and by Alia, and by Terry and James and Merlin. I could never go back to hunting psionics for a living. Your sister will be my last."

I shook my head. "You don't have to do this, Ed Regis. You don't have to turn Guardian for us."

"No more than you have to hunt your sister," Ed Regis replied evenly. "Besides, you're going to need people experienced in this kind of thing. Don't forget what I am."

"Terry?" I said, hoping she might talk some sense into the Wolf.

"Beggars can't be choosers," Terry reminded me. "We can't tell the Guardians or anyone else the truth about Randal Divine and Catherine. We can't afford to let anyone find out what you are, so it's just the five of us now."

"We're all in this together, Adrian," put in James. "It's not just between you and your sister."

"Alright, Ed Regis," I said slowly, "if everyone is in agreement, I suppose we could use a good soldier."

"You won't regret it," said Ed Regis, and to my own surprise I found myself believing him.

Alia had noticed it first during our time together, but now even I could no longer recognize the man who had once tortured me with control bands. Ed Regis was one of us, as trustworthy and reliable as I could hope for in any man. As I looked around the table at the four people who now shared my darkest secret, I realized that I could ask for no better companions on this most terrible mission we were about to start.

I said to them, "Just do me a favor, all of you, and stop calling Catherine Divine my sister, because she's not. Not anymore." I didn't know if that would help me very much in dealing with the idea of killing Cat, but it certainly couldn't hurt.

They nodded understandingly, and we finished our dessert.

"Master Howell," said Havel as we stood from the table, "the Historian wishes to speak with you again."

"Right now?" I asked. "I thought he meant in a few days, before we left this place."

"He wishes to speak with you alone this time, but I am to escort all of you to the waiting room."

We looked at each other. Terry and James shrugged. Whatever the Historian wanted with me, I would find out soon enough.

Havel quietly escorted us back to the waiting room, where he asked the rest of my team to wait with him. Ushering me into the Historian's office, Havel shut the doors behind me.

The Historian was sitting in his armchair at the end of the low table. I quietly sat down on the sofa and faced him.

"Welcome back, Adrian," the Historian said good-naturedly, showing his

311

missing front teeth as he smiled. "I can see a little sugar did you good."

I wondered why he didn't speak telepathically like Alia always did when she was alone with me, but then I heard the Historian's voice in my head say, *"I am quite capable of speaking telepathically, Adrian. Even to crowds when needs demand."* Then he continued with his mouth, "But I like to speak aloud."

"So do I," I replied evenly, hoping that he would take the hint and stop reading my mind.

"You are wondering why I have asked you back here," said the Historian. "It is for several reasons. First, I wish to apologize for what happened to your family as a result of me giving Ralph Henderson your surname. Know that I never bore you ill will, Adrian. I deal in information. I do not write the history."

Nothing personal, I thought wryly. *I get it.*

If the Historian heard my thoughts, he didn't show it. Instead, he said calmly, "I had offered to let you stay in this mountain for a few more days only because I expected you to take much longer to come to your inevitable decision, or conclusion if that is what you prefer to call it. But even I sometimes misread people. Since your mind is already made up, there is little reason to keep you from departing this very day."

I could think of several reasons. We had no equipment, no food or water, and no strategy for breaking through the Angels waiting for us outside. I imagined that by now there were enough Seraphim out there for them to all hold hands and make a big circle around the Historian's mountain.

"You need not worry about the Angels," said the Historian. "It is my intention to allow you safe passage through them and back to your part of the world."

I stared at him incredulously. "You're going to help us?"

"Know that I would never have supplied the Guardians with your family name had they not been so desperate, but things are worse than ever now. This is the least reparation I can make to you for my mistake."

"But I thought..."

"That I am neutral?" the Historian asked in an amused tone. "Just as many people incorrectly believe me to be some kind of oracle, many assume that I have taken a vow of neutrality. I have not. Such a vow would be impossible to keep. As you should know by now from your own failed attempts, there is no such thing as neutral. Existence alone negates the possibility. I merely dislike meddling in the natural course of events as long as some semblance of equilibrium is maintained."

"But it's not!" I argued, forgetting my manners again. "And your information changes the course of this war all the time!"

"I am well aware of the self-contradictory nature of my lifestyle!" the Historian snapped back. Then he shrugged, saying in a quieter tone, "That is what eccentric is supposed to mean. Believe me, if I used my powers, I would do much more damage than I would with my knowledge. I will not fight for you, Adrian. For you or the Guardians or the Angels or anyone else. Just this once, however, I will help you slip through the blockade."

"Thank you," I said stiffly.

"But I want something in return."

I looked at him apprehensively. "What?"

"That you will see your mission to its bitter end or perish in the attempt."

"I was planning on doing that anyway," I said evenly.

The Historian smiled diabolically. "But now you must promise *me*, Adrian, and there is no breaking a promise with the Historian."

"So Terry told me," I said. Then I asked carefully, "But why are you so interested in this, Mr. Historian?"

The Historian frowned. "Do not try to hide your thoughts with words," he chided. "You are wondering whether I was telling the truth when I told you that I do not know Catherine's whereabouts."

Nodding, I said, "You told me that you were tracking all five master bloodlines carefully, and that the only one you lost was mine. That means you knew about the Harrow family all along. You knew who the Angels' second master controller was back when the Guardians were looking for her. You knew that it was Angelina Harrow. You probably even knew exactly where she was living."

"I did know," the Historian confirmed in a casual tone, "but I was disinclined to provide the Guardians with that information at the time because the balance of power had not yet tilted so far as to merit such direct hints. I was hoping for the Guardians to solve that mystery on their own." The Historian grinned widely, adding, "And in the end, thanks in great part to you, they did."

The only part I had played in the Guardians discovering the identity of the Angels' second master was that of being shot, caught, tortured and blinded by the God-slayers. The Historian didn't need to make it sound like an accomplishment. I scowled at him.

"It is true that I denied the Guardians information," admitted the Historian, "but you are talking about a time when the balance of power still seemed recoverable. That was then and this is now."

"You really don't know?" I asked.

"I haven't a clue."

"Fine," I said. "But please answer my word question too. Why are you interested in this? What are you after?"

"Equilibrium, Adrian," replied the Historian. "I have watched this pointless conflict for seven centuries, which is a long time, even for me. Before the schism, the Guardian Angels were the bringers of peace and understanding for humanity. Now they are so busy killing each other that they are no different from power-hungry humans." The Historian paused once, sighing quietly before asking me, "Do you know how many psionics there are in the world today?"

I shook my head.

"Just over a quarter of a million," the Historian informed me. "Mostly found in Europe, Western Asia and now the New World. Two hundred and fifty thousand psionics, Adrian. Does that sound like very many to you?"

"Well, sure," I said unthinkingly.

"There are more then seven billion people on this planet," countered the Historian. "Seven billion people, and neither the Guardians nor the Angels of today will follow the old code. They cannot be permitted to rule humanity. You will kill the Angel master and restore the anarchy that will keep these wayward psionics in their place."

I asked, "If you're not sworn to neutrality, why don't you do something about it yourself?"

"I *am* doing something," replied the Historian. "I am helping you."

"I'm hardly your best bet, Mr. Historian," I scoffed. "If I fail, would you have the Angels win? Have them rule over this world forever?"

"It is not my place to choose the planet's future. I merely nudge it along as I see fit. Besides, there is no such thing as forever. Don't assume that any one person is capable of making a deep dent in the history of our world. You and Catherine are but one very small chapter."

I looked at the Historian defiantly. "If I succeed, it'll make a dent."

"Perhaps, young Adrian. History will tell," said the Historian, shrugging. "Speaking of which, in addition to your vow to never stray from your chosen path, you must promise me one more thing. Once you have dealt with Catherine Divine, you must allow your bloodline to end with you."

"I was planning on doing that too," I said. "Knowing what I know now, there's no way I'm ever having kids."

The Historian grinned mischievously. "So I trust you will make no more mistakes like the one you made with Laila Brown?"

"That is none of your business!" I said embarrassedly, and then muttered, "I should never have let you read my history."

The Historian chuckled. "I am a collector of stories, Adrian. I have seen many histories, and that little chapter of yours is not particularly unique. However, I must admit that I found other parts of your life quite intriguing, and I wish to know how your story ends. I shall be watching your progress with considerable interest."

I fought off the urge to call him a nosy bastard, and said instead, "Kill Catherine. End the bloodline. Is that all you ask in return for safe passage out of these mountains?"

"Do not agree to these terms lightly, for I will hold you to your promise," warned the Historian. "It is not too late to reconsider. Who knows? With companions like yours, you may yet break through the Angels without my help."

The Historian had spoken gravely, but I found it difficult to take his words too seriously. Promising the Historian what I had already promised myself seemed a small price to pay if it meant my team could avoid running the gauntlet a second time.

The Historian frowned. "Don't make the mistake of thinking that I don't know you, Adrian, because I do. I know you at least as well as you think you know yourself. Where you are about to go will test the very limits of your resolve. If I am to bend my principles and use my power to help you, then I will not see you turn away from your path. Do you understand me?"

I did.

"Then consider yourself under oath, as I most definitely shall too," said the Historian.

"Will that be all, Mr. Historian?" I asked.

"That is absolutely all I could ever ask of you, Adrian Howell."

I felt a touch of ironic sorrow in the Historian's tone when he said that, and I felt compelled to ask him, "If you could ask anything of me, what would you ask?"

"I already have your vow!" snapped the Historian. "You have nothing more that I want."

"But you must want something," I insisted. "Even if it's not mine to give, there must be something aside from *equilibrium*. What is it you really want, Mr. Historian? What do you want for yourself?"

"I have been alive for more than three thousand years," the Historian said stubbornly. "I have had plenty of time to get everything I could possibly wish for!"

"But there *is* something, isn't there?" I pressed, encouraged by the slight irregularity In the Historian's power flow.

Suddenly the Historian sighed heavily. "So subtly you exact your revenge for my meddling," he muttered, his power fading almost to nothing. "Fine, Adrian, I will tell you what I want. Have you ever been in love?"

"You know I have."

The Historian nodded sadly. "Then in but sixteen years, you have already lived more fully than I ever will. What do I want? I want my teeth to grow in. I want my feet to touch the floor when I sit in this chair. I want to be free of this ridiculous child and feel for myself what it's like to truly love a woman. I wish to have a family, and to someday die of old age. For all of my powers, I am incapable of these most basic functions that define us as people. That is why I collect stories and histories, Adrian. They are all that I can have."

"I'm sorry," I said, and I meant it. "I wish I could help you."

"Thank you," said the Historian, shaking his head, "but there is little hope I will ever get what I truly want in this life. That is one of the few things you and I have in common."

Before I could think of a reply to that, the double doors opened and Havel ushered the rest of my team into the office.

"It is time for you to leave," announced the Historian, hopping down from his chair. "Right now."

Terry looked aghast. "We at least need our mountain gear back, Mr. Historian."

"It's alright," I said to her as I stood up from the sofa. "He agreed to help us get past the Angels."

Terry's jaw dropped even lower. "What did you promise him, Adrian?!"

"Nothing I probably won't regret," I replied. "But it's okay, Terry. I know what I'm doing."

"That'll be a first!" Terry huffed loudly, but she seemed relieved nonetheless.

Looking around at us, the Historian said, "You will leave this place with nothing but the clothes on your backs. Where you go from there is your business, except for Adrian, who is now bound to his quest."

The Historian stepped up to Terry, saying in a solemn tone, "Teresa Henderson, you are a great warrior and I honor your dedication to your cause, and to Adrian. He will need your very best for this, and then some."

Terry nodded, carefully shaking the Historian's hand.

The Historian shook James's hand next. "James Turner, what an adventure this must have been for you. Your next one will not be nearly as easy, and I do hope you are up to it."

"I hope so, too," said James.

The Historian gave him a wink. "Your combat instructor thinks more highly of you than she is willing to admit."

Then the Historian turned to Ed Regis. "Major Edward Regis, you would have been the first Wolf to ever enter this mountain. I hope your decision leads you to a better life, or at least an honorable death."

"Which do you think it'll be?" asked Ed Regis.

The Historian grinned. "History will tell."

Ed Regis crouched and shook his hand.

The Historian turned to me again. "Adrian Howell... It would be meaningless to wish you good luck, but I sincerely hope that you find it in you to see this through. I honestly do not know where Randal and Catherine are, but you might find that information in the hands of those closer to this war. For now, learn to expect the unexpected."

I bowed silently. There was nothing more to say.

Finally, Alia. The Historian looked up into her face with kind pity. "Alia Gifford, I wasn't thinking of your feelings this morning when I told Adrian about his past. It was not something you needed to hear at your age, and I do apologize."

Alia smiled at him and said, "It's okay, Mr. Historian. Besides, not even you are right all the time."

"How very true," said the Historian, bowing his head slightly.

"How are we going home?" asked Alia.

The Historian looked up at Alia again, asking, "Have you ever seen the movie, *The Wizard of Oz?*"

"No, but Addy read the picture book to me like ten times."

"At least ten times," I confirmed.

The Historian chuckled. "Then you already know where this is going, dear Alia. Close your eyes."

Alia did, and then the Historian said to the rest of us, "Maybe you all want to close your eyes. It will make this slightly less painful."

I looked once more at Havel, the old man with whom I shared a distant ancestor. He smiled as our eyes met, and then bowed his head, saying, "The wise Historian believes it is meaningless to wish you good luck, Master Howell, but I am not as learned in these matters. I wish you the best of luck. Godspeed your way."

I returned the bow, and then closed my eyes.

My temperature dropped to zero. It felt like a billion tiny needles piercing every cell in my body, but when I tried to scream, the pain was already gone.

Opening my eyes, I found the five of us standing in the quiet white light of a nearly full moon, at the top of a lonely, grassy hill that overlooked a small farmhouse in the distance.

"Where are we?" asked James, gasping for breath.

"It was only a little past lunch when we left," said Ed Regis, looking up at the clear night sky. "I'm guessing that we're on the other side of the world now."

Looking around, Alia said unhappily, "For a minute, I thought he was really going to send us home. I forgot we didn't have one."

"Home is where you make it," Terry reminded her. "We'll find a place somewhere." Then she frowned at her left stump. "He could've at least let me go get my hook before sending us away."

"Nothing but the clothes on our backs," I said, touching my amethyst to make sure that I still had it. "So this is how it begins."

I was just as surprised as the Historian at how quickly I had come to terms with his information and what had to be done to restore the balance of power. It was only this morning that we had learned the true name of the last Angel master, but our meeting with the 3000-year-old boy felt like ancient history to me. Out of his mountain, back in my own familiar side of the world, I now felt the crushing weight of what I had promised him, and more importantly, what I had promised myself.

It wasn't a choice. Or, if it was, it was a choice that I had made long ago, back when Cat and I were still children innocently playing with our powers, trying them out on each other without knowing where they would lead us. Back then, I was her brother, and she was my sister. We were family. Now, years later, as we stood on opposite sides of a raging river, I knew that nothing had really changed but the weather.

How would I find her? How would I kill her? How would I live with it? I had no answers. I didn't even know what day of the week it was. But I knew what had to be done now. I had to put one foot forward and start the journey.

"So, um, where do we go from here?" asked James.

"Let's just walk down this slope a bit," I replied quietly, taking Alia's hand. "I'm sure we'll find something."

This pentalogy will conclude in

Adrian Howell's
PSIONIC

Book Five
Guardian Angel

About the Author

Born of a Japanese mother and American father, Adrian Howell (pen name) was raised for a time in California and currently lives a quiet life in Japan where he teaches English to small groups of children and adults. Aside from reading and writing fiction, his hobbies include recumbent cycling, skiing, medium-distance trekking, sketching and oversleeping.

Send comments and questions to the author at:
adrianhowellbooks@gmail.com

Visit the author's website at:
http://adrianhowell.com/

A Plea for Word-of-Mouth

The *Psionic Pentalogy* is an independently published work. Consequently, it does not have the big financial support of traditional publishing houses to promote the books, and instead relies much more heavily on reviews and word-of-mouth by readers such as yourself. If you have enjoyed this book, please tell your friends about it. Please give it a mention on any social networking sites you use such as Facebook, Twitter or Pinterest. Please also consider leaving a review on your bookseller's online site. Even if it's only a sentence or two, it would make all the difference and would be very much appreciated.

Adrian Howell's PSIONIC
Book Four: The Quest
First Edition

38139032R00183

Made in the USA
Middletown, DE
13 December 2016